I0591290

The Bratva Darling

The Ivankov Brotherhood

Sabine Barclay

OLIVERHEBERBOOKS

Copyright © 2022 by Sabine Barclay.

0 9 8 7 6 5 4 3 2 1

Published by Oliver Heber Books

 Created with Vellum

Thank you to my fellow authors who inspired and supported me as I jump head first into a new genre after writing Historical Romance as Celeste Barclay.

The Ivankov Brotherhood

Do you also enjoy steamy Historical Romance? Discover Sabine's books written as Celeste Barclay.

Chapter One

Laura

As I sit across from the four Kutsenko brothers, I press my lips together to keep from drooling. No four men should be so strikingly handsome. Not all from the same family, anyway. I fight a valiant battle against letting my gaze drift toward the eldest, Maksim, whose ice-blue eyes bore into me. After years of negotiating billion-dollar investment contracts while facing countless ruthless businessmen, I've learned to keep my expression studiously blank. But it's a true struggle today. Instead, I focus my attention on the squirrelly lawyer sitting across the conference table. While he's disingenuous with each comment, he's a good negotiator. But I'm better. How cliché am I?

While I feel Maksim watching me, I focus on Dmitry Yakovitch as he continues to argue the merits of the venture capitalist company I represent, RK Capital Group, merging with Kutsenko Partners. What he means is the merits of Kutsenko Partners acquiring RK Capital Group, then stripping

1

it and making it another money-laundering shell corporation. While most people in New York have little awareness of the Russian mafia, I do. The Kutsenko brothers' names appear on no titles or deeds anywhere in New York City, but it wasn't difficult to determine which shell companies likely belong to them. Their assumption that I'm unfamiliar with them is proving beneficial to me as they continue to whisper amongst themselves in Russian. I think they may even believe they're convincing me that they don't speak much English.

The senior partners of RK Capital Group know who I'm negotiating with, though they may not know I'm aware of these Russians' more nefarious operations. They've given me the go-ahead to agree to a merger with an eventual acquisition, but only for the right price. A price to the tune of twenty billion dollars. Considering an investment firm like Goldman Sachs is worth nearly one-hundred-and-twenty billion dollars, my clients' asking price appears reasonable.

"Mr. Yakovitch, I shall stop you now." I raise my left hand, pen caught between my index and middle fingers. When I have his attention, I lean back in my chair and casually twirl the pen over my index finger and thumb. "Fifty billion is my clients' asking price. You know that. Your clients know that. RK doesn't oppose the merger. What they oppose is the insulting offer you've made. It's nearly noon, and I'm hungry, Mr. Yakovitch. I have a delicious ham sandwich waiting for me. I even have three chocolate chip cookies waiting for me. If we aren't going to make any progress, I shall let you go, so I can move onto my eagerly anticipated lunch."

I cant my head just enough for me to appear as though my gaze rests solely on the opposing attorney's face, but I can see each Kutsenko brothers' reaction. My face battles yet again against showing my emotions as I fight not to smirk. Their muted but surprised expressions confirm what I already know.

"Please tell your clients to make a reasonable counteroffer, or I will conclude this meeting and enjoy my ham sandwich and cookies."

Dmitry glares at me before turning to Maksim and his three brothers. In rapid Russian, he doesn't interpret my suggestion. Oh no. There's no need for that. I can't catch every word because his voice is too low. But I catch something along the lines of "The bitch refuses to budge. What now? A fucking ham sandwich. More like a stick up her ass."

Maksim swivels his chair to look at his brothers. In Russian, he says, "Fifty billion is ridiculous. She's not so stupid or naïve not to know that. My guess is they'll settle for twenty billion. We offer fifteen."

"That's barely better than what we already offered," Aleksei, the second-oldest brother, argues. "She'll be eating the fucking sandwich and dipping her cookies in milk before we walk out the door. We need the buildings."

"We offer twenty, Maks," Bogdan, the youngest, insists.

As I watch the brothers discuss, their voices barely lowered, I pull my lunch sack from the black leather satchel by my feet and set it beside my laptop. It's a ridiculously pink floral bag with an embroidered monogram, the L and D overlapping. It's an empty prop, but they don't know that. I watch as five sets of eyes narrow. I offer a smile that would appear innocent in any setting other than this meeting. It's patronizing, and I know it.

"Fine. Twenty," Maksim concedes.

Dmitry turns back to me, shooting me a smug glare. "Twenty billion," he offers in English.

"Fifty," I shoot back. I'm not lowering my counteroffer yet. My clients may be willing to accept peanuts because they fear these Russian businessmen, but I don't.

"Ms. Doyle, be reasonable."

"I am. The company is valued at fifty-five billion. I'm

offering you a bargain." I unzip the lunch bag. I won't do more than that. There's a fine line between patronizing and stupid.

"Twenty-five," Dmitry blurts. Maksim's fingers curl slightly on the table. None of the brothers approved that amount. Dmitry cocks an eyebrow, to which Maksim's full lips purse.

"Are you going to tell your clients what you just bid?" I ask as I return to twirling my pen.

"They authorized me to continue negotiating."

No, they didn't. "Very well. Forty."

"You do realize that you're supposed to go down while I come up."

"I came down. It was fifty. Now it's forty." I stare into Dmitry's eyes, unblinking and unnerving him. "But the thing with negotiations is someone eventually gets to a point where they won't budge. I seem to have gotten there first." I lean back once more, casting a glance at my lunch and release a soft sigh.

"Just a moment." Dmitry turns back to the Kutsenkos, switching to Russian. "Now what? We'll be here all day at this rate. Fucking ham sandwich or not. Forty is reasonable."

"My guess is her clients agreed to twenty-five," Maksim replies.

"Forty is still a steal. And she looks like the type to walk and have a new buyer before she drives home tonight," Nikolai, the third-oldest brother, finally speaks up. "We need the buildings."

"Fine," Maksim concedes further.

"Ms. Doyle, my clients agree to forty billion. They still expect RK Capital Group to adopt their name and operate under their directive."

"That sounds a lot like an acquisition, not a merger," I reply. "The name changes, and they operate under Kutsenko Partners' auspices, but the company's day-to-day operations remain under RK's control. Those were the terms."

4

"You and I both know an acquisition is only months away."

"That may well be. But you offered my client a merger. If you wanted this to go faster, then you shouldn't have played a game you're not winning." I gather the documents in front of me and stand. I move to the side of the conference table across from the four brothers. As I hand the documents first to Maksim, I wait as his hand clasps the bottom. I don't withhold my smirk anymore.

"*Pozhaluysta, podpishite ikh. Vashi kopii budut dostupny do zakrytiya rabochego dnya. Ya ozhidayu, chto bankovskaya tranzaktsiya budet zavershena zavtra k poludnyu.*" Please sign these. I will have your copies available before close of business. I expect the wire transaction completed by noon tomorrow.

Maksim jerks back, his glare ready to set me ablaze. Aleksei, Nikolai, and Bogdan are mirror images of their older brother. Four sets of ice-blue eyes narrow and mouths set in hard lines.

"You speak like a native." Maksim speaks in Russian-flavored English. The same is true about Maksim's English. His grammar doesn't sound like someone who learned Russian later in life. Something as simple as using "a" tells me a lot. Russian doesn't use "a," "an," and "the" like English does.

"Thank you."

Maksim cocks an eyebrow at me. I raise both of mine. I don't owe them an explanation. Let them stew.

"Do you need a pen?" I offer Maksim mine, but he withdraws one from the small pocket near the left lapel of his suit jacket. All the Kutsenkos reviewed the contracts well before they arrived. Maksim skims over them as he puts the pen's tip to the paper, but he freezes. I can't help but grin.

"I thought it would be faster if I just went ahead and put in the agreed-upon amount." I knew the moment he read the agreed-upon amount was already typed in as forty billion dollars.

"Perhaps you should be our attorney." Nikolai grumbles as he rolls his eyes and shakes his head.

"I doubt you can afford me."

Maksim's eyes jump from the papers he's signing to me. He's still leaning forward, so he looks at me from underneath his dark brow. He takes my words as a challenge. But the heat emanating from his icy eyes has nothing to do with business. His gaze skims over me, resting on my mound, before jumping back to meet mine.

"It won't matter now that our companies merged." Aleksei crosses his arms as he rocks the seat back.

"Our companies did not merge, Mr. Kutsenko. Unlike Mr. Yakovitch, I am not in-house counsel. My firm is independent of RK Capital Group. They are my client, not my employer."

I watch as the brothers finish signing the documents before Bogdan passes them back to Maks. I reach my hand toward them, not quite halfway. It appears to anyone looking that my arm isn't long enough without leaning forward. But Maksim's glower tells me he understands. He won't ignore my offer, but he knows I'm making him reach more than halfway to meet me. The five men file toward the door.

"*Pakhan*, if I might have a moment." All five men freeze, much like they did when they realized I speak fluent Russian. I may have called Maksim "boss," since he's the CEO of Kutsenko Partners, but they know that's not what I meant.

"Only a moment, Ms. Doyle." Maksim's snarl makes my panties wetter—as if they weren't already soaked. I wait until only the two of us remain in the conference room, but I can see the others waiting in the lobby.

"I could spend hours searching for how you and your brothers make your money, but I know I won't find anything but shell companies. I don't have the inclination or the time to waste. What I know is that you're the Ivankov Bratva's *Kristney Otet.*" I call Maksim "godfather," and my pussy clenches. "Since there's no record that your branch even exists beyond a few mentions in police blotters, I can't be sure how you make your money. I don't doubt you'll use RK Group to launder your money, and I couldn't give a shit. But I will tell you that if you use a single building in their holding to warehouse victims of human trafficking, I will bury you."

Maksim's hands go to his hips, the gun holster under his left arm showing. It's no accident. He remains silent, and I'm certain he thinks his silence will intimidate me. I cross my arms. I can wait. He takes a step forward, forcing me to tilt my head back to keep our eyes locked on one another.

"If you know who I am, then you're foolish to make threats."

"I'm not threatening you, *pakhan.* I know that would be foolish. I'm promising you."

"*Malyshka.*" Baby girl. My clit throbs, his gravelly voice and the term make me ache. But I cut him off before he can continue.

I push my luck. "*Starik.*" Old man.

"I won't soon forget you, Ms. Doyle. That's rarely a good thing when I remember someone."

"If only my memory were so good. I can't say the same. Good day, Mr. Kutsenko." I can tell I've pissed him off. My tone. My words. And now my dismissal. But goddamn, he's hot to begin with. He's fucking scorching when he broods. Lucky bitches who share his bed.

He nods and leaves. As I gather my belongings, I consider going to the ladies' room to get myself off. Fuck, he's hot.

It's been two days, and I can't stop thinking about my meeting with the Kutsenko brothers. It doesn't help that I've had to file all the documents and debrief RK Capital Group's senior partners. But that doesn't explain why I've dreamed about Maksim for the past two nights. I've woken aroused and sweaty. Each time my panties are just as wet as they were when I left my meeting with them. I'd gone into the ladies' room but ended up removing them rather than pleasuring myself. Lord knows the last thing I needed was for anyone to smell my arousal.

My friends Lanie and Michelle are group-texting me, demanding that I come out to celebrate Michelle's birthday. It's not every day she turns a milestone-lacking twenty-seven. I'm exhausted after going for a three-mile swim that did nothing to clear my mind of Maksim. Usually, swimming allows my mind to go blank. All I focus on is my breathing and tucking tight for my turns at the end of the pool lane. This time, I spent ninety minutes fantasizing about a Russian mobster who's more likely to dump me in the bottom of Flushing River than fuck me.

Me: Fine. I'll come out with you. Give me 30 mins.

Lanie: Dry your damn hair, woman.

Me: You know I'm strictly wash and go. By the time we get there, it'll be mostly dry. It's August and roasting even at nine p.m.

Michelle: Wear that silver cocktail dress.

Me: Isn't that a little formal for a club?

Michelle: It's my effing bday tomorrow. I think we can dress up a bit.

Lanie: You wearing a ball gown and tiara?

Michelle: What if I am?

Lanie: What do you want for your bday? Maybe a...

An eggplant emoji appears.

Michelle: I'm not saying yes. But I'm not saying no either.

Lanie texts another eggplant emoji, then a taco.

Lanie: You get yours and I'll get mine.

Me: Things didn't work out with Teresa?

Lanie: No.

I wait to see if she writes more, but nothing appears. Oh, lawdy. That's going to be a few shots' worth of storytelling.

Me: Where are we going?

Michelle: I want to check out Envy first. If that sucks, we can go to Zebras.

Zebras isn't the official name. It's something like Lush, but they decorated the entire place in black and white. Not like one wall is black, and another is white. Or like one room is black, and another is white. All the walls are black and white. It's the gaudiest shit without being glitzy. But it's still a given that we'll have a good time there. The bartenders are generous, the DJs are great, and there's usually someone to hook up with if you're in the mood. Part of me isn't interested in the least, and another part of me thinks hooking up—not taking someone home, just making out—would be a great way to ease my sexual frustration.

Me: I'll meet you guys there. I'll Uber.

As much as I'd like to relieve my nonstop arousal, I don't have time. I hop in the shower and am out in five minutes. It's another five minutes for makeup and like two minutes to get dressed. I'm standing at the lobby door to my high rise when the Uber arrives.

Chapter Two

Maksim

I really didn't want to come to Envy tonight. I was here last night and the night before. I'm never here for enjoyment. But it was even less enjoyable than usual for the last two nights. Every brunette I see makes me think of that little termagant I watched negotiate the pants off my lawyer. We've been having more fights than usual, so all of us are here tonight instead of just Bogdan. We're all part owners, but Bogdan manages our nightclubs, bars, and strip clubs. Niko oversees the three casinos in Jersey that we own. Aleks is my second-in-command, so much like me, he doesn't have one specific area of our businesses that he oversees. My brothers and I are the majority in the Elite Group of our bratva branch. While I'm the leader, my brothers and I operate as equals in our business endeavors.

Organized crime. More like organized criminals. There's a rank and structure within the Russian bratva. I know it's left-over from the old Soviet days, but it works. Since my brothers are part of the Elite Group, I have no choice but to have a *sovietnik* and an *obshchak* who aren't my brothers. In English, they're known as the two spies. Really, they oversee collecting intel and carrying out our business transactions—the ones we prefer people not to notice. I keep it in the family with my cousins Sergei and Anton. They're floating around somewhere near the DJ.

"Are you just going to sulk all night? You've been a pain in the ass ever since the meeting. I know we paid more than you wanted, but we got what we wanted."

I glance at Niko. Let them think I'm pissed about the deal rather than them figuring out I'm pining over a woman who dared threaten me to my face. A promise. Bullshit. I sweep my gaze over the crowd as I lean against the bar to the far left of the entrance. I skim my eyes over blondes and brunettes, but none take my fancy until I spy a woman with deep chestnut hair. I can only see part of her profile, but my cock twitches just like it did the first time I saw Laura Doyle. It was fucking uncomfortable having a hard-on the entire fucking meeting. I've passed the age of sleeping with a hot chick I pick up at a club or a bar. But maybe this one can distract me from Laura. Maybe I can close my eyes and imagine it's Laura.

I push away from the bar and jerk my chin toward this woman's table. I can see she's with two friends. I cant my head toward them and wonder which of my brothers will come with me. It doesn't surprise me when all three of them follow me over. I'm curious to see who walks away empty handed. As we draw closer, I watch the muscles in her back shift when she picks up her drink. She has the taut physique of an athlete rather than the harsh ridges of a bodybuilder. But there's no doubt this woman works out, most definitely lifting weights, but there's a femininity to her strength. I wonder if she has endurance as well. I hear one of her friends speak when I'm nearly close enough to touch her.

"Those four guys are coming over here. That biggest one hasn't stopped staring at you. He looks like he's going to eat you for dinner."

"Too bad he'll stay hungry. Michelle, I told you. I'm not interested in fucking some random guy."

"Hook up doesn't mean you have to have sex." This woman's second friend doesn't look anywhere near as impressed as her first friend does. The woman, Michelle, is checking out all four of us. I hear Bogdan scoff, and I know he's staking a claim already.

"Hello, ladies." I practically purr, but the target of my attention stiffens. She'd been leaning on an elbow against the table, but she sits up straight. She twists in her seat, and we both jerk back. She grips the table to keep from falling off her stool.

"Ms. Doyle."

"Mr. Kutsenko."

We speak at the same time. I watch her glance at my brothers, but Bogdan is sidling up to Michelle. And I can see Niko and Aleks are already having no success with Laura's other friend. She says something about preferring tacos to sausages.

"Ms. Doyle, I can't say that I expected it to be you when I walked over."

"Mr. Kutsenko, I definitely didn't think it was you when my friend said there was a man rudely staring at us."

"Prickly." The back of my fingers glide along the outside of her forearm as I put my drink on the table. It's the smoothest skin I've ever felt. "Or maybe not. And it's Maksim."

Laura doesn't know what to make of me. I can see she's battling between continuing to keep her uptight persona and whether she wants to consider herself off the clock. I glance down at her glass.

"Can I get you another of whatever you're drinking?" I offer a conciliatory smile, but it makes Laura frown. I don't have to walk to the bar. I merely catch a waitress's eye, and she hurries over.

"What can I get you, Mr. Kutsenko?"

I look at Laura. She glances at me then looks at the waitress. "Whiskey sour, please."

"Vodka for you, Mr. Kutsenko?"

"Yes. On ice." Laura and I watch the waitress walk away.

"Not on a first-name basis with all the waitresses?"

"Do you call the man who signs your paycheck by his first name?"

"It's a woman. You own this club." It's a statement, not a question.

"My brothers and I." I can't believe I don't know what to say next. I notice the small gift bag on the table. "Celebrating something?"

"It's Michelle's birthday tomorrow."

Laura's friend looks over at us.

Bogdan grins. "Sounds like a night for champagne."

Laura watches my brother and her friend, and I'm certain she can perceive the things their body language doesn't say. I'd noticed she was observant during our meeting, but she seems to read people better than almost anyone I know. When the waitress returns with the drinks Laura and I ordered, Bogdan orders a bottle of champagne.

"I'd say it's a funny coincidence that my friends and I ended up in one of your nightclubs, but I suspect you own most of the best ones in Manhattan."

"We do."

"Then we've done business before. My friends and I have

invested a small fortune over the past few years." Her grin is infectious. Her eyebrows shoot up when I return her smile. "You can smile. I figured that brooding and intimidating is all you can do."

"From the way Dmitry bitched on the way back to the office, I'd call you intimidating, too."

"I didn't think he found me intimidating. I mean how could I be with a stick up my ass?" Her voice is like saccharine, but I can see the glint of humor in her eyes. She leans toward me. "Can I tell you a secret? Only if you promise not to tell your lawyer?"

"Of course." I can only imagine what she's going to say.

"There was no ham sandwich. Not even any cookies. The bag was empty."

I stare. My mouth drops open before I laugh. It doesn't happen often, so all my brothers gape at me. "Can we share your secret with my brothers? I don't keep things from them."

Laura's grin widens. "My lunch bag was empty."

"Shit." Bogdan, the most easygoing of all of us—perhaps because he's the baby of the family—laughs along with me. Aleks and Niko are a little more skeptical.

"Did you want to be there all day? I didn't. I use the lunch bag prop when I have morning meetings that are taking way too long. Sometimes it's a chicken salad sandwich and a brownie."

"Subtle." Aleks nods his approval. "I'll have to remember that trick."

"Mmm. I think a steel briefcase would suit you better than my floral lunch sack."

"Floral lunch sack?" Michelle huffs. "I gave you that."

"And I love it. It's super handy. I just don't carry food in it." Laura leans away as though Michelle might swing at her. But she doesn't remember how close I'm standing to her. Her shoulder and half her back press against my chest. My hand goes to her lower back, as if to steady her. She straightens slowly, but I don't remove my hand. Her gaze travels over me for the first time. I had plenty of time to observe her before we approached the women's table. She takes in the tight-fitting midnight blue button-down I'm wearing, with the top two buttons undone and the sleeves rolled up my forearms, allowing a hint of my tats to show; the charcoal gray trousers; and black loafers. It's far too hot in the club for a suit jacket. I dip my head to her ear.

"You look beautiful in a suit and a cocktail dress. I'm not sure which I prefer." I feel her shiver as my breath brushes her ear. She looks back over her shoulder at me. I'm not sure what I expected to see. I suppose I hoped it was lust. What I find is a challenge.

"Thank you. I can't ignore that you're handsome, and I'd be a liar to deny it. I prefer you without the blazer."

I realize that she's not looking at my chest or even my abs. She's looking at where my gun holster would be if I were wearing a jacket. Where it had rested when I flashed it at her in the conference room.

"Laura—"

"I used a lunch bag. You used a Glock. Same difference. We both made our point."

"I sound like an asshole when you put it that way. Your supposed ham sandwich is hardly as lethal as a handgun."

"I wouldn't be so sure. I once shoved a sandwich into Dave Holmes's mouth in middle school when he tried to touch my chest. He choked so hard they had to take him to the nurse's office."

"Are you teasing me?"

"Nope. Michelle."

"Yeah."

"Tell Maksim what happened with Dave Holmes when he snapped my bra during lunch."

"I thought you were going to be the first middle-school girl on death row. Murder by sandwich."

I turn my attention back to Laura, who shrugs. Thank God my trousers aren't as tight as my shirt. I've been hard since the moment I recognized her, and I think I just leaked. Her eyes glitter with humor as she nods along with Michelle's comment.

"Don't mess with her."

I look at her other friend, who I heard introduce herself as Lanie. There's an edge, a warning, to her voice. She's all bark and no bite. As I look back at Laura, I realize I wouldn't mind if she bit me.

"Will you dance with me?"

I know that made all three of my brothers stare. I never dance. We were all forced to learn ballroom dancing when we were children, but none of us enjoyed it, even if we were all good at it. I never dance with women at clubs. I might watch them dance, often on a pole, but I stick with sipping vodka. Laura hesitates, then nods.

"Sure."

I notice she isn't carrying a purse. I glance down and realize her skimpy cocktail dress actually has pockets. I can see a hint of her phone. I wrap my hand around hers and weave our way onto the dance floor. It doesn't surprise me when I see she's sex on a stick as she moves to the music. Her lithe body sways in time with the beat, no awkwardness at all. She dances because she enjoys it, and that's more alluring than any woman who's tried to seduce me by gyrating against me. I stand close, but I don't pull her against me like I want. If I do, she's going to know in an instant how hard I am for her.

My mistake though. I leave enough space between us for some asshole to think she's available to dance with. He wraps his arm around her waist and tries to pull her back against his chest. She steps around him and wraps her arms around my neck. I know the moment she feels me. But rather than going stiff like she did when she recognized me, she presses her hips forward. Our eyes meet. I've already wrapped my arms around her waist. Now one hand slides down to rest at the top of her ass.

It's my turn to shiver when one of her hands glides down my chest, and two fingers slip between the buttons of my shirt. We stay in that position throughout the song and the next one. During the third, I twirl her, then pull her back flush to my chest. My hand rests low on her belly, daringly close to her mound. She rubs her ass against my cock as my other hand grips her hip. I gradually apply more and more pressure, waiting for a sign that it's too much. But the sign never comes. Instead, she slides my hand from near her mound up to cup her breast. It rests there only a heartbeat before she spins back to face me.

"In case there's any doubt, I had two whiskey sours, and I hate champagne. You might have noticed I didn't finish the glass."

"Are you telling me you're not drunk?"

"Yes. Are you?"

"I've been drinking vodka since I was eight. Three shots are barely like a glass of water to me. And I don't like champagne either." I maneuver us away from other people and toward the hallway that leads to the kitchen, the storeroom, and Bogdan's office. No one needs to watch me slide my hands over the soft, ample ass that's now filling both hands.

"Can I tell you another secret?"

"Of course."

She glances down between us, then back up at me. "Since there's no hiding that you at least like touching me, if not

17

looking at me too, I'll confess that you made me ridiculously wet during our meeting."

"Did I?" I slide my right hand to the hem of her dress and bunch it, while my left fingers slip between her upper thighs. "Shall I tell you my own secret, *malyshka?*"

"Is it why you call me baby girl?"

"No. I'm not ready to reveal that secret. But I will confess that I was fucking hard the entire meeting. From the moment you greeted us at the conference room door until well after I got in my car."

"I had to take my panties off before I left the building. I didn't have time to linger." Her expression says what her words don't.

"I was glad I didn't share a car that morning. I had just enough time before I got back to my office. And since I have a driver, I could concentrate."

"If only I didn't have to drive myself."

I feel her hand rest where my thigh meets my hip. The other still has fingers tucked into my shirt. "I'm going to kiss you, *malyshka*. If you don't want me to, walk away now."

I wait, giving her a choice. Her hands cup my jaw and try to pull me toward her, but I won't budge. Confusion clouds her vision until she relents. When she does, I swoop in. My lips brush hers twice before I press them firmly to hers. She parts them without hesitation, and my tongue swarms the inside of her mouth, flicking and swiping the inside of her cheeks, the roof of her mouth, her tongue. I feel her fist my shirt as my fingers slide between her clenched legs, the heel of my hand resting at the bottom of her ass. I don't try to press into her. I just let them stay there, teasing her. I let go of her dress now that it's hiked up just high enough for my fingers to reach. My free hand tunnels into her hair, capturing a handful and keeping her head in place.

I devour her. My lips trail along her jaw, then down her neck. I nip at her collarbone before moving back up to her ear. I flick her earlobe before sucking it into my mouth. She shivers yet again, and I realize it might be one of the most arousing feelings I've ever experienced. It makes me want to rip her dress off, hoist her so her legs wrap around my waist, then thrust into her pussy. I know it's wet. I can feel it against my fingers. Her thong can't possibly keep the moisture inside. It's coating my fingers and the tops of her thighs.

"Do you think he's gonna fuck her right here?"

I pull Laura against my chest, shielding her face as I look over my shoulder. No recognition flashes in the college-age guys, but I see the immediate fear. I relish it. It took years to cultivate my aura into one that intimidates with ease. They scurry away, like little boys looking for their mamas. I look down at Laura, who remains pressed against my chest. As I peer down at her, I realize my reaction was driven by a desire to protect her, not my ego.

I stroke hair back from her face, shocked at my gentle touch. The women who've known me would hardly ever call me gentle. In fact, they would never call me gentle. I feel her sigh. I feel her relax against me, trusting me. God, how that is likely the most misplaced sentiment this woman could feel. But then again, I want her to trust me.

Why the fuck do I care?

The only trust I've wanted from women is for them to know I won't kill them while I tie them up and fuck them hard. I want them to know they're safe with me when I get rough with them. But the moment we're done and every minute leading up to it, I couldn't care less. With Laura, I do. I flashed my fucking gun at her two days ago, and now she's trusting me to shield her from prying eyes.

"*Malyshka*, they're gone. I'm sorry about that. I forgot

19

where we are." I'm not lying. All I'd known was how delicious she tasted and how much I wanted to do just what that guy said.

"I did, too. That was embarrassing. But I'm more pissed that they interrupted."

I take her hand and lead her farther down the hallway that ends with the office. Before that are the storerooms. I open the first one and lead her in.

"Do you want this, *malyshka*.?"

"It's all I want."

That's all I need to hear before I reach into my back pocket and pull out my wallet. So cliché, but I have a condom in it. She plucks it from my fingers and rips it open while I unfasten my pants. I push the wrapper into my pocket with my wallet while she rolls it onto my cock. I don't even remember picking her up, but her legs are around my waist and my cock's thrusting into her. Holy fuck. I've had enough sex to know what feels good and what doesn't. This is sublime. I guide her hips as she rides me. I surge into her over and over, careful not to slam her against the wall. I know several minutes go by, but it doesn't feel like enough.

"This feels so good...So big...I'm close, Maks."

So am I. Embarrassingly close. I don't want this to be a quicky, but that's all I can manage.

"I'm coming, Maks."

"I know, *malyshka*. God, you feel too good. I can't stop."

I feel my cock pulse as euphoria unlike any I've felt before washes over me. It's just sex, isn't it? Not with this woman. Not with my *malyshka*.

"Maks, that was—I don't even know."

"The same for me. I—"

I don't get to finish because the sound of shattering glass fills the air. I don't even remember what I was going to say. I yank the door open and look toward the bar, immediately spotting my brothers since we're among the tallest men in the club. We all stand at six feet five inches. I spot the shattered window and the broken shelf above the bar where a dozen bottles fell. I rush to fasten my pants, then I grab Laura's hand and pull her down the hallway, away from the ensuing chaos. I punch in the code to the office door and burst in. "Stay here. Do not open it for anyone but me. Not even if they say they're one of my brothers."

"What about Michelle and Lanie? I can't hide while they're out there."

"My brothers will protect them. Only my brothers know the code to the door. If it opens, it's one of them. But remember, don't open it for anyone but me."

"Yes, da—"

I don't know what she was going to say, though I want to imagine what it might have been. I press a quick kiss to her lips before slamming the door shut.

"She's in the office." I pass Niko, who's herding Lanie and Michelle toward where I just locked Laura into the safest room in the building. I hurry past the trio and out to the main floor.

Chapter Three

Laura

I look around the office as Maks rushes back into the fray. There's one sofa that looks perfect for taking a nap. There's another sofa that looks like little more than a wood plank. I can guess the comfy one is for the Kutsenkos, and the uninviting one is for—what? Business associates? Men who work for them and fuck up? When they come to appear before the principal?

The desk takes up much of the room. There's a leather executive chair pushed up to it. I opt to sit there. If I pick the sofa that's really more of a bench, then my back will be parallel to the door, and I won't see anyone coming. If I pick the comfy sofa, I'll have to sit sideways at the far end to watch the door. There is no way I'm waiting in here if I can't see someone approach my only safe way out.

Both computer monitors are off, but there are a few post-it notes stuck to them. The desk is tidy with next to nothing on it. There's a list of phone numbers with only initials next to them.

M, A, N, B, S, A. I can guess who the first four numbers belong to, but I have no idea about the last two. Curiosity tempts me to snoop. But the Kutsenkos don't strike me as the type to forgive and forget if I invade their privacy.

My head jerks up as I hear someone punching the keypad outside the door. I hear the lock release, then Niko is pushing Michelle and Lanie through the door.

"All of you stay here." Niko spins around.

"Laura!" Michelle rushes to me, Lanie on her heels. We embrace for a long time as we listen to the chaos outside the office. None of it gets louder or closer, but the sounds of yelling and breaking furniture fill the air.

"We didn't know where you went." Michelle shakes her head. "You went to dance, and then you disappeared. Niko had to practically drag us both here. We didn't want to leave you behind."

"He kept telling us you were safe with Maksim, but we weren't so sure." Lanie glances at the door. "It was only when he told us that the police would arrest us if we were there when they arrived that we agreed to come back here. Thank God you're here."

"Maks brought me here right away. He told me not to open the door to anyone but him. He said only his brothers have the code, so I knew it was one of them outside. It still made me nearly pee my pants."

"That would be all you need right now." Lanie grins at me, and it lightens the mood. I still don't want to sit on either of the sofas, but I join my friends on the soft one. I sit farthest from the door, but I have the best line of sight.

"I know it's only been a couple minutes, but it feels like an eternity since this started." Michelle looks at her phone. "It's two a.m. Maybe we should have gone to Zebras. We'd still be having a good time and waiting for last call."

I don't say anything. Despite the disaster the night has turned into, I don't regret coming here. I sure as shit don't regret kissing Maks or having sex with him. I might regret some of the things I confessed. But he's been all I can think about for two days. I doubt having him grope me, then fuck me, is going to do anything to make my sex dreams go away. Hell, it'll probably make them even more vivid. But at least now I know.

I know having sex with Maksim Kutsenko is the closest thing to heaven I've ever experienced. If I ever get to have sex with him again, I might see a choir of angels. The moment I felt how hard he was, I thought my legs might give out. I made him get hard. He wants me. I wanted to moan and rub myself against him like a shameless cat. He's huge. It felt like a Coke bottle pressed against my pussy. I know some women would worry if it would fit. Fuck that. I made it fit.

Another crash outside the office, much closer than any other, makes Lanie squeak. It pulls me away from my fantasy. What is wrong with me? This is like the worst time to be thinking about fucking Maks. But I can't help it. It's a good distraction to keep me from freaking out. As I look at my two best girlfriends, I realize I'm worried about them getting hurt. I'm worried about Maks and his brothers. But I'm not scared for myself. Maks told me I'd be safe here. I believe him. I trust him. I trusted him on the dance floor when that guy tried to dance with me and when that other asshole made the comment.

I can defend myself.

That's not just ego. I actually can. I can fight, and I can shoot. I know how to wield a knife. These were skills I honed in St Petersburg when I studied abroad. I might have lived the privileged life of a white college student, but I went to Moscow most weekends. That's not a place that's always safe for women. My boyfriend back then, Antony, taught me. He was French, but he'd grown up in Moscow. He insisted that if I wanted to go out at night with only my girlfriends, then I needed to practice.

We met two weeks after I arrived in St. Petersburg and started dating two weeks after that. He wouldn't let me go out at night alone for nearly three months. At first, it pissed me off. Then I saw what he meant. I watched a van drive up to three women, slow down, and then stop. Before I could do a single thing, the women were in the van, and it was speeding away. All I could do was stand there. I knew the police would do nothing. The men who kidnapped those women were probably bratva. It would be more dangerous for me to say something. The guilt still eats at me. That's when Antony insisted I improve how I could defend myself.

Michelle squeezes my hand. "What if someone breaks in here. It's getting louder."

I go to the desk. On a hunch, I pull open the top drawers on the left and right side. There's a handgun in the left drawer. "Give me your hairband, Lanie."

She takes off the rolled headscarf she had tied around her head. I quickly wrap it around my hand and pick up the gun. With the end of the scarf in my other hand, I check to see how many bullets are there. I never once wondered if it was loaded. I truly hadn't planned to invade the Kutsenkos' privacy, but I also didn't think there'd be an attack. This was no bar fight. "What happened out there?"

"I don't know. I was talking to Bogdan when all of a sudden, this canister breaks a window, and there's this horrible noise."

"A flashbang." I glance toward the door. "It was a stun grenade to distract everyone."

"Yeah. It worked. I screamed." Lanie swallows, and I can practically feel her fear.

"Then there was a gunshot, and the shelves behind the bar

collapsed. I don't know what happened after that. People were screaming and running around. Niko tried to get us to come with him, but we refused." Michelle wipes a tear from her cheek.

"You're safe in here now. Between the keycode lock and the gun, no one is coming in here without us knowing or without it being one of the Kutsenkos. I trust Maks."

"You've known him for like a minute." Lanie frowns at me.

"Remember the hot clients I told you about from the other day? You just had champagne with them, and we're hiding in their office."

"Holy shit!" Michelle suddenly looks far less scared and way more curious.

"Yeah. Didn't you wonder why we knew each other's names?"

"I figured you'd done business before. I didn't know they—he—was *the one.*"

"He's not *the one.*" I mock her exaggeration as I tell my pussy to shut up. "But I trust him about this."

"I don't. This is crazy. Who full-on attacks a bar? We've seen plenty of bar fights, but this was like a war zone." Once more Michelle exaggerates. None of us have seen a war zone. We're college-educated women who come from upper middle-class families. We've hardly faced hardship like people living in a war zone. I know I'm being testy right now, and I know Michelle doesn't mean anything by it. But I know from Maks and his brothers' accents that they grew up in Russia, even though I'd already noticed they spoke perfect English. That would have been in the late 90s. That wasn't a peaceful place to live. If they're bratva, they didn't have the luxuries I did.

"After tonight, you need to stay away from Maksim. Bogdan is nice, but I don't need this crap."

I don't look at Michelle now. My eyes are locked on the

door, wondering what's happening to Maks. She's probably smarter than I am about this. But if he asked me out on a date, I wouldn't hesitate to say yes.

"Good thing I'm not into dicks." Lanie's comment lightens the tension.

"You're the smartest of the three of us." I grin at her. It's not the first time I've said that. But she has her fair share of drama dating women. "Since we're stuck here, tell us what happened with Teresa."

Lanie shoots me a dirty look. I shrug. "She wanted a threesome."

"So? It's not like you haven't done that before."

Michelle and I have both heard the stories.

"With her ex-girlfriend who she broke up with four months ago, who she still sees every week—didn't know that until the other day—whose name she's called me twice in bed. Fuck that."

"That sucks." Michelle slings her arm around Lanie's shoulders while they sit on the sofa.

"It's fine. The sex was great, but she was annoying AF outside the bedroom. I stuck around for her tongue."

I snort. "You did say it was magical."

"No one's tongue is magical enough to make me want to ignore that she's thinking about someone else. The first time was when we just started dating. I thought it was because they'd just broken up. The second time was last week, just before she suggested a threesome."

"That's messed up." I offer her a sympathetic smile. Lanie hasn't had much luck in love. She's a serial dater. She always has been, at least ever since college. She came out in high school and didn't date much. But she's gorgeous, and girls noticed that in college. She's also got a big heart. People—women—take advantage of her. I hate it.

"Listen." I turn toward the window and peer into the dark. I can see flashing lights approaching and sirens blaring. I move to the office door, and I can tell it's getting quieter out there. There's still lots of yelling, but not as much stuff sounds like it's getting broken. I go back to the desk and pull my cell phone from my pocket. Thank God for dresses with pockets. I hate carrying a purse, especially to a bar or club. "I'm calling Maks."

"Do you even have his number?" Michelle's brow furrows.

"I think it's right here."

"Maybe you should wait. Didn't he say he would come get you when it was safe?" Lanie looks away from me to the door.

"You probably shouldn't distract him, Laura. What if he gets hurt because he's answering his phone?"

"Chelle, do you think he'd answer if he's in the middle of kicking someone's ass?"

"Kicking someone's ass. Is that what you assume he's doing?"

I can't answer Michelle. I can't tell her or Lanie that he's probably been in a knife fight. I don't doubt he's carrying a blade since I know he doesn't have his gun. Neither of them has asked why there was a gun in the drawer, and I hope they don't. I haven't heard any gunshots. I don't think any of the brothers are carrying guns, since none have suit jackets on. But I'm positive their security has them. All of the bouncers have jackets on. It's hot as balls in the club, so the only reason to wear them isn't to look spiffy. It's to hide their firearms.

"I'm calling him."

I dial the number on the list. It rings three times, then goes to voicemail. His phone is on. I bet it's because he doesn't recognize my number. I immediately redial. It goes to voicemail after the second ring. I try a third time. He answers. I hope he isn't pissed that I'm bothering him. I want out of the office because I want to know what's going on, and he needs a lawyer.

It also dawns on me that Yakovitch isn't here, but the police soon will be. If they want to stay out of jail for the night, I need to get to them before the police start questioning them.

When he answers, I drop the gun back into the drawer and slam it shut.

"Who is this?"

"Maks? It's Laura. I found your number on the desk. I hear the police. Let me out."

Chapter Four

Maksim

I'm running back across the dance floor when I spy Aleks with a man pinned against the wall. His forearm is against the guy's throat as he lands one punch after another into the guy's face and gut. Bogdan's foot lands against another man's ribs as I rush forward. I grab two handfuls of a man's shirt and yank him away as he prepares to launch himself at Bogdan. My right fist draws back before I land it against his nose. He staggers, but I watch him reach for his pocket. There's no outline of a gun, so I assume he's drawing a blade. My left fist lands an uppercut, snapping his head back, before my right fist hooks and lands against his temple. He's out.

I spin around as Niko calls my name. He's running toward me alone, so I assume the women are safe. I see the man he called out to warn me about. He has a bar stool in his hands. I dodge to the side as I draw my own knife. I may not be carrying my gun—fuck. I should have gotten that from the office—but I have three knives on me. I slash this guy's ribs. He howls, but it's nothing like the sound he makes as I drive the blade into his belly.

This is no drunken bar fight. I knew that the moment I heard the glass breaking. This was an attack. One glance at any of the men my brothers and I fight, and it's obvious they're Italian Mafia. What isn't obvious is why they're here. We're on decent terms right now. We stay out of each other's territory and each other's business. So why the fuck is the *Cosa Nostra* here?

Our security guys are dividing between those keeping the patrons away and those fighting the other dozen attackers. There are close to twenty men who came into a Kutsenko establishment and attacked. This is not something I will over-look. If my predecessor was still in control, this would be a declaration of war. I'm not so hotheaded. But it won't be ignored. The bratva working here tonight know not to kill unless it's their life or the Italians'. But despite everyone remaining alive, there's blood everywhere. Sirens blare as they approach. People are fleeing the two exits.

I look down at my bloodied hands. Only a few minutes ago, they were enjoying Laura's delectable body. A body that I wish was still pressed against me rather than hiding in the office. Niko dashes around the bar and grabs a handful of towels. He pushes them into a bucket of soapy water before he starts tossing them to our men. The Italians are either passed out or pressed together in a circle while our men use the wet towels to wash the blood from their hands, faces, and necks. They clean knives and hide them away.

Lena, a waitress whose grandfather, father, and brothers are all bratva, hurries around with an empty bucket to gather the towels. I watch her run toward the back door, and I know she'll dowse them in alcohol and soon have them ablaze. They'll be smoldering ash by the time the police find it.

My phone rings with a number I don't recognize. I glance at it and silence it. I don't have time to chat. It rings again, the same number. I silence it a second time. When it rings a third time, I answer.

"Who is this?"

"Maks? It's Laura. I found your number on the desk. I hear the police. Let me out."

"No. Stay in there until this is over. You don't need to get involved."

"I'm already involved because I'm here. Besides, you're going to need a lawyer. Let me out. Michelle and Lanie will stay here."

"You're not my lawyer."

"I know. But I'm still *a* lawyer. Let me out, or I'll walk out there on my own."

"You will not."

"You really want to argue about this? I can hear the police cars right outside. Maks, either you come and get me, or I'm going to find you."

"Fine. Wait a moment." I glance around the havoc before storming down the hallway. I punch in the code and burst open the door. Michelle and Lanie are cowering behind the desk. Laura is standing beside the door jam. I grab her hand, uncaring if I'm being rough. "We are not even close to being done discussing this. You do not issue me orders, *malyshka*. You do not put yourself in danger. You do not get involved in bratva business."

"You mean going forward. Because there is no way to avoid all of that tonight."

I spin around and pull her against me, my hand fisting her hair. "This is not the time for your sarcasm. I'll put you back in that office." My mouth covers hers, and my teeth tug on her lower lip. She opens to me without reservation. She accepts my harsh kiss with a moan. She lets me lead, dominate her. When we pull apart, I kiss the tip of her nose. "That is why I call you *malyshka*."

We both know she submitted willingly. She looks up at me and nods. It's more like an exhalation than a whisper. "Yes, sir."

"Fuck. Now you say it. When I can't rip your clothes off and taste your pussy." She doesn't blush. She doesn't look away. She merely nods again. I turn us back toward the main area of the club. We can hear the police, so I can't dawdle any longer. Laura spies my brothers being questioned at the same time I do. The police are talking, but my brothers remain silent. Laura steps past me.

"Officers, Mr. Kutsenko—all four of them—will not answer any questions without me present. I will decide which ones they do answer. I'm Laura Doyle. Their attorney."

We've been trained since we were young *shestyorka*—recruits—to never give anything away through our expressions or body language. I move to stand next to Aleks. We're lined up by age. We just seem to always end up that way. Laura positions herself between us and the male detective trying to step around her. She shifts each time, her smirk unflappable. I'm certain we look ridiculous. My brothers and I are easily a foot taller than her since she's wearing flat sandals. The detective is probably six inches taller than her. But she doesn't flinch.

"Detective Diaz." I watch Laura cock an eyebrow. I wonder how she knows his name when he hasn't shown her his badge. "I'm certain you passed a hearing test. Do not pretend not to hear me. I said my clients will not answer any questions that I don't approve. Direct them to me."

"Laura—"

"Ms. Doyle, *Detective Diaz*."

"Come on, Laura." The detective rolls his eyes. I want to punch him.

33

"Juan, I don't give a fuck if we've known each other since we were in diapers. Don't 'come on, Laura' me. You want to be a jackass and pretend like you didn't hear me, pretend like we're not both at work at a crime scene, then I'll be the same bitch who pushed you out a tree and stepped over you when you broke your arm. Remember why I did that?"

"Fine."

Bogdan can't help himself. "Why'd you do that?"

"Because he said I was too weak and too chickenshit to do it." Laura leans forward on her toes. "And I recall your mother told you, you deserved it. It wasn't the first time, you told me that. But it was the last. Don't push me tonight, *Detective Diaz*."

"Fine, *Ms. Doyle*. Do your clients recognize any of these men?"

Laura turns back to me and nods. I'm not accustomed to waiting for a woman, other than my mother, to give me permission to speak.

"I recognized their tattoos, but I don't know them."

Laura looks at each of my brothers, and they echo my words. She turns back to face her—what? Childhood friend? Childhood nemesis? Whatever he is, I want to knock the smug look off his face. There's too much familiarity for them to have just been old acquaintances. Something went on between them, and I hate it. I have no reason to. At least, no reason that a rational man could claim. But all I can think is *mine. Mine. MINE!*

"What do their tattoos have to do with anything? Who are they?"

Laura leans toward a man sprawled behind Detective Diaz. She looks at me, but her expression tells me not to give anything away.

"They all have a map of Italy. Hard not to recognize them.

It's on all their forearms." Laura points to one of the Italian foot soldiers.

"Why is the Italian Mafia busting up your nightclub, Mr. Kutsenko?"

"How would any of my clients know that? Do you think they got a text, a call, or an email giving them a heads up? Do you think there was much time to talk as my clients defended their patrons?"

"Defended their patrons?" Juan snorts. "Really, Lau—Ms. Doyle?"

"Yes, really. Do you think these guys announced their intention to attack this place tonight? How many criminals do you know who make declarations about a crime they're about to commit?"

"Fine. Have you had any recent conflict with the Italians?" Detective Diaz looks at me. I love how Laura answers all of his questions with her own. She's sexy as hell when she's being a lawyer.

"The Italians? Do you think my clients have a conflict with an entire nationality? They may be successful businessmen, but I don't think anyone's reach is so great as to have a problem with an entire nationality."

"Ms. Doyle."

"What?"

"You're testing my patience."

"You know better than to do this. Don't play chicken with a hawk, Detective Diaz."

"I gotta get some answers. If I don't, then I'll arrest the Kutsenkos. You won't be able to be in all four interrogation rooms at once."

I watch as Laura straightens to her full height and manages to look down her nose at a man much taller than her. Her face remains relaxed, but I can feel the energy reverberating from her.

"You and I both know that isn't a good idea."

"Since when did the Russian mob start employing you, Laura? I thought you had morals."

I'm ready to bash his face in. There was more than one loaded insult in those comments. My fists ball, and I shift my weight. But before I can say anything, Laura speaks again.

"Fuck you and the horse you rode in on, Juan. How's your *papi?*"

"That's a bitch move, Laura, and you know it."

"Don't speak to her that way." I'm snarling. I see red. It's only Laura's glare that stops me from wrapping my hand around the guy's throat.

"Maybe your father shouldn't have made that last run to Colombia. I warned him. I warned you. I don't judge you or your family, so don't you fucking judge me."

"We've always known what my family is. You—you were supposed to be far removed from all that. You were supposed to be good. You're a lawyer for fuck's sake."

"Bah." Laura snorts. "Like being a lawyer guarantees someone's ethics. And I was far removed as a kid. But I'm not a kid anymore. It's pretty damn hard to be a corporate lawyer in New York and not know people who break the law for a living."

Laura looks back at me before glancing at my brothers.

"Let's make this super simple. All four Mr. Kutsenkos were here at their place of business. They were away from the doors and the bar. The DJ was playing, and everything seemed normal. Then there was a loud crash, glass broke, and hell broke loose. My clients defended their patrons and their property. They are victims. Are you going to blame them for being attacked? Are you going to blame the victims? You haven't even asked if they and their men are all right. So much for looking after public welfare, Detective Diaz."

Juan snaps his notepad closed. "They better have you on retainer. I may not be able to charge them with anything tonight, but you know this isn't the last time they'll face the police."

"Fine." It shocks the shit out of me when they embrace. It's loose but yet again familiar. "Tell your mother that I'll see her for dinner on Sunday. And don't be late this time. It pisses my dad off, and then my mom and I have to listen to him complain when we're just as hungry as he is. I won't try to get them to wait this time."

"I almost got shot last week, Laura. That's why I was late."

"But you didn't. And you showed me your phone still worked. You should have called or texted. It was very thoughtless, Juan." Laura laughs. "I said a whole rosary for you."

"Goodnight, Laura."

I don't stop myself from stepping up to Laura when Juan kisses her on the cheek.

"Goodnight, Juan."

No one speaks until the last officer clears out. They arrested the Italians who were conscious and put the unconscious ones who needed medical attention in ambulances. With no blood on any of us, there was no way to prove who, if anyone, was involved, so there were no bratva arrests.

There are a few lingering patrons standing on the sidewalk outside while they watch or give statements to the police. The bartenders and waitresses are cleaning up what they can, but we'll have to have a crew come in tomorrow morning, or we won't be ready to open tomorrow night. I won't give the Italians the satisfaction of losing two nights' worth of business.

"What the hell was that?" Aleks crosses his arms and stares at Laura.

"Watch how you speak to her." I slide my arm around her waist and step closer, bringing her back against my chest.

"Whatever, Maks. Everyone knows she's yours. I want to know what the hell kind of conversation that was."

"*She* is still standing here," Laura snaps. "And what that was, was two people who've known each other their entire lives, facing off when business and pleasure don't mix. He might have been doing his job, and I might have been acting like your lawyer, but at the end of the day, he's still my oldest friend."

"Maybe we should put you on retainer." Aleks nods his approval.

"You couldn't afford me."

"You do know we're…" Niko cocks an eyebrow.

"Billionaires? Yes. But I also know what you pay Yakovitch. If that's the best your money can buy, then you can't afford me."

"How do you know that?" I lean around her to look down at her face.

"Because I learn as much as I can about my adversaries. And since we both know I couldn't find anything on you four, I found what I could about your lawyer. It wasn't hard to follow the money trail and figure out what he makes. I may not have looked at his bank account, but the way he spends money and buys expensive toys on credit tells me your in-house counsel doesn't make nearly as much as he likes to make people think he does. Discretion with his words or his actions is not his strength."

"Maybe we should hire you." Bogdan nudges Niko.

"Thank you, no. I like my corner office and my normal business hours. Just be glad I don't bill you for this. Like I said, you can't afford me." Laura turns to look at me. "Can we get Lanie and Michelle? They must be freaking out. The police aren't here to question them, and they don't have to see the busted faces and bodies."

"Yes. Then I'll take you three home. My car and driver are outside waiting."

"Thank you."

An hour later, Laura's friends are each in their apartments after I walked them to their doors. Now I'm alone in the backseat of my town car with the privacy glass up and a woman who still has me hard despite the shitshow tonight turned out to be. I tug her onto my lap, her legs straddling me. She doesn't hesitate to accept my kiss. My hand skims up her thigh, my thumb running along the inside until it gets to the juncture of hip. I can feel the heat coming from her pussy, and I can feel the moisture on her inner thigh. She's still soaking wet for me.

"Maks."

Her whispered breath against my ear makes my cock twitch for at least the twentieth time tonight. I slip two fingers into her and rub my thumb on her clit. She's rocking on my hand as I unfasten my pants. When she realizes what I'm doing she stops.

"I'm not fucking you the in a car tonight, *malyshka*. A store-room was bad enough for our first time. But I want to feel you against me. I'm just opening my pants. Rub yourself against my boxer briefs."

She glances down and nods. "I'd leave a stain on your pants anyway. I'm so damn wet."

"I know, baby girl."

I push her thong aside and work my fingers inside of her as she goes back to riding my hand. I press harder against her clit. When she moans, my fingers are digging into her ass. She's going to come. She's bracing herself by holding onto my shoulders. If I couldn't feel her pussy tightening around my fingers, I would know the moment her orgasm hits from the way she clutches my shoulders.

In one smooth move, I flip us, so she's half lying on the seat, and I'm kneeling on the car floor as I pull her panties down. I'm still finger fucking her, but now I'm tasting her, too.

"I've wanted to do this since I watched you take my company for forty billion dollars. I should have been pissed. But all I could think about was sticking my tongue in you and licking you dry."

"Maks. God. You make me so hot when you say shit like that."

"Good."

I bury my face between her legs and lick her pussy lips before flicking my tongue over her clit. As I work that little nub, my fingers are sliding in and out. Her hips rise and fall with each flick and thrust. Her fingers are gripping the edge of the seat. I feel the car come to a stop, but I'm not anywhere near done. My driver knows better than to open the door without my signal. I have a feast before me, and I'm famished.

"Maks, I'm close again."

"Come on my tongue, *malyshka*. Right now. Come for me." I rub my thumb hard over her clit while my tongue dives back inside her.

"Maks!"

Her back arches off the seat as she trembles. Her inner muscles clench around my tongue and fingers, and the gush of moisture coats my mouth. She's panting, and I've never seen a more beautiful sight than my baby girl properly pleasured and breathless. I slide her thong all the way off and sniff it before sticking it in my pocket. I'm going to be jerking off to this tonight and probably every night until she's in my bed permanently.

When our clothes are settled, I rap on the window, and my

driver opens the door. I'm helping Laura out of the town car, but I don't step back right away. I drop a quick kiss on her lips before I take her hand. We step off the elevator, and when we get to her door, she unlocks it. I can see a light is already on.

"Hi, handsome." My head jerks up at Laura's greeting. "Have you missed me? I've missed you. It's been a long night. I'm happy to see you, too."

My hand slams the door open. I want to know who the fuck she's talking to. Does she have a boyfriend? It better not be a husband. Why would she let me eat her out then walk her to the door if there's a man waiting for her? A deep growl answers the sound of the doorknob hitting the wall.

"Jesus, Maks." Laura frowns as she crouches down. An enormous mastiff wiggles his way to her. "This is Sebastian. I have a dog, not a man."

She grabs a leash from beside the door.

"I need to take him for a walk. Thank you for walking me to my door. Goodnight, Maks."

"I'm not leaving you to walk around in the dark at four a.m."

"Maks, Sebastian probably weighs close to what you do. He's a hundred and ninety-seven pounds. He's close to six feet tall when he stands on his hind legs. No one comes near me."

"Laura, I don't know who saw you with me tonight. He might bite, but that's no match to a knife or a gun. At least for tonight, please let me go with you."

Laura stares at me before she nods. She saw me untuck my shirt and stick a gun into a holster against my back before we left Envy. She snaps the leash onto her dog's collar before we make our way back to the elevator. The enormous honey-colored dog looks up at me. I feel like I'm being judged, and I'm not sure I'm impressing him. I reach out my hand for him to sniff. Apparently, I pass the test because he rests most of his weight against my shins, practically knocking me off balance. I stroke between his ears and listen as his tail thuds against the elevator wall.

"He likes you."

"I think he probably likes most people."

"He is a bit of a softie. But don't tell anyone. It'll ruin his street cred with the boxers, German shepherds, and the Doberman in the neighborhood."

"His secret is safe with me."

"There have been a few secrets shared tonight."

I cup Laura's jaw and bring her closer for a kiss. Our mouths fuse until the bell dings and we reach the ground floor. I enjoy the fifteen minutes I get to spend with her and Sebastian. Then I'm saying goodnight all too soon. I can taste her on my lips after our last lingering kiss at her door. I can still taste the whiskey sour and champagne on her breath. I can think of something else of hers I'd like to taste again. I'm sure she can taste herself on me. She agreed to go out to dinner with me three nights from now. We both have commitments before then. I suspect I'll be famished by then.

Chapter Five

Laura

I have a meeting with the Kutsenkos again today. I haven't seen Maks since the incident at Envy two nights ago. He texted me when he got to his place to say goodnight, and he texted me yesterday morning and this morning to say hello. I texted him at lunch yesterday and sent him a picture of a ham sandwich that I purposely made just so I could send him the photo. I don't know how I'm supposed to concentrate in a meeting where my clients and Maks will be seated facing each other while I address the transition.

I have just enough concentration to review my notes from yesterday's meeting with the RK leadership. It shocked the shit out of them how much I made them. The CFO had the audacity to tell me that I got them too much. I know it's because he's scared of the Kutsenkos. I could hardly reassure him that they would be on good terms with the brothers because the oldest one had his tongue in my mouth and pussy

43

and his fingers practically up to my belly button a couple nights ago.

My phone rings, and my heart stutters when I see the caller. Maks has never called me. We haven't talked on the phone except for when I demanded he let me out of the office.

"Hello" That hardly sounded as casual as I wanted.

"*Malyshka.*"

Well, there went another pair of panties.

"Hi, Maks."

"I know we have a meeting in an hour, but I wanted to call and give you a heads up."

"What for?"

"I won't be there."

"Oh?" Do I sound as pathetically disappointed to him as I sound to myself?

"My brothers know I'm personally pulling out of the deal. Dmitry amended the agreement to show three parties, not four, represent Kutsenko Partners. He emailed it to you a moment ago."

I check my computer, and sure enough, an email just came in. "Why?"

"Because I want to see you for more than just one dinner tomorrow night."

"Okay." I'm not following.

"*Malyshka*, if I remain a party to this deal, it will make us both look questionable if anyone finds out we're dating."

"We're dating? We haven't even been out once."

"Did you not just hear me say that I want to see you more than just tomorrow night?"

"Yeah. But how do you even know we're compatible enough to actually date? Fuck, yes. Date? I don't know."

"You have a dirty mouth, *malyshka.*"

"How else am I supposed to describe what we might do? I don't think you're the type to say make love. Is hook up better?"

"No." Maks snarls. I've heard that tone before, and it makes my belly clench. I love it. "'Hook up' implies it's only sex. I think we both know there's more than just physical attraction between us. I won't risk your reputation and career for the sake of being part of a merger that I'll have next-to-no role in."

I don't know what to say. "Thank you."

"I didn't want you to think I was avoiding you. And I didn't want you to get the email without me explaining first."

"I appreciate that, Maks. I still don't think you need to do this, but I appreciate it."

"I'll always look out for you, Laura."

I can't explain why that makes me want to twirl in a circle and beam. It echoes in my head over and over. What is it about the idea of Maks looking out for me, protecting me, that is so damn appealing?

"I want to do the same. Since I thought I was going to see you today, I didn't say anything yet. I had Sunday dinner with Juan and his family."

"Oh?" There's a note of warning. I couldn't ignore his possessiveness the other night. It didn't bother me when it would have irritated the hell out of me with someone else.

"Maks, Juan and I grew up next door to each other. He's seriously two weeks older than me. Our parents bought their houses within three months of each other when we were both two. I don't remember a time without him. We've had Sunday dinner together for more than twenty years. The only time we didn't was the four years we were away for college and my three years at law school. Even then, whenever we were home on breaks, we'd attend. Our parents still got together even without us there."

"I get it. Detective Diaz is an old friend."

"Yes. And as an old friend who happens to work for NYPD, he mentioned that white-collar crimes caught wind of the attack. They're digging, Maks. And they're trying to go deep. I know they aren't likely to find much, but I thought you should know."

"Did the detective tell you this in passing, and you happen to be passing this along? Or did he tell you so you could tell me?"

I pause. I'm not going to lie, but I know he won't like the answer. "Juan was warning me away from you. He doesn't want me involved if there's a sting."

"Do you believe what he does? That I can't keep you protected."

"Maks." I can't help my exasperation. "If I worried that I'm not safe with you, I wouldn't have agreed to go on a date with you."

"Do you feel safe with me, *malyshka?*"

"I—I don't know." I hear his intake of breath. "Wait. I mean, I feel safe from the rest of the world when I'm with you or think about going out with you. I just don't know if I'm safe from you." I'm practically whispering by the time I finish.

"Do you think I'd hurt you, Laura?" I can hear the pain in his voice.

"Not intentionally. At least not out of the bedroom and what's consensual."

"You called me sir that night."

"I know. You wouldn't let me kiss you at first. The moment I gave up trying, you kissed me. The way you fist my hair. Your entire personality. You're in control. I'm okay with that. I liked —like—it. But I don't want to think this is something it's not."

"What do you think it might not be, *malyshka?*"

"A relationship." I can barely get the word past my teeth.

"I'm going to tell you for a third time, and this better be the

46

absolute last time, that I want more with you than a good fuck or one date."

"I don't understand what you're saying. Are you a Dom? Is that what you're suggesting?" I swallow. I can't believe I'm having this conversation over the phone in my office, with a guy who I haven't even been on a date with, an hour before his brothers and my client arrive for a meeting he was supposed to attend. WTF?

"Have you had a Dom before? Is that what you want?"

"No. I've never been in a Dom/sub relationship before. I've been—I have some experience with Doms."

"Baby girl, this is a conversation better had in-person. I will tell you this, that if you want me as your Dom, we can explore that. But that wasn't what I meant." There's a pause. I wonder if he's going to clarify. "I want to be your boyfriend."

"You sound awfully rusty saying that."

"Because I haven't been one in five years."

"You haven't had a girlfriend in five years?" I can't help blurting that out.

"Laura, I'm no monk. But I haven't been in a committed relationship of any kind since I was twenty-five. What about you? When was your last boyfriend?"

I have to think a moment. "Like a year and a half."

"We'll talk about this tomorrow night. We'll figure out what we both want and what we can both offer."

"All right." I can't help feeling anxious now. I was excited and impatient before. Now I've added nervous to the list.

"Laura."

"Yes, Maks."

"We haven't discussed you issuing me orders to come out of the office into a crime scene. I think we both know that wasn't a wise way to go about getting what you wanted. Was it?"

"No, sir," I whisper.

"Good girl."

Why do those two words make me feel so hot? Why am I so pleased with that small acknowledgment? It eases much of my anxiety that cropped up only moments ago.

"Thank you, sir."

"Your meeting will start soon."

"I know. I have to head over there now."

"There's a car waiting for you downstairs. The driver knows where to take you. There's also a privacy screen, so you'll be totally alone. If you feel anything like I do right now, you'll appreciate the chance to take care of that ache."

"Are you suggesting I get myself off in your car?"

"Don't sound so shocked, *malyshka*. You already admitted you wanted to do that last time. Now you don't have to drive yourself."

"I—" I don't have a clue what to say.

"Don't doubt for a second that it's you I'm picturing right now as I unzip my pants."

"Maks!"

"Yes, baby girl?"

"Where are you? What the hell?"

"I happen to be at home right now. I'm in my office, but I'm not around anyone. I can even leave the door open."

"Maks." I'm hissing at this point. I can barely stand the images he's conjuring in my mind.

"Gather your things, baby girl." I'm following his order like he can see me or something. "I'm staying on the phone with you until you're in the car."

"Yes, sir."

I hear him groan. I wonder if it's from giving himself a hand job or from my last comment.

"I love hearing you say that. I'm fucking leaking. Hurry up, *malyshka*. I won't start until you're able to."

I'm practically sprinting to the elevator. Now I'm squeezing my legs together as I ride down to the lobby. I can see a man in a dark suit standing next to a town car as I approach the glass doors.

"Mr. Kutsenko sent me, Ms. Doyle."

"Thank you." I slide into the car and wait for the door to close. The privacy glass is already up.

"Are you buckled up, baby girl?"

"Yes, d—sir." What the hell is wrong with me?

"What were you about to say?"

Great.

"Dom."

"Don't lie to me."

"I'm not ready for that, Maks." I'm scared I'm going to disappoint him, but I can't bring myself to say what I'm thinking.

"When you are, I'll be listening, *malyshka*."

"Thank you." I lean my head back as I pull my skirt up my legs. I can't believe I'm doing this. But if I don't, I'm going to be a frustrated wreck. I slip my panties off and shake my head. No surprise they're damp. I shove those in the bottom of my purse where I'm not likely to accidently pull them out when I take my laptop out of my work bag.

"Okay, baby girl. I'll let you do your thing. Maybe it's still a little soon for full-on phone sex. But I will ask my brothers if you looked relaxed when you get there."

"Don't you dare, Maks! I don't want you asking them if they think I just gave myself an orgasm."

"I won't ask that."

"Why else would you ask them if I was relaxed? They'll figure it out. They strike me as just as horny as you."

"That is true. Fine. It'll be on the honor system. I'll get myself off, and you'll do the same."

"I don't doubt you will. Now if I'm going to have time, I gotta go, Maks." I can see from the window that there's enough traffic to delay what should be a five-minute drive to long enough for me to do my own thing. I can't believe I'm going to, but he has me worked up and tempted.

"I'll see you tomorrow night, Laura."

"I look forward to it, Maks."

I barely have time before we pull up to RK Capital's building to use the box of tissues in the car to clean myself up and squirt hand sanitizer from my purse onto my palms. I adjust my clothes and stuff the tissues in my skirt pocket until I can throw them away in the trash outside the building.

The meeting seems to go on forever. My clients kiss the Kutsenkos' asses and lick their boots. My clients keep shooting me alternating dirty looks and nervous glares. It gets so bad that Aleksei finally steps in.

"Ms. Doyle, you drive a hard bargain. We intended to way underbid, but you called our bluff. If you didn't have your job with your firm, Kutsenko Partners would hire you. Gentlemen, I hope you at least bought Ms. Doyle dinner. She made you far more than anyone else likely would have."

"Thank you, Mr. Kutsenko." I offer a quick, tight smile to Aleksei before my brow furrows at Nikolai and Bogdan, who are both trying not to laugh.

"Yes, well, we are pleased with Ms. Doyle's work. If she's good enough that you would consider hiring her, she's good enough for us."

Asshole. If I did work directly for RK Group, I would jump ship and go to the Kutsenkos—that is if I wasn't dating Maks—but I like the firm I work for.

That date cannot get here soon enough.

"All right, Sebastian. Be a good boy. I left Animal Planet on for you." I'm talking to my dog as I put the bouquet of mixed flowers Maks brought me into a vase with water. He looks too good to stare at right now. I need a moment to compose myself. My dog is a good distraction. I walk around the kitchen island and out to the living room where Sebastian is lounging on his bed. I know he'll be on the sofa before I get the key in the lock. I scratch behind his ears before looking at Maks.

He holds his hand out to me, which I happily take. He gave me a far-too-chaste kiss when he arrived, the bouquet in the way and keeping us from getting closer. We don't say anything until we get in the elevator.

"What are you doing?

Maks just hit the stop button on the elevator. Rather than answer me with words, both hands slide into my hair and cup my scalp before he presses me against the wall. I'm moaning as his lips meet mine. My hands wrap around his neck. I'm wearing three-inch heels tonight, so it makes it easier to reach him. I keep the pressure light with my palms, but when Maks slides his right hand to my throat, he holds tight. It's not enough to count as breath play, but it's enough to feel his control. I love it.

"This is so much better than I remembered. I've been starving to taste you again, *malyshka*."

I don't say anything. All I can think about is getting his tongue back into my mouth. Or better yet, between my legs. Like they did while we were on the dance floor, my fingers slide between the buttons of his shirt. I can feel his heated skin.

"If we didn't have a reservation, I'd spend all night right here with you."

Maks pulls away and restarts the elevator. I can only imagine what the other tenants in my building must be thinking when no elevator arrives when they call it. He leads me out to the waiting car. It's a different driver than who picked me up, and I can see another man in the front passenger seat. I look up at Maks.

"Michail is our driver tonight. Sergei is your bodyguard."

"My bodyguard? Maks?"

"Shh. Get in, and I'll explain." Once we're settled into the car, Maks wraps his arm around my shoulder and pulls me close enough to hold my hand. "Sergei is my cousin, and he's one of my most trusted men. If anything were to happen tonight, he knows that the only thing he's to do is get you somewhere safe. Laura, this is part of being with me. There is danger being seen in my company. You knew I was bratva, so you knew the threats before everything that happened at the club. Can you live with this?"

I nod. I remember Antony and how he hated me going anywhere without him or at least one guy friend. I suppose he saw himself as my bodyguard as much as he did my boyfriend.

"You don't seem surprised. I thought I might have to convince you."

"Maks, I spent a year living in St. Petersburg during my junior year of college. I went back for another six months four years later, after I graduated from law school. I spent the time studying for the bar. I've gone back a few times in the past two years. I understand why you have a bodyguard because I understand the threats."

"That's how you speak like a native."

"Yes. I went to Moscow a lot too. Are you from either of those cities?"

"*Da.*" God, his smile is gorgeous. "I lived in Moscow until I was fourteen, and we moved here."

"So half your life. Did you speak any English when you arrived?"

"A little but not much. We moved to Queens, where there

was already a Russian community. It meant there were always people there who understood me, but there were also plenty of kids to help me learn, so I didn't make too much of a fool of myself at school."

"You and your brothers are close in age, aren't you?"

"Yes. A year apart for each of us. I'm thirty. Aleksei is twenty-nine, Nikolai is twenty-eight, and Bogdan is twenty-seven."

The same age as Michelle. Too bad she's not at all interested. She tried to convince me not to see Maks tonight. I definitely didn't tell her or Lanie about my conversation with Maks yesterday, or what happened in the car after we dropped them both off at their places.

"What about your family? Doyle is an Irish name, isn't it?"

"Yeah. It was O'Doyle before my family moved to America in the '20s. But I'm pretty much only Irish on St. Patrick's Day. We don't really talk that much about where my family is from. My mom's family is Irish and German. My dad's family is mostly Irish, I guess. His parents died before I was born, and so did his older brother. There was a car accident that killed his family."

"That is a hard loss for your father."

I nod. "You said Sergei is your cousin. Do you have a lot of family here?"

"Some. My mother brought my brothers and me here. Her sister was already here with a husband and two kids. Sergei is one of them. My father's brother and his family came over not long after we did. It wasn't safe for them to stay in Moscow."

I want to ask more, but I don't know how much Maks can or would share. It's as though he reads my mind.

"You can ask what you want, *malyshka*."

"What about your father?"

"He was killed fighting the Chechens. He was KGB, and

53

after the fall of the Soviet Union, he was recruited into the Podolskaya Bratva. He wasn't given much choice, since they ruled our neighborhood. They weren't the largest bratva in Moscow, but they were vicious and methodical in recruiting and maintaining control."

"Is that...?" I bite my lip and raise my eyebrows.

"No. My parents fought to keep my brothers and me away from all things bratva. That's part of the reason why my mother had four children in four years. She was beautiful when she was younger. She still is. Too many men in the bratva noticed her when she married my father. He was terrified they'd take her and sell her or stick her in some whorehouse. My parents wanted each of us, but they had us close together because they knew the bratva would lose interest in a woman who bore so many children. It likely kept her alive. It definitely kept her with us."

I can only nod. What Maks tells me doesn't surprise me. I was the one who warned him about using any of RK's buildings for human trafficking.

"That's why you don't have to worry about us pedaling flesh. Our mother would kill us after what she went through to avoid being a victim."

"How'd you end up in the bratva if you didn't join in Russia?"

"The Ivankov branch is linked to the Podolskaya. It was impossible for people not to learn who my father was. Once news that we moved here arrived, my brothers and I were recruited."

"Bogdan would have been eleven."

"Yeah. But he was hardly the youngest they'd ever recruited. We started out as messenger boys. I got in a nasty fight with a Pole who tried to jump Bogdan. I beat the shit out of him. Vladislav Lushak was the leader then. He found out and decided to train me as a boxer. I became a prizefighter for him. I gained a reputation for not backing down, and as I filled out and got bigger, the betting got steeper. Vlad made me keep fighting."

I listen to Maks share his past, wanting to learn more about him. But when he mentions this man's name, his tone changes. There's bitterness and hate in it. I don't know if I should push for more, so I stay quiet. Maks doesn't offer any more, so I tell him about my family.

"I can't say that I experienced anything near that growing up in north Jersey, but I saw plenty when I was in Russia. I know parts of Queens and Brighton Beach run like they're in Russia, not America. I didn't know much about what Juan's father did when we were kids. I just knew he traveled for business a lot. Sometimes he'd come home with swollen knuckles or some bruises on his face. He and Juan's mother just told us that Colombia can be rough, and people tried to mug him. It wasn't until I was in high school that I realized Mr. Diaz was part of the Cartel. A senior part of the Cartel. He's been stuck in a Colombian jail for three months. The longest he's been in one is a year. Makes my dad being a stockbroker and my mom being a doctor look boring. My sister is a nurse."

"Is your sister older or younger?"

"Maddie is younger by three years. She works at a hospital in Albany. She went to school up there."

"Where did you go to school?"

I almost don't want to admit it. My life was filled with privilege, and Maks's was filled with hardship. But I worked hard to get into undergrad and law school, and I worked hard to get my job.

"I went to Princeton for college and Yale for law school."

"I knew you were smart."

"Yeah, a little bit."

"Don't do that." I jump at Maks's tone. I look up at him, startled. "Don't diminish what you've accomplished. Family money doesn't buy the intelligence I've seen. I know you worked for what you've gotten. Be as proud of what you've achieved, as I am to have such an accomplished woman beside me."

"Yes, sir."

Maks cups my jaw and kisses me fiercely before pulling away just as abruptly.

"Speaking of sir. We have the issue of you being so defiant the other night."

"Can't it be forgiven since I kept you and your brothers out of jail?"

"Maybe, but it won't be."

"Then how's that even close to a maybe?"

Maks's smile can only be described as wolfish. My thighs clench.

"We talked a little yesterday, but not nearly enough. Laura, I will turn you over my knee or bend you over a table and spank you if you defy me."

My chest tightens. I want to beg for a spanking right now. "Yes, sir."

"I haven't had a girlfriend in a long time. I told you that yesterday. The last woman I dated wanted me for my money and for my position."

When Maks pauses, I put my hand on his thigh. "You don't owe me an explanation, sir."

"I want to give you one. We started dating a month after I became *pakhan*. I didn't inherit this position, Laura. I took it. Vlad was far from the first man I killed, but he was the first one I killed to make a point. The men who helped lead back then kept telling me I needed a wife who could have a son and give me an heir. I believed them, but I just couldn't bring myself to

56

marry her. After two years, I couldn't ignore that I could barely stand her. When her infidelity became too well known and threatened to ruin my reputation, I cut ties with her."

"All right." I don't know why he's telling me this before we've even had dinner on our first date. But we haven't done a damn thing in the normal order so far.

"I didn't love her. I didn't even care about her after the first couple months. I did what was expected of me, not what I wanted. I haven't considered dating anyone since then because I felt weak by the time I broke things off. She played me for a fool. The leaders back then manipulated me through her. My brothers were barely old enough to be brigadiers, let alone part of the senior leadership. Until a week ago, I believed having any feelings beyond lust for a woman was pointless. Then this sharp-tongued beauty threatens to kick me out of a conference room so she can eat a ham sandwich. You're the only woman besides my mother I've ever admired."

My lips twitch. "Despite being compared to your mother, thank you for the compliment."

"The reason I told you all of this is because I care about you. I was willing to protect my last girlfriend because that was my duty. I haven't been interested in being gentle with my past partners. That wasn't the kind of sex either of us wanted. Laura, you won't be the first woman I've spanked—and I find I actually regret that—but you'll be the first one I've spanked because I care what happens to you. It's not just about sex."

My eyebrows shoot up while I blink once. That was a lot to take in. "Domestic discipline. Is that what you mean?"

"I suppose, sort of. I'm not sure."

"You said you would consider being my Dom if that's what I wanted."

"I've never been in a Dom/sub relationship beyond the clubs I go to. But I'm willing to try with you if that's what you want. But it's more than just me taking care of you, and you submitting. If I think you're putting yourself at risk, if you disobey me beyond just when we're being intimate, or you act out of turn in public, I will punish you."

"Yes, sir. I—" I don't have a chance to tell Maks that I want that. The car pulls to a stop. I live in Queens, so it took a while to get into Manhattan. A question unrelated to our conversation strikes me. "You said you moved to Queens. Do you still live there?"

"I have a house there, but I spend most of my time at my penthouse here in Manhattan."

"That was a long drive to pick me up. And it was a long drive the other night to drop Lanie, Michelle, and me off. I could have met you down here."

"No." Maks shakes his head. "I wanted us to have the time alone to talk. And I hate the idea of you Ubering or taking the subway at night. I know you've done it in the past, but you don't have to do it now. I'd rather you not do it now."

I gaze at Maks, and something registers with me. "You're worried about me. This isn't just doing what you think you're supposed to as a boyfriend or a Dom. You're worried something will happen to me."

"Yes. Bogdan told me someone moved his gun the other night. Between you and your friends, I'm guessing it was you. You've lived in Russia, and you live alone in New York City. It's obvious you can take care of yourself, but I still hate the idea that something or someone might hurt you. That risk goes up now that we're dating."

I nod. Maks knocks on the window, and Michail opens the door beside the curb. Maks slips out before he offers me his hand. I'm careful not to flash the world as I step out of the car. I look up and recognize the restaurant in front of us.

"Maks." My tone is anything but happy.

"I thought you would enjoy Italian."

"I do, but why would you bring me here? No. I'm not going in. I don't want to be in the middle of this shit. Is this the real reason you brought Sergei? You expect there to be trouble. You want to cause trouble. Take me home."

"*Malyshka*, you're overreacting. I didn't know you were aware of who owns this restaurant. It's the best Italian food in the city. I thought you would enjoy it. There was no other reason. I just wanted to give you the best."

"You know the risks of showing up at a restaurant owned by the Italian don when his men attacked you less than a week ago. Take me home or take me somewhere else."

"Look who's skulking around outside my door."

I don't need to see the face to guess who owns the Italian-accented voice. The exact man I didn't want to encounter. The exact man I'm angry Maks would bring me near.

"*Russkiy*, what are you doing here? Tired of eating potatoes and dogs? Come for real food?"

Maks ignores Salvatore Mancinelli and wraps his arm around my waist. He guides me toward the front of the car. I see a popular Asian fusion restaurant. I hope he's taking us there instead. I'm pissed, and I'm scared. I don't want a confrontation with the *Cosa Nostra* on the sidewalk. I don't doubt Maks can hold his own. But who knows how many men Salvatore has inside? It's Maks, his driver, and his bodyguard. I don't want to be in the crossfire.

"Your strip clubs are a few blocks over. Your woman won't find a pole around here."

Maks's arm tightens around me, but he says nothing. Salvatore doesn't give up.

"She looks more expensive than the sluts you usually fuck. How much for an hour with you after he's done, bella?"

I refuse to look at him. I keep myself tucked against Maks's side. Sergei is behind us, and Michail walks beside me, closest to the street. If this is a date with Maks, then I want no part of this. I want him. But I don't want him if he's going to tell me in one breath that he wishes to protect me and take care of me, then in the next put me in danger. Fuck that.

"Kutsenko, you and your shithead brothers can't be at every bar and club every night. I got a guy in Jersey with a head for numbers. He can keep track real good when he plays cards."

"Take Ms. Doyle inside," Maks instructs Michail.

"Maks, no. Please."

"Go, *malyshka*. I'll be there in just a moment."

"Please don't do this." I don't glance at Michail because I don't mean to insult him. "I don't feel safe without you, Maks."

"Listen to me and do as I say. I'll be there in just a minute. This is what you agreed to."

"No, it's not." I keep my voice down. "Obeying you, yes. Having you risk my life then abandon me, no."

"Laura, go."

I stare at him and know he won't budge. I nod and let Michail guide me away. When we get to the new restaurant's doorway, I refuse to go inside. I wait where I can see down the street. I can't hear what Maks says, but whatever it is makes Salvatore step back then go inside his restaurant. Maks and Sergei hurry toward me. He pulls me into his arms and holds me. I can't help but relax as he strokes my hair, but I'm still angry.

"If you won't take me home, I'll call an Uber."

"Laura, let's enjoy our evening."

"No. I told you what I agreed to. I know it's dangerous dating you. But you totally disregarded my wellbeing by pulling that stunt. You are too arrogant, and I'm not going to die for it. You might have thought you could protect me, or that no one would dare do anything, but I'm not convinced. Take me home, Maks."

"Laura—"

"You know what? No. I don't want to be stuck in a car with you for that long. I'm calling an Uber."

"No, you are not. I'll call for another car to take me home, but you definitely are not taking a fucking Uber after Salvatore Mancinelli just saw you with me."

"See. You know I'm in danger now, too. I'll accept the ride home alone. But don't call me or text me, Maksim. I won't answer. I don't want to see you again."

"Laura—"

"No." I can't help but snap. "I'm so fucking disappointed in you, Maks."

Neither Michail nor Sergei are watching us, but even with our voices lowered, there's no way they can't hear us. Maks nods, and Michail hurries back to get the car. No one says anything as Sergei and I get into the car. I don't want to look at Maks as we pull away, but I can't help it. He looks distraught.

I have no tears, but I'm so hurt and let down. I close my eyes for the entire ride home. Sergei insists upon walking me to my door. I draw the line at him checking my apartment. He refuses to budge past the doorway until I walk through and convince him that only Sebastian is there. I barely brush my teeth and peel off my clothes before climbing into bed. I think I should cry. I feel like I want to cry. But no tears come. I'm just numb now that my heart has broken.

Chapter Six

Maksim

Fuck me.

It's been a week since my completely disastrous non-date with Laura. She was right about it all. I was arrogant. I was selfish because I did put her at risk. I wanted to impress her with a private chef's table at the best Italian restaurant in all five boroughs, but I wanted it at the expense of her safety. It was about my ego, not her. I know she told me not to text her, but I still sent one that night to apologize. I knew she got home safely because Sergei called me from the elevator. She didn't respond. I've respected her wish that I don't call or text, but I sent her flowers three days ago. I hand wrote the card. *I'll regret that choice until my last breath.* She texted two words: thank you. That's all I've heard.

I rarely sleep more than four or five hours at night. I'm lucky if I'm getting two now. I can't stop thinking about her long enough to fall asleep. When I do, I dream about her. Either we're blissfully happy on a beach somewhere, or Salvatore is holding her at gunpoint while she's tied to a chair. I'm a mess. My men are staying away from me, and my brothers keep hovering. I'm certain Sergei told them what happened because none have asked. I don't have the energy to be pissed at Sergei for gossiping. It probably saves them all from a beating that I'm pretty sure I'd dole out if anyone asked what happened. I'm short tempered and looking for reasons to blow up at someone. I'm practically on the rampage.

We've had two men taken to our secure location since that night. We own a warehouse in Queens where we conduct business we don't want anyone to know about. It's where we deal with people who cross us. It was obvious the two guys my men picked up didn't know much, but they were involved in a botched burglary. I beat them until no one could recognize them. It was only Aleks's intervention that kept me from beating them to a pulp. They're dead, but it was a bullet between their eyes that did it, not my fists.

My hubris is my downfall with Laura. But now that Salvatore has seen her, it won't take him long to discover who she is. He might have called her a whore, but anyone who gets even a glimpse of Laura knows she's far from one. Sergei and Michail swore no one followed them, but I can't ignore that maybe someone did. I have two of my best men on twelve-hour shifts, guarding her from a distance. She doesn't go anywhere without one of my men trailing after her. Stalkerish? Most definitely. I won't kid myself. But I put her at risk. I can't forgive myself for fucking this up. My life would be a living hell if something happened to her because of me.

I've given Laura all the time and space I can bare. Ilya, who's the day shift, said he heard Laura talking in her office building's parking garage two days ago. Her mother and Juan's mother both have summer colds. They canceled Sunday dinner, so she's going out to brunch today with Michelle and

Lanie. Ilya didn't hear where, but he'll call when she gets to the restaurant. I wish I could be there first. It would look more like a coincidence. She'll know in an instant that I followed her. But I just want to apologize in person. I'll beg if she gives me the chance.

When my phone buzzes, I answer immediately. I sigh when I hear Ilya's voice on the other end. "*Pakhan*, she just left Mass. It looks like she's headed to Catherine's Bistro. She's walking."

"Thanks."

I spent the night at my home in Queens, working on the assumption that she would remain near home. Ilya watched her go to church last week. It was the morning after what I now think of as *the disaster*. He guessed she goes regularly, since she embraced the priest at the end of Mass and chatted with some people before getting in her car. Michelle and Lanie both live in Queens too, so it gave me more reason to think they wouldn't go all the way into Manhattan for brunch. I know where Catherine's Bistro is. I can be there in ten minutes on my motorcycle if I obey traffic laws. I can be there faster with how I drive. Lane splitting may not be legal, but it's common place. I have no fear weaving between cars.

I have my helmet on as the engine revs. As soon as the buckle clicks, I'm moving forward. I spot her from a block away. She's strolling rather than walking with the purpose she usually does. I take a right before I reach her and circle around the block. I park and pray that I make it into the restaurant before her. I have no way to explain why I'm alone. But maybe I can pull off making it look like a coincidence after all. I'm carrying my helmet under my arm as we both round opposite corners at the same time. She spots me the same moment I spot her. She stops and looks around.

I watch her spin as she whips out her phone. She dashes to

the corner and raises her arm to hail a cab. She must be calling Lanie or Michelle to tell them she won't be here when they arrive. She's that desperate to avoid me. A normal, sane man would accept the rejection and leave her alone. I'm pretty sure I lost my sanity around the fifth or sixth man I killed when I was fifteen. Or at least I lost most of my sense of right and wrong.

She glances over her shoulder, more eagerly waving her arm as she sees me approach. I grasp her forearm and pull it down as a cab changes lanes. I shake my head as I tug her back from the curb.

"Let go."

"Talk to me then."

"I have nothing to say, Maks. Leave me alone."

"Not until you let me apologize in person."

"Do it before the cab stops."

"Laura."

She ignores the warning in my tone and laughs. "Maks."

The snideness grates on my frayed nerves. We're close enough to a residential area that there are trees along the side street I'd first seen her walking down. I steer her toward them.

"If you don't want to make a scene, don't fight me, *malyshka*."

"Don't call me that. I'm not your baby girl."

"Oh, yes, you are. You're not fighting me very hard, Laura."

"What's the point? You're bigger than me. You're going to make me go where you want, so why hurt myself by fighting you?"

"I wouldn't let you hurt yourself, *malyshka*."

"You truly believe you can control everything."

"Not everything, but most things."

"That doesn't include me, Maks. You don't get it. I'm not angry or even sad. I'm disappointed. Angry and sad I can get

65

over. You let me down. I don't trust you or feel safe with you anymore. How can I imagine going anywhere with you or doing anything with you when I can't trust you to take me to dinner?"

"I messed up. I knew it that night. That's why I wanted Michail to get you away. It was pride and ego. I haven't let those two things rule me since I first became *pakhan*. But I wanted to impress you more than I had common sense."

"A restaurant isn't what impresses me, Maks. Not your money. Not your status. None of that. What impressed me was that you respected me. I could see it during the negotiations, even when you pretended not to understand. I saw it when we talked alone, and I'm pretty sure I pissed you off."

"No. I was never angry at you. I was impressed, and I was horny, but never angry. I didn't respect you by being so selfish. But I truly didn't realize how wrong I was until it was too late. If I didn't want to make a go of this, if I didn't want you to know me, I never would have told you any of what I did in the car."

"And that's what hurts the most. The Maks I saw in the car disappeared the moment we arrived. It was the *pakhan* I was with, not the man."

"You've been hiding away from me, *zaychik*."

I watch her eyes flash wide before she leans back against the side of the building we're near. I want to wrap my arm around her waist, lift her off her feet, and kiss her until she gives in.

"And I suppose you think this little rabbit should come out for you since you're the *solnste* the world revolves around."

"*Zaychik*, I'll be your sun, or whatever else you want if it'll get you to come out and talk to me."

"As much as Salvatore Mancinelli scared me, I'm more scared you're going to break my heart all over again."

"Again?" I step closer, pressing her against the wall. The shade from the building and the trees gives us some privacy.

"Yeah. This week has sucked so much, *solnste*."

"I'm sorry, *malyshka*. I really am. I know it was a big mistake. It's not like I forgot your favorite color or didn't show up to dinner with your friends. I get that this was a way bigger mistake than most boyfriends can make. But I don't want you to walk away again."

She looks up at me for so long, I wonder if she's going to say anything. Her eyes sweep over my chest, taking in my snug black t-shirt and jeans. My sunglasses are in my helmet, which I still have tucked under my arm. She sways toward me, and I think she's about to go up on her toes, but she stops herself. She casts her eyes down to our feet.

"May I have your helmet, sir?"

My brow furrows, but I hand it to her. She hooks the strap over the short fence we're close to.

"Sir, will you kiss me, please?"

I want to do a shit ton more than just kiss her. She's not only accepting me, she's submitting to me. She wanted to kiss me, take control, but she relinquished it instead. I squeeze my arm at her waist, and she leans into the kiss. Nothing has felt better. Not even our first kiss. This is like succor after a famine. It's like a bright blue sky after a tornado. She goes up on her toes, pressing the full length of her body against mine. Her passion matches mine as her tongue duals with me. Her arms went around my neck at first, but her left hand slides down my arm past my elbow but stops before reaching my forearm that's behind her. She pulls away.

"Sir, will you move your hand lower?"

"Show me where you want it, baby girl."

I'm so damn hard, I'm scared I'm going to come just touching her ass. She guides my hand to cup the full swell of one cheek. She's athletic, but her ass is just as soft and plush as her tits. I haven't gotten to explore them, but the brief moment I

67

had my hand on one in the club told me they're real. I want to bury my face between them after I've eaten her out. Why did I ride my bike? I should have had a car waiting for me. We could be in the backseat right now with no one around to see us. Her moan makes my cock pulse.

"Shit." She pulls away and reaches into her purse. I can hear her phone vibrating.

"Did you cancel?"

"I didn't get a chance to. You got to me as it went to Michelle's voicemail. I never got to call Lanie." She slides her finger across the screen. "Hey."

She stands there silent for a moment as she looks up at me questioningly. I nod.

"I'm almost there. I ran into Maks." She's quiet again. "Yeah, if you're okay with it."

She smiles at me, and I pray this means we've made up. That the kiss wasn't just impulsive and something she'll regret once she gets inside. But she slips her hand in mine as she hangs up.

"Would you like to have brunch with us?"

"Definitely." I lift my helmet from the fence and rest my hand at the small of her back until she steps beside me. I don't resist the urge to pull her against me, my arm pinning her in place. She wraps her arm around me and rests her head against my chest.

"I told them we had a disagreement, and we weren't going to see each other anymore. I didn't say what about. They don't know you're bratva. I don't think they'd even know what that is if I told them."

"Do I need to eat crow with your friends?"

"It probably wouldn't hurt. But I'm not going to reject you even if they aren't warm toward you again."

"Thank you. But I don't want to put you at odds with your

friends, Laura. That isn't my intention. I don't want you to feel like you have to pick."

"I don't. We're protective of one another, but once they see things are good between us, they'll come around. They encouraged me to talk to you in the first place."

I reach for the door and pull it open as Laura steps inside. She scans the dining area and waves when she spots her friends. Once again, my hand rests at the small of her back as we walk through the restaurant. For the first time, I notice what she's wearing. It's a knee-length dress with a cardigan over it. It's demure and completely appropriate for church. It doesn't stop a table of middle-aged men from staring at her chest. I shift her to my other side, so I walk closer to them. As a one, they look up at me, then dart their gazes away. This is Queens, and these men know who I am, even if I don't know them. They won't make the same mistake twice. They won't ogle my woman again. At least not if they want to keep their eyes.

"Maks."

Laura whispers my name, and I know she understands what I did. But this is one thing I won't apologize for. She's mine, and there will be no confusion in her mind or anyone else's.

"Maksim, small world."

"Good morning, Lanie. Thanks for letting me join you."

"What a coincidence."

I can tell Michelle thinks it's anything but. I don't care. I pull Laura's chair out for her. I wish we were in a booth. She moves to hang her purse over her chair, but I take it from her and hook it onto the back. I place my helmet on the floor between our chairs.

"How was Mass?" Clearly Michelle doesn't plan to pay much attention to me.

"The same as it always is. I feel better after, and I like the routine."

"You're the only single woman in her twenties I know who goes to church every week."

Laura shrugs at Lanie's comment. I sense she's heard it before. She looks at the menu instead.

"Have you been here before, *malyshka*?" My breath against her neck makes Laura jump. I slip my hand onto her thigh.

"No." I look at her friends and raise my eyebrows. They both shake their heads. "I recommend the stuffed French toast or any of their quiches. If Petey is in the kitchen today, steer away from the English muffins unless you like them like hockey pucks."

I don't get to say more before I feel a hand clap on my shoulder.

"Maksim, if I'd known you were coming in with such lovely ladies, I would have saved you a seat by the window."

"Hey, Danny." I've known the owner since I moved to America. He was an asshole classmate, and he's an asshole restaurateur. But the food is great here. He glances at each of the women, but he lingers over Laura. Lanie and Michelle are both attractive women, and by appearances, I know Lanie is more his type. He's only staring at Laura because he can see my hand on her thigh.

"How's business?"

Asshole.

"Good. How about you? I see the remodel went well. I'm glad my guys did such a good job." It's a subtle reminder that he didn't have much of a choice who did the work. The only contractors around here either work directly for me, or they take bribes to reject jobs, so my guys get them.

"Business is always good on Sundays. Best brunch around."

When I don't say anything more, Danny looks around and

signals a waitress. I want to groan when I see who it is. Liz is a woman I met a few times at one of the private clubs I belong to. She likes a lot of the same kinks as me. I've never gone out with her, despite the obvious offers she's made. I'm not exactly excited that a woman I've had sex with is about to serve brunch to the woman I want to have sex with.

"Hi, Maksim."

Her purring voice grates on my nerves just like it always has. Except I don't have a ball gag right now. I feel Laura's leg tense. She looks up and past me at Liz. The waitress's button-down black shirt is way too tight for this type of restaurant. Her black slacks are just as bad.

"What would you like, *malyshka*?" My attention is solely on Laura. I can sense Liz's surprise, though. I never used a pet name or endearment with her. Why would I? She called me sir or master. I called her nothing at all.

"I'll have the stuffed French toast with bacon, please."

Laura closes her menu and hands it to me. I hand both of ours to Liz, but I'm still watching Laura. I look at Michelle and smile, so she places her order next, then Lanie. Before I give mine, I ask the women if they'd like mimosas. Lanie and Michelle agree, but Laura's gone quiet. I move my hand from her thigh to the back of her neck. I rub my thumb over her shoulder and up her neck to her hairline. My fingers brush back and forth over her other shoulder.

"What would you like, Maksim?"

I finally look up at Liz. My piercing stare makes her drop her gaze. Laura's shoulders tense just like her thigh did. Damn. I wanted to make Liz back off. Instead, I made it obvious to Laura that the waitress is a woman I've dominated. There's no doubt to Laura that Liz has been a sub.

"I'll have the French toast and bacon, too."

When I kiss Laura's temple, I hope it's obvious that Liz

71

holds none of my interest. But Laura doesn't relax. I know Michelle and Lanie are watching, even if they're talking to each other.

"This isn't for show, *malyshka*. And I'm sorry. I had no idea she works here."

"It's fine, Maks. I'm sure that isn't the last time we'll run into someone from our past. I know you didn't like seeing me with Juan."

"But that's different, and I get it."

"Not really. Juan was the first guy I slept with, and he's a fuck buddy."

My ears buzz, and I feel like I just went twelve rounds in the ring. Her nonchalant shrug makes me want to hoist her over my shoulder, carry her into the ladies' room, and spank her. She's doing it to wind me up, and it's working. She turns her head just enough for our eyes to meet. I see the jealousy and anger. I don't doubt she sees the same thing in my gaze. I lean toward her again.

"She *was* someone I fucked. It's been at least a year. You said Juan *is* someone you fuck. When was the last time, Laura? Since we met?"

"No. Can we talk about this later?"

"We definitely are. After I redden your ass."

Rather than tense, she relaxes. I suddenly get why she said that. It wasn't just to make me jealous. She's insecure. I can't blame her. Liz is good looking and obviously didn't care that I'm here with someone. I know how I felt watching her hug Juan and get a kiss on the cheek.

"Baby girl, you have all my attention. You don't have to needle me to get it."

Laura's eyes dart to her friends before she leans against me. "Will you still spank me?"

"That was never in question. We need to talk about what we expect from each other."

"*Solnste*, I haven't been with him in months. You're the only one. I hope you see it the same way."

"*Zaychik*, you've been the only one since I met you in that conference room. If I hadn't run into you at the club, I would have found you some other way."

Laura pecks me on the cheek and beams at me before launching into a conversation with her friends, who graciously gave us time to whisper. I don't doubt they'll ask Laura what we talked about later. The meal passes quickly. Laura and I wait as her tipsy-off-mimosas friends get into a cab.

"I'll take you home, baby girl."

"Is it too soon to think about breakfast?"

I pull her against me and swoop in for a kiss that steals our breath. She fists my shirt, keeping me against her, even as I try to draw away. I'll let her have this moment of control because I don't want to let go either. When we finally draw apart, she rests her forehead against my chest as I kiss the top of her head.

"My French toast is even better than theirs, *malyshka*."

"Will you show me in the morning?"

"If I let you out of bed before tomorrow night."

"Take me home, Maks. And I want you to come with me this time."

Chapter Seven

Laura

I love my dog. I really do. More than just about anyone and anything. But never have I been more annoyed that I have to walk him than when I get back to my place with Maks. I've sat with my arms wrapped around his waist on the back of his motorcycle for the past twenty minutes. Between the feel of him against me and the vibration rumbling up my pussy, I'm ready to claw my way out of my skin.

"Come on, Bastian. This is a quick walk. No dawdling."

I reach for his leash as soon as I put my purse down. I look back at Maks and offer an apologetic smile, but he's staring at my ass as I bend over. I don't resist the temptation. I wiggle my hips. Before I know what's happening, a muscular arm that feels like a steel band is pressed against my belly and a hand like a wood paddle lands on my ass. I jerk forward, but Maks pulls me back against him before landing three more slaps.

"We are going to take your doggy for a walk. You're going to behave and not tempt me again. Then we are coming back up here. I'm going to strip you, spank you, then suck your clit. You will not come until I tell you that you can. Do you understand, baby girl?"

"Yes, sir."

I'm practically pulling Sebastian to the elevator. The poor dog is looking up at me with confusion, but he's so mellow he just goes along with whatever I do. He really is the best dog ever. We exit the elevator, and Maks takes my hand, weaving our fingers together. He holds the building door open for us, then we stroll along the sidewalk. It almost feels like we're a typical couple out for a walk with our pet. Except Sebastian is only mine, and we are nowhere near typical.

I glance over my shoulder when I sense someone following us. There are a few people on the street below my building. I don't recognize anyone, so I look forward again. But we don't make it another half block before I get the same sense again.

"It's Sergei, *malyshka*. I'm glad you're so aware of your surroundings. I worry a little less about you."

"When did he show up?"

"I texted him before we left the restaurant. He was at my place."

"Is your house far from here?"

"No. Actually, we can walk there in fifteen minutes."

"That is close."

"Maybe it means we were meant to be."

"But you said you spend most your time at your place in Manhattan."

"Now I do. My home here is the first one I bought. I was twenty. I lived there for five years."

Maks watches me nods, but I don't say anything. He guesses what I'm thinking.

"I've never lived with anyone, *malyshka*. Not even the woman I dated for two years. I don't bring women home with me. I like my places to be my sanctuaries. But I want you there. The house here in Queens or my penthouse in Manhattan. I want you to be comfortable at any of my places."

"Any? How many do you have?"

Maks can't help but laugh. "Five. Queens, Manhattan, Long Island, Moscow, and London."

"I'm not sure if I want to know this, but how many places do your brothers have?"

"A lot." He laughs again. "They have places in Paris, the south of France, Italy, Mexico, Montreal, Vancouver, St. Petersburg, and a few others I can't think of."

"What happens to them when you're not there? Somehow, I don't think they're listed on Airbnb or VRBO."

"No. Some stand empty most of the time. Others have family members who live there at times. We all travel a lot, so I can honestly say we put them to use."

I hesitate to ask. "So you're gone a lot?"

Maks sighs. I can tell he's not going to lie.

"*Malyshka*, I didn't mind traveling so much before. It's exhausting, but it was just work. Now I have someone to miss, it doesn't seem so appealing. You have a career, so I know you can't just pack a bag and come with me whenever I have to go somewhere. But I wish you could."

"Maks, we haven't even made it through a date yet. How are you so certain about us?"

"Because I get what I want, Laura."

"That's not how relationships work. Just because you want me doesn't mean we'll get along in reality."

"I think I know how to read people pretty well. I've seen the best and worst of humanity. I've seen people who are brilliant and those who are too stupid to put one foot in front of the other. I've been around people whose company I can't stand and those whose company I wish I never had to leave. I've learned to tell which categories people fall into very fast. It's how I'm still alive. I rarely misjudge someone. I don't think I've misjudged you."

I stop as Sebastian pees against a tree trunk.

"Maks, I don't want to be with a man who treats me like an ornament that he shows off for holidays and special occasions, then forgets about me. I know enough to know I'm not what most bratva men want. I met those women while I lived in Russia. I didn't realize it at the time, but now it makes much more sense."

"If I wanted a woman who only cooks and has babies, I would have married years ago, Laura."

I nod, but I still feel pensive. "Could I spend the night at one of your places this week?"

I don't think Maks expected that.

"I'd like that. Tonight at your place. Then, you pick which night and whether you want to be here in Queens or in Manhattan."

"I'd like that too. I think Sebastian is done."

"Then it's time we get started. *Malyshka*, I owe you a proper spanking. Do you know why?"

"Yes, sir."

"*Solnste*. I like it when you call me that."

"But..." I wrestle with my thoughts. "I said it at first to be sarcastic, but now I kinda mean it as a term of endearment. It doesn't seem right to replace sir with it."

His grin is smug, and he knows it. But what he says eases some of my worries. "The sun is the center of our solar system. Calling me the sun means I'm the center of your life. I can live with that."

"I suppose I should defer to whatever is the center of my life. It must be very important."

He tugs the hand he's holding as we step into the elevator. I step closer to him. His free hand tucks hair behind my ear. He kisses the skin just beneath my earlobe, inching up until he gets to my jaw. His tongue flicks my earlobe before he nips, then sucks on it. I shiver like I seem to always do near him. I know he feels it run through me. His cock swells, and I love knowing I do that to him. I make him that eager. I'm sure he can feel my nipples as his palm rests on one and kneads the mound. It feels better than I remember. He pulls my cardigan and the neckline of my dress aside as he kisses his way down to my cleavage and then over the swell of my breast. When he pulls back, my eyes are glazed, and he can tell I want to kiss him.

"Today, you can kiss me or touch me however or whenever you want, *zaychik*. No hiding away from me. You don't have to ask. I still expect you to submit, but I want you to be comfortable with me, too."

"Thank you."

I wrap my arms around his waist before rising on my toes. I flick my tongue against his lips, asking for entry that he seems happy to give me. I swoop in, and I wonder if he can tell I've been wishing to do that since he stopped me on the sidewalk. He lifts me high enough for my legs to wrap around his waist. I feel the tug on the leash in my hand and look down. Sebastian looks at me as if I'm crazy. I likely am. The elevator dings, and I let go, but Maks doesn't put me down. He peeks outside to see if there's anyone in the hallway. It's empty but for the three of us.

I drop the leash, and Sabastian trots toward my door. I hand Maks the keys, which he fumbles with like he's all thumbs. I'm kissing and nipping and licking his neck, making it impossible to concentrate.

"Unless you want me to fuck you where your neighbors can find us, let me think long enough to get the door open."

"Oh? Am I a distraction?"

"Malyshka," he warns. "Be a good girl."

"What if I don't want to be, da—"

He glances at me, but I'm back to kissing his neck. Or at least I'm trying to, but I can't because his head is turned toward me. He gets the door open and lowers me to the ground. I unhook Sebastian's leash and put it on the table. My dog goes straight to his bed, and I swear he starts watching TV. I left it on Animal Planet again.

"You've started to say the same thing three times, Laura, and you never finish."

"And I told you, I'm not ready to talk about it."

"I don't want secrets between us, *malyshka.*"

"And I don't expect you to divulge every thought to me."

He steps in front of me and fists my hair.

"You're mine, Laura. Do you understand what that means to a man like me?"

"You don't own me, Maks. Even when I submit, I'm still my own person."

"I may not own you, but you will not keep yourself from me, either. Your mind, your body, your heart. They're all mine, *malyshka.*"

"Is the same true for you? All three?" There's that challenge in my eyes and my tone that I think has turned him on since we met.

"They have been since we met. I told you that already."

"I doubt you would let me possess any of them the way you wish to possess me."

"Try me. I've been honest from the start, Laura. I've confided things to you that I haven't to any other woman. I've admitted how I feel, what I want. I've told you that I don't want anyone else. That if I hadn't run into you at Envy, I would have looked for you. Fuck. I barely made it a week without seeing you. I've been a dick to everyone. People are keeping their distance because they know I'm one wrong word away from exploding. Why? Because I fucking missed you. I worried about you. I wanted you to talk to me. I wanted to make things right. I wanted you to fucking want me as much as I already want you."

He unloads. It's like verbal diarrhea. He can't seem to stop. He watches me glance at my dog's bowls. I'm satisfied with what's in them, so I reach out my hand. When he takes it, and I lead him into my bedroom. I don't say anything. Instead, I kick off my shoes as I unbutton my cardigan. I lay it across the bench at the foot of my bed. I reach back and unzip my dress, letting it fall to my feet before I lay it on top of the sweater.

He's frozen in place as I reveal each inch of my body. I reach back again and unhook my bra. It's cream satin. It's obvious I didn't expect to undress for anyone since my thong doesn't match. Then again, I don't usually care if my bra and panties match. The last thing to come off is my green thong. I leave that pooled at my feet.

He watches me walk to the side of the bed and lean over it, my tits and cheek resting on the comforter. I grasp my hands at the small of my back. I position my legs wide enough for him to see my glistening pussy as he steps behind me.

"Tell me again why I'm going to spank you, *malyshka*."

"I gave you orders, *solnste*, when you were trying to protect me. I refused to obey you outside the restaurant when you were trying to keep me safe. I've ignored you for a week."

He must sense there's something else. He feathers his fingers over my skin, trailing them from my shoulders down my back and over the curve of my ass until his fingers glide across my drenched pussy.

"What aren't you telling me, baby girl?"

"I've made myself come every night since the last time I

saw you. I can't stop thinking about you, and I never stopped wanting you."

"Stand up, *malyshka*."

He sees my hesitation, but I obey. He turns me to face him and lifts my chin, so I can't avoid his gaze. I'm confused, and I think he can tell.

"Laura, you broke things off with me. And you had every right to. You didn't owe me your obedience or your loyalty. I don't want you to feel guilty about what you did. I jerked off morning, noon, and night thinking about you. From now on, your orgasms belong to me. They're mine to give, and mine to take away. But I will not punish you for touching yourself when I wasn't your boyfriend or your Dom."

"Thank you, *solnste*."

He hugs me and waits for me to wrap my arms around him. He gives me a peck before he guides me back over the bed.

"You will receive ten spanks on each cheek for giving me orders and demanding to go somewhere unsafe. I will give you five on each cheek for disobeying me in a dangerous situation. I will not punish you for ignoring me, *malyshka*. We were broken up. But you will not get away with it again now that we're together."

His hand rubs over my ass, squeezing hard enough to leave an imprint before he rubs it again. His fingers slide between my cheeks and along my lips until his middle fingertip taps my clit. I shift and try to squeeze my legs together to trap his hand against my pussy. His free hand gives me a quick hard slap.

"That doesn't count toward your punishment. If you keep trying to get me to finger fuck you before your spanking, I will add to it, and I won't let you come tonight. Do you understand?"

"Yes, *solnste*."

"Do you have a safe word?"

I think for a moment, then nod. "Cottage cheese. I hate it. There's no reason I would ever ask for it, so there's no way to confuse it for a request for more."

"Is that your usual safe word?"

"No. I just used red." Original. At least I know to have one.

"Before we start, is there anything off limits, *malyshka*?"

"I didn't mind when you put your hand around my throat before, but I'm not ready for breath play yet. I—I don't want to be called a slut or a whore."

He must hear something in my tone. He eases me to standing again. This time he steps around me. "What happened?"

"Nothing specific. But men have called me that before. Salvatore did the other night. I've heard it in more than one language. I don't like it."

"Do you like dirty talk in general?"

I press my lips together as I consider his question. "Not always. Sometimes it's annoying and distracting. But I think I'm going to like anything you say to me."

"As long as I remember what not to say."

"And nothing but you or sex toys in me."

He jerks back, stunned. That was not what he expected to hear. I'm guessing he wants to know what the hell has happened to me at those clubs or with ex-boyfriends. Or what freaky kinks I've heard about.

"Only toys you agree with and my hands, my tongue, and my cock."

I nod before I lean forward and peck his mouth. "Can I have my spanking now, *solnste*? Please?

"Yes, baby girl. Bend over." He pauses. It doesn't seem to be how he wants to do it. He sits on the bed and draws me over his lap. "This is better, baby girl. If you don't think you can keep your hands out of the way, then I will do it for you. Hold onto my ankle if you have to. If I hurt you by accident, I won't be pleased."

"Yes, *solnste.*"

He lands the first smack across my right cheek. He feels me suck in a breath, but I do nothing else. He lands the next three, and I still don't react. He swats each cheek, then lands a spank on each side where my ass meets my thighs. This makes me jerk and whimper. He lays three more on each horizontal crack. We're at seven out of the first ten. He moves back up to the meaty part of my ass and squeezes hard. I jerk on his lap and stomp a foot.

"Are you regretting your choice yet?"

"I regretted it before the spanking."

"I don't like that tone, *malyshka.*"

He delivers two more hard ones, his hand covering both cheeks at once with each swat. I scream.

"I'm sorry, *solnste.*"

"For what?"

"For my tone and for giving you orders."

"We're almost done with that part of the punishment."

He gives me the last two spanks on each cheek and finishes the first ten. He gives me a moment to breath, but he doesn't pause for too long. It'll only make it more painful for me. That's not his goal for tonight. He slides his finger along my pussy. It's soaked. He watched me get wetter and wetter with each slap.

"I don't know if naughty girls deserve to come."

"What?"

He has to tug me back against him to keep me from falling off his lap when I try to twist and look at him. I pray he'll make me come. I pray he's going to make me come over and over tonight until I won't be able to walk tomorrow without thinking about his dick inside me.

"Naughty girls don't get rewards for taking punishments they earn."

"But I thought tonight... Maks?"

"Hush. Keep being a good girl like you are now, and I'll think about it."

He dips his finger into my pussy and swirls it around before rubbing it over my clit. I moan, and he feels my first sob. He doesn't wait to rain down the next three slaps on each side.

"Two more on each side, baby girl. Are you all right?"

"It hurts so much. Fuck. You hit too hard."

"I'm not hitting you. And don't swear. That's two more."

"What? No."

He can feel my breathing increase as I sob. I'm clutching his ankle and shaking my head.

"Behave yourself like a good girl then."

"I'm sorry. I'm sorry."

My voice croaks as I cry. He knows my ass hurts. It must be bright red like a fire truck, and it's ablaze. He also knows I'm aroused to the point of pain. I don't doubt he can see my clit's swollen, and I'm dripping down my legs. And he knows I'm fighting wanting to rebel with wanting to surrender.

"Four more, baby girl. Can you do that for me?"

"Yes."

"Yes, what?" He lays a hard slap across my upper thighs.

"Yes, Daddy!"

His cock pulses like he's going to come. He probably guessed that was what I kept trying not to say the last three times I cut myself off. He lands the last slap, but it's light. He caresses my scorching skin. I can feel the heat coming from it. He's careful as he turns me over. He widens his legs, so he can cradle me against him with my ass in the space between them.

"You took that so well, *malyshka*. I wasn't gentle with you."

"No, you weren't."

He wipes my tears and kisses my forehead, then my nose, and finally my lips. He takes my hand and brings it up to his lips. He kisses each knuckle. When he's done, he presses our fisted hands against his heart.

"You made Daddy proud, *malyshka*."

I don't move except for my eyes to meet his. Slowly, I sit up and flinch when my ass touches his trousers.

"Maks, I'm not a little."

"I know you're not, Laura. I might call you baby girl, and you want to call me Daddy. But I know neither of us wants age play. You want someone who will stand up to you and take care of you. I get the sense you have a wild side, Laura. One that probably takes unnecessary risks. They might be calculated, but I'm pretty certain unnecessary. You need someone to either say no or to be there alongside you. That's why you want to call me Daddy."

"I've never called another man but my father Daddy. It scared me the first time I nearly said it. I was mortified when I did it again. I didn't understand at first, but being apart from you gave me time to think about it. What you just said is what I figured out. I just didn't think you'd want me to call you that."

"I'll be whatever you need me to be for you, Laura. But I don't want you to call me sir anymore. And I absolutely never want you to call me master."

"Do I call you *solnste* instead of sir?"

"Yes."

"I don't know when I'm allowed to call you Maks."

"When we're in public, when we're having a conversation that necessitates us putting our emotional and sexual relationship aside, or if you need to get my attention."

"All right, Daddy."

"Come on, *malyshka*. Let's take a shower. Some cool water on your backside will feel good."

"Daddy, I want to say thank you for my spanking."

He pauses. I bet he's hoping I'm thinking what he's thinking. He eases me onto my feet and stands beside me. I pull the shirt loose from his pants and push it up his abs as he kicks off his shoes. He lets me unbuckle his belt and then unfasten his pants. He pushes them off his hips once I've unzipped them. He watches as I stare at his cock. I glance up at him, waiting for silent permission to take off his boxer briefs. He nods and chuckles at how fast I yank them down, the elastic band catching on the tip. He pulls his socks off as he pulls each foot loose from his underwear. I sink to my knees and wait to see what's next.

Chapter Eight

Maksim

"**H**oly shit."

It's said with awe. I can't help but be flattered. I've seen women shy away from it. I've seen women curious. I've seen women want to master it. But the look of appreciation on Laura's face makes me want to strut like a fucking crowing rooster. It's obvious she didn't get a good look in the dim storeroom.

"May I touch, Daddy?"

"Yes, *malyshka*. I told you, tonight you can touch whatever you wish without having to ask."

She's not hesitant, but she is gentle. I almost jizz the moment her finger trails over the tip, swirling my precum over the head. Her fingers slide along the underside before she wraps her hand around it. She applies just enough pressure to make my hips move on their own. She strokes me twice before she leans in.

"*Malyshka*, you don't have to do this."

"I know, Daddy. I know you don't expect me to do this as part of my punishment or to say thank you for it. I want to. I've wanted to taste you since I sat across that damn conference table from you."

She dips her head and licks the length of me. She does it three more times before she slides her mouth down my cock until the tip brushes the back of her throat. I pull back and lift her off the floor and over my shoulder.

"I'm not coming until I'm inside you, *zaychik*. And I'm not ready to fuck you yet."

I carry her into the bathroom and twist the faucet to turn on the shower. I lower her feet to the floor. As the water warms, I back her against the counter. Our kiss is sloppy and out of control. When I reach back and find the water is just warm enough to keep us from being cold but cool enough to ease her sore flesh, I lead us into the shower. I position her under the stream and drop to my knees.

"My turn, baby girl. I'm starving."

She widens her legs and leans forward to brace herself against the wall behind me. It puts her ass under the shower-head. I spread her pussy lips and inhale. I kept her panties and sniffed them every time I jerked off while we were apart. This is so much better than I remembered. This is fucking heaven.

"Is this what my baby wants from Daddy? You want me to suck your cunt? You want me to finger bang you?"

"Yes, Daddy. I want it so much."

No woman has ever called me that before. Or at least a couple have tried, and I've ignored them or scorned them. Hearing that word come out of Laura's mouth makes me want to fuck her until neither of us can see straight.

I suck on her clit and make her moan. Her hand presses against the back of my head, trying to get me closer. I slap the outside of her thigh. Her ass is way too sore for me to spank that. That would be cruel. That's not the kind of pain I want to inflict. She immediately releases my hair but thrusts her hips forward. I grip them and hold them in place. I control how deep my tongue dips. I control how much pressure her clit gets. I control her, and she submits when she goes still.

"Pinch your nipples, *malyshka*."

She obeys immediately. I don't know if it's because she's been trained well or because she's naturally submissive. I don't want to think about that. I want to believe it's because it's me.

"Yes, Daddy. I'll do as you say. My body is yours, ma —*solnste*."

"Is that what you called them? Master?"

Why did I ask? Do I want to know what she says with other Doms? Says. Fuck that. Said. What she said because I'll kill any man who thinks he's touching my woman. I'll break his fucking hands before I tear them off his arms.

"I'm sorry. It nearly slipped out. I don't want to talk about the past, Daddy. I only want to think about being with you."

"I'm good with that, baby girl. I don't want to think about anything before us."

"There is no before us, Daddy."

She moans, and I watch her abs flex as I hit the sensitive spot inside her against the front wall of her pussy. I stroke it over and over while I suck her clit. She's right. There is no before us. There is only us and our future.

"That a good little—" I catch myself. She doesn't want to be called a slut. I'm fine with that limit. I've used the words she doesn't like before during sex, but the thought of using them about or to Laura is disgusting. I'd lose my shit if someone called her that. If Salvatore wasn't a don I'm trying to keep from going to war with, I would have beat the shit out of him for what he said to Laura. I play it off by running my teeth over her clit. "—girl."

"I want to be that for you, Daddy."

I feel her come. If she didn't scream my name, I'd still know from how her legs shake. I rise and wrap my arm around her as she falls against me.

"And I want to be a good daddy for you. I didn't tell you that you could come. But I'll let that go this time."

She opens her heavy-lidded eyes and offers me the sweetest smile I've ever seen before she burrows against my chest. I want to lift her up and thrust into her, but I don't have a condom. I never replaced the one in my wallet, and we haven't discussed birth control. I grab the bottle of body wash and forgo the poofy sponge, preferring to run my hands over her silky skin. I wash all of her as she continues to rest against me like a rag doll. When my fingers touch her inner thigh, she wraps her arms around me.

"Please."

I know what she's asking for. "We don't have a condom, and I don't know if you're on birth control."

"I take my pill religiously, and I'm clean. I was tested a few weeks ago. It was mandatory for one of my clubs. I haven't been with anyone since then."

"Same. It was a month ago, and I haven't been with anyone. Just this once, baby. We're going to be more careful in the future. But fuck, I want to be bare inside you right now."

"I want that too. I have condoms next to my bed."

I don't want to consider why they're there, but I can't stop thinking she has them for Juan. If I wasn't hard as a fucking plank, that would kill the mood. Instead, I'm suddenly driven to fuck her better than her little friend or anyone else she's been with.

"Hold on, *zaychik*. If I'm too rough, say your safe words."

"I understand, but I won't, *solnste*. I want it rough. Really rough."

I look into her eyes, and I see reflected in them what I'm feeling. "Laura, you don't have to prove anything to me. You don't have to outdo anyone. I've never wanted someone as much as I want you. Short of breaking my dick, I know you're already the best."

"And I don't want you to think about why I have condoms in my room. I'm in my twenties and was single. I'd be stupid not to have them just in case. You're all I want. No one has made me feel like you do."

I kiss her with all the need and hunger I have trapped inside me. She returns my eagerness and greediness as I hoist her into my arms. She clings to me like a fucking koala. I'm inside her with one thrust. Her moan sounds like it comes from her soul.

"The feel of you entering me is almost as good as coming, *solnste*. I want to feel that over and over almost as much as I want you to make me come."

"You will get what you want."

I turn us, so I'm under the water, and her back is against the tile wall. I brace my feet and start pounding into her. She rises and falls with my rhythm. I try to start slowly, knowing her ass is pressing against the wall and that her clit is probably sensitive from just coming. But she growls at me. Growls. She's growing frustrated with me. It tempts me to keep the gentle pace, but she digs her heels into my back.

"Maks, please. Tease me later. I need this too much. Spank me for using your name. Keep me from coming another time. But it hurts how much I need this."

I can hear she's almost in tears. "Shh, *malyshka*. I'll make it better. I'll give you whatever you want."

"I want you, Daddy."

I don't hold back. I pound into her with a savagery that I've never experienced before. I want to consume her whole until there's nothing left to ever walk away from me, to ever leave me again. Until she's so fucking addicted to me that she craves me with every breath. I want this because this is what she's doing to me. She's ruined me for any other woman, and I will be damned if she ever wants another man.

"I'm so close, Maks. So—close."

"Let me hear you, Laura. Let your whole fucking building hear you." She doesn't hold back. She moans with each thrust and pants with each withdrawal. "Come on my cock, baby girl. Give Daddy your cum all over my dick. That's it. I'm going to make you come so hard, Laura. You're mine."

"Fuck!" She claws at my back. "Maks!"

"Mine. All fucking mine."

I thrust two more times while she's still coming, and I explode. I feel my cum filling her then trying to drip free. I stay inside her, keeping all of me in there, not wanting anything to separate us. I rest my forehead against the crook of her neck. She strokes a gentle hand through my hair, her nails grazing my scalp.

"Maks?"

"Yes, baby."

"Are you all mine too?"

I lean back and gaze into her steel-gray eyes. I hate that there's a moment of uncertainty. I know she doesn't mean other women. She wants to know if my heart is all in.

"Yes, Laura. All yours."

"Are you still going to go to your clubs?"

"Only if you're with me, and only for scenes with you. Are you going to go to yours?"

"Only if you take me. Maks, I'm serious though. I won't share you. I don't even want—"

She snaps her mouth shut and won't meet my gaze. I'm curious what she was going to say. I open the shower door with her still wrapped around me, even though my dick is softening. I grab a towel and drape it around her. As I move us back to her bedroom, each step bounces her against me. I'm getting hard all over again. I don't know how. I didn't think there was anything left in me after that orgasm. It was the best I've ever had. I sit on the bench and run the towel over her as she straddles me. She rocks with a slow rolling motion, keeping us both aroused.

"What don't you want?" She shakes her head. "Laura, you're my girlfriend, not my sub. I realized that while I was getting off better than ever before. I might be the dominant one in our relationship, and you may submit to me. But I'm not your Dom, and you are not my sub. We are partners. Equal ones sharing emotions that go far beyond a Dom/sub relationship. We both can feel it. If there's something you want or need, I don't want you scared to talk to me. You can ask me to do or don't do things."

"I don't want you to go to strip clubs anymore."

She blurts it out then looks ready to burst into tears. That wasn't the statement or the reaction I expected. She appears to the world like the most confident woman anyone could meet, but she isn't. Just like she doesn't want to be in control when we're together.

"*Malyshka*, look at me." I tip her chin up. "I own five strip clubs. I can't promise there will never be a time when I go there. I do business there with people who don't want to be seen where the proper part of society can watch them making deals with me. They like the entertainment and want to measure their dicks. But I can promise you that I will never get another lap dance, I will never touch another woman, and I sure as shit have no reason to look."

I froze in place when she revealed each inch of her perfect body as she undressed. Now I'm holding her, and every part of her I can see and touch makes me crazy hungry for her. I can see the things she probably thinks are imperfections, but I already know I crave her more for them. And it's not just physical. For the first time in my life, I want a woman's body not just for pleasure but to show her how much she means to me.

She listened to me, but she only nods when I finish talking. It makes me wonder if something happened in her past to make her not trust men. Or is it just me? Does she not trust me? That creates an ache in my chest that threatens to steal my breath.

"You don't look confident in my answer, Laura. Do you not believe me?"

"I do. It's not you. It's me. I know that's so cliché. It's just..."

"What, *malyshka*? Tell me. You never have to hide anything from me."

"You're so hot. And I know women fawn over you. I've seen how they look at you. I saw the waitress. She's beautiful. She's obviously your type. I don't mean to be a bitch, but she looks like the type that works at strip clubs. The type you see whenever you're there. The type you want."

"The only type I have is you. I know her from one of my clubs. We've done scenes together but nothing outside of that. We have certain things in common, but not anything that compares to what I'm finding with you. I'm not anything like Juan, but I know you've been with him. He's got a career that's much better suited to you. He's good looking. And you have a way longer past with him than I do with any woman. I hate it. I fucking loathe it. But I'm forcing myself to trust you when all I want is to snap him in half, so he can never be my competition."

"We're a fucked-up pair."

"Did someone cheat on you?"

"No. That's not it. I just don't feel..." She shrugs. "I know your last girlfriend wasn't faithful. Is that why you feel this way? Why you're so possessive?"

"No. I don't think about her. I hadn't in ages until I told you about her. Liz and women from my past served one purpose. Most of the time it wasn't even outside a club. I want to share things with you, parts of me and my life, that I don't with anyone else. You're beautiful, Laura. You've got a smoking hot body. Your face is gorgeous. There is nothing any other woman has that surpasses you. We fit together like our bodies were made for each other."

She giggles. "It does feel pretty damn good."

"Only pretty damn good? I'm going to fix that."

I tickle her before tossing her into the center of the bed. She points to the bedside table. I pull a condom from the drawer and hand it to her. Her eyes twinkle with mischief. She tears the wrapper open with her teeth and crooks her finger at me.

"I have something for you, Daddy?"

"What's that baby girl?"

"A very wet and hungry pussy."

"Put it on me, baby. Then put Daddy where you need him. He'll make it all better."

She slides the condom down me and tosses the wrapper on the floor. She cups my balls as she lines my dick up with her pussy. I take her in one thrust. I didn't check to see if she was still wet enough. I took her word for it. I slide in with no friction. I grab her wrists and pin them over her head with one hand as the other grabs her thigh and hooks it over my hip.

"Are you too sore, Laura? Tell me the truth." She shakes her head as she tries to buck underneath me. I slap her thigh. "Answer me with words, *zaychik*."

"I'm all right. I promise, *solnste*."

I hold her in place as I rock into her and swivel my hips over and over. I feel her tug one of her wrists, but I don't let go. Maybe later I'll let her have a chance to lead for a few minutes, but not this time.

"Please come closer. I want to feel you pressed against me tight like we were in the shower."

Her request surprises me, but I realize I miss that, too. I was enjoying watching our bodies move together, but now I hate the distance between us. I release her leg, but it stays in place. My fingers entwine with hers as I lower myself onto my forearms and keep her hands over her head. I'm careful not to squash her, but it really does feel better being closer to her.

As I gaze into her eyes, I realize I'm in way deeper than I thought. This isn't just fucking. I think I'm making love for the first time in my life. It scares the shit out of me while being the best experience ever.

Chapter Nine

Laura

It's been a week since Maks and I reconciled. A sane woman would accept that Maks doesn't know what "no" means. But he's never done anything I don't really want. I was miserable while we were apart. I was tempted to go back to Envy on Friday and Saturday nights, even if I'd had to go alone. Instead, I'd stayed home and moped with Sebastian.

We spent all day and night in my bedroom after he cornered me at brunch. We only left long enough to walk Sebastian and to make food, which we ate in bed together. When my alarm rang at five, he convinced me that staying in bed with him would be better cardio than going for a swim. He proved he was right. We showered together, and I even considered what it would be like to see his shaving cream and razor on my bathroom counter or what it would be like to see his clothes hanging in my closet. I luckily had a spare toothbrush to give him, and I found I liked seeing it next to mine in the cup. No one's toothbrush has stood next to mine since I moved away from home and stopped sharing a bathroom with my sister, Maddie.

We were apart Monday night, though neither of us liked it. I think we did it because it seemed like the right thing to do. I was exhausted from barely sleeping Sunday night and having a long day at work, so I fell asleep right away. But Tuesday night was horrible. I didn't sleep well without him there. By Wednesday, we confessed to each other that we were miserable. He picked me up from work, and we were pawing at each other before the car even pulled away from the curb. I went back to his place that night. We'd already agreed, so I packed a bag with what I needed for Thursday, and a neighbor agreed to take care of Sebastian while I was gone. I had to call Michelle to grab me some clothes for Friday because I stayed over a second night. He came home with me Friday and has stayed here with me all of yesterday and through this morning.

I'm headed to church while he's at my place preparing brunch for my friends and me. I made the courtesy invitation for him to come with me, but I knew he wouldn't. Between being raised Russian Orthodox and his current lifestyle, he politely declined. I told myself I was being foolish when I wondered if he'd go to church if we were getting married, and I wanted the ceremony at one. What the hell? We've been together a week. I'm not quite bad enough to doodle Mrs. Maksim Kutsenkova or Mrs. Laura Kutsenkova on a notepad, but it's tempting.

I pull out of the underground parking garage beneath my building. I didn't even think about my car last week, but Maks had Michail drop by, grab my keys, and bring my car back since we rode Maks's bike to my place. It's about a twenty-five-minute drive to my Catholic church. As I pull into traffic, I glance left and notice a black town car like the ones Maks and his brothers have. I wonder if it's Michail or one of his other drivers just waiting around.

I know it's not when it pulls out from its spot with three cars between us. When I get to the intersection where I'm supposed to turn left, I make a quick right. The car follows me. I make a left at the next light, then another until I've doubled back. The car is still behind me, now with only two between us.

I tap the handsfree button and tell my car to call Maks. He answers on the first ring.

"Maly—"

"Maks, do you have someone following me?"

"No."

I can hear him set something down.

"A black car pulled out from my street when I came out of my garage. It's been following me. I've made turns I didn't need and doubled back. It's still two cars behind me. What do I do?"

"Where are you?"

"Mulberry between Oak and Sycamore."

"Okay. I want you to go to my house here in Queens. It's 614 Quincy Drive. If they get closer than one car between you, do what you have to not to stop until you get to my place. I'll have men waiting for you to get you inside. I'm right behind you, *malyshka.*"

I don't hang up right away, unsure if he's going to say more. I hear him call Sebastian to come to him and a snap that must be him attaching the leash. He's bringing my dog. My heart melts while I'm trying to avoid whoever is following me.

"I'm hanging up, *malyshka,* and calling my guys. I'll call you as soon as I'm done. I want you on the phone with me."

"Okay, Maks."

I hang up and tell my handsfree to put Maks's address into my GPS. I'm glad I decided against the red BMW coupe that tempted me. But I drive a silver BMW convertible. I might not stand out as much as if I'd picked the red one, but I have a soft top. I picture bullets ripping through it. It feels like forever until Maks calls me back, but a glance at the clock tells me it was only three minutes.

"When you get to my house, the gate will open. Go through and pull around to the right. A garage will be waiting for you. Drive in, and one of my men will close the door. Don't get out of the car until the garage door is completely closed, *malyshka*."

"All right."

"There are armed guards who patrol my property, even when I'm not there. Don't be surprised if you see men in black with earpieces and automatic rifles. They're mine."

"Do you think whoever this is will do something when they realize where I'm going? They must know where you live. They must know we're dating."

"I don't know, baby girl. Just stay on the phone with me and tell me if anything changes. Are they still two cars behind you?"

"Three. Someone cut them off. Thank God for New York drivers. My GPS says I'm four minutes from your house."

I have nothing to say. I keep glancing in my rearview mirror then looking both ways before looking forward again. My hands grip the steering wheel until they cramp. I still don't let go. My car tells me Maks's house is coming up in one hundred feet. I see a gate open.

"Is it the Tudor?"

"Yes."

"I'm going through the gate right now."

I glance back to see the gate closing behind me, and the black town car driving past. Three men at the gate raise their guns at the car, but nothing happens as I pull into the garage. I don't have the engine off before the door starts to close. I turn off my car but don't move. When I look toward the door into the house, I see Sergei coming toward me. He waits for me to unlock the door, then opens it for me.

"This way, Ms. Doyle."

I have my cell in my hand. It's switched back to the phone now that my car is off, and my door opened. "I'm here, Maks. Sergei is with me."

"I want you to go to my bedroom. It's upstairs and to the left. It's at the end of the hall. When you get inside, there's a reading nook that faces the backyard. Wait for me there."

"Yes, D—Maks." I almost realize too late that Sergei is with me. I tell him where Maks wants me to go, so he leads me there. He has a gun in his hand, but I don't even think twice about it.

"I'll be outside the door until Mr. Kutsenko arrives. Lock the door, Ms. Doyle."

"I will. Thank you."

I get into the nook, barely appreciating the size and furnishings in the bedroom. I glance out the window and see a backyard much larger than I expected. This is one of the nicest areas in Queens, and the houses have always belonged to old money. I wonder for a moment what Maks's neighbors must think if they have an idea what he does. I pull the blinds closed and curl into one of the oversized armchairs.

What if the men realize Maks followed us? What if they're waiting for him to slow down and turn into his driveway? His home feels like Fort Knox, but I doubt his car is bulletproof. He picked me up in his Mercedes on Friday. He didn't have a driver for the first time. My only consolation is Maks's Mercedes isn't the tank that taxi drivers have in Europe. It's small, with a rocket under the hood.

I strain to hear anything. Then I hear it. It's Maks's voice, and it's shouting orders. I can't catch everything until he's outside his bedroom.

"Laura, I'm here." I hear the door crash open. The next

thing I know he's lifting me out of the chair and holding me against him as he takes my seat. I curl into his chest. I can feel his heart pounding, and I'm not sure if it's just from him running up the stairs or because he's upset.

"Daddy." I can't help the whimper.

"I'm here, *zaychik*. I've got you, and I'm not going anywhere."

"Was it Salvatore's men?"

"I don't know. No one got a good look."

I lean away, my hands resting on his chest. "So it could be the Irish, the Italians, the Cartel, or even other Russians."

"Yes, baby girl."

I look toward the window. "Who else could it be?" I look back at him.

"The Polish or the Ukrainians aren't always fond of us."

"Do they have their own bratva?"

"They have their groups, but we employ a lot of them to keep the peace. They work for our construction companies. We keep money flowing into their neighborhoods to keep them loyal. We haven't had trouble with either group, despite what's been going on in our motherlands."

"What about other bratva?"

"They'd be from farther away. We are the bratva in the tri-state area. Everyone reports to me."

"Is there anyone who would rather people report to them?"

"There's always someone like that. But no one would dare."

There's a knock at the door, and Maks tells whoever it is to enter. He doesn't make a move to put me down or to get up. Sergei appears at the entryway to the nook. He doesn't bat an eye seeing me curled in Maks's lap.

"We swept the block. Whoever it was didn't stick around. I'm pulling the security feed and will watch it to see if I recognize anyone. All the doors are secure, and I've called in extra men."

"Thank you." Maks nods, and Sergei disappears. He strokes my cheek and watches me. He no longer looks scared for my safety. He looks scared of what I will say.

"Where's Sebastian?"

Maks's eyes widen. That clearly isn't what he expected. "He's downstairs in the kitchen. If I wasn't racing to get to you, I would have appreciated how ridiculous your monster dog looked in my sports car."

"Thank you for bringing him. Is he all right down there? He won't get in the way?"

"He's fine. Don't tell anyone, but Sergei is the Dog Whisperer. I guarantee Sebastian is already with him. He'll take your pup out when he needs it."

I nod. "Oh, shit! I have to tell Michelle and Lanie not to come over."

"And you need to tell your parents you won't make it to dinner."

I sigh. I'm not surprised, but I need to come up with a reason. I can't tell them that my mobster boyfriend won't let me come over because one of his enemies chased me in my car. If my parents don't freak, Juan will. He'll be staked out at my apartment until I get back. I fish my phone out of my pocket and call my friends. They're easy to put off. I tell them Maks got called into work, and I'm going with him. Not entirely too far off.

"Hi, Mom." I watch Maks as he strokes my back. "Hey. I can't make it this evening. Something came up out here that I need to deal with before work tomorrow."

"Is everything okay?"

I hear the concern in my mom's voice. It's not often that I cancel. But I also rarely give details when I do. "Yeah. I need to run a couple errands, and I don't think I can make it down there in time."

"Come for dessert."

"Not today. It's going to be a busy week. I don't want to drive all that way to just turn around an hour later."

"Laura, you're being cagey."

"I'm being twenty-six. I just have some stuff to do."

"Are you with him?"

"What?" My eyes dart back to Maks. I haven't told my parents about Maks yet.

"That guy Juan was talking about the other day. He warned you away from him."

"Yes. I'm with Maks. But that's not why I can't make it today. And Juan is a pain in the ass. He never likes anyone I date. He should mind his own business like I do when he's got a girlfriend."

"Yeah, well, you're not in love with him like he's in love with you."

I cringe. I know Maks heard because his thighs tense beneath me. I cup his jaw and shake my head before I lean back against him.

"Mom, I just can't make it this week. I have stuff going on at work that I can't divulge. I just need to prepare for it after I run some errands."

"All right." There's a pause. "Aren't you supposed to be at Mass right now?"

"Aren't you?"

"Laura, answer me."

"I decided to skip this week, Mom."

"Hmm. So did I."

"I'll talk to you later. Love to Dad."

"Love you too."

"Bye."

"Bye."

There have been plenty of times in my life when I've been eager to get off the phone with my mom, but I think this was the worst yet. Maks stays quiet and just holds me. I close my eyes and sigh. This is a messed-up situation, yet I'm completely content curled up with him holding me. I could fall asleep. I almost do.

"Are you hungry, *malyshka?*"

"Who knew middle speed car chases through Queens made you hungry?"

"I think it's everything we did last night and early this morning that made you hungry."

"Mmm. I am starving again." I glance toward his bed, which I can see from where we're seated.

"Let's have lunch, then we'll come back up here. We can get into bed and do whatever, even if it's watch TV. Anything you want."

"Thank you."

Maks shifts, but I'm in no hurry to move. I wrap my arms around his neck and wait. I want to kiss him, but I don't want to have to ask out loud. When he doesn't move, I lean forward. It takes my breath away how gentle the kiss is. I didn't expect that, but neither of us seems in a hurry to deepen it to something sexual. This is more emotional.

"Laura, I told you before. You can touch me when you want. You don't have to ask permission. This was a moment for affection, not for either of us to have control. I don't want you to shy away from that because you think I won't accept you."

"We're learning each other. But I'm glad you want to accept my affection as much as I want to give it."

"*Zaychik*, the only woman I've ever been affectionate with before is my mother. And that's entirely different."

He waggles his eyebrows at me and nips at my jaw. He

scoops me into his arms, bridal style, and carries me into the bedroom. We both stare at the bed for a moment before he walks to the door. He puts me down and lets us out. I see two guards with their backs to us halfway to the stairs. They're far enough away to give us privacy behind a closed door, but close enough to protect us against anyone coming upstairs. Maks slides his hand into mine and looks down at me. I nod. What else can I do? This is what I signed on for. I wish it weren't so, but I don't wish that enough to let go of being with Maks.

Chapter Ten

Maksim

"I can keep going all night."

My right fist plows into the man's face as he hangs from a meat hook. The force of the blow spins him around. I grab his neck and turn him back toward me before nailing him in his already-broken nose. I'm careful not to break his jaw. If I do, he won't be telling me anything.

"I told you. I don't know."

"And I've told you it's unwise to lie to me."

"I'm gonna die anyway, so what does it matter?"

"How you die doesn't matter to you? Fine. It'll be long, slow, and insanely painful."

"No."

The guy groans and sags against his outstretched arm. He's already pissed himself twice. He's been hanging here for two days, ever since Niko overheard the guy talking at one of our bars. He was bragging about scaring Laura when he chased her. Obviously, the guy didn't know Niko was behind him. But he figured it out when he woke up in our warehouse strung up like a side of beef.

"Tell me if it was Salvatore or someone else."

The guy is a hired thug. He isn't *Cosa Nostra* or any other affiliation. He takes money and does what he's told.

"I don't know. A guy called me and said he had a job for me. He didn't have no accent. He sounded American like me. He said there'd be an envelope of cash waiting for me outside my place with half the money upfront and a car running. He gave me your girl's address and said I should follow her. I asked if he wanted me to take her. He said just scare her. Afterwards I took the car to the empty lot where he told me to ditch it. There was the other half of the money under a barrel like he said. I didn't ask no questions. Ain't my business. My business was just to follow the chick."

I slam my fist into his gut. Laura isn't some "chick." And I'm pissed that he succeeded in scaring her. I catch myself before my left fist crashes into his jaw. I aim for his cheekbone, and it crunches. I don't fight for money anymore, but I still train at least four times a week. I haven't been this week or last because I've been with Laura most of the time or at work.

"Let me have a go."

I step back as Bogdan approaches. He has a pair of pliers that he waves in front of the guy's face. Without a word, Bogdan bends down and snips a toe from the guy's bare foot. The asshole screams like a little bitch.

"I can keep going. You still have nine left. Then there're your ten fingers." Bogdan puts the pliers to another toe.

"I'll talk!"

I step forward as Bogdan straightens.

"I truly don't know who hired me. It could have been the Italians or the Irish, but I'm pretty sure it wasn't the Cartel. Last I heard, you ain't got a problem with Triad, so I don't think it was them, either. Whoever it was made it sound like there was more work if I got this right. I think they want to mess with you and your woman for a while before anything serious happens."

It's Wednesday, and I still don't know more than I did when I got to my house on Sunday. I was terrified the moment I heard Laura ask if I had someone following her. I didn't that day. I should have. I should have had her with one of my drivers in a bullet-resistant car. But I know she hated my guys always being there. I thought in her own neighborhood on a Sunday she would be safer than a weekday in Manhattan. I'd hoped no one, including Salvatore, had taken notice of who I was dating. Not only did someone notice, but they may have followed me enough to know where I've been going.

The shitbag has passed out again from the pain, so I nudge Bogdan and jerk my chin toward the office. It's soundproofed, but it has a window that lets us watch captives without being out on the floor with them.

"Someone knows I've been spending time with Laura. They knew to target her."

"You haven't exactly kept it a secret. But you also haven't been seen in public together since you had brunch with her friends."

"I was thinking about what he said. A moment ago, I thought someone's been following me, but now I don't think anyone has been tailing me. One of our guys or I would have noticed. I think we have a leak. I don't know who it is or who they're working for. But it was someone close enough to know what I've been doing."

"That's not a lot of people. You know it wasn't one of us or Sergei or Anton. But Ilya, Stefan, and Michail know about Laura."

"And who have those three said something to? They may

have done it without thinking. Or they told one of their gossiping wives who told someone else's gossiping wife. Like a game of playground telephone."

"Do you really think they would be that careless? We've known them forever. They supported you when you overthrew Vlad."

"I don't want to. But I can't think of anyone else."

"Could Laura have told someone at work who has connections we don't know about?"

I shake my head. "I had Sergei check everyone out that works for her company. There's not a hint of anyone being connected to any syndicate."

"Where are Aleks and Niko?"

"At the gym. Want me to get them over here?"

"Yeah. I'll keep an eye on your guest."

I check my watch. I have two hours before I need to pick up Laura. She's been staying with me in my penthouse since Sunday night. I refused to let her go back to her place, even when she argued she needed clothes. I ordered her a full wardrobe that arrived before we got back from work Monday evening. I'm still not sure if she's angry with me about it, but she was very appreciative of the designer items. I had food, toys, and a bed delivered for Sebastian, since he is now my houseguest, too.

The dog refuses to sleep on his bed at night. I heard a noise just before I fell asleep Sunday night. Laura was already out, so I slipped out of bed, grabbed my gun, and almost tripped over the giant beast when I opened the door. He was camped out there. He's done it the last two nights, too. He doesn't whine to come in, but he won't let Laura get any farther away. He's Dog of the Year as far as I'm concerned.

"Get cleaned up. We're not getting anything out of him. I'll finish it, then I'll take a shower." Bogdan clicks the pliers together as he holds them up.

I nod as he leaves the office. I strip out of my blood-splattered clothes and dump them in a barrel we keep in the office for that purpose. I step into the shower and scrub all the evidence off me. When I'm certain I'm clean, I dry off. My brothers and I are the same size and can wear each other's clothes. We're worse than teenage sisters. We keep fresh clothes at the warehouse, including underwear and tailored suits. I finish dressing as Bogdan comes in and follows my routine. Once his ruined clothes are in the barrel, he pushes the dolly it sits on out the back door of the office. The clothes are soon ablaze. By the time there's nothing left but some ash that'll get dumped in Flushing River, Aleks and Niko are here.

"I think we have a leak."

"What?" Niko looks back at the unconscious captive.

"No one's noticed someone following me, but someone knows I've been spending time with Laura. Ilya and Stefan haven't reported anyone following her. So how the hell does someone know to target her? Unless it's Salvatore, no one else has seen us together. Besides brunch, we haven't been out anywhere together. We haven't spotted anyone watching me or showing up where I am. I think someone's selling information."

"What do you want us to do?" Aleks is the most direct of all of us besides me. He's patient to a point, then all hell breaks loose. I can tell my brothers are fond of Laura, and they know she's important to me. As far as they're concerned, she's family and must be protected as such.

"I'm going to take her away for the weekend. Somewhere out of the country. While we're gone, I want you to find out everything you can."

"Does she know?"

"No. I'm going to surprise her. All she'll need is—nothing actually. I'll make sure we have toothbrushes."

"Are you sure about this? She has a job that she can't just not show up to."

I know Niko is right, but I'll figure it out once I have her on our private jet and in the air. Hopefully, she'll think it's romantic. I've tried to be casual about it when I've asked how busy this week and next are. From what I can tell, she can miss Friday, and Monday is a holiday. It's also her birthday on Saturday. I just hope her parents aren't pissed that she's going to miss another Sunday dinner. We already have plans for me to meet them on Monday night. I'll make sure we're back in time, even if we fly into Jersey and go straight there.

"She'll only miss a day."

"You're really into her." Aleks watches me. I'm not sure why he states the obvious, but I nod.

"I never told you guys what she said when she asked to speak to me alone after that first meeting." I watch my brothers because I know they've been curious. "She warned me that if we used any of RK's buildings for human trafficking, she would bury us. I put my hands on my hips and flashed my gun. She didn't flinch. She told me she wasn't threatening me, just promising me. I called her *malyshka*, and she called me *starik*. She told me I was forgettable after I told her she was unforgettable."

"You *are* an old man." Bogdan snorts. Three years his senior, sometimes it feels like forty. He's the most easygoing and quick to laugh. It means plenty of people have underestimated him and not lived to make the same mistake twice.

"I knew right then and there that I needed to get to know her. If we hadn't run into each other at Envy, I would have pursued her some other way. I've never let any woman talk back to me the way she did. Most men would piss themselves before doing it. She didn't hesitate. She's understood from the start what I will and won't put up with, so she toes the line to challenge me. I never imagined I would enjoy that, but I do."

"Does she know the other things you enjoy?"

I scowl at Aleks. It's a fair question, but this is getting more personal than even what I'm willing to talk about with my brothers. "Enjoyed. We know each other's past. We have plenty in common."

That's all I'm willing to share. No man needs to know anything more about my sex life with Laura. I've boasted and jested in the past, but all three realize Laura is not the right woman to tease me about. I know I'm sensitive, possessive, and defensive about her in general. But this week has me even more on edge.

"You better get going if you don't want to be late to pick her up."

Niko's right. They assure me they'll deal with our guest. He'll be in a vat of acid before I'm out of the parking lot. I wish I was driving my own car just for the added sense of privacy when I'm with Laura, but none of my personal cars are rein-forced like the town cars and limos. And not driving affords me other benefits. I nod to Michail, who opens the back door for me. I slide into the seat and pull out my phone.

I had Laura add my brothers' numbers and Sergei's, Anton's—he's Sergei's equal but oversees a different part of the bratva, and Michail's to her phone. I have Sergei with her now instead of Ilya. I still trust Ilya, but short of my brothers or Anton, Sergei is the only other person I trust with Laura's life these days. She made me enter Michelle's and Lanie's numbers too. Now I'm glad she insisted. I dial Michelle.

"Michelle, it's Maksim."

"Hello."

I hear the surprise. "Laura gave me your number a few days

ago, just in case. Can you hold on? I want to add Lanie to the call."

"Sure."

I three-way call Laura's best friends. Once Lanie's on the phone, I explain why I called. "I'm taking Laura away for the weekend. We're going to leave tomorrow night. It's a surprise, so please don't say anything."

I'm praying I haven't just shot myself in the foot. Now that they're both on the phone, I don't trust them not to tell. I won't say where we're going. I can at least keep that a secret.

"I didn't want you both to worry when she disappears. She's with me, and we'll be back in time to have dinner with her parents on Monday night."

"What's going on between you two?"

I don't like Lanie's tone, but I remind myself that I felt like I owed my brothers an explanation. It's the same for Laura's friends, since she's so close to them.

"Laura's really important to me, and I care about her."

"If that were true, then you'd stay away."

"Lanie!"

I hear Michelle's shock. Either they haven't talked about me before, which I doubt, or they'd agreed not to say anything.

"What? He's dangerous. We almost died in his club, and Laura's suddenly secretive when she never was before. Maksim, you should leave her alone. She doesn't need to get killed just for a big dick she can get somewhere else."

I clench my jaw so hard it makes a buzzing sound in my left ear. I keep my mouth shut and remind myself over and over that Lanie is Laura's close friend. She just wants the best for Laura. If I don't keep repeating that, I'm going to say something I can't take back. I hear Michelle's panicked breathing. I roll my eyes before I lean my head back against the headrest.

"I get why you're worried. But I would never intentionally let Laura get hurt. She means the world to me."

"I asked Juan about you, Maksim. He told me you're Russian mob or something. Stay away."

"Lanie, you can ask whomever you want whatever you want about me. But that won't change whether I want to date Laura. Unless she ends it, I'm not going anywhere."

"If you cared, you would."

"Lanie! Stop. Don't piss him off."

I know Michelle knows I can hear her. "I'm not going to do anything to either of you. You're Laura's best friends, and you're important to her. That's why I called. I didn't want you to panic if you couldn't get in touch with her. I did this as a courtesy. I will never ask her to choose between us. I hope you don't."

"Why? Do you really think she'd pick you over us?"

"Either way, you'd hurt her. Is that what you want?" My temper is being sorely tested. I nearly told her I'd hold it against her, but the last thing I need is Lanie or Michelle running to Laura and saying I threatened them. I'm not thrilled Lanie talked to Juan, and he's a fucking idiot for telling Lanie what I am. He'll be my next call, since I also have his number. He left one of his cards with Bogdan.

"No." Lanie finally concedes, and I can't wait to get off this fucking call.

"Good. For Laura's sake, please don't tell her my surprise. She deserves something special right now, and I'd like to spoil her for a bit."

"Fine. I won't tell." There's a long pause before Michelle speaks again. "Lanie?"

"Fine. I won't tell either."

"Thank you. Would you both like to come over for dinner tonight?" I can be conciliatory for Laura's sake.

"Sure."

Michelle is quick to respond for both of them. I give them the details and hang up. I'm still pissed when I call Juan.

"Hello, Detective Diaz speaking."

"Diaz. Kutsenko.

"Maksim?"

"Yes. I just got off the phone with Lanie and Michelle."

"Is Laura all right?"

"Yes. But Lanie mentioned she chatted with you. She shared that you told her I'm in the Russian mob."

"She wanted to know if Laura is in danger with you. She is."

"You either underestimate me and my reach, or you're fucking stupid. Do you understand the danger you put Laura's friends in? Do you understand what could happen if they drop that little nugget to the wrong person? Are you fucking new?"

"Maksim—"

"Kutsenko. We are not friends."

"Fine. Whatever. She wanted to know why I want Laura away from you. I proved why you're dangerous and no good for her."

"All it sounds like you proved is that you're jealous."

"You motherfucker."

"You are stupid. I wouldn't speak ill of my mother again, Diaz. I'm only so forgiving."

"Laura is my oldest friend."

"Who you're also in love with."

"At least one of us is."

"You speak as though you know me. That usually proves to be a mistake for most men. Whether you like it or not, Laura has chosen me. But that's not the point of why I called. Fucking hate me all you want, but don't endanger Laura's friends. Keep your fucking opinions and what you believe you know about me to yourself. If I am what you claim, you're lucky Lanie and Michelle are important to me because they matter to Laura. I can't say the same for other men you think are like me. Shut the fuck up before you put a target on them."

I don't wait to listen to anything he has to say. I hang up. Besides, we're pulling up to Laura's office building, and I can see her in the lobby. I let myself out of the car and go to meet her. I'm looking around, and I know Michail is standing by the car, looking across the street. I can see Sergei with her.

"Hi, baby girl." I give her a soft kiss. One appropriate for where we are. It's not nearly enough, but I think I can manage for two more minutes until we're in the car.

"Hi, Daddy." She whispers in my ear just before I straighten.

We walk to the car and get in. As always when I'm in the car with Laura, the privacy glass is already up. We're tugging at each other's clothes before the car is moving. My hand slides beneath her blouse and up to her tits. Fuck. I love touching them. I press her backwards against the seat and push her bra out of the way. My tongue circles her nipple before I bite. Not hard enough to hurt, but just enough to give a little tug. She's fumbling for my belt. As she unfastens it and my pants, I alternate sucking each tit. Fuck. They're lovely.

"Daddy, do you have a condom?"

"Yes, baby. In my pocket. Here."

Better safe than sorry, even if she's on birth control. I sit up long enough for her to get it rolled down my cock while I'm pulling off her thong. I just need one quick taste. I lean forward, my hands sliding up her thighs and pushing her skirt out of the way. She's only worn pants twice this week, and we both agree that won't be happening again. I swipe my tongue along her pussy. I listen to her suck in a breath and wonder what sound she'll make with what I do next.

I slide my tongue lower, flicking her puckered star. She doesn't react. At least not more than a soft moan. We've never talked about anal, but I always assumed she hadn't done it before. We've talked about all sorts of things we like, and that was never something she mentioned. Maybe it was just because I didn't bring it up. I'd hoped I would get something no other man has. I wanted to take her anal virginity, but maybe I'm too late for that.

"Maks."

I look up at her.

"I—I've never. I didn't like the idea before."

"Of anal?"

"No. I don't mind that, even if I've never done it. It's someone licking me there."

"Do you want me to stop?"

"No. I'm just surprised how much I like how it feels. I feel kinda dirty that I like it."

"There's nothing dirty about what we do together, baby girl. Daddy will always take care of you."

I see something flicker in her eyes. I want to know what she's thinking. But I've already learned if I demand too much, she'll dig her heels in and shut down. I have to let her come to me with whatever's going through her mind, even if I hate not having that control.

"Always?" Finally, she asked.

"Yes, *malyshka*. I want it to be always."

"You know that already?"

"I've known it from the start. I've told you that."

"I have too. But I keep worrying you might be exaggerating."

I ease up to hover over her. I thrust into her so hard she scoots back on the seat. "You're mine, Laura. I've meant it every time I've said it. I'll keep saying it until you believe me."

"Good. I've wanted to hear it every time you've said it."

We're kissing and moving together until she arches beneath me, and I slam into her one last time before I'm shooting my cum into her. As I look into her eyes, I know she's the woman I'm going to marry. She's the woman I'm going to build a family with. She's the woman I'm going to grow old with, and I'll wipe anyone who tries to stop me from the face of this earth.

Chapter Eleven

Laura

Maksim waits until we're walking Sebastian to mention the two calls he made. They both shock me. It didn't surprise me that he told me that he called Lanie and Michelle, but it shocked the shit out of me that he called Juan. He told me what happened with both conversations. I appreciate him inviting my friends to dinner. I want the three of them to get along. And for the first time since the three of us became friends in high school, I don't think—no, I know—I won't choose them over a guy. Chicks before dicks ended when I met Maks.

I'm probably the world's biggest fool, but I can picture myself married to Maks, with kids running around. I can picture us with gray hair sitting in the backyard of his Queens house or up on the private rooftop deck of his penthouse. I don't know if he's the husband and father kind of guy. Maybe he thinks I'll just be a live-in girlfriend at some point.

I appreciate everyone's protectiveness of me, Maks's

included, but I'm fucking heated about Juan. Maks is right. Juan was stupid telling Lanie what he did, and he did it out of spite. He's a good detective, but that was fucking dumb. Lanie doesn't have loose lips, but I know it's dangerous that she knows who Maks is.

"If she asks, I'm not telling her the truth. I don't like lying to either of them, but for your sake and theirs, they don't need to know that you're Ivankov Bratva or what that means. I won't answer the questions that would open up a can of worms. Partly because I don't know the answers and can only speculate about half your business, and partly because I don't think it's anyone's damn concern. If I'm fine with who you are and what you do, then everyone else can just leave it alone."

"You've never asked me about my business."

We're still walking Sebastian, and he's stopped to seriously sniff the roses.

"I figured there's plenty you can't and won't tell me. What you want me to know, you'll volunteer."

"I appreciate that, but do you feel like there's too much you don't know about me? Do you worry that I'll keep too many secrets from you?"

I sigh.

"I don't know exactly what you did on Monday, but when you picked me up from work, you had a tiny bit of blood under two of your fingernails. I don't think you knew I noticed because it was gone before we had dinner. I saw you naked that night. There was nowhere on you that the blood could have come from."

I lift the hands we're holding and turn them so his is on top. His knuckles are split and rough. I look up at him as if to say I know what this means. He nods.

"You wore a different suit to pick me up on Monday than when we left your place. We went there just so you could get dressed. You're wearing a different suit right now than when we left this morning. Your clothes have been different all the way down to your socks and boxer briefs. I can only assume you take your shoes, watch, and belt off. Those are the only three things that have remained the same."

"You're very observant."

"I am by nature. It doesn't help that I'm dating the hottest man I've ever met, and I can't not stare at him."

He wraps his arm around my waist and lifts me off my feet to kiss me. It's a smacking, playful kiss. But we don't linger. We keep Sebastian's walks short when the sun's up. Maks didn't exaggerate when he said Sergei is the Dog Whisperer. I now feel like I have to compete for my dog's affection. Sergei takes him to the park at sunset and for longer walks once it's dark. Both Maks and Sergei refuse to entertain the idea of me being out past dark. I've told Maks that my curfew sucks. But I don't push the issue. I know they're both worried about me. I don't want to upset Maks, and I won't get Sergei in trouble with him.

When we get upstairs, I change into jeans and a tank top while Maks changes into jeans and a more casual button down. Except his more casual means the kind that hugs his biceps and pecs. If it were anyone else than my best friends, one of whom is a lesbian, I'd hate having dinner with two women who'll spend the evening looking at him.

"Do you want me to cook since I gave the invitation?"

I walk up behind Maks in the kitchen as he pours a glass of wine for me and a couple fingers of vodka for himself. I slide my arms around his waist and rest my head against his back.

"You can, or we could order Thai or something like that."

"That sounds good. Do you want to wait until Lanie and Michelle are here?"

"Nah. They always get the same thing at any Thai place. So do I."

I pull my phone out of my purse and pull up a website to find the closest Thai restaurant. I order online while we wait for the girls to get here. Lanie arrives first since she works closer to Maks's penthouse than Michelle. Maks tries to appear relaxed, but Lanie is practically hostile. I try to ignore it and hope it'll get better once Michelle arrives. It does, but only slightly. I'm going to have to talk to Lanie tomorrow.

"You've practically moved in." Lanie's voice hisses in my ear as she stands next to me to wash her hands at the kitchen sink while I pour two more glasses of wine. "You're making a mistake."

And I guess we're going to talk about it now. Fuck. "I know you talked to Juan. Do you want to tell me what he said? Or do you want me to go by what I heard through Maks?"

"I'd love to know what Maks said I told him."

"Fine. He said you talked to Juan about him, and that Juan told you Maks is Russian mob."

"And?"

"And what? Was there more that you didn't tell Maks?"

"No. I just figured he'd say there was more."

"Lanie, Maks doesn't lie to me. Please don't do this. I love you. I want you and Maks to get along. But if you can't, then don't piss in my Cheerios. I'm not breaking up with him because of you or what Juan said."

"You're picking him over me."

"This isn't fucking Red Rover. I'm trying not to pick anyone."

"You can't always get everything you want, Laura. No matter what you think or how spoiled you are."

I stand there blinking. I don't even know what to say. That fucking hurts, but I refuse to cry. I won't do it in front of Lanie and let her know how deep that cuts. And I sure as shit won't cry in front of Maks because he'll lose his shit. That's the last thing I need.

"I'm sorry. I shouldn't have said that. I didn't mean it."

"Oh, but I think you did. That came out way too easily for it to be something you just came up with."

"Have I thought you're spoiled before? Yeah. I'm sure you've thought not-so-nice things about me over the past ten years. But I said it to be mean on purpose. I shouldn't have. I'm being a bitch. I have never been jealous over a guy before in my life. I don't even like dicks. But I'm jealous now. And I'm scared for you. Juan said he kills people all the time." Lanie gets as close to me as she can without standing on my feet. "He said Maks is into human trafficking and sells women as sex slaves. What if he does that to you?"

"What the ever-loving fuck?" I'm shouting, and Lanie jumps away. I've been pissed plenty of times in my life, but never have I felt such rage. I grab my phone and march into Maks's room, slamming the door behind me.

"Laura?"

"Stay out, Maks. Leave me alone for a few minutes. I need to make a call. And don't fucking listen at the door, or I'll be even more pissed."

"What happened?"

"Don't worry about it, Maks. It wasn't anything you did. Just give me a few minutes to deal with something."

"Laura?" It's Lanie.

I rip the door open and tug her into the room. "Don't breathe a fucking word to Maks about what you just told me. It isn't true. I know things about Maks's past, things that happened when he was a kid in Russia. There is no way in hell he and his brothers are involved in human trafficking. And let's just say I'm positive he wouldn't let anyone he knows get away with it either."

I hear the doorbell. The food must be here. I look at Lanie then the bedroom door.

"Come on." I open the door. Maks is standing about ten feet away. I know he couldn't hear us. "You guys start dinner. I still need to make a call. It'll all be fine once I'm done. I'm having a temper tantrum, and I know it. I don't want to ruin dinner."

I walk to Maks and stand on my toes to kiss him. His arms were crossed, but he wraps them around me. I cup his face with the hand that isn't holding my phone. I see the worry etched in his furrowed brow.

"It's all right, Daddy. I promise. But it's something I don't want to talk about, so please don't push me. I don't want you asking Lanie either. It's something between the two of us."

"Fine. I don't like it. But I respect your privacy with your friend. I'm here if you need me, baby girl."

"I know, Daddy. Go eat before your food gets cold. I'll be back in a few minutes."

I go back into Maks's room, which I've really started thinking of as ours. I know I shouldn't, but I do. He has a walk-in closet, so I go in there to call Juan. I'm still livid, but I know how to hide my feelings from my face and my tone. It's a struggle, but I can do it in front of Maks and the girls.

"Laura, hey."

"Shut the fuck up and listen to me, Juan. Don't you fucking speak unless it's to answer a question. And if you fucking lie to me, I will never, ever, ever speak to you again. Do you understand me?"

"What the fuck happened?"

"You don't ask the questions. I swear to God, Juan. I'm two seconds away from coming to the station and beating the shit out of you. They can toss me in jail and throw away the goddamn key. Did you tell Lanie that Maks is Russian mob?

"I did because he is."

"How do you know?"

"Have you looked at him? Do you know what his tats mean?"

I do because I've asked. Most are bratva tats signifying different events and initiations. The stars on his shoulders signify his authority and mean "I kneel to no one." He has an eagle high on the right side of his chest that also shows his high rank. He has four cats grouped together on his back that represent his brothers and him as thieves, a roaring tiger on his chest across from the eagle to represent strength.

I want to know how Juan knows. But it dawns on me Maks must have been arrested at least once. They take photos of gang members' tattoos, and that probably includes any mafia members. If Juan hasn't seen them for himself, then he's looked them up in the records.

"What I do or don't know isn't what we're discussing. How do you know?"

"I've arrested associates of his who magically make bail or judges dismiss cases. He's fucking rolling in money, but there's no legal trace to how he makes so much. Construction and strip clubs don't account for it. People he does business with go missing never to be found. Not even a fucking fingerprint to trace. That's professional. And don't forget that little bar fight you witnessed. Do you know how I felt realizing you were there for that? Do you get how much danger you were in? What kind of man does that to his woman?"

"Don't do that, Juan. You've put me in plenty of shitting situations that were just as dangerous."

"When we were teens. Not since I became a man."

"A man?" I scoff. "You acted like a jealous asshole telling Lanie that stuff. You did it so she'd try to get me to break up with Maks. You did it because you're still pissed that you didn't love me when I thought I loved you. I've been over thinking we had a future for years. Now you just want me because I refuse to give in to you. You're such a colossal hypocrite! You became a cop when your dad's a senior member of the Colombian Cartel. You think I don't know you feed him information? I know you do. I've fucking heard you. Bet your bosses don't know that. Your fucking brother is going to inherit your dad's place. And you want me at your side. You're fine bringing me into the Cartel, but you whine like a little bitch when you think I might be with the bratva. You can go fuck yourself. Don't call me again. And don't expect to see me at Sunday dinner any time soon. And if one single thing happens to ruffle a single fucking hair on Maks's head, you will wish we'd never met."

"Come on, Laura. I can protect you better than he can. I have the law on my side."

"Even if Maks weren't in the picture, I don't feel that way about you. I told you that months ago. It's why we haven't fucked since last New Year's. You did this to yourself, and you didn't care that you were hurting me. That alone pisses me off."

"I didn't know you were that serious about him."

"I am. And if admitting that makes you try harder to keep me from him, I will make your life hell. You're not the only person who knows gang members. I have some interesting clients who appreciate that I speak fluent Chinese. I don't need the bratva to deal with you."

"Are you threatening me?"

"Why do men think I do that? I don't threaten, Juan. I promise. Stay away from me, my friends, and the Kutsenkos."

"Laura—"

"Get in touch with me again, and I will ruin your career with a restraining order."

"You wouldn't dare."

"You want to dare me? I double dog dare you, Juan. You've

gone too far this time. This wasn't about being my friend. This was about jealousy, and I'm through with it."

I don't say goodbye, and I don't let him say anything else. I hang up. I'm still so pissed I can barely see straight. I don't regret anything I said, but I have barely enough sense to know I shouldn't have said most of it. But I'm so fucking pissed!

I need fresh air, but it's already dark. Damn it. I have to get out of here before I deal with anyone else. I'm a shit friend and a shit girlfriend for acting like this, but I need space. I know that if the situation were reversed, and Maks threatened Juan like he did to Maks, I wouldn't be nearly as overprotective of Juan. It's something about thinking a friend of mine could harm Maks and his family that makes me stark raving mad. Maybe I wouldn't be losing my shit if it were a stranger. But someone who's practically family to me...I can't let it go.

I open the closet door and cross the room to the bedroom door. I take a deep breath before opening it. Three faces look at me, and I find Sebastian outside the door. I scratch his head and tap my thigh. I walk toward the door and pick up his leash.

"I know I'm rude. I'm sorry. I need some air. I won't be long." I'm ready to clip Sebastian's leash to his collar, but Maks is walking toward me. I know he's going to say no. "Please, Maks. I need a few minutes of air. I have Bastian with me. No one is coming near me with him."

"They don't have to be near you if they have a gun." Maks keeps his voice low. My shoulders sag. He's right, but I'm climbing up the walls. I want to be alone with my dog and sort through some of this and calm down.

"Can Sergei come with me to the roof?"

He looks toward the door where I know Sergei is standing guard. I can see he's hurt that I asked for his cousin instead of him. But if I don't calm down before talking to him, I'm going to unleash and vent everything to him. That's exactly the disaster I'm trying to avoid.

"Maks, please." My voice trembles. I'm barely holding on. "I don't want to talk about it with you. But I won't fight you about having someone with me. I need you to stay with my friends. We can't both walk out. I just want a few minutes with Bastian."

His eyes widen, and I see even more hurt. I shouldn't smile, but I do. I cup his jaw with both hands.

"Daddy, I'm not picking him over you. You have to know there's just something soothing about having an animal to pet. I promise to pet you an entirely different way later. Just five minutes."

"All right, *malyshka*. But I need you and Bastian to stay near the elevator where you're covered in three directions. It's too dark for Sergei to spot a shooter from another building. Stay behind him please."

"I don't want to make him a human shield."

"He's wearing a Kevlar vest, baby girl. He'll survive, but you wouldn't. Not unless you let me get you one, but I think you would hate that."

"If it meant I could go outside after dark, I'd wear one to bed."

"You don't wear anything to bed, *zaychik*."

"I know, *solnste*. I'll be back in five minutes."

Maks gives in and calls down to his security team to let them know where I'm going. Then he talks to Sergei, who looks over to me and offers a grim smile. Maks speaks to his men in Russian most of the time, but I never think much of it. But I notice the girls watching us. Since I understand Russian as well as I do English, it seems normal for Maks to switch back and forth. It must be odd to them. I smile and nod to them.

"I'll be back in five minutes. I'm getting some air with

Sebastian. I'll join you guys soon. I'm just pissed at you-know-who."

I'm certain Lanie told Michelle what Juan said, so I'm sure she knows who I talked to. It'll be fine. They've known me long enough to give me space right now. Sergei is waiting beside the elevator once I step out with Sebastian. We ride up to the roof in silence, which suits me just fine. When we get outside, Sergei holds up his hand to keep me from moving just past the elevator doors. He steps out of the covered area between the two elevators and the door to the stairwell. There's a solid wall to our left. He scans the rooftop and is about to turn back to me when I see red blossom on his right sleeve.

"Sergei!"

Now there's a hole ripped through his right pant leg. There's no sound as my guard and my boyfriend's cousin staggers backward. I see his body rock and can guess that a bullet just hit his vest. I watch as he falls backward. Sebastian is growling, and I'm trying not to scream. Sergei is reaching for his gun, but his right arm isn't cooperating.

"Give it to me."

"No. Get back in the elevator, Laura. Now."

He's never called me by my first name before. I push the button, but the elevator is already gone.

"Give it to me, or we're both likely dead."

I don't wait for Sergei to hand me his gun. I'm pulling it out of his hip holster as I order Sebastian to lie down and be silent. Thank God he's an obedient dog. I crouch and lean around the side of the building. There's a man dressed in all black with a black balaclava. All I can see are his eyes, which look dark as midnight. I don't hesitate. There's no silencer on this gun like there is on our attacker's, but I shoot twice. The first one lands in the middle of his forehead, the other lands between his eyes.

I hear someone at the stairwell door, and Sebastian is

barking and growling. I spin on my toes in time to see another black-clad attacker. This one I shoot in the throat. Blood sprays everywhere. Sebastian and I are coated, and it's splattered Sergei.

"We need to go."

Sergei is pushing to his feet as he gives the order. I'm happy to comply, but the elevator still isn't here. He's talking into his earpiece and telling someone to come up here.

"Do we take the stairs? We could be trapped." I don't know what to do.

"I know. The elevator should be here soon. There may be more coming up. We wait, Ms. Doyle."

I realize he used my first name a moment ago out of urgency, but we're now back to the cool professional distance we've always had. The deference had seemed rather formal; now it seems pointless after we both nearly died together.

Sergei draws a wickedly sharp knife that he wields in his left hand. When the elevator chimes, I raise the gun. I tell myself to wait a heartbeat before I fire, and I'm glad I do. I see a man in tactical gear, but that's not what registers. Maks is behind him and pushing past his guy. I put the safety back on and let the firearm dangle from my hand as Maks engulfs me in his arms. I feel someone take the gun from me, but I don't care.

"We heard the shooting just as my guys radioed up that they saw someone on the roof."

Maks and I are both trembling as he guides me toward the elevator. I glance back and see two guys sweeping the rooftop as two more go into the stairwell. There are three men in suits still standing with us as Maks, Sergei, Sebastian, and I get into the elevator. I try to look at Sergei to see how badly he's injured, but Maks won't let go enough for me to move. I relax against his shoulder.

"Why were you holding that gun?" Maks's voice is quiet, but it's a demand, not a question.

"That's my fault, *pakhan*."

I twist this time and look at Sergei. His entire sleeve is red as he presses his hand against his wound.

"No, it's not." I will not let Sergei take the blame. "They shot him in the arm, the leg, and the chest. I didn't give him a choice. I took it."

"She kept us both alive, *pakhan*." There's a mixture of shame and pride in Sergei's voice. I never knew the combination could exist.

"What the fuck happened?"

It's only now that I realize the gravity of what I've done. I've not only shot two men but killed them both. No guilt. Just fear of the consequences.

"I killed them both."

I know my mouth is saying the words, but I'm not sure if I utter them aloud. The buzzing in my ears is too loud, and my heart is racing so hard now that I can barely breathe. I know it's the overdose of adrenaline still pumping. I can feel my body shaking harder.

"What?"

Maks isn't looking at me. He looks like the next murder will be Sergei's. He's trying to push me behind him, but I won't let go.

"Maks, Sergei got hurt. He didn't ask for it. If he hadn't stepped out to check the deck, we'd probably both be dead. He made me wait. He took three bullets for me, so don't you fucking dare blame him." We're already at Maks's floor and standing outside his door. I didn't even notice us walking. He's reaching for the door, but I pull his hand back. "Lanie and Michelle?"

"We heard the gunshots from here, and they were there when my men called. I told them to stay put."

"I don't want them to see me like this."

I wave my hand up and down, then look down at Sebastian, who seems completely unfazed now that the threat and noise are over. One of his men offers me his suit jacket. I can tell Maks isn't thrilled about me wearing another man's jacket, but what else am I supposed to do? The guy is as big as Maks, so I'm drowning in it, but it covers all my ruined clothes.

"I'll take Sebastian to get cleaned up."

"You need medical attention, Sergei." I know that he has an apartment in the building, but I'm worried about him.

"The doctor is already on his way, *malyshka*. You know he can't go to a hospital."

I hadn't thought about it, but I understand why. Gunshot wounds equal the cops getting called. Then there are questions no one wants to answer.

"What about upstairs? Will the neighbors have called the police?"

"I doubt anyone heard, and there aren't any sirens." Maks opens the door, but I don't see Lanie or Michelle. I look up at Maks, terrified they ran out and are on the street somewhere or in a cab. "They're waiting in the spare bedroom."

Maks nods to where I can see two sets of eyes peeking out. Maks's bedroom is across the apartment, so I head there while Maks tells them I need a moment to get cleaned up. They must have seen the blood on my face. When Maks reassures them that none of it is mine, I know for certain. I hurry into the bathroom and peel off the clothes. I look around for where to put them. I grab one of the oversized bath towels and lay it on the shower floor. I take off each item and fold it before laying it on the towel. Once I'm naked, I have a neat little bundle with no blood touching any surface. It's only my hands and face that are dirty, so I scrub them in the sink.

Once I'm certain there are no traces of blood left on me, I look beneath the sink. Thank heavens for small mercies. There's a bottle of surface cleaner and a roll of paper towels. I clean the sink and the counters before tossing the two pieces of paper towel into the toilet and flush. I leave the bundle where it is and hurry to find clothes that now hang in Maks's closet. I pause to appreciate how it feels to have my stuff next to my boyfriend's. I know Maks wants me to move in. He hasn't said it outright, but he keeps clearing more space for me. I was considering it before. Now I want nothing more.

I head back to the living room and find Maks standing with Lanie and Michelle, who rush to me when they spot me. I embrace them, but I'm looking over their shoulders to Maks. What the hell are we going to tell them?

"He is Russian mob, isn't he?" There's no accusation in Lanie's question. I don't know if I'm allowed to answer that question, so I opt for evasion.

"He's a wealthy and powerful businessman. His family controls a lot of different companies with influence throughout the city. Not everyone likes him."

"So by extension, not everyone likes you? Laura, this has to stop. You nearly died." Michelle's crying.

I feel guilty. But I'm not leaving Maks. Maybe it's the time I spent in Russia that makes me accept the situation with such ease. Maybe it's because I love Maks—which I'm certain of—or maybe it's because I'm certifiable. I don't say anything.

"Would you ladies like to spend the night or go home?"

Maks's question has us pulling apart. I appreciate his offer. I'm not certain if it's entirely altruistic. I don't know where they are better off. Did whoever this was see them arriving? Are they targets now too? Will they be collateral damage?

"We're going to my place."

Good. Michelle's building is more secure than Lanie's.

"I'll have my driver take you."

It isn't an offer. It's clear Maks isn't letting them use public transportation, which is fine with me. I can see them hesitate, but then they both nod. I glance at the dining room table and see the empty to-go containers and plates with food.

"Do you want to take your leftovers?"

"Leftovers? That's what you're thinking about?" Lanie's aghast. I don't want them to go hungry. I shrug as I meet her gaze. My heart races again.

"Don't tell him. Do not call him and talk to him about this, Lanie. I'm serious."

"You nearly got shot, and I don't see any police swarming the building. That's what usually happens when there's a shooting. So tell me why there aren't any here? Why aren't we calling them?"

"Don't ask questions I can't answer, Lanie. You call them or tell Juan, and I'll be the one in prison."

Neither Lanie nor Michelle knows what to say to that. They're not sure what I'm confessing to.

"Don't take the blame for something you didn't do. It's your mobster boyfriend."

"Lanie, lay off. I get you're trying to protect me, but don't make me choose. You can disagree all you want. You can be scared for me, and I get it. You can think I'm the stupidest woman alive. But enough. You have to accept my choices even if you disagree. That's what friends do. Otherwise..."

"You are choosing. Fine." Lanie gathers her purse.

Michelle just stands and stares until she seems to find her voice. "I'll talk to her. I get both your sides. I hate this, but you're happier with him than I've ever seen you. You were miserable while you were apart. We've been friends since first grade. I know you better than nearly anyone, and I can remember nearly everything. Be careful."

Michelle's right. We've been friends nearly as long as I've been friends with Juan. We met Lanie in high school and soon became a trio. But Michelle's seen parts of my life that Lanie hasn't. She visited me in St. Petersburg and traveled to China with me one summer. We also went to law school together.

"Please make sure she doesn't talk to Juan. I hate saying it, but I don't trust her with this."

Michelle sighs. Lanie's already waiting in the hallway. "I don't either. Laura, you need to prepare for her to do that. She loves you, and she's scared."

"I know." I can't blame my friends. In the normal world that I used to belong to, you called the police in America. But that's not the case in much of the world. It's not in Russia, or parts of Italy, or Mexico, or China apparently. These organized crime syndicates operate like they're still in their motherlands, and they are the law. I don't know why I get that so easily, but I do.

"*Malyshka?*" Maks turns me against his chest as Michelle closes the door behind her. I inhale his fresh scent that's woodsy and spicy at the same time. I love it. It's as calming as feeling him hold me. He scoops me into his arms and carries me to the sofa, where I sit on his lap. "I'll have men follow them for the next few weeks and keep them stationed outside their apartments and offices. They'll never know."

"Thank you, Maks."

"Can you tell me what happened?"

"We got out of the elevator, and Sergei held up his hand for me to stop. Sebastian and I waited in the covered area while Sergei stepped out. It was instantaneous. His sleeve was red, then there's a hole in his pants. A third bullet hit his vest and knocked him backwards. He tried to pull his gun, but I think the wound is too close to his elbow. He couldn't bend it. He refused when I told him to give it to me. Sebastian was growling and barking. I commanded him to sit and be silent. I took Sergei's gun when he sat up. I looked around the wall and saw the guy. He was in all black with a balaclava. I shot him twice. The first landed in the middle of his forehead. The second between the eyes. Sebastian started growling again, and I heard someone at the stairwell door. I spun around and shot the guy in the throat. Then you were there."

Maks is silent. His hold on me is so tight that I can barely breathe. He's murmuring to me in Russian so softly that I can't understand. I can feel his heart still racing. Holding me may be making me feel better, but he's still upset. I tap his chest and push away. He eases his hold but not by much. I twist to straddle him. He cups my face and gives me the most tender kiss I've ever felt. There's a depth of feeling from us both that I can't explain, and I'm not sure either of us is ready to speak it aloud.

"*Meelaya*, I can't lose you. I can't."

My darling. That's a new one. I want to hear it for the rest of my days. My towering and intense boyfriend is looking at me with the softest gaze. A month ago, I would never have imagined a man so intimidating could be so gentle and kind. I don't think anyone else has ever seen this side of him. Maybe his mother. But that's not the same. I kiss his cheeks and his neck and the dip at the base of his throat. Then I come back to his mouth. He's letting me take the lead, but when our lips meet, I melt against him. I don't want to be in control. I just want to feel safe and protected again. Maks does that for me. I know he's what put me at risk, but he's also the only one I feel can save me.

"*Meelaya*, are you hungry?"

That makes me think. I'd forgotten about dinner. "Starving. Is that normal?"

"Is what?"

"To think about food after killing someone?"

"We should talk about that, Laura. This is something that will stay with you the rest of your life. You're still in shock right now. When you wake up, you will feel very differently about this."

"Things happened fast. It was fight or flight and instinct. But the moment I killed the second man, I knew why. They would have killed Sergei, they would have killed Sebastian, then they would have killed me. After that, they would have gone for you. I may have wanted to protect my bodyguard and dog. But what I wanted most was to keep any of them from getting to you. I know that's why I did what I did. Can you protect yourself? Yeah. But that didn't stop the overwhelming need to keep them away from you. I will never regret that."

Maks looks at me for a long time, and I wonder what he's thinking. I know what I'm thinking. I love him. Ridiculous as it may be after such a brief time and after what we've already dealt with, but I have never felt such a connection at such an elemental level with anyone.

"I hate that you had to do that, *meelaya*. I never wanted that for you. But I can't help but feel—special? My men protect me because they pledged their loyalty. My brothers because we are blood. We are one. You are neither of those, but you chose me."

"Maks, I'm always going to choose you."

"And I'm always going to choose you."

We reheat our dinner and eat in silence, enjoying the companiable quiet. After we wash the dishes, Maks takes my hand and leads me into the bathroom. I totally forgot about my clothes. When he sees how I've bundled them and smells the disinfectant, he turns to me.

"I didn't think I should let someone else's blood touch anything, but I didn't know what to do with them."

"You did the right thing, *malyshka*."

He takes the trash bag out, and I realize it's a kitchen-size bag. He dumps everything, including the towel, into the bag and ties it shut. The large bag in the tiny trashcan isn't a coincidence. This isn't the first time bloody clothes have been discarded here. But neither of us comments about it. Maks turns on the bathtub and waits for the water to run warm before putting in the plug and squeezing in bath gel. The bubbles form immediately, and I smile.

"I'm going to give you a bath, then I'm taking you to bed. I'm going to make you forget about earlier. At least for a few hours. I'm taking care of you."

"I need that."

"Do you submit?"

"Yes, *solnste*."

Our sex has been rough since our first night together, but it hasn't been kinky. I'm not sure if Maks thought I was still upset from the car chase and needed to be gentle, or if he wasn't sure how kinky I really like it. But I am so ready for this.

He strips me and helps me into the tub before he takes off his own clothes. He climbs in behind me and sits, then he pulls me onto his lap. I rest back against him, our arms crossed over my belly. It feels divine, but I want more.

Chapter Twelve

Maksim

My baby girl is in my arms where she belongs, but I'm still rattled. How can I not be? She was arguing with Lanie in the kitchen, then she insists on making some call alone in our room. Yeah. It's ours, even if we haven't talked about it. Then she's angrier than I could have ever imagined possible. She's demanding to go outside, and I let her against my better judgement. This is why I like to be in control. When I'm not, everything goes to shit. I nearly lost the woman I love. Yeah. I know that, too. I don't think she's ready for that declaration, but it doesn't make it any less true. I thought soulmates was bullshit. Then I met Laura.

We're soaking in the tub together, but I can't stop seeing her standing, covered in blood, with a gun pointing at the elevator. There wasn't fear in her eyes. There was determination. She would have shot without hesitation if she'd believed my men and I were a threat. Part of me is relieved that she won't go down without a fight. But a much larger part of me is wracked with guilt. She only needs to defend herself because of me.

I don't want to make her relive any of tonight ever again. But this isn't nearly through. I will find out who those men are. I will find out who hired them or who they're affiliated with. Then I will round up whoever is responsible and take them to my warehouse. I will do unspeakable things to them for coming anywhere near my *malyshka*. I will draw it out until they're begging everything under the sun to release them from their agony. Only when I have gotten my pound of flesh will I consider killing them. I will torture them for information. If I get none, then I will torture them for revenge. I don't enjoy killing. There is no thrill in it for me. I don't look forward to it or glorify in it. But I won't hesitate if it means I protect the people most important to me, to end a threat.

Maybe this weekend's trip is a mistake. What I should do, if I had any decency, is break up with her. Put as much distance between us as possible and keep my lifestyle as far from her as possible. The thought hurts more than any gunshot wound or stabbing I've taken. It threatens to paralyze me. I feel myself tightening my hold around her as we recline in the bath, like I'm scared someone is going to rip her away from me or that she might walk away. But she's relaxed and limp against me. She doesn't want to go anywhere since she linked her fingers through mine.

That still doesn't change what I need to do. I can't keep her and be that selfish. Is it worse if I make love to her, then break up with her in the morning? Or do I do it before we can have sex? I want to spoil her tonight. I want one last chance to take care of her. But it seems cruel to take her to bed only to break up with her in the morning. The conflict raging within my head is making it pound. I have never wanted to be more selfish in my life than right now. This is a piss-poor time for my conscience to suddenly stand up and be heard. Then again, if ever there was a time to think about right and wrong, it's where Laura's wellbeing is concerned.

"Maks, what's going through your head? You're tense, and you keep holding your breath. You're squeezing me so tightly that it's hard to breathe. What's going on?"

"I'm struggling, *malyshka*."

She leans forward, forcing me to release her. I want to grab her, pin her to me, and refuse to let her leave me. But she's just turning around. She straddles my legs and sits on my thighs again. She's searching for something in my eyes, and I don't know what she sees. Whatever it is has upset her more. Tears are streaming down her cheeks, and I reach to wipe them away. But she bats my hand away.

"If you're about to break up with me, don't pretend like you care enough to wipe away my tears."

I sit there slack jawed.

"I can see it in your eyes. You're regretting being with me. You feel guilty. So rather than us figure this out together, you're going to push me away. Fuck. If this is how you felt when I refused to talk to you, I don't know how you survived."

"You were right back then, and your friends are right now. My lifestyle is too dangerous for you. You didn't grow up with this. I'm certain this isn't what your parents will want for you. It's going to corrupt you and warp you until you have no sense of right and wrong. It's going to force you to tell lies to people you care about. And worst of all, it's going to keep putting you in danger. You could have died today. I can't and won't keep you in a gilded cage, keep you from having a life. But that would be the only way to ensure no one ever gets close enough to hurt you."

"So what? Now you're going to ignore my calls and texts? You're going to avoid me and ignore me? That sucked enough when we barely knew each other. Do you know how badly that will hurt me? How badly you're hurting me right now?"

"You'll move on."

"Don't you dare tell me what I will or won't do, Maksim. You can't command my heart and my mind, even if you can my body. You'd throw this away because—what—you got scared? I thought you were braver than that. You didn't strike me as a coward."

"Don't bait me, baby girl. You can hurl your insults because you're pissed and hurt but know that I will take it out on your ass. Except I won't make you come. I'll pack your shit and take you home."

"Then what? Go to one of your clubs and get some stripper to jerk you off? You're fucking hard now, and you like to fuck too much to stay this way. Maybe I'll call—"

"Don't you dare say his fucking name, Laura. I know he did something to piss you off. You'd do that just to fucking spite me. He's barely staying alive at this point. You touch him, and I'll fucking torture him before I kill him."

"You're breaking up with me. You don't get to decide who I bang."

I see red. My baby girl is about to learn that I am the wrong Russian bear to bait.

Chapter Thirteen

Laura

Maksim roars and stands with me in his arms. His fingers bite into the underside of my thighs as he carries me into the bedroom. He doesn't bother with towels. He tosses me onto the bed. Thank God it's soft because I land hard. He bends over and pulls something out from under the bed. I try to lean over the edge to see what he's doing, but his massive hand lands on my chest and pushes me backward. Then he's pulling my right arm over my head and clapping a handcuff on my wrist and attaching it to the headboard. He does the same with my other arm. He twists me over, so my arms are crossed.

I shriek with the first spanking. It isn't his hand. I'm sure of it. It's some type of paddle. He lands four slaps before flipping me back over. He reaches down again and pulls out a spreader. All I can do is watch as he moves around, positioning me how he wants, doing what he wants. I want this so badly. I want him fierce and impatient. I want him to control me. In my twisted head, I know it means he still cares. I was baiting him. I was unnecessarily mean. But the idea of him getting pleasured by someone else popped in my head and out of my mouth. Then I wanted to hurt him as much as that idea hurt me. He did nothing to me. I did it to myself, and now I deserve my punishment.

I whimper as he spreads my legs as wide as they can go. My ankles are attached to it, and I can't move beyond writhing. I'm watching him as he moves back to whatever bin he has with his —tools.

"I thought you said you don't bring women home with you. You seem to be plenty ready for a woman in your bed."

"I bought all of this for you."

There's that snarl. My pussy clenches. Whatever he's going to do, I hope he starts soon. I turn my head and watch him retrieve a ball gag and a long wand vibrator. It's even purple, my favorite color.

"Since you have so much to say, and I don't want to hear any of it, open wide."

"I can't say my safe word with that in."

"I'll respect your limits always, Laura. If it's too much, snap your fingers, and I'll stop. But if you do it because you think you can avoid your punishment, I will lock you in here all weekend and keep you on edge until you think you're going to die from needing to come."

Fuck that's hot.

"Yes, *solnste.*"

His nostrils flare, but his gaze is cold when he turns to look at me. This isn't the man I'm used to going to bed with. This is a Dom. This is a man who has complete control, and I'm willingly surrendering. He fits the ball gag into my mouth and fastens it, careful not to catch my hair.

"You're trying to break up with me, remember. I'm not your *solnste* anymore, am I?

My eyes widen as I realize how badly I've messed up. Tears spring to my eyes and trail down my cheeks. What the fuck was I thinking? Why did I have to hurt him to try and keep him from hurting me?

"I won't bother trying to wipe away your tears, *malyshka*. I know you don't want me to."

All I can do is moan and nod my head. I want him to. I want to make things right. I want him to make things right. Fuck.

He starts the vibrator and skims the foam head over my right instep. My foot twitches, but my leg can't move. He trails the wand up my calf, his lips following. He continues until he's at my inner thighs.

"Wet for me already, *zaychik*. You can't hide from me now any better than you did when you thought to run from me the first time. Your cunt knows what you need better than your head. I'd say better than what your mouth knows, but I'm certain *that* knows it wants my cock down your throat. I'll take that gag out in a while and put in a lip spreader and prove it. You'll take my dick and swallow all of it. My cum and everything."

I'm nodding furiously. I shift my gaze to his hand with the vibrator. He's skipped my needy pussy and is now rolling it over my belly. My abs keep clenching, pulling my upper body from the bed, but the handcuffs won't let me move very far. My moans are muffled, but I'm begging for relief. He laughs before he trails the vibrator over my clit. My hips buck, but he turns it off. Then he steps away from the bed.

I watch as he strokes himself. I'm jealous of his fucking hand. I want to be doing that. I want my mouth or my pussy to be doing that. And he knows it. He's doing it slowly to taunt me. He's not trying to get off yet. He's reminding me of what I'm already missing. The tears are falling faster and harder. He does this for five minutes. I know because I saw the clock. When he eventually comes back to the bed, I'm praying he'll touch me somehow. And he does. He licks my nipple, then bites hard enough for me to scream behind the gag. He moves to the other side.

"Even wetter than a second ago. You like the pain, *malyshka*. You like submitting to me and letting me do what I want. Are you going to run back to your club and try to find a Dom who can do this for you? Do you think you're going to want someone else as much as you want me?"

I shake my head furiously.

"What about if I fantasize about you, but you won't come near me? Who will I act out those fantasies with? I'll have to find someone at one of my clubs."

I scream and thrash. I'm sobbing and choking on the gag. I can take the physical, but that's too much for me. I gag, and I think I'm going to be sick. Maks is quick to get the gag off me. I wail as I think about what he just said. I can't breathe even without the gag.

"Laura, look at me."

It's a command. I'm trying, but I can't seem to get my mind or my body to do what he or I are commanding it to do. He's cupping my face and looking into my eyes, blowing cool air against my temple. It's helping. I can breathe again, but I can't stop crying and panting.

"I went too far with that. I didn't think it would upset you that much, baby girl. I'm sorry."

"Can't breathe—when I think—about you—doing this—with—someone else. Hurts. No—one—else—for—me. Don't want this ever with someone else."

I can finally string a sentence together by the end. The panic is subsiding, but the fear is still there.

"Laura, I canceled my memberships before I went to find you at brunch. I thought if we ever wanted to play, we would go where you belong. I'm not going back. It holds no appeal to me anymore."

"I canceled mine that Monday morning. It didn't feel right to belong to a BDSM club anymore. I thought the same thing you did. If we wanted to play, we would go to your club. I can't do this with anyone else ever again."

"I'm still angry with you, but you just scared the shit out of me."

"I scared the shit out of myself."

"I'm going to leave the gag off, and I will not use the other one tonight. But I am not done with you."

"But Maks—"

"No, *malyshka*. I was trying to work out my thoughts, what would be best for you. I didn't voice them. You're the one who tried to end it. If you're so hell-bent on breaking up with me, then I will make sure you remember exactly what you'll be missing."

"I don't want to—"

"Then I will punish you for toying with me, trying to hurt me, trying to break us up."

"I thought I wanted to."

He turns on the vibrator and presses it against my clit. "Then what do you want, baby girl?"

"You, Daddy!" I scream. I know his guards outside the apartment had to hear. The people below us probably did, too. I don't care.

"I apologized for freaking you out. Yet I haven't heard anything like that from you."

He plunges two fingers into my pussy while he keeps the vibrator teasing my clit. I'm ready to come, and he knows it. He pulls away, turning off the wand again. He licks his fingers and looks at me expectantly.

"I'm sorry, Daddy. I'm so sorry. I never should have said any of it. I wanted to hurt you like I thought you were going to hurt me. God. I'm selfish." I'm not sobbing anymore, but I'm still crying. He walks up next to my head, and I turn to him, mouth open, praying he'll let me suck him. I want to show him how badly I want to be with him, please him. But he just kisses my forehead and steps back.

"I know why you said what you did. I know you didn't mean it, and I know you regret it. But you will learn that treating me like that, treating our relationship like that, is unacceptable. I don't deny that I was considering breaking up because I thought it would be better for you. Unlike you, I didn't lash out. Not today and not the last time. Tell me right now exactly what you want for us, *meelaya*."

"To be together. No more doubting or being scared the other is going to walk away. Whatever we face, we do it together, Maksim. I don't want to do this on my own anymore."

"Me neither, baby girl. No more walking away, no more threatening to walk away. We solve our problems together, and it's us versus them, not me versus you."

"Yes, Daddy."

"Can you take more tonight, *meelaya?*"

"Yes, Daddy. Please only Russian endearments. They feel more special."

"Okay, *malyshka*. You are special."

He kisses my forehead again before he reaches down and pulls out nipple clamps that are connected with a thin chain. Another chain dangles from the center, and I realize it's a clit clamp. He sits on the edge and licks my right nipple. He's slow and gentle again. It's so at odds from how we've been. He switches to the other one once my right one is a tight and aching dart. When they're both standing at attention, he bites hard on my left nipple, and I nearly come off the bed. Need shoots from inside my tits to my clit. He fastens the clamp, then does the exact same thing on the other side. He climbs between my legs and kneels. His hands grasp my ass and lift my hips as he bends forward. His tongue is finally there, finally where I need it. He's licking me from top to bottom.

"This is going to be mine tonight, *meelaya*. All of you will be mine before the sun rises."

"*Da, papochka.*" It's the first time I've ever called him daddy in Russian. The way his eyes bore into me and the fierce attention he pays to my clit tells me I've pleased him.

"Say it again."

"*Papochka. Moy papochka.*"

"I am your daddy."

The rumble of his voice near my pussy and the feel of his lips around my clit bring me to the precipice, but he pulls back. He attaches the clit clamp and once more climbs off the bed. He surveys his work as he strokes himself again. Fuck. I want to be doing that.

"*Papochka*, please let me do something for you."

"You are. I'm enjoying myself. Can't you tell?"

He strokes his dick toward me, and I can see the shiny precum on the slit. My eyes are feasting on him as he draws closer again. He taps the top against my lips with the tip, and I open to him. My tongue comes close, but I don't touch him without permission.

"You can still touch me when you want, *meelaya*."

"Then let me have my hands back."

"No. I also still decide what you can and can't do,

malyshka. You are not in control. Do you think you deserve my dick yet?"

"Yes, *papochka.* Please." I still feel remorseful. He may enjoy the control he has, but he's not receiving the same physical satisfaction I'm getting along with my need to submit.

"Very well, *malyshka.* Open for your *papochka.*"

Chapter Fourteen

Maksim

Laura's words cut me to the quick. Part of me doesn't want a relationship with someone who hurls her words like a knife when we argue. But today's been extreme for her. She's not accustomed to any of this, let alone killing two men in cold blood. On top of that, she was already upset about something Juan said or did.

It scared the shit out of me when she started having a panic attack. I meant to strike back and make her feel shitty, too. I never imagined how deeply this part of our relationship affects her. This is the first time we've done anything kinky. I've fucked her hard, and I've fucked her gently. But with the trouble we had in the beginning, then the car chase, I wasn't sure jumping into BDSM was the right idea. Now I think we both would have benefited from it. It's obvious this type of intimacy means a great deal to Laura.

Then again, maybe that would have made tonight even worse. We're already deeply bonded. Adding that connection then threatening to take it away and share it with someone else might have been more than she could handle. The thought makes me feel sick, but it shifted something in my baby girl that I didn't mean to hurt.

I'm going to keep her on edge for as long as I think she can handle it. Then I'm going to fuck her hard in her pretty little cunt before I finally take her ass. I'm going to let her rest, then I'm going to make love to her the rest of the night.

I climb onto the bed and straddle her neck. I guide my cock to her lips, and her tongue darts out. Holy shit, that feels good. Her tongue's swirling around my tip, and I'm leaking. I may need to come right now to keep from sticking my dick in her pussy and ending this too soon. I'm careful at this angle not to choke her as I slide into her. She lifts her head and bobs, but her restraints make it difficult. As I rock my hips, and she takes my cock, it reminds her yet again who commands and who obeys. Her face is relaxed, and she's stopped crying. Her tears tore at my heart. I hated that she wouldn't let me wipe them away in the bath. I couldn't do it in here at first because her rejection hurt too much.

But as I slide my cock along her tongue to the back of her throat, she's relaxed again. Her eyes look like she's smiling, and they're soft with an emotion I hope is love. I graze the back of my fingers along her cheek before I stroke her hair. She sighs, and her eyes drift closed. She's hardly falling asleep though. She increases the pressure, and I can't stop.

"I'm going to come, and you are going to swallow every drop for me. Do not let any of it dribble."

"Mhmm."

I can feel my cum racing to be released. When the first squirt hits the back of her throat, I feel her swallow and practically take my cock with it. I lean forward and grab the headboard, resting my forehead against my forearm. Fuck, that came on hard and fast. That's what she does to me. When I pull back, she licks me clean before licking her lips, catching a drop that spilled out.

I scoot back and kiss her, tasting myself. I reach for the wand as I move to kneel between her legs. I turn it on a higher setting than before and torture her nipples. Her breath is soon labored, and I love hearing her pant. When I know I'm on the cusp of taking it from pleasure to real pain, I move the vibrator to her clit. I press it against the tip sticking out from the clamp. It's super sensitive, and I know it. She screams again, and I hope the whole damn world knows I'm pleasuring my woman.

I slide two fingers into her as I release the right nipple clamp, my mouth ready to lick and suckle as sensation rushes back in. She whimpers with the pain, but she's soon moaning as I tend to her aching bud. I repeat the process with her left one. But I'm not ready to remove her clit clamp. I flick it, and she almost comes off the bed. I draw my hand away and lick my coated fingers. I lick my ring finger before I slide the first two back into her. My third finger presses against her rosebud. She sucks in a breath, then forces herself to relax. I slide in to my first knuckle, then second, then my entire finger.

I remove the clit clamp and suck until I know she's right on the edge before I pull my mouth and hand away. She wails. I retrieve something else from my treasure trove beside the bed. I managed to just jerk off that Monday night after we had brunch. But by Tuesday, I was online ordering everything I could imagine we'd like together. Now I grab the bottle of lube and an anal plug.

"*Malyshka*, this is a medium-sized one. I'm going to start you here while I eat you out. When I think you're ready, I'm going to move you to one that will get you ready for me. I'm going to fuck you. I won't let you come while I'm licking your cunt, but if you're a good girl, I'll let you come on my cock. Then you're taking me in the ass. Do you understand?

"Yes, *papochka*."

"Is this what you want?"

"Yes, but can I ask for one thing, *papochka*?"

"Yes, *meelaya*."

"I love when you call me your darling." She seems side-tracked for a moment. "When you're ready to give me your cock, will you please release my hands?"

"Why should I do that?"

"Because I'm really struggling right now, Maks. I need to feel you hold me, and I need to hold you. I like this. But I'm barely holding it together. I still don't feel right. I'm still scared I ruined everything."

As much as I want to keep drawing out her edging, I can't ignore her request. Part of being a Dom, and one of the most important parts of playing her daddy, is taking care of her emotional needs. She's admitting what she needs, and I won't reject her request. I grab the key from the bedside table and unlock her hands, leaving the cuffs still attached to the headboard. They might stay there permanently. I reach back and release each ankle. I rub her hips as she moves her legs closer, knowing she's sore. Then I rub her arms and hands as the circulation comes back into them fully.

She's cupping my jaw as I wrap my hand around her throat. I know she doesn't want breath play, so I add only enough pressure to remind her of our roles. I flip us, so she's on top. She guides my cock into her pussy and slides down. I watch her throw her head back as her tits bounce. She may be riding me, but my hands on her waist control her motion and her speed. I dig my heels into the mattress as I surge into her over and over. She falls forward, her hands on my chest before she lowers her chest to mine, her legs curling up. If I didn't have my dick in her cunt, it would almost be like cuddling. But I'm holding her hips down as I thrust into her over and over.

"Daddy."

She reverts to English on a moan.

"Yes, *malyshka*. You can come."

She rubs her clit against my pubic bone twice, and she explodes. I can feel her core clamped tight around my dick. I just came not too long ago, so I'm ready to keep going. She rides me through her orgasm, but I don't let her rest. I press her up and make her bounce on my cock.

"Daddy?"

"Yes."

"Can I be on the bottom? I know missionary isn't very exciting, but I like it best."

I didn't expect that, even if I've noticed she prefers it. I roll us, so she's on bottom. Her hands glide over my abs, up my pecs, and then over my shoulders. She watches my muscles flex, and I can see the lust building in a way it hasn't so far tonight. She seems to truly enjoy my body. Her hands slide down my back until she grabs my ass. Her moan is deep and satisfied.

"You like that?"

"So much, Daddy. I like the feel of you on top of me. You're so much bigger than me. It's like you're dominating me and shielding me. And I love watching your body. I never imagined a man's shoulders flexing could make me want to come. But I love seeing how powerful you are. Even when we're rough, and I know you could hurt me, you don't. I know you could over-power and force me, but I know you won't."

"I will never force you, Laura. I will only take what's freely given. And I will always shield you and protect you."

"Thank you, Daddy."

She cups my cheeks, waiting for me to nod or lower my

mouth to hers. I do both. I feel her come again as our tongues twirl. I can't stop myself. I thrust and hold as I shoot my load into her. It's only after my cock stops twitching that I realize we didn't use a condom. It's only the second time, and I know she takes her pill on schedule. I don't regret it. The thought of a family with Laura is the most appealing idea I can come up with. I stroke hair away from her temple and press soft kisses to her lips before we roll onto our sides. I draw her close as we wiggle under the covers. Her body is limp against mine. Today went from a shitshow to heaven. None of it played out how I thought, but it ended perfectly. My baby girl is in my arms, and we're where we belong.

"Thank you, Daddy."

"You're welcome, *meelaya*."

We'll see what morning brings. I hope I'm not making a mistake deciding to go ahead with the trip.

"How was your day, *malyshka*?"

I dropped her off this morning, and we were both still wrapped in a blissful, post-coital bubble. I abandoned the plan to keep edging her or to have anal. I stuck with the making love to her throughout the night. We slept a few hours and then made love for an hour all throughout the night. Then we did it again in bed this morning and the shower. It's like we've recommitted ourselves again. Neither of us brings up what happened at all yesterday. That will inevitably come up later.

"Busy this morning, but it was winding down by noon. I think a lot of people are taking an extra-long long weekend. I don't think there's going to be much going on tomorrow."

Good. Now I have one less thing to worry about. I loosen my tie and take it off as we get into the car.

"I have a surprise for you, baby girl."

"You do? What is it?"

"I can't tell you. It'll ruin the surprise."

She seems genuinely unprepared, so I guess neither Lanie nor Michelle told her today. Hell if I know if they're even still talking to her. I'm not bringing it up if she doesn't. I twist her shoulders and lift my tie over her head to blindfold her.

"It really is a surprise."

I don't expect lighthearted laughter after the heaviness of yesterday. I know she hasn't forgotten, but she seems to want to enjoy whatever I have in store for her. I lift her into my lap. I know we should wear seatbelts. I shouldn't take these kinds of risks, but I always feel unreasonably safe in the town cars and limos.

"We have a bit of a ride, so rest against me. Tell me more about your day."

"To be honest, it started out crappy once you dropped me off. I didn't even make it to the elevator before Lanie called. She chewed me out for ten minutes, and I just let her. I know she's worried and pissed, so I let her vent. What I didn't realize was that Michelle was already on the line while Lanie unloaded on me. She went easier on me than Lanie, but she didn't hold back either. I'm glad I have a door to my office that locks."

"Are you all right?" I hate this is happening to her. It makes me feel guilty all over again, and my doubts from last night resurface. But the way she's curled into me, her arms tucked in, and her legs pulled up, tells me she feels better with me than she would apart.

"Yeah. It sucks. I know why Lanie is being like this, though. She dated a girl in grad school who abused her. We tried to tell her to leave the girl, but she swore up and down that they loved each other. It wasn't until she wound up with a fractured arm and a concussion that she finally ended it. They were living together. It was a horrible scene the day she moved out, and I had to file a restraining order for her. I know she's scared that I'm making the same mistake she did."

"Does she believe I would abuse you?"

"I don't think so. But I do think she's scared I'm going to get hurt physically. Coming back to your place covered in blood didn't help. And I think she's worried that if—or when, in her head—we break up, she and Michelle are going to have to pick up the pieces."

"That makes sense."

"I do know that she hasn't spoken to Juan. She promised she hadn't and that she wouldn't. I believe her because he's texted me four times and left three voicemails. Nothing makes me think he knows what happened last night. He thinks I'm just really angry about him talking to Lanie, which I still am."

"That anger goes a lot deeper than him telling Lanie that I'm bratva."

She sits up but doesn't try to move the blindfold, even when she turns to look at me. She fumbles until she finds my hand and entwines our fingers.

"Maks, he claimed you do what I feared you might when I first met you."

"He told her I'm a sex trafficker."

"Yeah."

"And she believed him."

"At first. I didn't divulge anything you've told me, but I did tell her that I know things about your past that make me positive you would never do that. And you would never let anyone you know do that."

"Do you think she believes that?"

"Yeah. She said she did when I talked to her. She's pissed at Juan now too because she feels played."

"Did you talk to him?" I'm trying to stay calm. I don't want to tense because she'll feel it. It takes every ounce of self-control that Vlad drilled into me as a teen. He would taunt me and scream in my face. He'd slap me and punch me, even kick me. If I showed any response, any emotion, he'd take it out on my brothers, especially Bogdan. I learned to hide my feelings fast after he broke Bogdan's nose and Aleks's fingers.

"No. I can't. I don't trust myself. I don't want to have to end a twenty-four-year-long friendship if I can help it. And it would make things horrible between our parents. But disliking you and what he believes you do is one thing. Claiming that you buy and sell people to be raped is more than I can forgive right now. I'm not sure how you forgave me for my accusation."

"I was too busy thinking about bending you over the table and fucking you until you screamed. No one stands up to me like that. Definitely no woman has. I was practically coming from how turned on you had me."

"We deserve each other. We're just as twisted as the other. I thought you looming over me was going to make me come. I held my own, but God, if you'd pushed me against the table or the wall, I would have hiked up my skirt for you. I knew then that I didn't have to be scared of you. It was controlled anger, or least that's what it looked like. I didn't fear you actually harming me."

"I never would have. And not just because you're a woman. It's you. I couldn't do that to you."

"How was your day?"

Now there's a loaded question.

"Good."

"Can you not tell me about it?"

"Not all of it, baby girl. But I stopped by two construction sites, then met with my brothers at the gym and worked out. I went a few rounds with Niko and checked in with them just to know how the merger's going. And took care of a few things."

She's silent for a moment, and I wonder what's going through her head.

"Can I ask you two things? Then I'll try not to ask more in the future."

"Of course. I'll do my best to answer you."

"When you have to go take care of things, could you please tell that's what you're doing, so I don't worry if I can't reach you or you come home with busted knuckles? I don't need or want specifics."

"Yes. When I can, I always will."

"Juan mentioned your tattoos, and I realize that you must have been arrested before. Either he's seen them in person, or he saw the photo records. What do I do if you get arrested or you're taken to a hospital? I want to know where I go, who I can trust, and what I can say."

"If either happens, you get to one of my places or my brothers' as fast as you can. They'll call you, or you call them. If it's safe for you to come to the hospital, one of them or Sergei or Anton will come get you. You haven't met Anton, but he's a cousin on my father's side. I don't think you know much about bratva structure, but Sergei and Anton are equals. Their positions are known as the two spies. Sergei heads the security group, which handles intelligence and security. Anton heads the support group, which plans and executes operations. You can trust my cousins and my brothers. If it's a situation like my arrest or being in the hospital, you trust no one else unless those five say you can. Under no circumstances, and I'm fucking dead serious, Laura, are you to go to any police station and pretend to be my lawyer. I know you think Dmitry is an idiot, but he's our corporate lawyer, not our defense attorney. You have to stay away."

"And what do I say if I'm questioned?"

"The truth. You know about my legitimate businesses, so stick to that. If they ask you about anything illegal, tell them you don't know. I will do what I can to shield you from that. What you don't know, no one can try to get out of you."

"All right."

She accepts that and leans back against me as though she didn't just ask me to let her know when I'm going off to torture or kill someone, or what to do if she has to flee and hide from the police or deal with me getting hurt. I suppose I can offer her a little more than the vague answer I gave before.

"The two times you noticed I changed, I was taking care of men involved in the car chase. I will not tell you what I did or what was done to them. I didn't get any definitive answers, so I am not keeping anything from you. But I do have some suspicions that someone is leaking information. That's why I'm very specific about who you can trust, and it's why only Sergei has been your bodyguard until today. I let Ilya do it because you know him, and you said you didn't have to leave your office today."

"Maybe's it's a good thing I don't know any of your men. I would be suspicious if a stranger told me something on your behalf. But if I knew them, I might be trusting. I've seen you with your brothers, and I know Sergei. If Anton is anything like them, then I know I'll be as safe with him as I am with you."

"Yes, *meelaya*. They know how much you mean to me. Last night, what you did with the clothes and the disinfectant was exactly right. I'm guessing that's from being a lawyer and understanding crime scenes. Where my brothers and I take care of things is a warehouse in northern Queens. It's not listed on any city plans. It's been abandoned for years, and no one questions who it belongs to. We have a method for how we handle things. We never wear personal items in front of anyone. We wear booties and burn our clothes. We shower there. We do everything there, and we leave it all behind there."

"Is that what you did with my clothes?"

"Yes. I need you to promise me something, Laura."

"I will if I can."

I regret she's blindfolded for this. I reach and pull the shades down on the doors before I turn her to straddle me.

"I want to see your eyes for this. Do not look out the windows. Look at me. Understood?"

"Yes, Maks."

I slip the tie up to her forehead.

"There may be times when I come home worse than you did. It means something unexpected happened and wasn't within our control. When that happens, I need you to leave me alone. I need to concentrate on getting cleaned up and disposing of things. And I need to calm down. If I need something, I will ask you. Please don't ask and please don't try to help. Just leave me alone when I'm like that."

"Yes, Maks. I promise."

"I know it'll scare you, and I know you'll want to help. The best thing to do is go into one of the guest rooms. All right?"

"All right."

"I'm sorry if I'm scaring you."

"You're not. It was scarier not knowing what to do. Thank you for telling me."

"You're welcome, baby girl. Now put your blindfold back in place. We're almost there."

Chapter Fifteen

Laura

Maks won't tell me where we are. We got out somewhere where there was a breeze and machine noise. I'm straining to determine what the sound is. It sounds like propellers. He scoops me into his arms, making me squeak.

"I can walk, Daddy."

"I know you can, baby girl, but I don't want you to."

Maks walks a little way, then we're going up metal steps. I sense someone else is there, but no one speaks. I'm completely confused now. I hear some thunks, then the noise goes away, like a door closed. But the engine sounds are much closer. He places me in a comfortable chair and drapes a blanket over my lap.

"You can rest for a little while."

"Maks, where are we? Where are you taking me? A blanket. Propellers. Luggage thumping. What's going on?"

"You, little girl, are too perceptive by half."

He kisses me, but he still won't tell me anything, and he hasn't said I can take off the blindfold. I know enough not to do it myself without being told to. I feel him fasten a belt across my lap. Then he sits down beside me, takes my hand, and tugs me against him as he wraps his other arm around my shoulders. It's just easier to give in.

Only a few minutes later, we're moving. I can tell we're taxiing, then the engine revs louder, and we're hurtling forward. My head and back press against the backrest as the plane's nose lifts up. Then we're in the air.

"Now will you tell me? I can't get away."

"Yes, baby girl. Take your blindfold off."

I slide it off and look out the window beside me. I can see the city's skyline and the bay as the plane continues to rise. Then it's turning south and banking. I look down at something Maks is handing me. It's a brochure for a villa somewhere. I open it and gasp. It's a beachside villa in Turks and Caicos. I've always wanted to go. I can only stare at it, then at Maks.

"Happy birthday, baby girl."

"Thank you, Daddy." It comes out a whisper when I wrap my arms around him and squeeze. But then I remember it's only Thursday. "Maks, I have work tomorrow."

"Call in sick. You said it was a quiet week, and you even said it seems like a lot of people are taking an extended long weekend."

"Yeah, but it'll look suspicious that I'm suddenly sick rather than having requested the time off."

"Then tell them your boyfriend has whisked you off to a romantic weekend getaway where he intends to ravish you six ways from Sunday."

"Maybe just the beginning part. I need to call L—"

"I told them yesterday before I invited them to dinner. I didn't want them to panic when you disappeared."

"That's part of why she was in a bad mood. Makes more sense. I'm certain she doesn't approve."

"I don't think she does."

"I need to tell my parents I'm going to miss another dinner. Good thing we're going Monday night. We will be back in time, right?"

"Yes, baby girl."

"Oh, you are my *lapochka*!" I can't help it. I'm so excited that I smother him in kisses as he chuckles. I doubt anyone has called him "sweetie pie" before.

"That is definitely one you're keeping to yourself. Don't let even my brothers hear that."

"Especially not your brothers?"

"Especially. Are you happy about this? I was worried you wouldn't like the surprise."

"If I'd known, I would have felt guilty about work and Sunday dinner, and I would have worried this is too extravagant. Thank you."

I'm so close to saying it. To revealing how I feel. But I don't want to be the one to say it first and not hear it back. That would crush me.

"Damn." I just realized something that has just ruined every ounce of excitement.

"What? I packed our toothbrushes. That's all we need." Maks squeezes my thigh. "And there might be a tiny string bikini somewhere."

"I don't wear string bikinis."

"All the better. I prefer you naked."

"No. Not when someone can see me."

"It's a completely private beach. The staff will only be there at specific times. They know to stay the hell away otherwise. But what made you say damn?"

"It's more like fuck, but I know you don't like me to swear. I might not be going to Sunday dinner, but Juan probably is. He's going to fucking poison my parents against you. Fuck."

"We'll deal with that Monday night. Call your parents now and tell them I'm taking you away. Then spend the next three-and-a-half hours coming up with all the ways you want me to make love to you."

We both freeze for a heartbeat, not sure if we should acknowledge what Maks just said. I reach for my cell phone, but he unfastens my seatbelt. I look around for a sign that says it's safe, but there's nothing.

"I wanted to wait until the perfect moment to tell you, *moya lyubov'*."

My love. I hold my breath. I was just scared to tell him what I hope he's about to tell me. Please let it be what I'm thinking. I want to say it so badly.

"Laura, I love you."

"I love you."

I don't know who kisses who. I couldn't give a shit. All I know is that we're clinging to each other, ravishing each other's mouths. I feel Maks unfasten his seatbelt, then he's standing and walking to the rear of the plane with me in his arms. I hear a door close, then I'm lying on a bed with Maks on top of me. I glance around and realize that there's a private cabin aboard the jet. I didn't even get to appreciate the main cabin, but now we're tucked away.

"I've been wanting to say that for days, but then I decided I wanted to wait until the perfect moment on this trip."

"This was perfect. I almost said it right before you, but I was scared you didn't feel that way."

We sit up, then stand up, so we can peel each other out of our clothes. Maks pulls a condom from his pocket and tosses it on the bed before his pants hit the floor. We're naked and tumbling onto the mattress. His hands are roaming everywhere he can reach as he kisses my neck, my cheek, the tops of my tits, then back up again. When our mouths meet once more, I nip at his bottom lip before enticing his tongue into my mouth. I suck gently, reminding him how much we both like it when I give him head.

"I need you, Maks."

"I want to be inside you right now."

"I'm ready. I don't want foreplay, just you."

Maks reaches for the condom and unwraps it. He slides it on, neither of us in the mood for me to tease. I widen my legs, inviting him to lay between them. His cock finds my pussy like it's always belonged there. We grasp hands, and they rest beside my head as he thrusts into me.

"Laura." It's a masculine groan that makes my pussy drip and clench. He rocks into me slowly as our eyes meet. It's achingly sweet as my hulking boyfriend moves as though I'm the most precious thing he's ever beheld. Love and affection mix as I let go of his hand and run my fingers through his hair as my body undulates beneath him. I cup his jaw as he rests his forehead against mine.

"I love you, *malyshka*."

"I love you, *papochka*."

Our pace speeds up as need consumes us. The gentleness and finesse fall away as passion controls us. Our bodies slide together as sweat rolls between my tits, and I feel it between his shoulder blades once he releases my other hand, and they roam over him. The sound of our bodies colliding and our heavy breathing fill the cabin, and it's better than any symphony.

"Come for me, baby girl."

"I'm so close."

"Come on my cock. Your tight little cunt is going to milk me dry."

"Fuck, Daddy. I'm coming."

"That's it, baby. Fuck, you're so tight. Your pussy feels so good. I may have died and somehow found my way into heaven."

"Do I have a magical pussy, Daddy?"

"Yes, baby girl."

He grunts as he slams into me. This roughness is what we know, and we both crave. Tenderness was what we needed in the beginning. Now the need to control and be controlled puts us back into our desired roles.

"Let me hear you. I know you're going to come again."

"I am. Goddamn, I'm so fucking close. A little harder."

Maks happily obliges as he thrusts into me so hard the bed hits the wall. I'm certain any flight attendant can hear us. Let them know. If it's a woman, I hope she's jealous as fuck. My boyfriend is the hottest man I've ever seen, and he fucks like a god.

"Maks!"

"Laura!"

Our voices cry out in unison. The feel of getting off at the same time is unreal. Knowing how we feel about each other only makes it better. As the high wears off, we lie together panting and grinning. He rolls off me and pulls me against his chest. His fingers stroke my back, and my eyelids feel heavy. I'm exhausted but blissfully happy.

"Sleep, *malyshka*."

"Will you stay with me?"

"Nothing is dragging me away from you."

"Do you think you can fall asleep too?"

"I'm struggling to stay awake as we speak."

We tug down the covers and slip inside.

"Is this your plane?"

"Kutsenko Partners, so all four of us can use it."

"Did you tell your brothers where we're going?"

"Of course."

"Good."

"Oh?"

"Yeah. You can brag that you had real sex on the beach when we get back."

"Is that so?"

"Yup."

"Go to sleep, baby girl. I've just joined the mile-high club."

I sit up for a moment. I shouldn't ask. I shouldn't ask. I shouldn't ask. Fuck it. "You weren't a member before?"

"No, baby girl. I don't travel with women."

"Ah, you have one in every country."

"You think I'm some sort of Casanova. I had the clubs, and that was it. There was nothing outside of that for years. No romantic interests or even hook ups or escorts."

"In that case, I'm happy to induct you in the mile-high club."

Maks's face is a thundercloud. "You've done this before?"

"No. But why should you get all the credit?"

"Baby girl..."

So much for our nap. The plane is making its descent when we finally get redressed and return to our seats. I realize that I haven't called my parents. I just want to get it over with.

"Laura? Hi, sweetie."

"Hi, Dad." God, I will never, ever consider calling my father Daddy ever again. I haven't in at least ten years, but definitely never again.

"The connection isn't very good. Where are you?"

"About to land in Turks and Caicos. Maks surprised me with a birthday trip. We won't be back until Monday."

"That sounds like fun. Oh, here's your mom."

"Laura?"

"Hi, Mom. I was just telling Dad that Maks surprised me

with a trip to Turks and Caicos. I'm going to miss Sunday dinner again, but we're really looking forward to Monday." I'm not really. Not now that I know Juan is going to talk their ear off before I can get home.

"That's two weeks in a row, Laura."

"Mom, isn't it enough that I'll be twenty-seven tomorrow and still come home almost every weekend?"

"We were going to celebrate with the Diazes."

"I know. Mom, Juan and I got in a massive argument the other day."

"About your new boyfriend?"

"Yeah. If he's there on Sunday, I'm sure he won't have nice things to say. He tried to scare Lanie into trying to break us up. He made some ugly accusations about Maks's businesses. It's disgusting."

"What did he say?"

"He's a hypocrite, Mom. We know what Luis does and what Pablo is being trained to do. Juan accused Maks of being the same type of guy. Except instead of drug running, he accused Maks of way worse."

There's a long silence on my mom's end. I wonder if I've royally fucked up trying to take a preemptive strike. I look up at Maks, and I can tell he isn't pleased. But I don't know if it's at me for saying this much or just the situation. He must be able to tell that I just got nervous because he tugs me against him and kisses the top of my head while he holds me close.

"Mom, the plane's landing. I gotta go. I'll call you on Monday when we set off, okay?"

"Yeah. Have fun and be careful."

"I will. Just remember, whatever Juan says, it's because he's pissed at me."

"He's jealous. Laura."

"Yeah."

"If Maks is mixed up in stuff like the Diazes, be extra careful with Juan. He was a jealous, moody, and spiteful kid. He's not much better as an adult."

"If you knew this, then why did you let us be friends?"

"Because you two got along, and you rarely had problems. But I've heard things, Laura, from Luis and Margherita. I saw how he played with Pablo. He hated being the younger brother. He doesn't share well."

"He's never acted like this before. I think he's using Maks being Russian as an excuse."

"I can tell from how you say Maks's name that you're serious about him. Anyone can. Juan can. Your dad and I will make our opinions based on meeting your boyfriend, not what Juan says. Just watch out. Juan's not a petty little boy anymore. He has a gun and a badge."

Wonder-fucking-ful. Now my mom tells me this. But truthfully, she isn't telling me anything I don't already know about Juan. I've just never been on the receiving end like this before.

"Thanks, Mom. I probably won't get to talk to you tomorrow, so happy birthing day. Thanks for having me."

"Smarty pants. Happy birthday. I love you."

"I love you too. Bye."

"Bye."

I look up at Maks, and I know he heard the entire conversation. He looks pissed, but he doesn't say anything until the wheels touch down.

"We'll deal with him when we have to. I'm not letting that piece of—I'm not letting him ruin our first vacation together and your birthday."

"He is being a piece of shit. And I won't let him. First. Hmm. That implies there will be others."

"Plenty. Maybe one a month."

"I have a job, and you have an empire to run."

"An empire? Maybe you'd like to see the emperor's new clothes."

"Your birthday suit is the finest one you own, Daddy."

"Cheeky. I might have to put you over my knee for your birthday spanking."

"Yes. Please. With one for a wish, and one to grow on." I can't stop my giggles as I reach between Maks's legs.

"Something will definitely grow, baby girl. Now give Daddy a kiss before we go find our love shack."

I snort. "Love shack? You mean the billion-dollar luxury home on a private beach?"

"That one. My kiss."

I'm happy to kiss him now and whenever he wants. I'm glad neither of us is letting what's happened recently spoil this trip. I can't wait to see what Maks has in store for me.

Chapter Sixteen

Maksim

I made the right decision. Laura is already more relaxed, and her smile hasn't left her face since we walked down the airplane's steps and got into the waiting car. It was a quick drive to the villa, so we are already changed into our bathing suits for a dip in the sea before dinner. I hadn't lied when I said I packed a skimpy string bikini. There's just enough to cover her nipples and her pussy. I'm wearing board shorts, which do not meet Laura's approval. She complained they cover far too much of me. I plan for her to discover they're still easy to get off.

"Are you ready?"

Laura's got a towel under each arm, so I pick up the frosty fruity drinks waiting for us as she stands eagerly at the door that leads to the covered veranda. Just beyond it is a private swimming pool. Then it's out to the sand, where there are two beach lounge chairs calling our names. As we make our way to the water's edge, I sense Laura's nervous about someone spying her in the barely-there bathing suit. I know no one is here, and I'm loving walking a few steps behind her.

"Are you going to hurry up?"

"No. I'm taking my time and enjoying the scenery."

She looks back, shakes her hips, and sticks out her tongue. She jogs to the chairs, knowing I can't hurry unless I want to spill our drinks. She's already charging into the surf by the time I put the glasses on the table between the chairs. I'm quick on her heels and scoop her under her arms as she wades in.

"What shall I do with such a sassy *malyshka*? A spanking?"

I flip her over my shoulder and give her ass a resounding slap. She giggles and kicks her legs. I've never seen her so carefree. I definitely didn't expect it after yesterday. I wonder if she's in denial, and it still hasn't registered. Or has she decided to make the most of our vacation and deal with it later?

"An orgasm."

"I don't think you get how this type of counteroffer works, baby girl."

"You can have one too. I'm not greedy."

"Yes, you are."

I can't help but laugh along with her. The early evening sun turns her dark chestnut hair gold and red, and her eyes are luminescent. She has no lines when her face is at rest, but fine ones crinkle around her eyes and bracket her lips as she grins. I pretend to drop her toward the water, and she squeals. She leans back and splashes water at me.

"That does it, baby girl."

I wade out until the water is to my chest, and I know she can't stand since she's a foot shorter than me. I wrap her legs around my waist and slide my hand over her ass until I can reach between her legs. That's not the seawater making her wet. She pulls her bikini top apart, revealing her perfect tits.

Women would pay a small fortune to have what she developed naturally. She leans back and presses them together in offering.

"Daddy."

It's said on a sigh as I work her tight little cunt around my fingers. My teeth graze along her neck as she fists my hair, her nails scratching my scalp and making my cock jump. I pull at the drawstring to my boardshorts and pull open the front panel. My sinful temptation moves her hips, allowing me to push our clothing out of the way before I surge into her.

"This has always been a fantasy, Daddy."

"Making love in the sea?"

"Yes. Or on a beach or in a pool. Just anywhere with water."

"We've satisfied your bath and shower fantasies then. Several times."

"Mhmm." She's breathing soft moans beside my ear as she clings to me, her face burrowed against my neck as she nips and sucks.

"Do you intend to mark me?"

"Would you let me?"

"Of course. I'm yours."

"As long as I keep it where no one could see it?"

"While we're here, I don't care where. When we get home, then below my collar. I don't want anyone to think I've been with an escort or a whore."

"I like it when I look down and see your love bites all over my tits."

"I know you do."

My grin is predatory, but it only makes her giggle more. With a growl, I latch onto her nipple and suck while I drive myself into her over and over. She's meeting my pounding with her own. Making love to my girlfriend—my soulmate—while we're standing in the water on our first vacation moves me more than I expected. My chest swells with how much I love her. Most people would say we're ridiculous for believing we've fallen in love so quickly. It was definitely lust at first sight, but our connection is deep. I think that's why last night was so wretched for us both when we nearly split up. It would have been like losing a limb or an organ. I would no longer be complete if Laura walked away. The idea drove her to a panic attack, and I get it.

"Oh, Daddy. I'm—can I—God, I need to—Maks, please."

"Yes, *meelaya*. Come for me. I want to feel you."

Her legs clamp around my waist, her strong swimmer's thighs squeeze my waist as she grinds against me. I dig my fingers into her ass and press her hard against me as we come together. I tilt my head back and groan. Will I ever get enough of her? I pray I never do. I carry her out of the water and grab a towel to wrap around her before I lay her on the lounger and follow her down. We're still moving together, our need not nearly satisfied.

"Maks, I love you."

"I love you, Laura. I want to make you happy until my last breath."

We keep saying these things, hinting at a permanency, but I don't know if she views our future like I do. I want more than just a girlfriend. I want Laura as my wife. I don't know if it's too soon to ask, but the question is constantly at the tip of my tongue. At the very least, I want her to move in with me. Or hell, if she prefers, I'll move in with her. My places may be where we spend most of our time, but her place feels so much more like a home. My fancy furniture and absurd square feet don't feel anywhere near as inviting as Laura's apartment.

She cups my face and gazes into my eyes. I hope she sees the sincerity, and I think she does because she nods. She lifts her chin, hinting that she wants a kiss. I love that she lets me know what she wants, but she still lets me lead. I'm happy to oblige. Our kiss drives my need to come again until I'm smashing into her with no finesse. Her rasping breaths tickle my ear, making me even more aroused.

"I'm close, *meelaya*. I'm not coming without you."

"Just keep doing this. I'm close too. I want to make you come so badly. I want to do this for you."

"You do. Over and over. I don't know how I have any cum left after each time we fuck or make love."

I feel her muscles spasm as her hips lift off the lounger, a testimony to the strength in her legs with my considerable weight pressing her down. I drive into her once more and spill. I can feel my cum shooting into her over and over, and I feel completely drained. I'm careful not to squash my baby girl as I settle some of my weight on her. She pulls me, silently demanding that I give her more. I'll always keep some of it off her, but I relent since I know how much she loves us being chest to chest. I do too.

A noise in the distance tells me the staff is arriving to make our dinner. Laura hears it too because she's trying to scramble out from under me. I sigh, not at all excited to pull out. But I know she'll be beside herself if anyone sees her in this bikini. As much as she joked on the way to the water, I know she feels self-conscious. I adjust my trunks before I stand and wrap her in the beach towel. We forgot all about our now-melted drinks. We carry them back to the house.

"Take the first shower. I'm going to check that everything is on track for dinner. We can eat outside and enjoy the sunset if you want."

"That sounds amazing, *lapochka*."

I grin and shake my head. I never imagined anyone would call me sweetie pie. Not in seriousness or in jest, but my baby girl seems to like it. So who am I to argue? I walk through the villa and check with the chef and his two assistants. He has everything he needs and is already setting up, so I leave them to their work. I cross back to the bedroom and am ready to join Laura in the shower when my phone buzzes. I brought one that only my brothers and cousins have the number to. This must be important.

"*Privet.*"

I greet Niko in Russian since I know the chef and his staff won't understand. I close the bedroom door and can hear the shower running. Niko continues in Russian.

"We have a problem, Maks. Pussycats was vandalized and broken into just before it was supposed to open this afternoon."

"What? How'd I not hear about this before I left?"

"They knocked one guard out and killed the other. But they must have gotten one of them to disarm the alarm. It wasn't until Gregor arrived to open that he discovered what happened. Windows shattered, graffiti outside and inside, furniture broken and ripped with knives, and they took a bat or pipe to all the bottles. There are bullet holes in the walls."

"That's thousands of dollars of damage. Salvatore?"

"We don't know. The guard didn't see anyone coming. He has no idea what happened."

"Do you think that's the truth? Or is he lying to cover his ass?"

"Truth. He has a massive lump at the back of his head, and they worked him over. Three cracked ribs, and there's a chance he might never father a kid."

"Fuck."

"Maks, that's not the worst of it."

"What else is there?"

"They left a message in the office spray painted on the wall. I'm sending it to you now."

I wait until my phone pings, then pull up the text. My heart feels like it stops before it races.

Such a pretty slut you're fucking. My turn is coming soon.

"I need you, Aleks, and Anton here now. I'm sending the jet back. Once it refuels, I want you three on it. I can't hire the security I need here, and I don't trust anyone."

"Aren't you going to cut your trip short?"

"And bring Laura home to a threat I don't know where it's coming from? Hell, no. But I'm not comfortable with being the only person guarding her here. I need Bogdan and Sergei to figure out who did this."

"Do you think it's *Cosa Nostra*?"

"Maybe?" I run my hand over my face as I look toward the bathroom. Laura's probably waiting for me to join her, but she'll only wait for so long. Then she'll be out here looking for me. I don't want her to hear this conversation.

"Who else could it be?"

"I really don't know. Salvatore is the only one I know who has definitely seen us together. But I wouldn't put anything past her pissed off ex-fuck buddy."

"Who?"

"Diaz. And don't tell a single person I just said that. I wasn't thinking."

"You said this morning that she got in a fight with him."

"Yeah. A colossal one. She told him not to call her, and she ignored his calls and texts today. I was sitting next to her when she called her parents to tell them we were going away for the weekend. Her mom didn't sound surprised that he's trying to interfere. She said he was petty and vindictive as a kid, but not to her. She warned Laura that he's still the same but now has a gun and a badge. Were the cops called?"

"No. No police report. I figured Diaz would hear about it and get involved. I didn't think you'd want that."

"You're right. I want him followed. I want everything you can find on him. Where he spends his money. Who he's fucking. Whether he's dirty."

"I already know his dad and brother are Cartel."

"Yeah. Laura told me. Hey, I gotta go. Laura's almost out of the shower, and I don't want her overhearing this. I want to tell her myself. Get your asses here."

Fucking-a. I planned to take Laura on a charter boat tour of the island tomorrow and out to swim with dolphins on Saturday. Now I don't know if we can even leave the villa. I don't know if whoever this fuckhead is knows we're away from the city.

"Maks?"

"I'm coming, *malyshka*."

"I'll let you go. I'll text you when we set off."

"Thanks."

I hang up with my brother and call the pilot to let him know about the change in plans before I make my way to the bathroom. I have no idea what I'm going to tell her. I don't want to ruin our getaway. But if I don't, and she finds out, she'll be pissed. I know I definitely don't want to show her the picture, so I delete it from my phone. It's not like I think she's going to snoop, but I don't want to scare her.

"I thought you might come wash my back."

She turns her back to me as I step into the shower and draws her hair over her shoulder. I can't resist kissing along her shoulder, up to her neck, and behind her ear. She does that shiver that I love so much.

"Sorry. Niko called to check in. There was some trouble at one of the clubs. A break-in."

"Is everything all right? Do we need to go back?"

"No, baby girl. That's the good thing about having three brothers. There's always someone to take care of business. They're more than fine without me."

"Do you know who it is?" She turns toward me, her eyes wide.

"Not yet."

"Do you think it was Juan?"

"You think a cop would break in? Whoever it was did a lot of damage."

"You heard my mom. Besides, who better to get away with a crime than a police officer? He knows what to hide, and he bleeds blue alongside the others."

"I don't like the guy, but I'm not ready to believe it was him. It was more likely the Italians."

"Because of what happened at Envy?"

"Yeah, and because Salvatore saw us together."

"What does that have to do with anything?"

She's running the bar of soap over my chest and back as I scrub the saltwater from my hair. What do I say? I want to tell her the truth, but I'm definitely not telling her that I told Niko to get our brother and cousin and come here. I promised her it was already safe here.

"I don't know all the details, but I think you caught Salvatore's eye."

She just stands in front of me and blinks. I don't know what's going through her mind, and I hate it.

"Do you think he knows who I am?"

"I don't know, but it wouldn't surprise me if he does. You're not exactly a public figure, but you've handled some big cases that he'd know about. And you and your friends are on social media enough for there to be a path to find you."

"Do I need to close my accounts?"

"I would just let them snooze for a bit. I don't think you need to close them."

She studies me before she goes back to soaping me down.

"I think in general, I need to be more selective in what I post. If we're together, then I get there's always a threat. I might become a foodie and just post pictures of omelets and cake or stick with posting books I like. No more posting anything that can give people an idea of where I am or what I look like."

"That's probably for the best."

Guilt tugs at me for not telling her the entire truth. Hopefully, she can understand that I'm trying to protect her. I'll figure out what to do next once my brothers and cousin arrive. The best I can do is plan for them to guard the property. Despite what I told Laura, I did pack more than our toothbrushes and bathing suits. I had a dress ordered for her that I hoped she could wear to dinner at a resort on Sunday night. I suppose I'll be canceling that. I don't even know if I should have dinner on the beach with her tonight.

"Daddy? Where'd you go?"

"Sorry, baby girl. I was just thinking about the club."

"Did anyone get hurt?"

"Luckily, none of the dancers were there. One of the guards got roughed up pretty badly, and they killed another."

She listens to me, and I watch her. I think she's startled by how nonchalant I am when I talk about someone dying. I have to remind myself that this is still new to her. I hope she never becomes as jaded as I am.

"We don't have to stay, Maks. If you need to take care of things, or if you're going to be distracted, then we should go back."

"Absolutely not. I told you. My brothers can take care of it. This is your birthday weekend, and I think we need the time alone together. No more distractions from the outside world.

We'll have to face all of that soon enough. For the next four days, it's just us. You promised me sex on the beach, baby girl. And I'm thirsty for my favorite treat."

I press her back against the wall of the shower and sink to my knees. Our fingers look like raisins by the time we get out of the shower. I wrap my *malyshka* in the thick robe and wring the water from her long hair with a towel. I slip on my own robe before we make our way out to the table on the veranda. A bottle of wine awaits, and we can smell the aroma of fresh fish grilling. For now, the world only includes us, a chef, and two servers. If only it could stay that way.

Chapter Seventeen

Laura

There's something more going on that Maks isn't telling me about the break-in. But I trust that he's doing it to protect me, not to intentionally keep secrets from me. Yesterday sucked hard. I'm not in the mood to let anything ruin our weekend away, so if he thinks I don't need to know—at least for now—then I'm content to keep it that way.

Dinner was delicious. It was one of the best meals I've ever had. It was course after course with salads and cheeses and fish and the most decadent molten chocolate cake I've ever had. We enjoyed that in the privacy of our bedroom where we fed each other the cake and licked the chocolate from one another's bodies. I'm stuffed and replete. I've gorged myself on food and Maks because, of course, our dessert wasn't just food.

It's late when I go into the bathroom to get ready for bed. All I've seen from home so far are our toothbrushes and that bikini. Maybe Maks told the truth. Maybe I am going to be naked the entire weekend. I can't say that I'll complain. As I reach for my toothbrush, I notice just how bare the counter looks. Neither Maks nor I use many products, but there's stuff on our counters at his place and mine.

Fuck.

My birth control isn't on the counter. He packed the toothbrush I keep at his place, but I don't think he thought to look in the medicine cabinet for my pack of pills. I doubt this evening did any damage, but we need to be more careful from here on out.

I can hear Maks on the phone speaking Russian. We usually brush our teeth together. How domesticated is that? If he's still on the phone, I'm guessing it's business. I wonder if it's about the break-in. I head into the bedroom and slide the robe off. As I drape it at the foot of the bed, I realize I left the door open. I can hear Maks without any effort.

"Take turns tonight. I want one of you at the front door and one on the back veranda. There's a security room just inside the front door to the left. I haven't been in, but I know there are cameras all over the property wired to that room. Be quiet when you get here. We're about to get to bed. You'll scare the shit out of her if she hears you."

What the fuck?

"I'm already scared, Maksim. Who's coming here?" I don't bother with the robe. He spins around at my voice.

"I have to go." He hangs up without waiting for whomever is on the other end. He hurries over to me, but I step back from his embrace.

"Who's coming?" I repeat myself, and I'll keep doing it until I get an honest and complete answer.

"Niko, Aleks, and Anton. I should have brought security with us, and I regret it now that there was the break-in. I don't know what these people are after, but there's a reason I always have a bodyguard with me. I shouldn't have been so careless."

"So this is about you?" I don't believe him. Why are there three guys coming?

"Both of us. Aleks will guard you, and Anton will guard me. Niko is here to rotate with them."

"You said there are cameras all over. Have they been recording us? Is there now footage of us having sex?" I spin around and look at the ceiling and walls. Are there cameras in here?

"*Malyshka*, there are cameras in the hallway and pointing at the bedroom doors, but none in them."

"And they're on? Do they go to some security company? Is someone monitoring them outside that room?"

"No. I chose this villa for its seclusion. That's also why I want them here. There is no one monitoring the property."

"Does Bogdan have extra guards now?"

"I don't know. It's not that we're having extra guards, *malyshka*. We're just having a guard each."

I still feel like there's something he's keeping from me. Maks doesn't lie. But he is overprotective to a fault. He thinks he's shielding me from whatever's going on. I feel less safe not knowing. "Maks, if there's more to this, then tell me. I don't like feeling unprepared."

"We are prepared. Niko, Aleks and Anton just landed. They'll be here in half an hour. I'm just being cautious."

"Fine. Maks, did you bring condoms? You didn't pack my birth control."

"Shit. I didn't think about that. Yes. I brought plenty."

He winks at me and waggles his eyebrows. I can't help but smile. I'm still uneasy, but Maks has been handling security details and travel since long before I was in the picture.

"Are you coming to bed?"

"Yes, *malyshka*. You know that's one of my favorite times of the day."

I roll my eyes. The sheets usually wind up in a mess before he gets a chance to tuck me in. I slide into bed, and he follows. A massive yawn escapes. I didn't mean to, but the moment I rest my head against his chest, I suddenly feel exhausted. He tightens his hold on me and strokes my back.

"Sleep, *meelaya*. I'll get up to meet with the guys when they get here, then I'll be right back in bed beside you. It shouldn't take me long. You shouldn't even notice I'm gone."

"Okay, Daddy." I can't help it as my eyes drift closed. I'm out with the next yawn.

The sun is shining brightly the next time I open my eyes. It's well past when I usually wake, even on weekends. Maks is next to me, and I can tell he's awake.

"Roll over and go back to sleep if you want, baby girl. There's no rushing around this weekend."

We're spooning, so I roll over and snuggle back against his chest as he shifts onto his back. I enjoy the heat radiating from him and the scent that never seems to leave him. Woodsy and spicy. It's become as comforting as my favorite scent, lavender. I close my eyes, but I know I'm not going to fall back to sleep. I'm tired but not sleepy. I still feel exhausted, but my mind is jumping from one thing to another. It settles on the day before yesterday. The day I killed two men. Before I know what's happening, I'm trembling, and tears are leaking from my eyes.

"Shh, baby girl. I know it's scary, and I know you feel guilty. You did what you had to. I never wanted you to kill anyone ever, but I'm so fucking proud that you protected yourself and Sergei."

"Don't forget Sebastian." I can barely get the words out as I sob. I was fine yesterday, but it just hits me. I feel guilty because I don't feel guilty about killing those men. I did it without batting an eye, and I could just as easily do it again. What kind of person does that make me? And if I'm judging myself for that, how can I not judge Maks and his entire family? They kill all the time. God. That sounds horrible. How can I be sure this won't come back on me? Or worse, come back on Maks.

"I could never forget Sebastian." Maks rolls to look at me. "I know it's shocking when you realize what you've done and the ease you did it with. Do you regret shooting them?"

"No. That's the only thing I feel guilty about. I have no remorse at all for what I did. I never could have imagined I would so blithely kill someone—two someones—and not have a moment of second thoughts. It was easy. Too easy."

"It's not about how easy it was. You're loyal and protective to your core. You did what you felt you had to. That's admirable. It's just unfortunate that it had to be so extreme. But you were right. They would have killed you, Sergei, and Bastian. Then they would have come for me. And when they did, they would have found your friends."

"That's not helping, Maks. Now I feel like shit for having Lanie and Michelle anywhere near me. I don't want to lose my friends, but I can't put them in danger."

"You don't have to lose your friends."

"How can I not? They'll be linked to me. I can't expect you to put a security detail on them for the rest of their lives, and they won't want that."

I sit up, and Maks follows me. I'm sitting cross-legged, naked, having one of the most serious conversations of my life while on vacation in a tropical paradise. A month ago, I couldn't picture anything like this. Not a bratva boyfriend. Not a threat to my life and to the lives of my friends. Not an island getaway.

"Are you saying you would let your friends go for this life with me?"

I know the answer. I don't have to pause. "I would."

Maks takes my hands and runs his thumb over the back, but he doesn't say anything for a long time. It feels like he's choosing his words carefully.

"Laura, your life took on a different type of value when you started dating me. If we make a future together, people will know you matter to me. I haven't made a commitment to anyone in years. People will notice. It makes you a target. But Lanie and Michelle hold no value to the people in my world. Not unless someone believes they know things that you've passed along. Not unless I bring you into the inner circle, the Elite Group. That's not a place women are usually welcome, and I would keep you away from it for your safety. There are things I will never discuss with you. Things I will always keep from you. Not because I like secrets. I don't want them. But I have to, to protect you and the men I lead. Is that something you can live with?"

"I realized that the moment I accepted our first date. I understood it when we ran into Salvatore. I accepted it when we got back together. Maks, we talk about that week as though we broke up. We were never officially together. Our first date was a bust, but we talk as though we were already a couple. We both knew, even then, that something exists between us. That something intends for us to be together. I know the manner of man I'm with, and I'm all right with that. Don't keep secrets about anything else though. That will be harder to forgive, and you'll break my trust, *lapochka*."

"I know, *meelaya*. I never want that. I know I'm asking for an incredible amount of trust from you. I never want to abuse that."

"I love you, Maks. Don't shut me out, and I will follow where you lead."

"I love you, Laura. I want you by my side, but I will always put your safety first."

I nod. It's the best I can ask for. What he says about Lanie and Michelle makes sense, and I hope it holds true. I can keep sharing my life with my friends, but even before this conversation, I knew I would never share things about Maks's life. He's already trusted me with things he's not told other people. I'm more than willing to trust him, even if it's inevitably going to be hard at times.

"I'm starving. Is there anything left after your brothers and cousin got to breakfast? I'm assuming they've already eaten."

"They better have stuck to cereal. Those pastries are ours."

Maks offers me the most boyish grin I've ever seen. I like seeing him joke about his family. This vacation is good for both of us. Not just as a couple. I know he planned this before the incident on the roof. He needs the time away just as much as I do. He might have done this for me, but I'm glad he's getting a break too.

We slip on our robes and head out to the living room. It must be mid-morning from how bright it is. I can't believe Maks stayed in bed that late. I slept through the night without waking once. It's a first for us, but I feel better catching up on the sleep. I never felt him get up to talk to his family. I wonder if he got up this morning and just came back to bed to be there when I woke.

There's a lavish spread of fresh pastries, fruit, cereal, yogurt, and juices. There are things under silver domes being kept warm with chafing dishes. I push back the swivel lids and discover three types of eggs, French toast, bacon, ham, and sausage. All my absolute favorites. Maks knows that.

"There is way more food here than the two of us can eat."

"All right. I may have texted the chef and told him that we'll need more food. But my brothers and cousin are on strict instructions not to touch anything until after you've had first choice."

"Maks! They've been up for hours. Did they even sleep last night? They must be starving. I'm fixing them plates."

"They slept on the plane. Or at least, they should have. And they can fix their own plates."

I'm not sure if he's serious. "Are you jealous that I might make them a plate of food, but I haven't offered to make you one?"

"Maybe."

"Daddy," I hiss. "I'm making them plates. You can fix your own. Where should I take them?"

"I'll tell them to come inside to eat."

"I'm only in a robe!"

"There's a bag inside the closet with more clothes for both of us."

I close my eyes and shake my head. Of course, there is. I hurry back into the bedroom and toss on a pair of pajama shorts and a tank top. Thank heavens for shelf bras. The guys are already inside by the time I come back. They're looking expectantly at the food, and I think I see them drooling. I scowl at Maks, who stands with his arms crossed, guarding the spread. I hurry to serve myself then make room for them. Maks at least has the good graces to go last. We sit together at the dining room table after Maks introduces me to Anton. It amazes me how much Sergei resembles Maks and his brothers, yet so does Anton, but the cousins are from opposites sides of the family. Sergei is Maks's mother's sister's son, and Anton is Maks's father's brother's son.

"How was your flight?"

I try to be welcoming, since none of the men sitting across

from me planned to babysit me this weekend. I hope none of them had plans. I have no idea if Niko or Aleks have girlfriends, or even wives. I assume they don't since they tried to talk up Lanie at Envy. I know nothing about Anton.

"Not bad. We slept." Anton answers, but I see Maks's smirk. His expression clearly says I told you so.

"Thank you for changing your weekend to come here and help."

There's a shift in each man's body language. I look at Niko, thinking I might figure out what happened because I know Maks has closed down. But there's no hint to what just happened.

"It's our job to protect the *pakhan* and his family." Anton's answer is crisp, and I wonder if it's the word "help" that bothered them. Did it diminish what they do? Wait. Family? I'm not family. Does that mean I'm just an added chore? Is that why they're now pissed? I finally look at Maks, but I can't tell anything from his expression. I feel utterly out of place now. Breakfast no longer holds much appeal.

"Did you pack anything less revealing than what I wore last night?" I want out of here.

"Yes. One." Maks's tone isn't cold, but it no longer holds any of the jovial notes it did before. Fuck. How did one sentence change the whole mood?

"Excuse me. I'm going for a swim."

"Aleks."

I look up when Maks speaks and see him tilt his head toward the pool. My shoulders slump. They can't even eat their breakfast in peace. I don't know how to get out of this without making a scene, and I don't dare dawdle, even if I want to give Aleks more time to eat. I slip out of my seat and hurry to the bedroom. I search through the bag. The bathing suit I find is barely better than the one last night. It's not quite what I usually wear when I swim laps, but it'll have to do. I tie my hair back and switch clothing. I cover myself with the robe and hurry outside from the door in our bedroom. I can guess Maks will be annoyed that I went out without Aleks, but I want to be in the water before his brother sees me practically naked. There will be no flip turns today. I dive in. When I surface, Maks is rushing outside.

"Laura." There's censure in his voice, and I hate it. "You didn't give any of us a chance to sweep the grounds. Do you not get why I called my family here?"

"I do, Maks. And I also get that I'm humiliated walking around in this bathing suit, which is barely better than last night's floss. I just wanted to be in the water before any of them see me."

Maks looks chagrined. I know he didn't plan for anyone else to see me in either bathing suit. And I know he wouldn't be thrilled with another man watching me walk around in either of them, even if they're his brothers and cousin. He turns back to where the others have spread out on the veranda. "I'll stay poolside."

Aleks, Anton, and Niko disappear into the house. I assume they're headed to the security room and spots out front. I don't wait for Maks to say anything else. I kick off the bottom and move into freestyle. I keep going for an hour. The pool is a little shorter than standard, but I guestimate that I've done nearly two miles. Maks hasn't tried to interrupt, so I didn't stop. I feel better for having the time to clear my head. I didn't think about anything but my strokes and my breathing. I don't usually count strokes and breaths, but it kept me from dwelling on what upset me before breakfast or that our trip isn't what I thought it would be. I know Maks is still trying, and I have to give him credit for that.

When I finally stop, I turn toward where Maks is sitting on

a lounge chair. He's at the edge rather than reclined. I watch as his gaze scans the beach. Now I feel like shit. This is his vacation too, and he just spent an hour doing nothing but watching waves. And not relaxing. Instead, he's waiting to see if some threat emerges from the surf. He's doing this for me, so I can basically sulk. Fuck. That's not what I meant to do, but that's what it looks like. That's how it feels now. I wanted to do what I wanted to do because I feel uncomfortable being around the others.

Maks notices that I've stopped, and I notice that at some point he put on trunks rather than the robe he wore to breakfast. He slides into the water and walks over to me. I'm hesitant. But he isn't. He pulls me into his arms and presses my head against his chest.

"I'm sorry for coming out here alone. And I'm sorry for what I said at the table."

"Why are you sorry about that? You didn't say anything wrong."

"I did. All four of you changed. Was it because I said they were here to help? Did it insult them?"

Maks laughs, the sound rumbling in his chest. "No, *malyshka*. I heard them before you woke up. They were joking about me. They didn't say anything about you—I would have beaten the shit out of them—but their jokes were rather off-color. You reminded them that this isn't their vacation."

"But Anton said they protect the *pakhan* and his family. I'm not family. I'm inconveniencing them."

"Don't ever say you're an inconvenience. And that's ridiculous. Laura, they've figured out that I'm in love with you without me saying anything. That's part of what they were joking about. I've never felt this way about any woman, and I've never brought anyone on vacation with me. I don't even take vacations. As far as they're concerned, you are family. You're mine. That means they protect you with the same loyalty as they protect me."

"I feel so good when I hear you say I'm yours. There's such fierceness in it. It's impossible to not believe you."

"Because you are mine. I will never let you go, Laura. We agreed to that the other night."

"Yes, *solnste*."

Maks's nose flares, and he pulls me tighter. I slide my hand into the front of his board shorts and wrap my hand around his length.

"Can you be quiet, *malyshka*?"

"I can try, *solnste*."

I love the command in his voice. It makes every part of me tingle. He releases me and walks back to the pool wall. I'm practically drooling as I watch him pull himself out of the water. It's like one of those expensive cologne ads as his muscles flex, and the water drips from him. He reaches out and grabs the belts from both robes and is back in the water before I can wonder what he's doing.

"Come here, *malyshka*."

I'm quick to obey. He tests the limits of my flexibility and endurance once he has my legs stretched wide, my ankles bound to my wrists. He backs me against the far pool wall. He can still see the beach, and I can tell he's scanning our surroundings in between kisses and thrusts. But he fulfills another fantasy: sex in a pool. Maybe I can convince him to do it again tonight, with just moonlight and the underwater lights to illuminate us. That would be an ultimate water fantasy come true. There's a sensuality to my imaginings that gets me more aroused. Between my thoughts and what Maks is doing, I barely keep quiet. My teeth dig into his shoulder as I keep from screaming. His groan is what will surely give us away.

"That was amazing, Daddy. Thank you."

"You're amazing, baby girl."

"Is it safe to walk along the beach? I know that means they probably have to come too."

"It should be. I'll ask two of them to come while you get dressed. You are right. I don't want any man seeing you in these suits."

We climb out of the pool, and he bundles me in a towel before I slip back into our bedroom, and he goes to find the new additions to our romantic holiday.

Chapter Eighteen

Maksim

"Don't kill the delivery person. I have a couple items arriving for Laura while we go for a walk."

Niko volunteered to stay behind and keep an eye on the villa. Aleks, Anton, and I are all wearing earpieces and have two-way radios. They're far faster than dialing cell phones. Niko will see the more appropriate swimwear before Laura, which dulls some of the excitement of surprising her, but none of us would allow a package into the house or near Laura without checking it first. The store agreed to take a photo of the delivery person and send it to Niko and me. If anyone else shows up, they will find themselves either running or with a bullet in their head.

Laura emerges from our room in a little sundress she hasn't worn with me before. I stopped at her apartment before picking her up from work. I packed a variety of clothes, some casual and some dressier. I still want to surprise her with the dress I ordered, but now I wonder if I should wait. I'm not convinced I can take her away from the villa. I don't want to give her a shiny toy, then tell her she can't play with it. It would be an asshole move.

She heads to the kitchen and fills the blender with ice before going to the bar and gathering a bottle of rum and simple syrup. She combines them with fruit and sugar. I know she prefers sweeter wines and cocktails. This might give me a cavity. But I watch her pour, and she's liberal with the amount of rum she adds. We soon each have a glass of strawberry and banana daiquiri. There's a soft breeze that lifts the wisps of hair from her neck that escaped her messy bun. She's not wearing any makeup, and I think she's never looked more beautiful.

I slip her hand into mine as Aleks takes off ahead of us, and Anton trails behind. They give us enough space that we can talk quietly but not so far that they can't protect Laura. I slipped a shirt on while she got changed. I don't think she's noticed yet that I have a gun tucked against my back.

"Thank you for bringing me here, Maks. This is so lavish. I never imagined coming to the Caribbean and staying in a private villa with a private chef. I know this isn't quite what you planned, but this is beyond anything I've dreamed of."

"You're welcome, Laura. I'm glad I'm able to do this for you. Despite everything, you seem more relaxed here."

"I am. I would live along the water in a heartbeat. I like mountains and forests, but the water is my happy place. It always has been."

"Did you and your family vacation much?"

"Yes. We traveled a lot when Maddie and I were kids. We went all over the Med and Caribbean, but I've never been to Turks and Caicos before. My parents aren't into cold weather, so I've never learned to ski. But I can surf and scuba dive. I love to sail, too."

"And you went to study for a year in the great white tundra. Why did you choose Russia?"

I realize I've never asked why she chose the language since she said her family is mostly Irish. And she speaks like a near-native. Even my English is flavored heavily by my Russian accent.

"I went to China each summer in high school because I thought learning the language would be useful in corporate law. I had the chance to add Russian to it when I was in college. I learned it for the same reason, and they have both proven useful."

She winks at me, and I remember my meeting with her. The damn ham sandwich she sent me a picture of the next day. She'd thrown us all off when she suddenly told us in Russian that she'd have the papers ready and that we'd better pay on time. She could have worked for Anton as an enforcer with that air of command when she demanded the money.

"You sound like a native, though. How did you manage that?"

"Oh, that's easy. My professor was a former Soviet college instructor. He drilled it into us. I heard *nyet* a lot. Then he would make us repeat until we got it exactly right. I didn't appreciate it until I went to Russia. Sounding like a local probably saved my life more than once. My boyfriend back then took a long time to convince that I could go out without him or any of my guy friends. He was just as insistent as my professor that I not have an accent. Antony didn't want me to sound like a tourist."

"Wise boyfriend." It was years ago, yet I want to know who this man was, whether she loved him, whether she misses him. I want to know how long they were together. I want to know if they once planned a future together.

"Maks?"

"Yes?"

"I'm still friends with Antony, but we've been over for a long time. We broke up when I came back to America. We saw each other when I went back the summer after graduating law school. I met his wife and two kids."

"That must have been hard."

"Why?"

"To see someone you loved with another woman, with a family."

"Maks, I didn't really love him. It was puppy love at best and mostly friendship and lust. We got along well and had fun together, but we always knew I was coming home, and he was staying there. We never thought it was more than it was. It's not like we were together for long, and I considered marrying him."

I hear the edge in her voice. She's told me one boyfriend's name, and I know she and Juan have slept together. I haven't told her anything specific about the woman I was with for two years. "I am not in touch with Nadia. I haven't seen her in a couple years. She could be married with a family or even back in Russia. I don't know."

"She isn't still connected to the bratva?"

This isn't easy to explain without sounding like a chauvinist pig. "She was a girl I knew from high school because there were plenty of Russian kids there. I went to prom with her my senior year, then we didn't see each other for three years. I was rising through the ranks, and Vlad reintroduced us. I wasn't interested at the time, but we hooked up whenever we felt like it. When I took over, the members of the Elite Group back then pushed me toward her. They thought she would be a good Russian wife. She might have been if she could have remained faithful. As my power increased, so did her need to be the center of attention. When I broke things off with her, no one took an interest in her. She no longer served a purpose.

The men who fucked her could no longer brag that they were banging the *pakhan*'s girlfriend behind my back."

"Did you know she cheated?"

"Yeah. Pretty much from the beginning. I didn't care that much because I never intended to marry her. She was good for taking to events and a good lay. But I never considered her for my wife. It was only when her infidelity stopped being discreet that I ended things."

"Were you faithful?"

"No." I won't lie to Laura. But I can hear how horrible it sounds. All of it.

"But you will be now?"

"*Meelaya*, I'm seven years older than I was when I entered that relationship. I don't think with my dick, at least not around anyone but you. She knew I didn't love her, and I knew she didn't love me. We both knew the leaders wanted us together. I would have been faithful if we'd ever married, but neither of us considered our relationship as serious as everyone else did."

"Did she know?"

"At the end."

"So she thought all along that you were faithful while she wasn't?"

"Yes."

Laura is quiet as she digests what I've told her. We continue walking along the beach until she turns to look out at the water. I slide an arm around her waist and pull her back against my chest.

"You know she thought you were in love with her."

"No, she didn't."

"If she thought you were faithful for two years while she screwed around, she believed she had you hook, line, and sinker. How did she take it when she learned you hadn't been faithful?"

That gives me pause. It was finding out that I wasn't that caused the argument that finally broke us apart. She was livid and screaming. I pointed out all the men who I knew she'd fucked and said I was sure there were plenty more. She didn't even flinch. She didn't look guilty for a moment, but she was pissed about me cheating.

"Not well. I assumed it was pride."

"It was. But she must have really thought she was secure in her position as your future wife. You've really never seen her since then?"

"She was around for the first year after we broke up. She wanted to get back together, but I refused to even consider it."

"You said you haven't seen her. Have you heard from her?"

"A few times. She'll text, and she's tried to call, but I never answer."

Laura is quiet again, and I wonder once more what she's thinking. She leans her head against my chest as she finishes her drink.

"When's the last time she reached out?"

"A couple weeks ago."

"After we hooked up at Envy?"

"Yeah."

"What a coincidence."

I hear the sarcasm, and she pulls away. She continues walking, but she's no longer holding my hand.

"What's that supposed to mean?"

"How long had it been since the time before that?"

"I don't know. Like eight or nine months."

"More people than Salvatore know about me, Maks."

"You think she knows about you?"

"She just happens to reach out a week after you get a new girlfriend when she hasn't been in touch in nearly a year. That's not a coincidence. That's a slighted woman."

"I don't know how she would know, Laura. We hooked up that night, but the only other time we've been seen together was at brunch."

"And as we got out of the car at Salvatore's place, and ever since brunch, you've picked me up from work or dropped me off. There have been plenty of opportunities for people to see us."

"Maybe she did see us or heard about us, but that doesn't mean it matters to her. Maybe she was curious. Maybe she was jealous. But what of it?"

"You're sure she has no more ties to the bratva? What about somewhere else? If she wanted the position and glamor of being the *pakhan*'s wife, would she seek out someone else who can give that to her?"

"Who knows? Maybe. But that wouldn't matter. If you think she's behind any of this, that makes no sense. She would use her new boyfriend or husband to get back at me? What man would agree to that?"

"I don't know. But I'm willing to consider Juan might have had something to do with the break-in, and it's been nine months since the last time I had sex with him. Same amount of time since the last time she tried to reach you. I'm not ruling anything out."

"Fine." I can't ignore that there is a sliver of possibility, even if I think it's not the case. I speak into my radio and ask Niko to get Sergei to look her up while he's recuperating. We'll know where she is by dinner.

"Thank you."

We've reached the end of the beach, so we turn back. We're almost to the villa when it starts to rain. It comes down in sheets, but I know it won't last long. We run back to the villa with Aleks and Anton close behind. I've already gotten confirmation from Niko that he'll have Sergei work on it, so I know all is fine in the house. Laura and I strip off our soaked clothes on the veranda outside our room while Anton and Aleks go to find their own dry clothes.

"What do you want to do while it rains?"

Laura's glancing at the bed, but I'm considering whether it's safe for us to go on the cruise I planned. I still haven't canceled it. I look at my watch and decide to call the charter and see if it's possible to add three more people.

"I have a surprise for you. Get dressed and grab a sunhat. There's sunblock in the top bathroom drawer. Pack a couple towels in the beach bag near our bags."

"Are we going somewhere?"

"Maybe."

I swat her backside and point her toward the closet. I grab a pair of shorts, boxer briefs, and a shirt before I head to the living room. I don't care if the guys see me naked. It won't be the first time or the last. I call the tour director and arrange for my brothers and cousin to join us before I call for a larger golf cart to take us to the marina a couple miles away.

By the time Laura comes out with our bag packed, we're all ready to go. She looks at my family, and I see her small sigh, but she doesn't say anything. She offers them a warm smile before following me outside. The golf cart pulls up, and Aleks climbs into the seat beside the driver. Niko and I sandwich Laura between us, and Anton sits in the third row facing backwards.

"I'm glad you said you like to sail, *meelaya*."

We pull up to the marina, and there's a large sailboat docked in front of us. I'd considered a speedboat or a small yacht, but I thought she would enjoy this more. I wonder if this is the type of sailing she meant. It takes only a moment to realize it was. She kicks off her shoes and boards without help. She moves along the deck, avoiding the rigging as though she spent her life on a boat. I'm close behind, but the rocking motion affects me more than it does her. I have to try to walk without looking like a klutz. I hear the guys chuckle until it's their turn to find their sea legs.

"Mr. and Mrs. Kutsenko, I'm Captain Michaels."

I watch Laura freeze at the greeting. I only gave my name on the reservation, but I'd said it was meant to be a romantic couple's outing. I'm certain he's wondering why there are now three more men aboard. I slide my hand into hers. When she looks up at me, there's a bright smile on her face, and her eyes twinkle as though we share a secret. She doesn't appear opposed to the title.

We set sail for our three-hour tour of the islands. Captain Michaels has a five-person crew, but it's not long before he lets Laura help with the rigging, then he's letting her captain the boat. It's obvious that she's experienced as she calls out orders to the crew. I think she's impressed everyone, and she looks utterly in her element. Breathtaking and at ease. I think I will buy a sailboat and an island when we return home. The afternoon passes quickly, and it's soon time to head back to the dock. When we get back onto land, I catch her taking a last longing look at the boat. I'll have a boat christened with her name by the end of the week.

"Maks, that was wonderful. Thank you."

She wraps her hand around my neck and tugs my head toward her as we take off on the golf cart. She kisses my cheek, then rests hers against my shoulder. I wrap my arm around her, and her sigh feels like bliss. She's almost asleep by the time we get back into the villa. Since we skipped lunch for the walk on the beach, we have a quick late lunch. Then, despite her protests, which are half-hearted, I carry her into the bedroom. She slips off her shorts and tank top and is soon asleep. I head back into the living room to talk to my family.

"Why'd you want me to look up Nadia? I thought you

hadn't heard from her in years." Niko stares at me, and I can tell there's something that's put him on edge.

"I haven't seen her in years. She tries to contact me every once in a while. She texted me right after Laura and I started dating. I hadn't heard from her in eight or nine months."

"Laura wants to know where she is?" It's Aleks's turn to ask questions.

"No. But she thought it was suspicious that I hear from Nadia out of the blue just after I get a girlfriend for the first time in five years."

"She's smart."

Nikos states the obvious and hands me some papers. I scan over them and glance back at the bedroom. There's financial information that shows Nadia just bought a unit in Laura's building a week ago. There's a flight manifest from Moscow showing she arrived back in the U.S. a day before she called me. She got a job at a boutique a block from my office building. Fortunately, I'm almost never there. It's a front for the Kutsenko Partners company.

"Fuck. This does not look good."

"What're you going to do?" Niko takes the papers back. I don't want them left lying around for Laura to stumble upon.

"I want her followed. The arrival and work could be a coincidence, but I do not like her moving near Laura."

"Are you going tell Laura?" Anton looks skeptical, and I know he thinks I shouldn't.

"Yes. There are enough things that I can't tell her. I'm not keeping secrets when I don't need to. And God forbid Nadia tries to contact her, I want Laura prepared."

I'm about to ask if there's more I need to know, but Niko's phone rings. I watch him look at the screen before he looks at me.

"It's Sergei." He answers and puts it on speaker. "*Privet.* I'm here with Maks, Anton, and Aleks. We can hear you."

"Hey, Maks. I didn't mean to disturb you. That's why I called Niko."

"What's going on?"

Maybe that means it's not that urgent. Or maybe that means he wants to prepare Niko before I hear whatever this is.

"We identified the guys on the roof. They're hired guns, like the guy who followed Laura after church. We traced them back to Robert Simms."

Wonderful. Robert Simms is a ghost. He's never seen in person, but he basically runs a temp company for mercenaries. He takes no sides. He has no allegiances. The only thing he's allied with is the almighty dollar. I knew him when he was still a mercenary. I hired him several times. And apparently helped fund his own business endeavors. There are rumors that he got injured and can't go on any ops himself. Others say he's older than people thought and can't keep up. So now he hires out men and women to do the killing for him, taking a significant cut in the meantime. I haven't had to hire him since the early days as *pakhan*, but I'm always aware of him. Now I want to know who the fuck hired him.

"And what are we doing to figure out who brought Simms on?"

"You know that's practically impossible. The man keeps his money under his mattress. He has no digital footprint. He probably still uses a flip phone for his burner."

"Practically. That means it's not entirely impossible. I want to know why someone is after me through Laura."

"I'm working on it, Maks. How is Laura? I saw what it looked like up there. She blew one guy's brains out and nearly blew the other guy's head clear off his shoulders. She's too good a shot for that to be dumb luck."

I hadn't really thought about that. I was impressed, but I didn't question it. That shows how rattled this has me. "I don't know for sure. But it wouldn't surprise me that she learned either to get ready for or while she was in St. Petersburg. It sounds like she had a protective boyfriend back then."

"Like your level protective?" I don't appreciate Aleks's snicker.

"I don't know about that. Is anyone Maks-level possessive?" I scowl at Niko. Ass.

"He said protective. And I don't deny I'm possessive about Laura."

"Seems like there's a lot you don't know about your girl-friend, yet you've practically had her move in with you." Aleks's eyebrows rise as he glances toward the bedroom door.

"What're you getting at, Aleks? Do you think I shouldn't trust her?"

"Just an observation."

"No. Say what you mean."

"How do you know that she was really followed? How do we know that the roof wasn't just a botched op?"

"What the—"

"No." Sergei interrupts me. He's adamant even with a single word. I wait for him to continue. "She was terrified when she got to the Queens house. There was no faking that. She pulled herself together by the time Maks got there. But she was scared shitless. And maybe you don't remember, but I was there on the roof. The look on her face when she saw me get shot is one I will never forget. You can't fake the shade of white her face went."

"But she doesn't seem that shaken up."

"How the hell would you know, Aleks? Last I checked I'm the one who's been with her in private."

"Just playing devil's advocate."

"Just being a dick." I don't get pissed at my brothers often, but Aleks is pushing me. I know his role is to question me to make sure I make sound decisions, but suggesting Laura is to blame for what happened isn't okay.

"Did Niko share what we found about Nadia?" Sergei brings the conversation back around.

"Yeah. I want her tailed and kept away from Laura. Take her to the fucking warehouse if she gets anywhere near Laura."

"We don't take women there. We don't kill women."

I can hear the surprise in Anton's voice, and he's right. But if Nadia is a threat to Laura, then she's a threat to me, too. That makes her a threat to the whole organization.

"I didn't say kill her. I didn't even say string her up. Just take her there. Scare the shit out of her, and it'll keep her away from Laura."

"Maks, no one leaves the warehouse alive." Anton says what we all know. No one leaves breathing. They usually leave as ash or ooze.

"She always liked winter. Her ass can end up in Siberia with a reminder that she isn't welcome back in the U.S. She stays away from Laura."

"She's been with some guy in the Security Group of the Podolskaya for the last year-and-a-half." Somehow what Sergei shares doesn't surprise me.

"Then why'd she text me at Christmas about missing me and wanting to know how I'm doing? Then I don't hear from her until I get a girlfriend a month ago."

It's Niko's turn to join the conversation with his observations about my ex-she-devil. "She always wants something. I don't know if it was a Christmas gift or something else back then. But she probably wants you back now that she believes she can't have you."

"Niko, she hasn't been able to have me for five years. I don't respond to her texts or answer her calls. How has she not gotten that?"

"I don't know, but she moved into your girlfriend's building and got a job down the street from where she thinks you work. Aleks, I'd be more suspicious of her than Laura being involved in her own attacks." Niko is about to say more, but we all hear the door to the bedroom opening. Laura doesn't look like she's slept at all. How much did she hear?

"So does this mean I can't go home? Or will I just have to have more guards?"

Guess that answers that. She heard most, if not all, of it. I shoot my brothers and cousin a look, and they take off back to their posts. I pour Laura a whisky sour and a vodka for me, then gesture toward the veranda. Once we're out there, I pull her onto the lounger in front of me. She settles between my legs but decides she doesn't like it. She turns and rests her legs over mine.

"I don't know what it means yet. You can always stay with me in Manhattan, or if you want your own space, then my Queens house."

"And if I want my own home? The one I pay for and like living in."

"Then it means more guards until I know what's going on."

"What the fuck is up with the people we used to fuck?"

I don't have an answer to that. But as I think about the situation, I realize that it might be safer to have Laura move in with me, but there are two problems with that. The bigger one is I don't want her to think I'm asking because of this. When I ask, I want her to know without doubt that it's because I love her and want to share my life with her. The other problem is I like her place and wish we could move in together there. She has a home, whereas I have places I sleep.

"Maybe you could spend a few nights with me at my place.

Unless you don't want to chance running into her. Maybe that isn't such a good idea after all."

I can see what she wants. That's why she suggested it. I hate seeing her doubt herself. "I don't want to let her chase you out of your home if it turns out to be nothing."

"There are plenty of other places she could live, Maks. Why my building? I didn't even know there were any vacant units or that anyone was selling."

"I don't have a solution right now, *meelaya*. But we will come up with it together."

"Thank you for not keeping this from me. I admit I was listening. I heard you say you wouldn't hide this or lie to me. At first, I truly was trying to fall back to sleep. I woke up with pins and needles in my hand. It was bent funny. Then I couldn't because I was too anxious about what I heard."

"I don't think she's connected to what's already happened. She wouldn't know how to contact Simms. He's a guy who hires out mercenaries. Any problems we're going to have with her haven't started yet."

"Wonderful. But Sergei said she's connected to the bratva in Moscow. Maybe she does have a way to get in touch with this Simms guy."

"I don't know yet. The guy following you and the rooftop could be connected to each other, or they could be separate. I don't even know if the incident at Envy and the one at Pussycats are connected and if they have anything to do with what happened to you."

"Do you usually have this many mysteries all at once?"

"Mysteries?" I can't help but laugh. "There's always something, *meelaya*. But this went from a little inconvenience with the Italians to something way more when whoever it was got you involved. Maybe it's all bad timing or one big plan, but whoever this is, is poking a bear."

"Mmm. Bears are big and lumbering. I think you're more like a *volk*."

"A wolf?"

"Yes. An apex predator. Cunning and stealthy but unrelenting. Besides, you travel in a pack with three brothers and two cousins, plus all your *boyevik*. That's what bratva men are called, right? At least the regular guys."

"Yes. Warriors. Some are *bratok*. They have special jobs and work for an *avotoritet*."

"I don't know those two words."

"*Avotoritet* is a brigadier. I doubt you had reason to learn that unless you studied the military. They run small groups of *boyevik*. These men usually have special jobs or roles—ones that are not legal—and are called *bratok* or sometimes *patsan* or *brodyaga*."

"I know those words. *Bratok* is brother. Isn't *patsan* a word for boy? And isn't *brodyag* like—um—what's the right word—like a vagabond? Do you know that word?"

"Yes to all three. But they don't have the same connotation in Russian."

"Do Ilya, Stefan, and Michail fall into one of these categories? Are Anton and Sergei Avotoritets and the two spies?"

I can't help but chuckle. "I appreciate you taking an interest in my life. But I'm not sure yet whether it's safe for you to know the bratva hierarchy. I need to think about that, *malyshka*."

"All right."

"But for now, Anton and Sergei are not currently brigadiers. Ilya, Stefan, and Michail have had several positions over the years including *boyevik* and *bratok*. I won't say more until I give this some more thought."

"Fair enough. I'm starving. Lunch was nice, but the fresh air has made me hungry. When's dinner?"

Chapter Nineteen

Laura

Maks got me a bikini that actually has some material to it. It's bright, florescent colors and reminds me of something from Miami in the 1980s. I love it. He also surprised me with an emerald-green cocktail dress. I don't know how he knows my size, and I'm not sure I want to ask how he's so good at picking out women's clothes, but I love that, too.

We swam with dolphins on Saturday, and it was amazing. I'd done it before in the Bahamas, but this time I actually got to swim alongside them rather than in a pool where I really only got to pet them. There were five other people on the excursion, and I thought Niko, Aleks, and Anton might have strokes trying to keep Maks and me separated from the other people while in the water. Thank goodness all five of us are strong swimmers.

We went to a resort on Sunday evening for dinner. It felt odd to be around so many other people after being so reclusive. The restaurant was full, but we had a chef's table and were able to enjoy an exclusive menu. I'm unaccustomed to such lavish experiences. I feel utterly spoiled.

We're pulling up to my parents, and I don't know what to think. The car met us at the private airport in north Jersey. Maks didn't want to take any chances that we might get stuck in city traffic and be late. I grew up just outside the city in an affluent neighborhood, but nothing I experienced growing up prepared me for the whirlwind that has been dating the obscenely wealthy Maksim Kutsenko.

Aleks, Anton, and Niko are still with us. I offered to order them pizza or suggested we pick something up along the way. They were aghast. I think it was only partly in jest. Michail is the driver and will stay with the vehicle. The other three guys will fan out around the property. I don't know whether we should keep their presence discreet or if we should tell my parents. If either of them sees what they think is a man skulking about, they'll call the police before they say anything to anyone.

"Laura. Welcome back. You look like you enjoyed your trip. You got some sun."

"Hi, Mom. It was wonderful. And it is nice to not feel so pasty at the beginning of September."

I've always tanned well, but it inevitably fades. Maks's skin is permanently suntanned, and it makes me wonder if he spent a lot of time outside as a child. I don't think of Russians as being particularly dark skinned, but Maks and his family have a perpetually sun-kissed look. I'm wearing the sundress I wore to walk along the beach, so it shows off my tan well. I turn to beam up at my equally suntanned boyfriend and think about how mesmerizing his already-piercing blue eyes are. They are remarkable against his darker skin.

"Mom, Dad, this is Maksim. Maksim, these are my parents."

"Dr. and Mr. Doyle, it's a pleasure to meet you."

Maks extends his hand, and my parents return his cordiality as they shake his in return. I watch my dad, and I'm certain he squeezes just a little harder than he needs to, but Maks takes it in stride and doesn't bat an eyelash. His other hand rests at the small of my back. I love it. It's protective and possessive without being vulgar in front of Mom and Dad. We make our way into the living room, where we each find a seat. Maks and I sit on the loveseat while my parents choose their recliners. It's a picture of domestic tranquility, but I'm nervous as hell.

"Tell us what you did on your trip?"

I pray my face doesn't turn beet red. I can't believe my mom is asking a couple what they did on a romantic getaway to a secluded island. What does she think we did?

"A few walks along the white sand beach. I took Laura on a sailboat, where she looked like she'd lived all her life. She was right at home. We swam with dolphins and had dinner last night at one of the resorts."

Thank you, Maks. That's the highlights, and for some reason, hearing it from him makes it feel like my parents won't think I'm covering for all the time we spent having sex. Which we did a lot.

"There was a private pool, so I was able to swim every day. And the beach was private too, so I laid out for a few hours each day."

I know it's horrible for my skin, but I love the feel of the sun baking me. And since the bathing suits Maks initially brought with us were barely there, I have no real tan lines. That's a first. My mom goes to check on dinner and returns with a bottle of wine. I know Maks prefers vodka, but he graciously accepts the glass. We pass the next fifteen minutes with small talk before we move to the dining room. The spread my mom's prepared is far more than what we usually have for Sunday dinner when

216

the Diazes come. I can't help but wonder if she's trying to impress Maks.

"Dr. Doyle, this looks fantastic. I hope it wasn't too much trouble, since I know you hosted Sunday dinner last night."

I watch as my parents exchange a millisecond glance. My mom smiles at Maks and says it's no big deal. I want to know what the big deal was the night before. What the hell happened? I know my parents, and I know what that look meant. It was "don't tell the kids."

"Mom, what happened last night? I saw that look."

"It was a little strained."

"What does that mean? Mom, what did Juan say?"

"He didn't know you'd gone away together. We mentioned it, figuring it would have come up."

"We're not talking. I told you that on the plane to Turks and Caicos."

"Yeah, but you've never been at odds long, so I thought it might be resolved. I realized it wasn't by Juan's reaction."

Maks's hand rests at the base of my neck, his thumb stroking it. It's soothing at first, but it soon annoys me as I wait for my parents to elaborate. I shift, and he stops. But he doesn't withdraw his hand, and for that I'm glad. It's my dad who starts explaining.

"He accused Maksim of some unsavory crimes, and he claimed there'd already been death threats made toward you. He said that you thought it was exciting dating a bad boy, but you're more likely to end up dead or in jail or..."

I look at my dad and wait for him to continue, but he's staring at Maks.

"A Russian whorehouse."

I'm shocked that Maks said that out loud, but my parents both nod. I look at Maks, and I have no idea what to say. He looks perfectly calm, but his hand suddenly feels much heavier on my neck. I can tell he's holding himself back.

"Dr. and Mr. Doyle, I was born in Moscow and lived there for the first fourteen years of my life. My parents had four children in four years to ensure that never happened to my mother, who is still a beautiful woman. There is no way that I would ever engage in what I'm sure Detective Diaz accused. It would be an insult to my parents' efforts to keep my mother alive and with her family. I have no stomach for buying and selling flesh, and neither does any part of my family. As for Laura ever ending up somewhere like that because of me, that I can promise you will never happen."

There's such finality to Maks's voice that it's impossible not to believe he means every word he's said. His promise is as good as written in stone. My parents noticeably relax, but I wonder what else Juan said.

"Did he tell you anything else, Mom?"

"He showed us Maks's police record."

"What?" I can feel my rage returning from the other night. That's not entirely confidential information since an internet search can share the same information, but to bring it to my parents was as fucked up as Juan has ever gotten.

"*Meelaya.*"

Maks's voice is soft and reassuring, but I'm still fuming. It keeps me from saying anything else, but I want to defend Maks. I look at him, worry and unease in my gaze. He slips his hand from my neck and takes my hand, lacing his fingers through mine. I don't know if I want to cry or scream.

"Dr. and Mr. Doyle—"

"Please. It's Susan and Killian."

My dad interrupts, and I take it as a good sign that they want to be on a first-name basis with Maks. They haven't done that with any guy I've dated since Antony, when they visited me for Christmas in St. Petersburg. Other men have made the mistake of assuming they could address my parents informally, and it never went over well.

"Thank you. My past isn't a secret from Laura or anyone else. It's all a matter of public record. But they were crimes committed as an adolescent and a young man. We were not wealthy when we arrived here. I'm the oldest of four brothers. My father died before we immigrated, so many responsibilities fell onto my shoulders. I did things I'm not proud of, but I did them to provide for my mother and younger brothers. There are arrest records for all four of us. I won't keep that a secret. We didn't have a father here to protect us from some of the rougher Russian influences in our community. My brothers and I did what we had to."

I watch my parents, and something flickers in my dad's eyes that I don't know how to interpret. It's not censure; it's more like understanding and sympathy. My mom doesn't look fazed in the least. She nods and offers us more wine as my dad begins to pass dishes to us. Maks releases my hand because he has to, and I feel the loss keenly. It was like an anchor keeping me from flying away to find Juan and... I don't even know what. I'm still just as angry despite my parents taking Maks's explanation so well.

"Our family isn't without its past. Killian and I both have family that did what they had to, to make ends meet when they were newly arrived immigrants. They lived in rough neighborhoods where they didn't always have much choice about who they worked for or what they did. We won't judge."

My dad nods along with what my mom says. It makes me wonder what stories they never told me about my family's past. They've always been vague. Both sets of grandparents on my dad's side died before I could remember them. My mom's side of the family had some rough beginnings when they were newly arrived from Ireland, but it didn't seem like anything interesting from the few stories she told. She's told me more stories about her German side.

"You've done well for yourself, Maksim. Susan and I both noticed the dates, and it's been five years since the last incident. We trust Laura's judgement, and it's obvious that you already care deeply for our daughter. Juan is bitter that his chance came and went. He took you for granted, Laura. He still does. But be careful. I know your mother already warned you, but he has a long reach now that he's a detective. It's clear he intends to cause more trouble before he lets go."

So now what? Dating Maks will bring unwanted attention to him and his family. Juan is like a dog with a fucking bone when he wants something. I was the only one he could never browbeat. His father gave in because he felt guilty for always being away. His mother gave in because her role in the family was to support the men, not to disagree. Pablo gave into his younger brother because Juan was bigger despite being two years younger. But now, Pablo has skills and connections much like Maks's. I doubt Juan goes toe-to-toe with Pablo anymore. Is this what will end my relationship with Maks?

"*Meelaya*, don't even think about it. He doesn't get to come between us."

Maks's voice is quiet, but I know my parents can hear him. I nod as I look up at him. He kisses my temple before serving himself scalloped potatoes. He's so calm, at least on the exterior. I can only imagine what he's thinking and planning. I don't know if I dare ask in the car or whether he would even tell me. I don't know if I want to know.

Dinner progresses smoothly as Maks asks about my parents' work, their childhoods, and what they wish to do as they approach retirement. For his part, Maks shares stories about his brothers and how they grew their business. Obviously, he glosses over most of it, but he lets my parents get to know him. And for that, I'm really appreciative. Maks helps my mom clear the table. While they're in the kitchen, my dad leans toward me.

"There're more unsavory things to his past than your mom and I will ever know. But the way he is with you can't be faked. It just can't. If you can live with the secrets he has to keep and the danger that comes along with a man like Maks, then we aren't going to say anything against him. But know that if it ever gets too much, and you don't feel safe, you can come to us. No questions asked. You can always have a home with us."

"Thanks, Dad."

My mom gets out photo albums to show Maks some of the vacations I'd told him about. It's fun reminiscing with my parents, but I feel a little guilty because I know how different and privileged my childhood was compared to Maks's. But his light hand on my thigh and an occasional squeeze reassures me. He laughs with my parents, and I think he's having a genuinely good time. When it's time to leave, both my mom and dad embrace him. It's not a formality. There seems to be actual fondness between my parents and Maks. I couldn't be more relieved.

Juan doesn't come up until we're back at Maks's place in Manhattan. There's not a chance in hell that I'm going back to my place with Maks. I don't know if I ever want to go back if Nadia is there. It's petulant and childish, but I just know we'll "accidentally" run into her. Yes, air quotes and all. I'm certain she's gorgeous, and I just don't want to deal with feeling insecure after such a wonderful time together. I'll deal with that another day.

"*Malyshka*, you're still angry. You can't control Juan or what he says to other people. He's ruined his relationship with you and with your parents. They don't seem fond of him anymore. He's going to do what he's going to do. But don't let him ruin our relationship. We're not letting him come between us, so you can get rid of any idea that you'll valiantly break up with me to protect me. We already know how well that goes between us. We're done with that. You are mine, and I am yours. End of story."

I'm in the bathroom washing my makeup off as he speaks. He slips in behind me and swats my bare backside. We're brushing our teeth when I remember about my birth control. We were careful after that first day, but as I look at the missed pills, I can't help but wonder. I pop out the one for today and swallow it. Part of me daydreams about having a family with Maks, but right now is not the time to start one.

"Come, *malyshka*. I think you need a distraction."

Maks lifts one of the handcuffs that's still attached to the headboard. Since I'm already naked, I'm more than happy to climb onto the bed and look expectantly at him.

"Face down."

"Yes, *solnste*."

I'm soon handcuffed with my wrists crossed. I'm in the center of the bed, so I can't see what Maks reaches for. I never had the opportunity to dig through his magic bin. I close my eyes as he slips a sleep mask over my eyes. Losing one of my senses heightens the others. I listen as he moves around, taking more things out of his arsenal. I jump when I feel leather drape between my legs.

"You remember your safe word, *malyshka*?"

"Yes, *solnste*. Cottage cheese."

"Good girl. This is not a punishment. It is purely for our pleasure. Do you understand?"

I nod, and what I realize is a flogger lands across my lower back, ass, and upper thighs. It stings, but it doesn't hurt. That was just a warning.

"Yes, *solnste*." I'm quick to correct my error. Maks trails the flogger over my left foot and up my legs. I widen them, hinting at where I want his attention. His hand rains down a slap on each cheek.

"I decide what you get and when you'll get it. If I wanted your legs wider, I would have commanded that. For that, you can now put your legs together."

I swallow my groan. Fuck me for trying to be helpful. I roll my eyes beneath my mask. Thank God, he can't see me.

"Don't roll your eyes at me, baby girl, or I will edge you and not let you come."

How the hell did he know?

"I saw the mask move."

"Are you a mind reader too, Daddy?"

"Only yours, baby girl."

The flogger once more comes down across my back, butt, and thighs. This time it has some bite to it, and I flinch. He trails the falls up the crevice of my ass. That's somewhere he still hasn't been. He forgot to pack lube, and he refused to consider doing that without it. Now he tempts me and builds my curiosity. I hear him moving around as the flogger swishes over me hard enough to make me flinch again but without any real pain. I hear the lid of something snap open, then he's pressing my legs apart. The cool liquid drips down my crack before he slips the tip of his finger inside, working the lube into my ass.

"We're going to start with that medium plug, Laura. If it's too much, speak up. I wish to bring you pleasure with some pain. It's not my goal to harm you. Do not take it for me if it's going to hurt you. Do you understand?"

"Yes, *solnste*."

He presses the metal plug past the puckered ring and lets me adjust. Just like the first time—the night I almost ruined everything—it's an odd sensation but not painful. I nod, sensing he's watching me. The flogger cracks through the air before the tails land across my ass. The contact is centralized to just my cheeks. I jolt, unprepared for the feel of the flogger or how squeezing my ass cheeks makes the plug feel deeper. He brings the flogger down over and over, and I can feel the heat building in my ass cheeks and my pussy. He presses my legs open and trails the tails across my pussy. I can't help but shift restlessly.

"You're already so wet, baby girl, and that's the first time I've touched you there. Do you like this?"

"Yes, Daddy."

He flicks it once more, bringing it down across my pussy lips much harder. I can't keep from screaming. I kick my feet, but I make no complaints. He twists the plug, sliding it in and out a couple inches. My scream turns into needy moans. I lift my hips, but they're met with a stinging slap of his hand. He slides his fingers into me, and I nearly come right then and there.

"Uh-uh, *malyshka*. I didn't tell you that you could come. You haven't earned it yet."

"What do I have to do, *solnste*?"

"Be patient."

"You would ask the impossible."

The flogger cracks against me before he presses his fingers into me again. This time his thumb rubs my clit.

"Cheeky."

"Only for you, Daddy."

"Now it's flattery, is it? You're still not going to come until I decide you can."

He continues to torment me, driving me to the edge then pulling back. Sweat beads on my brow before Maks takes a break. He runs his hand over my burning skin. It's cool and gentle, soothing much of the sting. He warns me as he switches to a larger plug. It feels enormous. I fight to relax as it goes in, wondering how it won't tear me in half. But once it's in, I admit that I like the full sensation. When he finger fucks me, he finally lets me come. He groans as my muscles contract around his fingers, and I'm sure he's imagining the same thing as I am. His cock inside me, pressed against the plug with a thin wall separating them.

He flips me over onto my back and slides off the blindfold. He's stripped off his shirt and tie, leaving him in his trousers and boxer briefs. He slides those off and leaves me watching him stroke himself. I glare at him, and all he does is laugh. He knows I hate it when he doesn't let me touch him, and instead, does it himself. He knows I hate being teased, and he knows I hate that it feels like he's denying me the chance to give him pleasure.

"All right, baby girl. You can quit giving me the evil eye."

He climbs onto the bed and settles between my legs. I cry out as his tongue sweeps across my pussy. He dips his tongue into me and swirls. My hips rise on their own accord. I can't help it. They need him, and they have a mind of their own. His teeth skim my clit then nip as he uses his hand on my lower stomach to press me back against the mattress. His hooked fingers inside me press back against his hand on my stomach, hitting that spot inside me that feels so amazing. His tongue might very well be magic. He makes me lightheaded every time he eats me out. He's the first guy I've been with who never expects a blow job in exchange for going down on me. I know he won't turn one down, but I don't have to give him head just to get him to do the same for me. I suppose it's not a big deal, but it feels like one. It makes me feel special in a way none of the other guys in my life have. He works my pussy like he relishes what he's doing. It's not just foreplay to get what he wants.

"Don't tell your mom, but you're a much better dessert than her flan."

I can't help but laugh. "I never would."

He kisses my inner thigh then up my belly until he suckles each tit. His tongue flicks over my nipples before he grazes his teeth along my throat. As his mouth reaches mine, he aligns the head of his cock with my entrance. His dick enters me at the same time as his tongue. I catch it and suck, matching the rhythm as he thrusts into me.

"Come for me, *malyshka*."

"I'm so close, Daddy. Harder, please."

"Anything you want, baby girl."

He obliges, pounding into me. He reaches for the key on the bedside table and releases me. My hands go into his hair, pressing him toward me. For once, he doesn't fight me on it. I indulge in controlling the kiss and having free roam of his body. I love every moment of it. I watch the harsh lines of his face as he concentrates. He is the definition of masculine beauty. And he looks at me as though I'm the only thing in the world that matters to him. Right now, he's the only thing in the world that matters to me.

"Daddy!"

The orgasm consumes me. I feel it to my toes, which curl as I dig my nails into his back, the muscles rippling beneath them.

"Are you ready for me, *malyshka*?"

"Yes, *solnste*."

Maks withdraws and grabs the bottle of lube. He draws the plug out of me and squeezes the bottle, a cool dribble landing where the plug was only a moment ago. Then he coats his dick. I watch every movement as he prepares me. I assume he's going to tell me to flip over doggy style. Instead, he presses my legs back, my knees coming to my chin. He's slow and careful as he nudges his way into my back channel. This isn't the way I've seen it done in porn, but I like it. I like being able to see Maks looking at me, looking into my eyes. The feeling of fullness is almost too much, but I feel like I can take anything while I feel this connected to Maks. He flexes his hips once he's inside me, ever so careful not to hurt me.

"You're pretty little cunt is so tight, but this—this is so fucking tight, you might just squeeze the cum from me. Fuck, it feels good. Are you all right, baby girl?"

"Yes, Daddy. It feels a bit strange, but not in a bad way. Just so full. And I'm curious."

"I know, baby. Tell me if it stops feeling strange and starts being painful. I never want to hurt you."

"I know, *solnste*."

"I love you."

"I love you too."

He rocks against me, moving a little faster as he continues to flex and thrust. His thumb works my clit. I'm surprised he's trying to get me off again, but I should have known. Nothing about the way Maks makes love to me or fucks me is selfish. Not really. Even when he's dominating me, he's still considering my needs and making it good for me. My hands cup his neck as we continue to gaze at one another. I can feel another orgasm building. I move as much as I can, trying to get his thumb to press harder against my clit.

"Are you getting close, *malyshka*?"

"Yes. Are you?"

"I'm holding back for you."

"Don't. More. Make me come."

My wish is his command. He picks up his pace, and his thumb rubs faster and harder. The sensation as it hits me is overwhelming. My abs contract, and my shoulders lift off the bed. My mouth is starving for his kiss. His arms scoop under my shoulders and hold me close as we come together. Never had I imagined something so intimate as making love to a man by having anal. I mean, the act is about as intimate as you can get. But the way we look at each other, what I feel we're sharing. That is an intimacy I never fathomed with a partner. With everything happening outside the penthouse, I wonder when real life will once more intrude. It feels like it'll be all too soon.

Chapter Twenty

Maksim

Laura and I have been home for two days, but it feels like two years. Reality rushed back into our lives on Tuesday morning. Michelle dropped Sebastian off on her way to work. She took him when walking the gentle giant proved too much for Sergei's injuries. I have never seen a dog wiggle and thump his tail like Sebastian did when he saw Laura. He glanced at me but barely showed any interest. He didn't even care when Sergei arrived to take him to his apartment. He was glued to Laura, and she happily indulged. It seemed like we were off to a good start, but it fell apart as soon as I got to work.

A few of our latest construction projects are hitting one roadblock after another. The city planner—Alberto Mancini—suddenly denies our permits. I can guess who got to the Italian-American bureaucrat. Suddenly, supplies and equipment aren't available for my men at three sites. These urban condo developments are worth millions to us, and it's already costing us thousands every day we can't work. No work means no pay for the workers. No pay means they will turn elsewhere. As it should be, they are loyal to their families before they are loyal to me.

Who happens to be successfully continuing their builds? The Italians. My men aren't going to be mine much longer. Salvatore is poaching left and right. He's offering more money and guaranteeing weeks of work.

What's worse are the three bodies that show up today as we break ground on a strip mall. I'm pulling up now. Niko and Bogdan are already here, and Aleks and I are sharing a car. We have no idea what's about to greet us, but it's sure to be a shitshow. It's only Wednesday, and the week is already feeling screwed. Someone already called the police. My Russian and Polish men know to contact my brothers or me first, but not everyone is aware of our more nefarious dealings. I can't blame whoever called, since we don't exactly announce we're bratva.

"What happened?"

Aleks and I step out of the car, and I don't bother to greet Bogdan or Niko. I want and need answers before I speak to the police. I scan the area and want to scream. Diaz. He's here and in the thick of things. Just what my day needs.

"Our guys were running the excavator in the northwest corner. One of them spotted a leg in the bucket. They stopped and looked around. Two more bodies were in the hole. All three are women."

Fuck. That just complicated things more. The cops will automatically assume we're burying whores we don't want or women we couldn't sell. There has never once been even a hint that we traffic, but people are still convinced that we are the stereotype. It doesn't help that we own strip clubs.

"Wonderful." Aleks is a man of few words.

"Any idea who put them there?" I need to get straight to the point.

"Yeah. They all have a C carved on their left breast."

Niko looks over his shoulder as he shares that little nugget. Cartel. I wonder if Juan has heard about that. This is likely his dad's or his uncles' work. But why they buried them here is beyond me. This land has been owned by private investors for years. It's in a no-man's land of sorts. None of the syndicates have staked a claim until we bought it to develop the strip mall. I feel a perverse sense of satisfaction that Juan cannot pin this on us. He'll know as quickly as we did who did this. Or at least who is being blamed for it. I'm not convinced the Cartel is so lazy as to bury bodies rather than dispose of them more permanently. I just don't know why they're on our land.

"Are they fresh?"

I need to know how long ago they wound up here. Is someone using us to wage their own war? I want nothing to do with it. I don't need these complications when we're still trying to figure out who broke into Pussycats and why Salvatore attacked Envy. He hasn't sent any message about what he wants or what he's holding the latest grudge about.

"A few days. Niko and I talked to the night security. They were just about to leave when the men found the bodies. We're trying to figure out how the fuck someone got onto the site long enough to bury them, and no one noticed. We requested the footage, but the cameras don't cover the entire site. They're mostly focused on where we store the equipment."

I listen to Bogdan and think about how our progress was already slowed by the city planner. Is this Salvatore's way of making sure we can't get anything done? Does he want the site, and he's trying to drive us away? Why? And does he really think we'd sell over this?

"Kutsenko."

Bastard. Juan is walking over, and his smug look makes me want to bash his face in. My brothers and I face him. Our arms are crossed, and our disinterested expressions match. He steps into our trap. We shift, making it look like we're making space for him to talk, but we've encircled him. We won't do anything while there are other cops here and too many witnesses. But he will soon understand that he's picked the wrong men to flex his muscle against. He looks over his shoulder, immediately realizing what he's walked into. Each of us now has a hand in our pocket. The slight widening of his eyes tells me he knows we each have a hand on our blade. A little intimidation never hurt anyone.

"Diaz. You seem to work several precincts. That must be a lot of time spent listening to the dispatcher."

He covers the area near Envy. There's no reason for him to be here other than because he wants to be in the middle.

"I was called in since I'm still working the Envy case, and this concerns you too."

"Have you seen the bodies?"

I'm curious to know whether he's taken the time to investigate or just spread speculation.

"The coroner is bagging them."

"I hear someone left their calling card. I'm sure you'll recognize it immediately. Maybe you've left that calling card before. I know your *papi* and *trunco* have."

I watch the surprise he can't catch and keep to himself. He doesn't like me mentioning his father and brother. I don't think he expected me to know the Spanish slang either. Does he not know about the carvings? Or does he not know that I'm aware of his Cartel connection? After what Laura hinted at when they talked at Envy, my brothers did some digging. He doesn't seem dirty, but I have no idea how he passed a background check with his family connections. There's no way he should have a badge.

"Are you surprised that I know your nose isn't so clean? Or are you scrambling to think about how to bury—if you will—this little family connection?"

I shouldn't taunt him, but I want to see his reaction. Seems he didn't have the same training the bratva gives their men to hide their emotions. His face tells me everything. The answer to both my questions is yes. I wonder what else I can get out of him.

"Maybe you should take a look at what my brothers already saw."

As a group, we walk to the coroner's truck. The bags are still open. It's gruesome even for me. They might have been buried here recently, but they've been dead for a while. Either they've been moved, or someone has been holding onto them to use later. Juan pulls the zippers lower until each woman's chest is visible. The etchings are small, but if you know what to look for, they're obvious.

"Do you want us to give you a moment to call your *trunco*? I know you can't reach your *papi*. He's still unavailable in Colombia."

"Bitch."

He mouths the word, but I see it. I lean close, so no one but Juan and my brothers can hear. The coroner conveniently disappeared.

"Call her that again, and you won't make it home. She didn't tell me anything. You're easy to track, Juan. You and your family boast too much. Your egos are your downfall, and whoever did this, knows that. Either your family is fucking careless, or someone knows you like to claim your kills."

"They aren't mine."

"They may as well be. The coroner won't be able to hide

233

this. I'll make sure of it. I wonder what the IG will think about you working a case involving your family."

"You wouldn't. It would only involve you more."

"If it ruins your career, I will gladly. Stay away from her. Call her or text her again, I will make your life hell. You may speak to her if *she* decides she wants to talk to you. You can make this easy on both of us. Or you can make yourself miserable. But if history is any indicator, your family doesn't come out on top against mine. Would you like to test that?"

"Fine. I'll stay away. But I've been around a lot longer, and I've been fucking her for years. Only one of us will last. She always comes back."

It takes everything in me not to kill him right there. The coroner's already here. He could take him away along with the other bodies. But no. If I need to, he will be a guest at the warehouse.

"We had dinner with her parents. She knows what you did."

Juan's face pales, and the bravado is gone. He glances at me and nods. It's not defeat that I see, but there is some resignation. He'll plot and regroup, and I'll be ready. Like hell he's going to get near Laura again. Fuck. I might have to keep her from killing him.

"Take care of this, Diaz. Today."

My brothers and I walk away. There's nothing more to be gained. I have Aleks and Niko stay at the site. Bogdan needs to check on our clubs to make sure there aren't any surprises there. I have an errand to run. I've already decided that Laura is my future. I intend to make that clear before the end of the week. I already wanted to make her my wife, but our trip away and dinner with her parents solidified that decision. I want her to meet my mother before I do anything else. But I have some shopping to do.

Chapter Twenty-One

Laura

Maks and I spent last night at my place. We've only done that a couple times. I wasn't thrilled at the possibility of running into Nadia, but I needed more clothes. Maks knew I was anxious the entire way up in the elevator last night and the entire way down this morning. Rightfully so. She's standing right in front of me. She's beautiful. Like so beautiful it makes us mere mortals feel like we aren't from the same planet.

Maks recognizes her and tries to steer me away from where she's standing in the lobby, but it isn't large enough for us to escape notice. I watch her eyes rake over Maks as though she's a panther deciding how to strike. Then she sees me and how Maks's arm is around my waist. There's anger and jealousy in her gaze, and I want to scratch her eyes out. I now understand the possessiveness Maks feels toward me. It verges on violent. We have no choice but to stop.

"Maks." She purrs his name just like the panther I imagine. She continues in Russian, assuming I don't understand. I stand and listen, too curious to interrupt.

"It's been a long time, my love. You didn't answer my text letting you know that I was back. I'd hoped to run into you. Who knew it would be so easy?"

"Have a good life, Nadia."

Maks tries to maneuver me around his ex-girlfriend, but she blocks us. I need to get to work.

"Maks, you can spare five minutes. Send her to your car and let's talk. We have so much to catch up on. I missed you. If this is who you're seeing these days, you must miss me. I know how much you appreciated my, shall we say, more substantial assets."

"Move, Nadia. I have nothing to say. Speak about my woman like that again, and I will make sure you never speak again."

"Mmm. You haven't changed at all. You used to talk about me like that."

My gut clenches, and I know Maks feels me tense. I hate hearing this. That special feeling I had that we share emotions that we've never had with anyone else evaporates.

"No, I didn't. I said what was expected of me about you. I never talked about you like this because I didn't care that much."

Oh, Maks. Is it wise to say that out loud? She doesn't look like the forgiving type.

"Testy, Maks. Did you not get off this morning? I know how much you like morning sex. You don't have a good day without it. I can take care of that."

I've had enough. I need to get to work, and I'm not listening to this bitch proposition my boyfriend any longer. I join the conversation in Russian.

"Touch my boyfriend, and you will come away a hand short. I know he fucked plenty of other women when he was with you. So don't pretend you held his interest. He's not away from me long enough to fuck anyone else. You moved into my building thinking you could have a scene like this. You think you can have him back. Do you know why we're here? To get my clothes to take to his place. He mentioned he's never cleared space for someone else's clothes before mine. Hmm. I guess he does like my morning sex since he wants to wake up with me."

"You speak Russian?"

"You didn't do all your homework, Nadia. You found my building, but you should have learned more about me. I don't share. I don't give in. I don't give up. And I will come out the winner. I know Maks hasn't shared his home with you or any other woman. But he shares it with me. Move. I'm late for work."

"You're going to let her talk to me like that, Maks? After how long we were together? You wanted to marry me."

"No, I didn't. Igor and Alexandr wanted that. There's a reason in two years, you never came to my homes and why I never proposed. Now, like my girlfriend said, move."

"Maks—"

"Sell the place you have here. Today."

"You're threatening me?"

"Yes."

I listen as Maks and Nadia go back and forth. Beyond her initial shock that I understand our conversation, she's once more forgotten about me. Nothing about Maks's tone makes me think he misses her or is considering reuniting. He sounds as pissed as I did talking to Juan. I don't know much about the warehouse, but if she were a man, I think she'd be on her way there now.

237

"I won't."

"I know you didn't buy this place with cash. You have a mortgage. You will soon find yourself without the funds to pay it. You will find yourself suddenly in default. You will not have a place to live by morning if you don't sell today."

"You'd make me homeless?"

"Yes."

"You hate me that much?"

"No. I feel nothing for you. But I love my girlfriend, and she likes her place. Move, or Sergei will move you."

Maks doesn't wait. He steps forward, forcing Nadia to move. His hand is now in mine, and he's practically pulling me out the door. As much as I want to smirk and sneer, I keep my eyes forward. I refuse to acknowledge her again. I can hear Sergei repeat Maks's threat. His tone is even icier if it's possible. We're in the car and pulling away the moment Sergei closes his door. All I can do is look at Maks. I don't dare say anything.

"I'm sorry, *malyshka*. I should have listened to you when you said you didn't want to stay here last night."

"Did you mean everything you said? Don't lie. I will know."

Maks looks deeply insulted, and I regret questioning him. But I need to know. The rational side of my brain processed everything that happened, but the emotional, insecure side is quivering.

"Yes. I don't want her near you. I will never pick another woman over you, *meelaya*. I didn't want to ask you during the trip because of her arrival. And I don't want you to think that I'm asking now because of her. I'm asking because I don't like this coming back and forth for your clothes."

"What are you going to ask, Maks? You've just talked in circles."

"Laura, will you live with me? I want us to live together. It

238

can be at your place, one of my places, or we can buy something together. I just don't want anymore his and hers."

"I love you, Maks. But are you sure you want to make this commitment so soon?"

"I am. Are you not sure you want to make this commitment so soon?"

"I am. I just don't want you to regret it and change your mind."

"You mean, you don't want me to dump you for Nadia. That isn't going to happen. I'm not picking anyone else, Laura. Not today. Not tomorrow. Not next year. Not ever."

"Didn't you think that—"

"No. I never thought that about her or any other woman. You know that. I told you I never intended to marry her. We were together for two years, but you know what our relationship was. It wasn't even remotely the same as what we have."

"All right. I want that too."

I can truly say that without reservation on my part. I know how I feel, and Maks is so steadfast and unwavering that I believe him. My insecurities silence themselves as he pulls me onto his lap and kisses me. This is where I belong. And it's a pain in the ass that we get to my office faster than I wanted. I could spend all day kissing Maks and having sex with him in the car. We've barely finished before Michail pulls to a stop.

Maks walks me to the door and watches as I get into the elevator. His phone rings as I cross the marble floor. I glance back and see his expression as he answers. Something's wrong, but he smiles and waves at me. I make my way to my office. Fortunately, I didn't miss much on Friday, so yesterday wasn't too bad. But I have plenty to do today. I need to prepare for three meetings tomorrow. I can't afford for any to run long, or I won't stay on schedule.

RK Group is trying to buy a smaller investment company,

hoping they can leverage more equity to delay Kutsenko Partners' acquisition. I'm helping them with this deal, but I've already recused myself from any further dealings with Maks and his brothers. I have two other clients trying to invest in Chinese businesses, and it's not going smoothly. They want to operate like Americans, and the Chinese are digging in their heels. I'm, of course, stuck in the middle.

My assistant was thoughtful and picked up a chai for me on her way in. I'm at my desk for an hour, sipping my now-tepid drink as I answer an onslaught of emails between reviewing contracts. She knocks and sticks her head in.

"This envelope arrived. It was couriered. There's no return address and only has your name on it, no address for the firm."

"Did you have to sign for it?"

"Yeah. But the guy said he didn't know who it was from. It was dropped off at his boss's office by another courier. Weird, huh?"

"Yeah."

She brings it to me, and I examine the envelope. I'm suspicious. I look for any hints of residue or any discoloration. The manila envelope appears totally normal. I grab my letter opener —yes, I still have one of those—and slice it open at the top. I can tell before I pull them out that they're eight by ten photos. The first one makes me gasp. The second makes me feel ill. The rest have me shaking. The last terrifies me. One after another, there are photos of me with Maks. We're having sex in all of them. There are photos of us in his place, my place, and on vacation. There are ones of us having sex against walls and on his desk. Ones of us doing it on my kitchen island. There's at least two dozen. The last photo is from less than an hour ago and shot through my office window.

I force myself not to look out the large glass pane. I slide the photos back into the envelope and consider what to do. I glance at my cell phone on my desk then the landline. I push the envelope off to the side as though I will deal with it later. I turn back to my computer and force myself to answer two emails before I leave my office.

"Katie, can I borrow your phone? I just spilled my drink all over mine. I managed not to get any on me, but I soaked it." Luckily, there isn't any glass between my office and the open area where the administrative assistants and paralegals have cubicles.

"Sure."

"Thanks." I'm glad I memorized Maks's number, or I'd be screwed right now. I punch it in and send a text.

911. It's Laura. Something's happened. Call me on this number not my phone.

Reception must be good for us because Maks calls within seconds.

"*Malyshka?*"

"I need to come to you. Or I need you to come to me. I think my office and phone are bugged. I can't say more."

"I'm coming."

"Can you bring your brothers?"

"What—"

"Maks, please."

"We'll be there in twenty minutes."

"Faster if you can."

"All right."

I'm trying not to shake as I end the call. I go into the call history and delete the number, then I do the same in the text log. I'm sure a forensic analyst could trace the number, but for now, I don't want to leave anything on Katie's phone linking either of us to Maks. I head back into my office and sit back at my desk. I don't open anything on my computer, but I look as though I'm working. Someone is watching me. Fortunately, the sun has shifted and is creating a glare on my monitor. I use the remote and slide my blinds closed. The moment they are shut, I'm back in the hallway. Katie looks at me, but she senses enough not to say anything. It feels like an eternity until the cavalry appears.

Maks is hurrying toward me, and his brothers are close behind. If I wasn't so fucking freaked out, I would appreciate how intimidating the four Kutsenko brothers appear when they look like they're on a mission. Maks leads me to my door, but I stop and shake my head. I stand on my toes and wait for him to lean forward.

"I'm almost positive my office and my phones are bugged. The landline and my cell. I hoped your brothers could make a sweep while you stay with me. Someone is watching me."

"How do you know?"

"I'll show you once your brothers are done. Please, Maks. I'm not overreacting."

Maks nods and tells his brothers in Russian to go and search my office. They're in there five minutes before they come out. Their faces are grim, and they each have their hands curled around something. I turn my gaze to Maks, struggling to keep myself under control.

"I need to get a manila envelope off my desk."

"No. Niko, can you get it, please?"

I watch as Niko slips into my office and returns only a moment later. I don't want to go back in there. I don't trust that the conference room isn't bugged either. I look around before I decide.

"Come with me."

I lead them to the stairway and take them down a floor. Most of the office suites are empty. The restrooms don't need a key, so I knock on the men's room door. When no one answers, I go in, knowing the brothers will follow me.

"What's going on, Laura?"

I don't look at Maks. I look at his three brothers instead. This is so fucking humiliating. I thought Maks's brothers and their cousin seeing me in the string bikini was bad. I thought the scene with Nadia was bad. This is so much fucking worse.

"I need to show Maks some photos. I don't want you to see them, but I know I may not have a choice. Can you give me a moment to show Maks and let him decide what to do? Please?"

Aleks, Niko, and Bogdan step back, and Maks takes me into the disabled stall. I hand him the photos and watch his expression. He's calm as he examines each picture. Bringing it close to search all the details and flipping it over to see if there are any clues on the back. I don't understand how he isn't more worked up. But then he looks up at me. I take a step back. The look in his eyes makes my blood run cold. This is the ruthlessness he wanted to keep from me. This is the man who kills without remorse. This is the man who can ruin someone with a single word. He holds up the photo of me in my office.

"That was taken less than an hour before the envelope was delivered. Someone got it printed immediately."

"I'm assuming you didn't see anything fly past your window."

"No. Nothing like a drone caught my attention. But maybe I just didn't see it. Or it could have been taken from the building next door or even a mile away. I don't know."

"Get your belongings. We're leaving. Tell your boss that you are taking an indefinite leave of absence."

"What? I can't do that. I have three client meetings tomorrow. I can't just not show up. I'm the sole counsel on all of them."

"Laura."

Maks's tone tells me that I can argue until I'm blue in the face, but I won't dissuade him. How the hell do I tell my boss that I'm walking out today and have no idea when I'm coming back? If I'm coming back. She's going to flip. She knows I'm seeing Maks because I recused myself from any further dealings with him. But she doesn't know what the Kutsenkos are. At least, I don't think she does. How do I explain I need to be gone because someone is threatening me because my boyfriend is a rival, or pissed them off, or they're just having fun at my expense?

"Now, Laura."

"Yes, *solnste*."

I can barely get the words out. He holds the stall door open for me once he has the photos back in the envelope. His brothers look at us, but none of them say anything. I pray he explains to them what's in the envelope without having to show them, and I hope he does it while I'm talking to my boss. We head back to my floor. I'm about to turn toward my boss's office when I think of something.

"Did any of you check my purse or satchel? My phone?"

"We took your SIM card out of your phone. It was too easy to unlock, and there are two trackers on it. We checked your bags. They were clean." Aleks appears sympathetic for the first time. I think all three of Maks's brothers understand this is serious.

"How does that even happen if no one has had it?"

"Not right now, Laura. Aleks can explain it later. Go talk to your boss."

Maks says he'll get my stuff while I try to plan what I'm going to say. I knock on the door and wait to be told to enter.

"Hi, Emily."

"Hi, Laura. Did you have a good weekend?"

I hear the censure for not coming in on Friday and calling

out last minute. Wonderful. I'm so screwed. Should I just quit on the spot?

"It was good. Emily, I need to take some time off immediately. I just got some news that concerns my family. I don't know if I'll be able to work remotely or not, and I don't know how long I need. I know this is unprofessional, and I'm sorry. But I really can't come in for a while."

My boss leans back. Her silver hair is coiffed like Meryl Streep in the *Devil Wears Prada*. She's just as much a shark as the Anna Wintour-like character. She looks at me, and it doesn't take a genius to deduce she's pissed. Like super pissed.

"One day didn't matter, Laura. It was almost a holiday weekend. I didn't appreciate you deciding to call out last minute, but whatever. But this? No. You may not have the time off. You have clients who expect their attorney to appear when they have meetings. Meetings that some of them are flying halfway around the world for. You can't just phone it in. Give me a better reason than family concerns."

What do I say? I'm usually quick on my feet, but nothing is coming to me. My legal brain is cotton.

"There have been some threats, and it's best for my family and me if I take time off."

"Because of your boyfriend? Don't think I didn't notice all four Kutsenkos arriving when I know they don't have an appointment here with anyone. It's a little early for your boyfriend to take you out for lunch."

"I don't know what's happening."

That's the truth, but it only seems to make it worse.

"If you don't know what's happening, then I don't need the threats rolling over to this firm or its clients. Your cases are reassigned as of today. Take all the time you need. But you will not receive a severance package, and you will not be able to claim unemployment."

Holy fucking shit. I just got fired. She didn't say it outright, so I have no grounds for wrongful termination. She granted my request, but she made it clear I'm done. I just lost my job. Fuck. I stand tall and nod.

"It's a shame so many documents haven't been translated yet, Emily. I hope someone finds time before tomorrow's meetings. I can't recommend any interpreters or translators since you've never needed anyone but me. I hope you find someone the clients are willing to work with. A little time off rather than not having me at all would have pleased the clients more. Good luck getting them to trust someone who doesn't speak their language. You know that's why each of them hired this firm. I wish you well."

I watch her stunned face as she realizes everything I said was true. Our Chinese clients had been more amenable to a female attorney than some of our Eastern European ones, but once I demonstrated I was more than capable, they returned for more business. Every client I've represented has put us—this firm—on retainer because of me. She thought she was putting the business first and being a hard ass with me. She cut off her nose to spite her face, and I'm too fucking terrified of what's going on in my own life to care. I turn around and walk out. Maks looks at me, but I shake my head. I'm not saying anything until we get to the car. I don't want anyone to hear, and I need time to compose myself.

I go into the copy room and remove reams of paper from a box, then carry it into my office. All four brothers watch me from just inside. I pack all my personal items. I sit at my desk and transfer what is proprietary to the company's cloud if it wasn't already there. Then I wipe everything else from my laptop, which is mine. I leave my notes in the files and all the documents just as they are. Many are only half complete. I pull out a tube of disinfectant wipes. I take two out and toss it to Bogdan.

"Wipe down whatever you touched."

I clean my desk, my chair, and the filing cabinet I touched this morning. My trash can is empty, so I toss my remaining chai into it with my dirty wipes. I pull the bag loose and hold it out for the guys to drop their wipes into. I press the air out of it, tie it, and drop it into my satchel. I'll dispose of it somewhere else or leave it to them. I can't change that people saw them here, but I'm not leaving any evidence behind that they searched my office.

I lift my box, but Maks takes it from me. He's watched me in silence, not missing a single move I've made. When I walk out of my office, I smile at Katie.

"Thank you for everything you've done over the years. You've been invaluable to me, and I appreciate it. If you ever need anything from me, a reference or something, just let me know."

"What's going on?"

All I can do is shake my head again. I give her a hug and turn toward Maks. I walk in the center, Aleks leading, Niko and Maks beside me, and Bogdan bringing up the rear. When we get down to the street, it surprises me to see a limo. The brothers must have come together. A driver I don't recognize takes the box from Maks and puts it in the trunk. I slide in and look out the side window while the men get in. Maks pulls me against him, and I gratefully rest my head against his shoulder.

"Know anyone who wants a mafia-affiliated corporate attorney? This good one I know is looking for a job."

My comment is met with silence. I look up at Maks, and he looks just as dangerous as he did in the bathroom stall. I close my eyes and shake my head. That's all I seem to do right now. I don't need him terrorizing Emily into giving me my job back.

I've worked long and hard for that company. I know I was ambiguous about my request, but she didn't even bat an eyelash before she sacked me. Fuck her and the horse she rode in on. Let her figure out how to appease the clients. Not my circus, not my monkeys. I exhale as I settle closer to Maks.

"Can we just go home?"

"No, *malyshka*. We have an errand to run."

Chapter Twenty-Two

Maksim

My heart has been racing since I received Laura's text. I was about to get out of the car at the jewelers when I got it. I called her as fast as my finger could hit the buttons. Her cryptic message freaked me out. When she asked me to bring my brothers, I wanted to demand an explanation. But I knew she was at work. I trust her discretion, too. Something was happening, and she knew she needed to be cautious.

Luckily, Bogdan hadn't gotten to any of the clubs yet and was still near the job site. Aleks and Niko hadn't left since the police had cleared out only minutes before I sent the group text. It took us nearly thirty-five minutes to get to Laura, and I was in a silent panic the entire time. I was utterly unprepared for the photos. I never could have imagined that's why she needed me. The clarity and closeness have me even more freaked out than just knowing they exist. The problem is

249

whoever took this could have been half-a-mile away for all I can tell. A good telephoto lens made this possible. The photos taken on our vacation had to have been shot from a boat. My brothers and cousin would have spotted and shot down a drone. There aren't photos of us anywhere but at the villa. The only picture I showed my brothers was the one of Laura at her desk.

I'm holding her against me, wishing she would say something more than her quip about needing a job. I never wanted her to get fired. I admit there are times when I thought life would be easier if she quit, but this isn't how I wanted her career to go. I keep telling myself she just doesn't want to say anything in front of other people. But I'm scared she's withdrawing from me. Between knowing someone is stalking us and getting fired, I can't blame her for being overwhelmed.

The car pulls up outside the jewelers, and Laura looks out the window past me. Her brow furrows as she looks at the sign, then me. She looks at my brothers, but they have no idea why we're here either. They look just as confused.

"Maks, why are we here?"

"We're picking out your engagement ring. We're getting married."

"We are not."

Laura looks like she's ready to punch me. Maybe that wasn't the most tactful way to put things, but I'm not exactly at my best right now. I'm scared shitless right now.

"The best way for me to protect you is to make you my wife. I planned to ask you anyway. This just moved things along."

"Planned to ask? You just told me. No. Take me home. Fuck Nadia and whether she's still there. I want to go to my place. Alone."

"Laura, I'm not arguing this with you. You already agreed

this morning to live with me. This is just the next progression. I know you would have said yes. We both know that."

"So that assumption makes it all right for you to command me? This isn't sex, Maksim. You don't get to be in control."

She's so angry, she doesn't care that my brothers can hear. That's their cue to get out. They tumble out as fast as they can. They sense the storm brewing, and they don't want to be caught in the eye. I wait until the door closes before I continue.

"Laura, I love you. More than anything. I will do whatever it takes to keep you safe. I want to marry you because I want you at my side every day for the rest of time. But marrying sooner rather than later gives you protection that you can't have as just my girlfriend. My brothers may already consider you family, but as my wife, all my men will owe loyalty to you. They will be sworn to protect you too. There's an unwritten code among all mafia in this city. Wives and children are off-limits. The fight is between the men. Until you're my wife, you don't fit under that provision. That's why whoever this is has been threatening you."

"Wait. Threatening? Not threatened, as in this once. What else happened besides the car following me and the roof? I'm certain something else did."

I sigh. I shouldn't have kept this from her. I went to Pussy-cats yesterday and saw the office wall for myself. I took a picture, and it's still on my phone. I pull it up and hand it to her. She sucks in a loud breath then glares at me.

"You knew about this in Turks and Caicos. You didn't tell me that there was a specific threat against me. You let me think that nothing serious was after me. You asshole, Maks. You let me go to work yesterday and today totally unaware. What the fuck?"

"Now do you understand why it's urgent that we marry?"

"It's not really because you love me. It's because you feel obligated."

She pulls away and turns toward the window. I fist her hair and make her look at me. The anger simmers there, but I can't miss the hurt. My mouth crashes against hers, and she relents after a heartbeat. She fists my shirt as she clings to me. I feel her tears against my cheeks, they slip between our lips, salty on my tongue. When we pull apart, she burrows her head against my chest.

"Did that feel like obligation?"

"No. It felt like lust."

"Laura, don't do this. This isn't ideal, and I know it isn't fair. But don't pretend like we weren't moving toward this. We're just hurrying it a little."

"A little? I suppose the wedding will be next month. No long engagement."

"The wedding is in two days."

"Two days? Maksim, I haven't even met your mother yet. This will break my mother's heart. She's always wanted to help me plan my wedding."

"We don't have time, but I will make sure you have everything you want. The florist, the cake, the food, the reception. All of it, baby girl. It just will be in two days."

She looks at me for a long moment, and I wonder if she's about to bolt. She looks like the little rabbit I sometimes call her. But I want to be the sunshine that leads her to safety, to our life together.

"Is this for real, Maks? Or is this just convenience?"

"What do you mean real? How could it be anything else?"

"I mean, do you really intend this to last, or do you see a way out if it's no longer convenient?"

"If I was worried about convenience, I would still be alone."

"Fuck you."

She tries to reach the door on the street side, but I pull her back and into my lap. I wrap my arms around her and tug her hair.

"Sit still, *zaychik*, or I will turn you over my lap. It will not be a fun spanking for either of us. You know you're purposely misconstruing my words. You are a liar if you can say being in a relationship is easier than being single. That's all I meant. I am not marrying you out of duty, obligation, guilt, or anything like that. I'm marrying you because I love you. I'm marrying you in two days because nothing means more to me than you being safe. Marry me, Laura, and have some semblance of your usual life. Refuse me, and I'll lock you away in my penthouse, and you will not even go for a walk with Sebastian."

"Your solution is to force me?"

"I'll do whatever the fuck I have to for you to be safe. You are mine, Laura. You know that. Don't pretend that you don't know what type of man I am. You've known from the start. I'm possessive. I'm overprotective—and as you can see, there's a reason. I'm unrelenting in getting what I want. And I love you. Now decide."

"You pretend there is a choice. But you make one of the options so undesirable you know I won't choose it. But I should. I should accept being your prisoner and then make your life a living hell."

"And you know I would cuff you to my bed, smack you until you think you need the fire department to put the burn out, then I would fuck you raw. That doesn't exactly sound like a hardship, does it?"

Her cheeks flame, and I know she agrees. She looks once more at the jewelers before she nods. I lean to kiss her, but she gives me her cheek. I kiss her temple and let it go. She's been through enough, and I know I've bullied her into this.

"If this is for real, then I want a real ceremony. A Catholic or Russian Orthodox priest. It can be outside if you don't want it in a church. But if you don't intend to end this, then I want it as binding as it comes."

I know this isn't what she wanted, and it's not what I wanted. It sure as shit isn't what I pictured the first time I arrived here today, but it's for the best. I knock on the window, and Fyodor, my regular driver, opens the door. I help Laura out and find my brothers milling around by the building. She doesn't look anywhere but straight ahead.

A security guard opens the door, and the salesman greets me by name. I called to postpone, but I can tell Laura's even more pissed. She probably thinks I'm here often, buying jewelry for other women.

"Mr. Alden, it's nice to meet you. Thank you for making time for us. This is my fiancée, Laura. We'd like to look at rings. Whatever Laura wants."

She doesn't react at all. Not to me clarifying that I haven't been here before. Not to me referring to us as already engaged. Not to me saying she can have anything in the store she wants. She's silent. She forces a polite smile and follows the older man to a chair near a display case. He pulls out a tray of loose diamonds, then a tray of settings.

"How long would it take to set a ring and have it ready?"

Laura's jaw clenches when I ask. I can see the muscle bulge before it relaxes.

"May I see those?"

Laura points to trays of rings that already have stones.

"*Meelaya*, if there's a style you like, then I'm sure Mr. Alden can customize it with the stone you choose."

She won't look at me.

"This is easier. I'll pick one of these."

I switch to Russian. "*Malyshka*, you will wear this every

day for the rest of your life. Don't be spiteful. You will regret it. Pick a ring that you want and will love."

"I want and will love? How is that supposed to work when I'm being forced to choose because you're coercing me to marry you. Just pick something, Maks. I don't care. Better yet just brand me. That's more permanent than a ring. Then everyone will know who I belong to."

"Don't be awkward."

We're both keeping our voice light, neither interested in the salesman knowing we're arguing. But my brothers can hear me. I can see Bogdan, who's standing near the window behind Laura. My brothers are near the doors and windows, not to gaze outside but to watch for any threats. Bogdan shoots me such a look of disgust and disapproval that I feel like I'm the younger brother. I glance at Aleks, who shakes his head. He doesn't seem in any more agreement with what I'm doing than Bogdan. I sigh and turn as though I'm looking at the display cases, but I glance at Niko. He's fuming. And I don't think it's because Laura is being awkward. He pushes away from the wall and approaches. I'm certain I'm not going to like what he says. Like us, he speaks in Russian.

"We had no idea this is what he planned. If you want me to take you home, I will. We wouldn't have let him do this if we knew."

"What the fuck, Niko? This isn't your business."

"Oh yes, it is. You want her to become our sister, then we will look out for her like a sister. Mom will kill you when she finds out this is how you proposed. And none of us will stop her. She is going to be so disappointed in you."

"Stay out of this."

My temper is reaching its limits. I look at Laura, and it's clear she's considering Niko's offer. What the hell do I do? All I want is to protect my *malyshka*. I want her to know that I would lay down my life for her. That I will stop at nothing to make her happy and to give her a good life. That I will do anything to make up for who I am and what I'm bringing her into.

I offer her my hand. She looks at it as if she's not sure if she should take it. It's breaking my heart, but she finally puts hers in mine and lets me pull her out of the chair. I draw her against me and lean to whisper in her ear, switching back to English.

"Laura, I know I've done this completely wrong. I know I've ruined what should have been one of the most special moments of your life. That's not what I intended. This isn't about obligation and duty. This is about me loving you so damn much that I can't breathe when I think someone might hurt you, might tear us apart. It's about me wanting to share my life with you now, not waiting. Has this shitstorm made it feel more urgent? Yes. But I didn't decide I wanted to marry you because of this. I've wanted to marry you since nearly the moment I met you. And it wasn't lust. You know that. It's always been more."

I lean back and look at Mr. Alden. He's watching us, not even trying to hide his curiosity. I suppose this isn't how most couples go about picking out a romantic piece of jewelry.

"Thank you for moving my appointment this morning. Something came up, but I'm glad you had time for me now."

"It's not a problem, Mr. Kutsenko. It was only two hours. I think many brides like to be part of the process."

Laura looks up at me and swallows. Tears brim in her eyes as she realizes I planned to come here all along. Maybe if I'd proposed properly, gotten her the ring, then suggested we practically elope, that would have been better. I did everything completely out of order. This will be memorable for her, but in the worst sort of way.

"I'm sorry, *malyshka*. I didn't do this the way you deserve.

But I was outside the door when you texted. I was already here to surprise you. I was going to do it tonight. I was going to take you to meet my mother this afternoon then out to dinner."

I pull out my phone and open a text thread with the manager of the Michelin star restaurant that's known as the best in New York. I hand it to Laura and watch as she reads.

Me: Tony, it's Maksim Kutsenko. I need a table for two tonight.

Tony: I can try to squeeze you in, but no promises.

Me: Do more than try. This is a special occasion. I want a private table where no one can overhear while I have dinner with my girlfriend. We don't need everyone listening and watching tonight. I want to ask her to marry me without an audience.

Tony: You're proposing? I didn't even know you were dating. She must be amazing if she's got you settling down. That alone is enough to make me get you a table. It's done. What time?

Me: 7.

Tony: See you tonight.

Tears slide down Laura's chin as she nods and hands the phone back to me. She slides her arms around my waist, and I gladly hold her tightly against me. I kiss the top of her head, and she squeezes tighter. I feel her take a shuddering breath before she steps back. Her smile is radiant. I know this doesn't make up for everything I got wrong. But she knows that I didn't do this out of guilt. She turns to Niko.

"Thanks for the offer, but I'd like to pick out my ring. Your brother sucks at communication."

Niko and the others chuckle. Mr. Alden looks at us, not understanding Laura's Russian or when Aleks replies.

"You get him to talk more than anyone else can. He's a fucking chatterbox with you."

"Enough."

My command is halfhearted as I lead Laura back to the seat. For the next two hours, she tries on practically every premade ring and every setting. She chooses a round diamond set in tulip prongs. There are smaller rounds along the sides until the band touches her other fingers. It's a vintage-inspired style, and it looks perfect on her. I see her eyeing a much larger stone than what she picks. When she looks up at me, I shake my head. I cock an eyebrow and nudge my chin toward the bigger stone. Her eyes widen, and she suddenly looks shy.

"Something you'll love every day, *meelaya*."

"Mr. Kutsenko is right. This is something you'll only get to pick out once."

I glare at the salesman. I don't need his help, and his wish for a bigger commission doesn't need to be so obvious. Laura glances up at him, and her expression says she doesn't need his help deciding. He takes a step back. With the jewelry tongs, she carefully sets the larger stone among the prongs. It's stunning. When she looks at me again, I nod. She looks back at the jeweler.

"This, please."

"Very nice, miss. I will take this back to my master craftsman. It'll be ready in a week."

"Tonight."

I cross my arms and watch the man stutter as he tries to come up with a response. My expression tells him everything. He glances at my brothers who are back to staking out the doors and windows. He looks at Laura's now-eager face. He nods vigorously as he spins around and heads into the backroom. A younger woman steps out. She ignores Laura and looks at my brothers and me. The trays of stones, settings, and rings are still out, so it's obvious what we're here for. She leans forward, flashing ample cleavage as she puts the trays back into the cases. I'm watching Laura, whose newfound excitement is quickly wearing off.

"Is there something else you want, Mr. Kutsenko?"

"No. I have everything I want already."

Laura stands and positions herself in front of me, as though she's a blockade. Never mind that there's a foot of me that towers over her head, and my shoulders are nearly twice as broad as hers. There's no hiding me, but I like it. We're a matched pair.

"I could show you—"

"No, you can't."

Laura isn't interested in pretending the woman isn't there. I've just botched our engagement, and she's had another horrible day. I don't blame her for being short tempered. I wonder what she will say next.

"Tell Mr. Alden to cancel the order."

I didn't expect that. My hands slide around her waist. She links her fingers with mine.

"What?"

"You heard me. We're finding a ring somewhere else. We aren't giving money to a store with an employee who shamelessly flirts with a man who came here with his fiancée to pick out a ring. Nope. Cancel it right now."

"I—"

"Don't lie. And you can put your breasts away. I've seen mine and plenty others, so I don't need to see yours. My fiancé isn't looking anyway. Besides, he likes natural ones."

I press my lips together. She's right. But I didn't expect her to say that. I'm certain she'll wish later that she hadn't said anything, but I won't deny I like this side of her. I know she's doing it as much to show me as she is to show the sales assistant that I'm hers, and I love every moment of it. Mr. Alden reappears, but he soon senses the shift in atmosphere. It's tenser than it was when Laura and I were at odds. Laura looks at the young woman and cants her head toward Mr. Alden.

"Tell him."

The saleswoman opens her mouth then shuts it. She looks around, but no one sympathizes with her. My brothers might have chatted her up in a bar or club, but they're turned off by her attitude. She could have flirted with any three of them.

"Dad, uh, she doesn't want the ring anymore."

"What?"

"Tell him why."

I stare at her as I demand she explain. Laura may have done the talking before, but I don't want this woman to doubt I feel the same way Laura does.

"I flirted with Mr. Kutsenko in front of his fiancée."

"Go in the back. Now, Lisa. I'm so sorry, Mr. Kutsenko, Ms. ..."

"Mrs. Kutsenko works." I love saying that, and from the way Laura's cheeks pinken, she likes hearing it.

"How can I make it up to you? You haven't chosen either wedding band. I could work with you on that."

Work with me indeed. Like I need a fucking discount. I'm buying a flawless four and a half carat diamond set in twenty-four-carat gold with nearly two carats of stones in the band. I don't think I need a discount if I can afford an eighty-thousand-dollar ring.

"I already know which one I want."

I look at Laura in surprise. Two hours ago, she barely wanted to look at anything. Now she has an engagement ring and wedding band picked out. She points to an eternity band with stones inlaid in the gold. It's a beautiful compliment to the engagement ring. It's more subtle, so it keeps the combo from looking ostentatious. The stones are still flawless, like my *malyshka*.

"Do you see a band you like, Mr. Kutsenko?"

Laura and I walk to the case with the men's rings. I watch what her eyes go to. She surveys the different shades of gold, then the platinum, and finally the tungsten. She turns back to me and keeps her voice low, even though she once more chooses Russian.

"Don't get the tungsten, Maks. If anything happens, it can't be cut off. They'd have to take your finger. Gold or platinum. I don't want to regret what you choose."

"You choose, *meelaya*. I want what you pick."

I see her surprise, but I also see my request makes her happy. She turns back and immediately points to a broad yellow gold band with platinum borders. She looks up at me, and I can't help but grin. It's what I wanted, but I would have gladly accepted anything she chose. Knowing how close he was to losing his enormous commission, Mr. Alden doesn't charge me for my band. By the time he's ensured the wedding band fits Laura, sized my ring, and processed my credit card, the engagement ring is ready. Laura looks at me expectantly, but I grin and shake my head. I love her little pout. She's in a much better mood than when we arrived. Thank God.

We step outside, and my brothers and I surround Laura again. Unless someone is aiming their camera from above, she's virtually invisible since we're all so much taller than her. Once we're all in the limo, she once more looks at me expectantly. I shake my head again.

"Do you think the restaurant manager could get us a bigger table?"

"How much bigger?" I don't want to share this evening

with anyone but Laura. But her suggestion is impossible to turn down.

"Could we invite your mother and brothers? I feel horribly that we're getting engaged, and I haven't even met her. It's rude, and it feels really wrong. I don't want her to feel left out. If your mother can come, then I want it to be a family meal."

I don't have to look at my brothers to know they're touched by her thoughtfulness. I am too. I nod, too choked up to say anything. The only woman I have to compare to Laura is Nadia. Never would that woman have considered my family or involving them in such a special event. I planned to take her to meet my mom today, but I like this idea better.

"Do you think your parents could come?"

"Probably. But Maks, we've already made time to have dinner with just my parents. I don't want to hurt your mom's feelings by not giving her the same attention."

"All right. But I'm sure that if I can get Tony to find us a table for six, he can find a table for eight."

"He could barely get you a table for two."

"*Malyshka*, he'll make room. He'll see the dollar signs that such a large party—especially one celebrating—will bring him. He'll cancel half the other reservations if he needs to. Call your parents, and I'll call my mom."

"Can we please make it three days, Maks? I don't know that my family can make it to a Friday wedding. Can we do it on Saturday?"

"Yes, *malyshka*. I'll agree to that."

It's all arranged by the time we arrive at the penthouse. We've dropped off my brothers at their nearby apartments. We all have lavish places at the top of the most desirable buildings. Our mother lives not far from my house in Queens. I texted Sergei to tell him about our plans, and he offered to pick her up.

I've convinced Tony to find us a table for ten. I've extended the invitation to Sergei and Anton, too.

I made a mess of our first date when I chose an Italian restaurant. Actually, I've made a mess of a lot of things, but Laura still loves me. I hope that this Italian restaurant, one Salvatore Mancinelli doesn't own, proves a better choice. I just want one thing today to go right.

Chapter Twenty-Three

Laura

My nerves are getting the better of me. I chose the emerald-green dress Maks bought me for our vacation. It's shockingly appropriate and covers far more of me than you would expect considering his choice in swimwear. But then again, he intended me to wear it to dinner at the resort, and he would have had a fit if I wore something that drew too much attention from other men.

We're already at the restaurant with Maks's brothers. Tony didn't look thrilled when we arrived, but Maks ordered three bottles of champagne and a bottle of top-shelf vodka before we even got to our seats. The restaurateur's attitude immediately improved. Now we're waiting for my parents and Maks's mother. I know almost nothing about her. I still feel guilty that she's meeting me on the day her son proposes. At least my parents got a chance to meet Maks and form an opinion before we announced we're committing ourselves to each other for life.

"Did you tell her why we want her to join us? Does she know?"

"*Malyshka*, yes. I talked to her while you were in the shower. You know that. Stop worrying. You haven't met her, but I've told her about you. She knows how I feel. She's known since the beginning. That week we were apart was hard. I talked to her every day. She's the one who convinced me to give you space. I wanted to kick down your door the next morning."

"I didn't know that. Why didn't you tell me?"

"I'm thirty years old. I didn't think it exactly sounded manly that I needed my mommy to help me with my broken heart."

"I like that you talked to her. I like that you wanted her opinion and her help. There's nothing unmanly about that. Just the opposite. It shows you trust your mom's opinion and advise. I like knowing you're close to her. It makes me wonder if spending so much time with me has kept you from seeing her."

"No, *malyshka*. I know I don't see her often enough these days. But I didn't ignore her because of you. Don't think that."

"Look."

I point toward the door. My parents are walking in with Sergei and a stunning blonde, middle-aged woman on his arm. If I didn't know better, I might think she was a cougar and Sergei's date.

"People think she's our girlfriend or Sergei's or Anton's all the time."

I look at Maks, whose eyes crinkle with laughter. I understand why. She doesn't look like she's anyone's mother. She looks like a runway model. No wonder Maks's father was worried about her safety. Now I understand. Maks greets his mother as my parents arrive at our table.

"Mama, this is Laura Doyle and her parents, Dr. and Mr. Doyle. Laura, this is my mother."

I greet her in Russian, and she beams. "It's so nice to meet you, Mrs. Kutsenko. I wish it could have been sooner. Your sons have been very welcoming, and Maks is—well, Maks."

She chuckles as she kisses Maks's cheek, then mine. She winks at her oldest son before responding in English.

"My son is quite the character. They all are, but Maks has always been the ringleader. And not just because he's the oldest. He found trouble when there was none to be had. He's told me much about you. I think you must be perfect if you're willing to take him on. God bless you, *moya devushka*."

She calls me her girl, and I can't help but beam. Her sons look so much like her, except for the blonde hair, which is the same shade as Sergei's. It explains why Sergei resembles them. I assume they get their dark hair from their father. It makes sense why Anton looks so much like them too, with his black hair and brown eyes.

"And it's Galina, not Mrs. Kutsenko. I don't think we need to be so formal."

Galina turns to my parents and greets them. They agree we should all be on a first-name basis. Maks introduces his brothers and cousins to my parents, and I'm happy to see how at ease everyone is with one another. We take our seats at a large round table. It's interesting to watch how the brothers position themselves. It seems like Bogdan, the youngest of them all, draws the shortest straw and is the one with his back to the main door. He looks ill at ease. Sergei and Niko position themselves to put Galina between them, with Niko next to Bogdan. Anton sits next to Sergei and has my father on his other side. My parents sit beside one another, and Aleks sits between my mother and me. Maks is between Bogdan and me.

My parents, Galina, and I all have walls to our backs. As I watch my parents, then Galina, as we take our seats, I thought my parents wouldn't notice the intentional seating arrangements. But I feel like my mom and dad both recognize how they're positioned with their backs protected. It doesn't seem to surprise either of them. Galina glances at the wall behind her before she takes her seat. Something about it just strikes me as odd, but I'm not sure why. But once the food and drinks start arriving, I don't think much of it.

I love seeing Maks's family together. Galina's love for her sons just radiates from her, and her sons' affection for her is genuine. They all beam when she smiles at them in turn. Sergei and Anton treat her like a second mother, and she laughs with them as though they are her sons, not her nephews. They joke about coming to America and settling here. Galina tells stories about the brothers serving as acolytes at their church in Moscow when they were young boys. I can't help but shoot Maks a questioning look. That's something he's never mentioned. He leans over to me.

"If you want an hour-long Orthodox wedding ceremony, then we can do that, *malyshka*. But if you prefer a shorter Roman Catholic one, then we can do that instead."

"I don't know anyone who would think a Roman Catholic wedding Mass is short."

"You don't have to stand as long as you do for a Russian Orthodox one. If we do that, I suggest you don't wear heels."

Maks kisses my temple, and I feel better than I have all day. My feelings are still hurt by what happened in the limo and when we first arrived at the jewelers. I understand now what I didn't at first. I'm bummed that my one and only marriage proposal was an order rather than an offer. I can see how hard Maks is working to make it up to me. He didn't ask for the photos to arrive and interrupt how he wanted to propose. I didn't ask to get fired and have that put me in a foul mood. But the night is redeeming itself.

When they bring out the desserts, I notice Tony is among

the three servers. He carries a plate toward me that has far more on it than the cannoli I ordered. I strain to see. When he places it in front of me, I'm speechless. There are edible rose petals arranged like the flower around the edges. In the center is a strawberry and honeydew arrangement that looks like the strawberries are the flowers, and the melons are the stems and leaves. In the very center of the plate is the ring box. Maks pops it open as Tony sets it down. Mr. Adler didn't show us the set ring, and I never saw Maks slip the ring to anyone after we left the store. I have no idea how he arranged this, but it takes my breath away.

When I look at him, I can see all the love he feels for me pouring forth. Everything that I should have seen and felt this morning is there now. He pushes back his chair and takes my hands as he gets down on one knee. I realize that I never imagined my hulking, brooding, sometimes-downright-terrifying boyfriend ever getting down on one knee for anyone. It seems almost too humbling to be comfortable for me. I'm used to him —I prefer him—being the dominate one.

"*Meelaya*, you were a magnet the moment I met you. We thought we could fool you into believing we didn't understand your negotiations. We thought we could outmaneuver you. Not only did you run circles around us, but you impressed me more than anyone ever has. When we ran into each other at Envy, it was like my life suddenly made so much more sense. You're the most intelligent person I've ever met. You're kind and loyal to those who you love. You're tenacious and driven when you want something. You're forgiving and accepting when I'm at my worst. And you bring out the best in me—parts of me I didn't even know were there. I want to spend the rest of our lives making you as happy as you make me. Will you marry me, *zaychik*?"

I nod, trying to swallow the lump in my throat. When I answer, it's more of a croak. "Yes, *solnste*."

Maks slips the ring on my finger, and it feels just right. It's like I'm Goldilocks. All the others were too big or too small. Too flashy or too dull. This is the only one that is perfect, like it truly was made for me. I cup Maks's face and lean forward to kiss him. Just before our lips touch, I whisper.

"I love you, *papochka*."

"I love you, *malyshka*."

People have noticed what's happening, so other diners applaud and cheer. Our families congratulate us as Maks takes his seat. He feeds me a strawberry, a promise for later glimmering in his eyes.

"Congratulations, boo bear."

My mom has called me that since I was a baby. She doesn't say it in front of other people anymore, but I don't mind. That was a beautiful proposal, and I'm ecstatic. My hand is tucked into Maks's as he accepts well wishes and teasing from his brothers. I hear Galina scolding Bogdan for an inappropriate comment I'm certain he thought she couldn't hear. I try not to laugh, but I squeeze Maks's hand.

"Congratulations, *moya devushka*."

"Thank you, Galina. Thanks, Mom."

"Do you think it'll be a Christmas wedding?"

My mom's question stops me cold. I turn to Maks, who waits to see what I say. I know what he wants, and I have to admit now that my initial anger at his highhandedness has worn off, I love the idea of getting married in three days.

"No, Mom. We're not exactly eloping, but sort of. We talked about it earlier. We want to get married in three days."

"What?"

It's my dad whose voice booms. He leans around my mom and me and glares at Maks. He's about to say something, but something else catches his attention. I see his hand move to my mom's thigh. She looks away from me and to my father, but he's looking straight ahead. I don't understand what's happening.

"Mom?"

"Is that Donovan?"

My mom is speaking to my dad, not me. Maks's head whips around to look where my parents are. Then he glances at my dad. What the hell is going on between them? I look at the other men at the table, and I see they are as tense as my dad and Maks. Only my mom and Galina seem all right, but I can tell they're both extremely aware of what's happening around them. I hate feeling like I'm the only one not in the know. It's scary.

"Maks, what is going on?"

I keep my voice low as I watch a russet-haired man walk near our table. It's like everyone collectively holds their breath until he takes a seat with a group of men. I hear them speaking another language, but I don't know what it is. It's not one that I can recognize. It's definitely not a Romance language or a Slavic one.

"That's Donovan O'Rourke. He's the head of the Irish."

"The Irish?"

Once I ask, I realize what he means. The guy is the leader of the Irish mob. He's Maks's equal. I get why the Kutsenkos are ill at ease, but I don't understand why my parents are. We're only Irish on St. Patrick's Day, Christmas, and Easter. I look at my parents, who seem more relaxed than they were a moment ago, both eating their desserts, but I can tell they're acutely aware of what Donovan and the men at his table are doing. Donovan has his back to us—he's either snubbing Maks or has too much bravado—but a couple of his men keep looking over at us. One of them locks eyes with me, and I feel a chill run down my spine.

"I think my wedding gift better be a crash course on who's who, Maks."

He doesn't find any humor in my comment, and I don't really intend any. He starts to relax when no one from the Irishmen's table makes a move toward us. Slowly, the tension fades, and we go back to our desserts. But I know Maks and his family are keenly aware of where each Irishman sits and when any of them leave the table. I can also tell that Maks and everyone but me are trying to draw out dinner until after the Irish leave. No one seems to want to walk past their table, which is inevitable if we want to get out of the restaurant. Fifteen minutes after they go, we finally slip on our coats and jackets. Maks settles the bill while I corner my parents as they move away from the wall at our backs.

"What was that?"

"What do you mean?"

I glare at my dad. I am not in the mood for this. "How do you know Donovan O'Rourke, the head of the Irish mob?"

"He's a prominent businessman who happens to be one of my firm's clients."

"Is he one of your clients?"

"He was a few years ago, but he was moved to another broker when I started working with more international clients."

"Did that leave you on bad terms or something?"

"Donovan is the type who is on bad terms with everyone."

"Mom, how did you know Donovan? You recognized him too."

"I met him at some of your dad's work parties. Anyway, I'm just glad we didn't have to say hi. He's not the politest young man. Why are you getting married in three days?"

I decide to let it drop. I'll ask Maks later.

"We're already practically living together. Maks asked me to move in, and I already said yes. I've never wanted a big

271

wedding. I'm happy to have you, Maddie, Michelle, Lanie, and a few other family members there. If we can't have that, then I'm fine with just you two and the girls. I really hope Maddie can make it down in time."

"I talked to her this morning. She's coming down anyway. She wanted to surprise you and meet Maks. I guess she has ESP, since this is good timing."

"I guess so. When does she arrive?"

"She's flying, so by noon tomorrow."

"I haven't had a chance to talk to Michelle or Lanie since I got back. They're not thrilled about Maks. They're scared for me. Juan got to them. I don't know if they'll come to the wedding. I want them to go dress shopping with me, but I don't know if they'll want to or can even make time. I was going to go tomorrow afternoon. I hope you and Maddie can come. I want to ask Galina, too."

"I'm sure Maddie will be thrilled, and I can clear my schedule tomorrow afternoon. I don't have any patients or rounds."

"Good. Let me ask Galina." I turn to Maks's mom. "Would you like to come dress shopping tomorrow afternoon with my mom, my sister, and me? I'd love it if you could."

"Yes. Thank you for inviting me." Galina embraces me, and it's almost as comforting as my own mom's hugs.

"Your sister is coming?"

I slide my hand into Maks's as I let go of his mother. He must have heard some of what we said.

"Yeah. Mom told me she wants to surprise me and come down to meet you. I'm glad she is. She can be my maid of honor."

Maks sees something in my expression because he draws me against him.

"What's wrong, *malyshka?*"

"I barely spoke to Michelle when she dropped off Bastian. I haven't talked to her or Lanie since we've been back. I didn't talk to them while we were gone. I don't know how they're going to react to the news. I hope they'll come shopping with me tomorrow, and I hope they'll be in the wedding as my bridesmaids, but I don't know if they'll even come."

Before Maks says anything, something else dawns on me. Fuck. Fuck. Fuck. I turn back to my parents.

"Are Mrs. Diaz and Pablo going to expect an invitation? Do I have to invite them? I absolutely do not want Juan anywhere near my wedding. I'm not that comfortable having them there either."

"You don't have to have anyone there you don't want, boo bear. It's your and Maksim's day."

"Won't that make it awkward for you?"

"Things are already a little strained. I don't know what Juan said to Margherita, but she's been rather cold the last few times I've seen her. Pablo won't look at me or your dad. But it's fine. She's his mom. She can side with him, as she should. But you're my daughter, and you will always come before anyone outside the family. You, Maddie, and now Maksim come before everyone else."

"Thanks, Mom. Do you think Aunt Mary Rose and Aunt Patrice and their families can come on such short notice?"

My mom's really close to her sisters since that's pretty much all the family we have around. My dad's family died before I was born. His extended family was small, so no one is really left. My mom has her sisters, their husbands, and my cousins. That's only ten people combined. I've never wanted a huge wedding, but I hope at least they can be there. But who can or can't attend won't change Maks's mind about having the wedding so soon, and I find I'm just as eager. And that's without thinking about the looming invisible threat.

"I'll call them in the morning. Do you know where and when?"

"I'm going to call Father Howard in the morning and see if we can do it at St. Mary Immaculata. Maks said we can do Catholic or Orthodox. He doesn't mind. I would like to do it at my church, and it's a service everyone can understand. If we can't then, I'll figure something else out."

"If you can't, then we can do it in the backyard. Maybe one of the priests at our church can do it. They've all known you since you were a little girl."

"All right. I'll call first thing in the morning."

I still need to tell my parents that I lost my job, but that's a subject I don't want to deal with tonight. I want to end this on a happy note. The day has been fraught enough. I don't need to add to it. But I have no idea how to explain why I got fired if I don't mention needing the leave of absence. How can I mention the leave of absence without mentioning what's happening? My parents will freak. And I can't blame them. Between now and tomorrow afternoon, I need to come up with something that will keep them calm, or my parents might kidnap me from my own wedding.

"I really want you both to come, Lanie. Please."

I'm on a three-way call with her and Michelle. It's painful. She's barely letting me get a word in edgewise. She's already accused me of only asking them to be in the wedding party because I can't get anyone else. That hurt. We all know that's not true. I've told them since high school that both of them and my sister would be in my wedding party. My sister would always be the maid of honor, and they would be my bridesmaids.

"I'm busy washing my hair."

"Lanie!" Michelle keeps saying our friend's name, but she isn't saying anything more. She sounds appalled, but she's not sticking up for me either.

"I'll text you the bridal boutique address and the time. Come if you want. If you do, we'll pick out gowns for you. If you don't, then fine. I'll text you the time and the place for the ceremony. I hope you make it to both, both of you."

"You expect us to just drop everything because you want to get married all of a sudden to your thug boyfriend. Is his dick really that great?"

"Enough, Lanie. You're pissed. I get it. But I'm not going to listen to you insult Maks. You want to have a go at me. Fine. Go ahead, but I'll hang up if you say anything else about Maks."

"So you are picking him over us."

"For fuck's sake, Lanie. I'm marrying him. This isn't about you. I love Maks, and I'm marrying him. You can think this is a dumb idea. You can disagree with me. But you don't get to ruin my day, and you don't get to be rude about him. Of course, I'm going to stand up for him. He's going to be my husband by Saturday night."

"Fine. You made your choice. I'm making mine. You can scratch my name off the guest list."

"Lanie!"

"Are you going to say anything else, Michelle? Are you coming?"

I never used to think I was closer to one of them over the other, but I realize now I've always been closer to Michelle. I hope she still understands like she did before I went to Turks and Caicos.

"Yes. I'll be at the fitting, and I'll be at the wedding. I'll stand beside you."

"What the fuck, Michelle? You can't stand Maks."

"But I love our best friend. Lanie, you're the one who is wrong about this. It's not your decision who Laura marries. You're supposed to support her."

"Even if she's making a massive mistake?"

"It's her mistake to make, Lanie. Not yours, and not mine. But I don't agree with you. I don't think Maks is the wrong choice. And I never said I can't stand Maks. I hate the danger this relationship puts Laura in. I pray he isn't into what Juan claimed. But I like him. Don't put words in my mouth."

"Whatever. I'm done."

I hear the click. Lanie hung up. I'm actually kinda glad. I don't want to hear any more from her.

"I'll be at the shop on time. I'm excited for you, Laura. He makes you happy. Lanie doesn't believe in soulmates, and I didn't used to. But you and Maks. If there is such a thing, then it's the two of you."

"Thanks, Chelle."

"I'll see you in a little while. Love you."

"Love you."

Big sigh. I secured the church this morning for late Saturday afternoon. Maks pulled whatever strings he can, and he secured a ballroom at The Peninsula. Apparently, as *pakhan*, there are plenty of people who expect to attend. There won't be a lot of people at the service. He wants to keep that secure. But there are city officials, businesspeople, bratva members, and more who he says will want to attend. I can't imagine how they can be available on such short notice, but he says they will be.

Juan has called twice this morning. I guess somehow he heard. Probably from Lanie. I talked to her and Michelle last night when we got back to the penthouse after dinner. I hoped this morning's call would go better with Lanie than last night's attempt. Obviously, it didn't.

The one good thing about not having a job is I have time to plan this last-minute wedding. I couldn't do that with the three meetings I had scheduled. Emily called this morning, but I sent it to voicemail. I listened to it and promptly deleted it. She wanted me to brief her in time for the meetings. I don't work for her anymore, so I don't owe her my time. She sent a series of texts that went from polite and cajoling to scathing and hostile. Maks was there when they were coming in. Thank goodness she's a woman. I don't know that she would have survived if she weren't.

Maks is at the site where the bodies were found. He told me about that last night after I talked to my friends. I asked if I could swap with him. I'd deal with the bodies if he dealt with Lanie. He declined. Lucky bastard. Before I forget, I send Michelle the boutique information. I'm meeting Maks for lunch then the others for the fitting. I take a quick shower before Sergei escorts me out to the car, where Michail is waiting. Maks still insists that I only trust him, his brothers, and his cousins. I asked about Michail. It unnerved me when he said only when one of the men he trusts most are there. What does that mean? This is a new life to adjust to.

I meet Maks at a restaurant near his office building. I know that he rarely is there and that it's a front for the shell companies he uses. But it's a good spot since the shop is around the corner. He's already at a table when I arrive. Sergei walks me over then finds an unobtrusive spot near the door. I already spotted Anton near the rear fire exit.

"How'd it go?"

"Shitty. Michelle is coming with me to pick out a gown, and she'll be in the wedding. Lanie won't do either. She's pissed that I'm picking you over her. This isn't dodgeball. This is my life partner. If she can't get that and get behind this, then she's the one who's made the choice. Maybe some more time and distance will help. Maybe it's the end of the friendship for good. I don't want that, but it's out of my hands. It's her decision now."

"I'm sorry you're going through this, *malyshka*. I know it's hurting you."

"It is. But it's not your fault. It's her choice. She didn't like Antony when I was dating him, and she didn't even meet him. She just didn't like thinking I might stay there for him. I never even considered that, but she was convinced that I would. The only guy she's never questioned was Juan, and that's because we never really dated."

"Can I ask you something that might offend you?"

"Yes."

What's he going to ask?

"Did you ever experiment with Lanie at some point?"

"No. I've never been with a woman. I haven't even kissed one. Why?"

"If I didn't know better, she sounds as possessive as I am. She sounds jealous."

"Of the guys I'm with? Then why doesn't Juan bother her? He's been around a long time."

"Maybe because she knew there was no chance it would get serious. He wouldn't take you away from her."

"I've never once gotten that vibe from her. I'm not even her type. She likes leggy blondes. You two seem to have more similar tastes."

"*Malyshka*, that's not fair."

"I know. I'm super testy right now. Lanie hurt me a lot. I'm nervous about meeting more of your men. I want the wedding to be just right. I don't know who's even coming. It's a lot right now, Maks."

"I know, baby girl. I know we just went away last weekend,

but I still want to take you on a honeymoon. Where would you like to go?"

"I suppose I have the time."

I can't help but grin. I liked my job a lot, so it surprises me that I'm not more upset about losing it. But in the grand scheme of all that's going on, I'm barely fazed now that the initial shock and anger has worn off.

"So where do you want to go and for how long?"

"How long can you be away?"

"I have three brothers. The roof won't fall down around us if I'm away. I haven't been on a vacation ever. I think I'm due another one. Last weekend wasn't nearly long enough."

"I don't know. Maybe we could wait a couple weeks and plan something without rushing."

"If that's what you want. Where are you headed this afternoon?"

"There's a boutique a block from here. I thought we could start there. I have a feeling I'm going to find what I want there. Maks? What's wrong?"

His face falls, and he looks uncomfortable. I can't tell if he's angry or embarrassed or what.

"I don't want you to go there. Nadia's still employed there. She sold the condo like I told her, but she's still working there."

I lean back in my seat. I suppose her moving out is a step in the right direction, but of course, of all the boutiques I could pick, that's the one where everyone is meeting me. Son of a bitch.

"How do you know?"

"Ilya's been following her. I got a copy of the closing documents for the condo, and Ilya said she packed up yesterday morning. She left the building. She took my warning seriously."

"Maybe she'll quit today."

"No. She's staying with the owner. The woman is Russian,

and they've known each other since we were kids."

"Wonderful. Whatever. There are plenty of other boutiques. I'll go to a chain shop. I don't mind. This is a huge city. Now that she isn't in my building, and you don't really work down here, we shouldn't have to see her."

"That's what I'm hoping."

Our food arrives, and we eat in silence until something occurs to me. It curdles the food in my belly.

"Your men know she isn't welcome at the wedding or the reception, right?"

"I hadn't said that to anyone. I assumed they would figure that out. But it might pay to make it clear. I don't want her there, *malyshka*. I don't want anyone near us who will ruin the day."

Maks reaches his hand across the table. We finish the rest of the meal chatting about the wedding, and I can tell he's as eager as I am. I look up a different bridal shop to go to and text everyone the new address. The afternoon turns out wonderfully. I'm so happy my sister is here. She and Michelle have always gotten along. Galina and my mom are practically besties. A flash of sadness hits me that Lanie isn't there, but it surprises me how fleeting it is. My family, my friend, and my future mother-in-law make it a perfect experience.

It doesn't take me long to find the absolute perfect gown. While I'm getting fitted, we find gowns for Maddie, Michelle, my mom, and Galina. We're done in three hours, and everyone has what they need. Michelle invites Maddie and me to spend tomorrow night, since all four of them insist it's bad luck to see the groom before the wedding. I have no idea what Maks is going to say to that. We haven't been apart in weeks.

He's surprisingly good-natured when I tell him that I'm staying at Michelle's. He's waiting with a bubble bath already run. The bath turns into sex in the tub. Then there's some kinky hanky-panky before he lets me pack my overnight bag for the next day. That man's tongue is a national treasure in two countries.

My sister and best friend treat me to a spa day with a massage then a mani-pedi. We go to my apartment to gather the things I most want to have at the penthouse. I've already brought a lot over in dribs and drabs. I think about what I want to get rid of since we don't need doubles of furniture or household goods. We make a list of what the movers Maks arranged will pick up on Monday and what I intend to donate. It turns out to be a wonderful day with Maddie and Michelle. I really couldn't ask for a better one, and it's been ages since I've spent time with just the two of them. It reminds me of when we were kids.

I make what I intend to be a quick trip back to the penthouse. I know Maks worked from there this afternoon since he took on many of the arrangements for the wedding. I told him what I wanted, and he promised to make it happen. I can only imagine how much that costs him. Of course, nothing is quick between Maks and me. He tempts me with what he swears is just a preview to our wedding night. I meant to be there less than an hour. Two and a half hours later, I'm hurrying out the door as he laughs.

I can't believe how fast my wedding day dawns. I thought I would be a bundle of nerves, especially since I wasn't involved in most of the planning. I'm usually a bit of a control freak about things like this. My perfectionist side is known to have a silent temper tantrum if things aren't just right. It turns out for the best that Maks is even more controlling than I am. All I have to do is sit back and enjoy the day. The hair stylist and makeup artist meet us at the church. The hours fly by. The hair stylist has just placed my tiara and veil over my hair. It's time to officially become Mrs. Maksim Kutsenko.

Chapter Twenty-Four

Maksim

I'm standing beside Aleks at the altar when he nudges me. Laura was worried about excluding any of my brothers since she only has Maddie and Michelle standing up for her at the ceremony. She insisted that all three of mine be there, even if the numbers are unbalanced. I turn toward the door as Aleks whispers that they've opened. The music begins, but I hear nothing and see nothing but my *malyshka* walking down the aisle toward me. I barely register that her dad is walking beside her. She's the most incredibly beautiful sight I've ever beheld.

Her white gown looks as if it had been tailor-made for her. It fits like a dream, and her long train fans out behind her. A veil covers her face, so I can only see hints of her features, but I can't miss the way she looks at me. Never have I felt more special in my life. Never have I felt more loved, needed, and desired. I could float away. I'm not nervous like I thought I might be. But I am impatient. I want to speak my vows and pledge the depth of my love to her. I want to hold her in my arms and kiss her once we're pronounced man and wife.

I want to know that we are bound together in this life and the next. And it happens faster than I imagined. She takes my hand after her dad gives her a kiss on her cheek. We're reciting our vows, and it's as though there is no one there but us. I barely even notice the priest. We go through all the steps of the Mass, which are mostly familiar to me after the years that I attended with my parents and the time I spent as an altar boy. Then we're sealing our commitment with a kiss. I ease her veil back over her head and cup her cheeks before I slide my arms around her waist. We're slow, disregarding the witnesses. We are determined to make this first kiss special, and it is. It's tender and loving, both of us pouring forth all we feel. There's no doubt that we both want what we're doing, that we are all in. Before we know it, we're greeting our guests as husband and wife.

"Mrs. Kutsenko, over here."

The photographer is speaking to my *meelaya*. For the first time in years, I hear the title and know that the man isn't speaking to my mother or my aunt. This time, it's to my wife. My stunning bride who radiates happiness. Most people usually say I'm dour in photos, but I know I have a ridiculous grin on my face. I can't help it, and I don't want to.

We stand on the steps to the church, and the photographer encourages us to kiss. Neither of us needs to be asked twice. This one, outside the sanctity of the church, is far more passionate. It's a promise of things to come. Once we've both caught our breath, our family surrounds us for a formal photograph. We kept the guest list short, only our families and top-ranking members of the bratva. I've had no time to introduce Laura to them, but she will meet them at the reception. Those not involved in the photos are milling around, but I can tell Laura knows that they are security as much as they are guests.

While Laura takes photos with her parents and sister, Aleks leans toward me. I follow his gaze and see what he's about to point out. Nadia. Somehow she discovered not only the wedding, but the location and time. I didn't see her inside because I wasn't looking anywhere but at Laura.

"When did she get here?"

"I don't know. I didn't see her inside, but I wasn't the one who was supposed to watch the guests. I'm going to find Ilya and Stefan. They better have a good answer."

Aleks leaves my side as I signal Anton. I want her gone before Laura notices.

"Get Nadia out of here. Make sure she doesn't make a scene. Take her to the place where she's staying to get her passport and whatever she can't live without. Then take her to JFK and put her on the first plane anywhere in the former Soviet bloc. Stay with her until the damn flight takes off. It'll be booked by the time you get there. I want her gone."

Sergei walked over with Anton and heard everything. He has his phone out, and I know he's already booking the ticket. If they can't get her on a commercial flight, then they'll put her on the jet and take her themselves. I was clear with all my men that she was unwelcome.

"What's she doing here?"

Well, fuck. So much for Laura not finding out until after the fact.

"I don't know, *meelaya*, but Anton and Sergei are taking care of it. She'll be out of the U.S. before we cut the cake."

"She's got some balls showing up here."

I watch Laura, but she's looking at Nadia. I squeeze her waist until she looks back at me. I can feel the tension in her body. This is ruining her day, and it's just what I wanted to avoid. I turn her back toward the church doors.

"We need to sign the register, baby girl. Let's take care of that now."

I guide her inside and to where the priest waits for us. It only takes a couple minutes, then we're alone for the first time. I look around and spot a crying room in the hallway. I tug her in and shut the door. There's no lock, so we can't linger overly long. I press her against the door and plunder her mouth. Finally. I get to kiss my wife how I really want. She's just as eager. As she does so often, her fingers find the gap between my shirt buttons. She slides her fingers inside, and they rest over my heart. I gather her dress in my hand and hike it up until I can skim my hands over her thighs. I feel the garters, but when I slide my hand to her pussy, I discover she isn't wearing any panties.

"You're a naughty little girl."

"Only for you, Daddy."

"What do you want, *malyshka*? Do you want to wait until tonight?"

"No, Daddy. But do we have time?"

"For a taste. Hold your dress up, baby girl."

I hoist my wife high enough to flick my tongue along her pussy. I position her with her leg over my shoulders. Her gown is flowing around us, and I can only imagine the sight we make. This is a better feast than the wedding breakfast we're about to enjoy. I'm starving for her. One night apart, and I'm a wreck. My brothers have mostly handled things at the warehouse since Laura and I started dating. I know I can't neglect my responsibilities much longer. There will be times when I'm away for days. I haven't explained this to her yet, and I dread it. I dread not having her beside me at night even more.

"Maks, fuck. Like that. Yes."

Her voice is like music from heaven. Her moans make my balls ache. I work her little cunt as she writhes on my face. We don't have much time, so I can't tease her like I usually do, like we both enjoy. It's a full onslaught as I work her clit.

"I'm close, Daddy. More."

I can feel when her muscles contract then when she shudders her release. My mouth floods with her juices as she grasps my hair. Her nails graze my scalp before she tugs. It should hurt, but it only makes me work harder to prolong her orgasm. When she finally sighs, I ease her back to the floor. I wipe the back of my hand over my mouth, wiping away the evidence of what we've been up to. I give her a quick hard kiss before we return to our guests. A few people shoot us knowing looks, but most pretend not to notice our absence.

It's a pleasant drive from the church in Queens to The Peninsula in Manhattan. Our wedding party, Laura's parents, and my mom join us in the limo. I can tell from how Laura's hand fidgets in mine that she wishes we were alone again. I can't disagree, but the conversation flows around us. Everyone is lighthearted until my mom notices that Sergei and Anton are missing.

"Where are your cousins, Maks?"

"They're taking care of something before they join us at the reception."

My mom's face tightens. I know she assumes they're at the warehouse. She doesn't know where it is or exactly what goes on there, but she knows it exists. I give my head a small shake, but Laura's parents notice. Laura isn't as subtle.

"Maks's ex-girlfriend showed up. Sergei and Anton are escorting her to the airport. She wanted to say her goodbyes, but we were too busy. They want to be sure she doesn't miss her flight."

My brothers pick up their conversation, hoping they can

avoid this one. Susan, Killian, and my mom nod. None look very convinced, but they don't push the subject. I wrap my arm around Laura and kiss her. I don't care who watches.

"I love you. You're brave to say that. I know she upset you."

"She did. But I refuse to let her ruin our day. You chose me."

"And I always will, baby girl."

She kisses me back as we pull up to the hotel. Guests are already arriving as we get out of the limo. It's early evening and a black-tie affair. Laura watches in awe as she recognizes the mayor and various members of the city council. She recognizes influential businesspeople she's either represented or gone up against. There are many who she doesn't recognize.

As we enter the ballroom, she realizes the event is bigger than she imagined. Part of me wishes it could remain a small private affair. But part of having these events is the opportunity to rub elbows with people who can help our business. Part of it is also facilitating other people rubbing elbows, then reminding them later who they owe that chance to.

We take our places in the receiving line and greet our guests. I introduce Laura to those she doesn't know. She glances at me from time to time, and I notice she's unsure why my tone has changed. I'm not the gushing groom I was at the church. I'm now Maksim Kutsenko, the businessman most fear and few cross. She doesn't understand why I'm not as excited as I was. I can feel her attitude change to match mine. She becomes more reserved and says far less to each guest.

When I lead her to our places at the head table, she only nods when I pull out her chair. She laughs with Maddie and Michelle, but she's now cold to me. When I take her hand under the table, she moves to place them on top, but I keep my arm down. She glances at me, confused.

"This isn't the time."

"Isn't the time? We got married an hour ago. How is our reception not the time to be affectionate?"

"Because this is business, too."

She looks at me and swallows. She doesn't know what to say. I thought she understood when I explained why people who aren't close to us would want to attend our reception. I assumed she would understand that my attitude in business will always be different than how I am with her.

She plasters a smile on her face and keeps her tone light when she speaks with our guests. But each time someone taps their glass for us to kiss, her lips barely respond to mine. The look in her eyes chills me when she does look at me. I've ruined her day. Will I ever get anything right?

We talk throughout the meal to keep people from wondering why things are so strained between us. When we move away from the table for our first dance, she's stiff in my arms. I have to pull her closer.

"Isn't this a little inappropriate for propriety's sake, Maksim?"

"Don't call me that, *malyshka*."

"This is a formal event. It's business, so I intend to keep it professional."

"It's not business between us."

"You can't have it both ways, Maksim. You can't turn cold on me and expect me to fawn all over you. You want to put distance between us for the sake of appearances, then you shall get what you want. You'd best hope I remember when to tell the difference."

"Are you threatening me, *malyshka*?"

"Never, Daddy. Remember? I only make promises."

The sarcasm in her voice grates on my nerves. I'd hoped the dance would soothe things between us. That it could be a chance for us to be more affectionate, but I sense she thinks it's for show now.

"I have my own promises to keep with you tonight, baby girl."

I feel that involuntary shiver, and I know she can't help how my words make her react. When she meets my gaze, I see the hurt once more.

"I'll make this up to you tonight, *meelaya*. I know I should have explained. I don't know why, but I assumed you would understand. You know how people perceive me. This isn't the time to change that."

"You mean, you don't want to look weak. The only thing you look like, Maksim, is an asshole being cold to his bride. I didn't realize that everyone else's opinion mattered more than how you make me feel. I guess they outnumber me."

The song ends, and she pulls away. She still has that phony smile on her face that she turns to those around us. She gathers her dress and turns toward the ballroom doors.

"Where are you going?"

"The restroom."

"I'm coming with you."

"No, you aren't. I don't need you to hold my hand while I pee. I've done that on my own for twenty-plus years."

"Sergei and Anton aren't here. I'm not sending my brothers to do it. You aren't leaving this room without a guard, Laura."

"Even at our wedding? You think someone would attack us here?"

"I think anything is possible, *malyshka*. It's no secret now that we married, and everyone knows we fell in love."

"Do they though?"

She doesn't wait for my answer and starts weaving her way through the tables, accepting people's well wishes. When she enters the hotel hallway, she looks around and takes off toward the restroom, not caring if I'm at her side or not. I knock on the door before I let her go in. A woman's voice answers, so I nod. She shoots me the dirtiest look I've ever received from her, and I've gotten several.

Two women leave before she comes back out. It feels like she's in there forever. When she finally emerges, I can see where her eye makeup is smudged. She's been crying. I pull her away from the door and pull her into my arms.

"Laura, I'm sorry."

"You say that a lot, Maks. When are you going to start doing better so that you're not always apologizing? You wanted a wife. Now you have one. You need to think about how your actions affect others before you take them."

That pisses me off. It shouldn't, but it does.

"All I have done since I was twenty-three is think about how my actions affect other people. Believe it or not, you are not the only person I have to deal with."

Fuck.

"Deal with? Don't worry, Maks. I shall make it very easy for you the rest of the night. You don't need to deal with me once we leave this fucking reception, which better be soon, or I will walk out. We go in, cut the cake, look like we're enjoying ourselves, then I'm leaving. I don't care whether you come with me or not because I'm done with you for tonight."

"You don't mean that."

"Don't I? You keep trying to make up for how you fuck up. How about you just don't fuck up in the first place? A big ring and a nice dinner don't make up for the fact that you ordered me to marry you. An expensive reception doesn't make up for the fact that you forced me to marry you with three days' notice. You sending your ex-girlfriend wherever doesn't make up for the fact that she was at our ceremony. You trying to cover your ass right now doesn't make up for being such a dick to me when this is supposed to be the happiest day of our lives. And despite everything, it was enough until you decided your public appearance is more important to you."

She spins on her heels and marches back to the ballroom. Once she passes through the doors, she's once again graceful and smiling. She makes her way to a member of the catering staff, who hurries away. Only moments later the cake arrives. She takes her place and picks up the knife, waiting for me expectantly. I cover my hand with hers before we perform the tradition. It should be to celebrate, but I ruined that. She feeds me a bite of cake, and her eyes warn me not to smash any in her face. I never would, but I can tell she doesn't trust me. We kiss, a pro forma one, not a loving one. Then I announce that we're leaving but everyone should continue to enjoy themselves. We say goodbye to our family and head to the elevator. When I put my arm around her waist like I have countless times, she doesn't move. She doesn't look at me as we enter our suite. Is my bride even going to let me touch her tonight, let alone consummate our marriage?

"Are you going to ignore me all night?"

"No. After the crap you pulled tonight, you owe me a good fucking."

"You have a foul mouth, *malyshka*."

"What do you think is going to happen, Maksim? You give me the cold shoulder for most of the night, act as though showing me any affection is a chore, and you think we're going to make love? Uh, no. I want something between us tonight, Maks. It's our wedding day. But I'm not feeling quite as mushy as I was four hours ago. We like fucking. That's no secret, and we're good at it together. Maybe that's not what I thought was going to happen tonight, but that's where we're at."

"So you want angry sex on our wedding night."

"For fuck's sake, Maks. I'm not angry. I'm hurt. It feels like

I feel this way as often as I feel loved. It shouldn't be equal. I'm new to being a bratva wife. I'm new to being a wife, period. If you'd just told me that there were appearances to keep up, then I would have been prepared. How could you assume I would understand? I'm not from your world."

"You aren't. So can you trust me a little to know what's best?"

She turns her back to me and points over her shoulder.

"Can you help me with my dress, please? I can't do it myself."

"Aren't you going to answer me?"

"You're asking more of me than you're willing to give. I don't want to cry on my wedding day. At least not anything but happy tears. I just want to get into bed with my husband and forget for a while that there's a world outside this suite. I'm still hurt, and I'm not feeling as tender toward you as I did this afternoon. But I love you, Maks. I just want my husband."

Some of my worries ease. She's not rejecting me despite how I made her feel rejected. She's right about it all. She's learning how to be a bratva wife without any lessons or warning. I'm learning to be a husband. She married into my world, not the other way around. I need to remember that.

I kiss her neck and shoulder as I slip her gorgeous gown from her shoulders. As it glides down her hips, it reveals a backless camisole. I only know what the thing is called because she told me once. Her bare ass is perfection even if I know she doesn't think so. I gently lay her dress over the back of a chair before I turn her toward me. I can't help it. For once, I don't want it even a little rough. I want her to take control. She looks up at me expectantly. I nod as I place my hands on her waist. She stretches to kiss me. She tries to make it more aggressive, but I keep it light. She adapts after a while, then takes control as our passion spikes. My touch is soft, and she matches it.

I help her as she peels off my tux jacket then pulls my bowtie loose. We work together to shed the rest of my clothes. I step back as my boxer briefs hit the floor. She's still in her camisole and garter belt. I had no desire to do a garter toss, so I'm glad she didn't want to stay downstairs longer. I don't want anyone seeing something so intimate as me sticking my head up her gown or watching me remove any of her lingerie. That is for my eyes only. That is for us only.

She waits for me to guide her toward the bed, but I only take her hand. When she realizes I'm not going to move, she tugs my hand. I immediately follow her. She picks up on the shift between us and pushes me onto the bed. She tosses the camisole aside and crawls over me only wearing the garter belt, her garters, and her thigh-high stockings. She's the most sensual and erotic woman I've ever met. I put the condom I'm holding on the bed beside me. We haven't talked about whether we want anything to change.

She glances at it then turns her attention back to me. She pecks my lips before shimmying away. She moves back to kneel between my legs. She locks eyes with me as she strokes my cock. It's tortuously slow and light. I try to raise my hips, but she lets go and cocks an eyebrow. When I settle against the mattress, she goes back to teasing me. She moves her other hand to my balls and rolls them. I fist the sheets to keep from lifting her pussy onto my cock.

She leans forward and licks away the precum leaking from my tip. My abs contract at the first touch of her tongue. She slides it along the underside from root to tip before flicking the head with her tongue. It twitches, and she smiles this completely wanton expression. She knows she's in control. She uses her mouth and her hands to bring me to the brink over and over. I suddenly regret every time I've edged her since she's paying me back now. It's almost unbearable how much I want to be inside her and how much I want to come.

"The need is almost too much, isn't it?" She reads my mind. I nod. "That fine line between pleasure and pain when your partner pushes you toward pain, and you doubt for a moment that there will ever be pleasure. That lack of control."

"You're in control tonight, *malyshka*. Whatever you want."

That makes her pause. She looks at the pillows before she snatches one and tugs off the pillowcase. She does the same to another.

"Give me your wrists, *solnste*."

I obey without hesitation. She uses one pillowcase to bind my wrists. She surveys the headboard. She leans over my face as she lifts my arms over my head. Her tits purposely brush across my lips.

"Suck."

Gladly. Your wish is my command, baby girl. I work her tits as though they're my last meal. She secures my arms and gives the binding a little tug. Satisfied that I can't get out of my pillowcase cuffs, she presses her tits together. I can't get enough, and I know she enjoys how hard I'm sucking and biting. She doesn't bother to control her moans. She reaches back and presses my cock between her ass cheeks. She lifts and lowers her hips before shifting and letting my cock fall between us. She slides her soaked pussy along my dick, coating it.

When I tug against my binding, forgetting that I can't control her, she laughs at my frustration. She moves back down my body again and grasps my cock. She spits onto it, something she's never done before. But I love it. It's like she's marking me as hers, that she's in charge. She strokes me until my balls tighten, and I groan. She lets go. She rises on her knees and slides her fingers along her smooth pussy. She makes me watch as she finger fucks herself before rubbing her clit. I'm practically pulling the headboard loose as she makes herself come.

"It's my turn to control when we both come, *solnste*. Not so much fun watching me do what you want to do yourself."

"But I've never made you watch me come without you."

"Maybe not. But we both know part of you enjoyed it. You've never gotten yourself off because you know I wouldn't like it. It arouses you, but you know it would have hurt me. We know that about each other, *solnste*. We know what we need together. We know what makes us right for each other."

She leans forward and releases my hands. She guides them to her hips as she lines my cock up with her pussy.

"We have to be partners, Maksim. Not just in bed but in life. You might dominate me in here, and I may love to submit. But in our marriage, we have to be equals."

"Yes, Laura. I want to do better. I will do better."

Together we lower her onto my cock after she slides the condom on. The passion explodes. It's somewhere between making love and fucking. It's unlike anything we've shared before. There is no space between our bodies as we take turns being on top. There is no leader or follower. We are equals. When neither of us can hold out any longer, we come together. We cling to each other long after the euphoria subsides. Whatever tomorrow holds, we will do this as partners.

Chapter Twenty-Five

Laura

We've been married a month and a half, and most of the time has been surprisingly blissful. Since I don't have a job in Manhattan anymore, and Maks usually works from home most days, we decided to move into the house in Queens. Sebastian is in heaven that he finally has a yard to himself, rather than hoping I take him with me to my parents when I visit. My condo is on the market with plenty of interest. The bids keep getting higher. We've talked about selling the penthouse, but we both agree having a pied-à-terre in Manhattan still has its benefits.

We haven't seen or heard from Nadia since the wedding. Sergei promises that she's back in Moscow. Apparently, the man she was dating was less-than-thrilled when she stole a few thousand dollars from him and disappeared. According to Sergei's intelligence, he's kept her under lock and key. It's obvious her bratva man isn't as patient as mine.

We spent two-and-a-half weeks in Greece for our honeymoon. We left five days after the wedding with a far larger entourage than I expected. We were joined by Sergei, Michail, Ilya, Stefan, and four men I didn't even know until we boarded the plane. To their credit, they were like ghosts for most of the trip. Apparently, flying in a private jet internationally makes it far easier to have an arsenal at your disposal. When I wondered aloud how each man traveled with twice the luggage I did, I soon discovered what they carried. I felt practically invincible. Maks made it the most perfect honeymoon anyone could have. Beautiful accommodations, excursions of a lifetime, and plenty of time alone with his own arsenal of devices.

Despite not having a job, I've kept busy. I've done some redecorating at the house, but not much. Maks asked me to review several prospective contracts before he let Dmitry look at them. He wanted my opinion before he asked his hired attorney. He was not thrilled with several of Dmitry's valuations for upcoming negotiations. I also devised some workarounds that have gotten the construction projects back on track. The city planner knows Dmitry and took that relationship for granted. He wasn't prepared for me. Maks and his brothers agree to keep Dmitry on since he's been the bratva's attorney since before Maks became *pakhan*, but they're diminishing his role.

Maks and his brothers still haven't figured out who is responsible for the break-in at Pussycats. Salvatore took responsibility for Envy, but he steadfastly denies having anything to do with the strip club. The only two bones of contention I've had since we got married are the nights Maks has been away at the warehouse and when we've made public appearances. The day after we returned from Greece, he told me he'd be gone for a day and a night. He was honest and said it was to the warehouse. But when it stretched into two days then three, I panicked. I went to Galina in tears.

She soothed me and explained that they turned off all their

personal devices and couldn't receive any outside communication. She was none-too-pleased that Maks hadn't explained that to me. She told me what she could about what goes on there, but it wasn't much. She knew they took people there to be questioned. She knew that no one left there alive. The amount of time her sons were gone depended on the circumstances. Some people broke and confessed faster than others. Sometimes they took people there on suspicion and had to wait to gather all their evidence. She suspected that's why all of her sons had disappeared for so long. She told me that the longest she'd been out of touch with them was eight days. That freaked me out even more.

But it was Maks who was in a full-blown panic when he got home, and I wasn't there. I brought Sebastian with me and stayed with Galina for the night. I took Bastian for a walk and wound up at my mother-in-law's house. For the first time in ages, Ilya was my only bodyguard. When I got to Galina's, he left because he was taking his wife to Atlantic City for the weekend. Galina has her own security detail, so we thought that would be enough. It clearly wasn't by the time Maks found me.

I'd left my phone charging in the bedroom where I spent the night. Galina and I were enjoying the mid-autumn day and were sitting by the pool talking; she had also left her phone inside. Maks burst through the backdoor, and without a word, he hoisted me over his shoulder and carried me inside. Galina laughed, but I didn't find anything funny about it. He was smacking me by the time we were halfway up the stairs. Once we were inside and the door was locked, I was over his lap with my dress up by my ears. He ripped my panties off, leaving them in tatters around my toes.

He was careful not to harm me, but he unleashed. In between slaps, he told me about how he went back to the house and couldn't find me. He told me that he called me five times, but I never answered. He called Ilya but couldn't get in touch with him either. He knew I'd taken Bastian for a walk, and Ilya came with me. But Ilya never notified the other guards at the house that I was staying with Galina. None of Galina's guards left a message at the house or with Maks.

Since his brothers and cousins had been with him, they didn't know where I was, either. He tracked my phone to his mother's house, but by the time he discovered where I was, he was beyond reason. Once my spanking was over, he was beyond tender as he explained how terrified he'd been. He treated me like I was porcelain and he was afraid I might break. We made love for nearly two hours. We went back to our house with ridiculous smiles on our face, and I had an ass still on fire.

Since then, he's been gone again, but he's done better about letting me know when he's going to be away longer than he originally expected. He refuses to talk to me when he's there. He says he doesn't want me to hear how he gets. But he texts, and I can accept that. I make sure he knows where I am if I leave the house. It's not that I feel obligated to report to him, just like I don't think he feels obligated to report to me. We just know that it makes us both feel better. There's enough danger in our lives without creating unnecessary fear.

The only other thing that bothers me is when we go out together, and we're not alone. We've had dinners outs with people who are connected to Maks's businesses. He always takes me, but he's back to being cool like he was at the reception. I accept that he has a public persona, and I adapt to that. But he doesn't always realize the things he says make me feel diminished or trivial. I often feel like the trophy wife I told him I didn't want to become. Other times, I feel like he trots me out like a show pony to show off his accomplished attorney wife.

Tonight, we have our first real public outing since our

wedding; we are attending a fundraiser held by the mayor. I'm more excited to attend than Maks is. He's more of a homebody than I ever imagined. Now that we know that we're coming home together, and there's no question of where our relationship is headed, I thought we might not spend quite so many nights at home. I'm happy to stay in, but I thought Maks would want to go out more often. We've gone out to dinner at least once a week, ensuring we have a date night together. But this is a formal event. Maks is in his tux once again, and I can barely keep my hands off him. He's not much better with his hand up the high slit of my silver gown. His fingers trail along the inside of my right thigh. I can't stop squirming, and he's reveling in it.

He gave me a surprise tonight while I was getting dressed. Since meeting Maks, half my panties have wound up torn and in the trash. The other half never get worn. So I was unprepared when I opened a box and found a lacy pair of red panties. As I lifted them out, I realized immediately why he wanted me to wear them. There's a tiny vibrator in them. He's been turning it on and off the entire drive to Gracie Mansion, the mayor's official residence.

"Maks, do you want everyone in there to know when you make me come? I don't know that I'm going to be able to hide it."

"You'll have to try very hard not to come. Not until I tell you, you can."

"Maks, I'm practically there already. If you keep teasing me with this, it's going to happen no matter how hard I try not to."

"I'll just have to punish you, *malyshka*, if you don't obey me."

"You're setting me up to fail, Daddy. This isn't fair."

"I know, baby girl. Come here."

Maks lifts me onto his lap to straddle him. He turns off the vibrator and pulls my head against his chest as he slides his hand into my pussy. I shudder as he works me into a fervor before his thumb finally circles my clit. I can't stop my moan as I cling to him. The moment my orgasm is done, he pulls his hand away. He licks his fingers as he turns the vibrator back on. I cry out. My clit's too sensitive. He turns it back off and grins. He helps me out of the car and shields me as I adjust my skirts. His hand rests at the small of my back as we make our way inside. I leave my wrap at the coat check, and we head toward the receiving line.

Unlike our reception, I'm prepared for Maks to be cooler toward me in public. I don't like it, but I remind myself that this is business for Maks. If we were at a work engagement while I still worked for my law firm, I wouldn't want him pawing me. But it's not just his unwillingness to even hold my hand. It's his tone. I see people notice, but there's nothing I can do.

"Mr. Mayor, you remember my wife, Laura. Thank you for having us join your event."

"Mrs. Kutsenko, my wife and I enjoyed ourselves at your reception. You were a beautiful bride. Maksim outdid himself, and no one even knew he was dating."

I can tell Maks doesn't appreciate the observation.

"Thank you, Mr. Mayor. We were very happy that you could attend. We're homebodies and enjoy each other's company."

I sense Maks wanting to move us down the line, but the mayor isn't ready to let us go.

"Maksim, I hear that your construction projects are finally back on track. That Yakovitch was on his game finding those loopholes. Mrs. Kutsenko, I know you're a lawyer. Maybe one of these days your husband will let you look over his attorney's shoulder."

I grit my teeth, waiting for Maks to correct him. He says nothing. I know he's worried that I'll risk getting disbarred if word gets out that I'm involved. But he hasn't involved me in any of his less than legal dealings. Everything I've seen has been on the up and up.

"Maybe one of these days I will." What else can I say? If Maks isn't going to speak up, then I can't correct the man.

"If you'll excuse us, I see some other people I should introduce my wife to."

Maks steers us away with barely a nod to the mayor. He reaches in his pocket and clicks on my panties. I nearly jump out of my skin. He really means to torture me. I glance up at him, but he's looking straight ahead. I recognize two men at the bar that we're approaching. They're in capital venture, and I handled hostile takeovers of their company. They are not who I want to greet.

"Maks, I don't want to talk to them. I represented a company that put them out of business and cost them millions."

"I know. Won't they be surprised."

I bite my tongue. I don't know what I expected about tonight. Maybe I thought I could be what I assumed was a good bratva wife. One who is quiet and looks pretty on my husband's arm. I didn't expect him to parade me in front of people who wouldn't mind seeing the back of me before having another conversation with me. He isn't doing this because he's proud of my accomplishments.

"Taylor, Hanson. I believe you've met my wife, Laura, before."

"Gentlemen."

What else do I say as they stare me down? They look at me as though I'm dirt under their shoes, even though they came out the losers. I just stand there, waiting to see what Maks wants to talk about.

"I believe it's been a while since you've done business with my wife, so I thought I would reintroduce you."

"Mrs. Kutsenko, it's nice to see you again."

Tom Hanson looks anything but pleased, but he greets me formally. Maks may have introduced me with my first name, but the man is wise enough to know Maks doesn't want them on a first name basis with me. His partner isn't so smart.

"Laura, it's been a while. You're just as lovely as you were when you took my company for all it was worth. You did it with such a pretty smile."

"You don't sound so eager to see my wife, Larry. And I thought to suggest you might want her as your legal counsel since you're trying to go public. She's opening her own firm, but if you aren't interested, I'm sure you'll find someone competent."

I am? What the hell? Since when am I opening my own firm? And why the fuck would I want to work for them? But I watch as their expressions change.

"I thought to do you a favor, but never mind."

And there it is. Maks used me as a lure to make them indebted to him. But he knew they wouldn't accept the suggestion. What would have happened if they did?

"I didn't realize you weren't at your old firm, Laura. If I had, I wouldn't have been so quick to disagree. If you're now in private practice, perhaps we can work something out."

"Maybe you could. We'll be in touch."

Maks answers for me, and I try not to grimace. Before I know what's happening, Maks picks up two glasses of wine and guides me away from the men who keep staring.

"What was that? I'm not opening my own practice, and even if I was, I would never take them as clients."

"They have foreign investors that I want. If they owe me a favor, then I can get them."

"You used me. What if they'd said yes?"

"I knew they wouldn't. I'm going to let them stew for a bit."

"Then what? Hire me out without telling me?"

"No. If you want to open your own firm, then you can. But I won't pick and choose your clients."

"It kinda sounds like you just did. You might have let me know."

"I didn't think of it until we started talking to them. I want them indebted to me, I just didn't think of playing it that way."

"Playing."

I mutter the word, but Maks hears me. He guides me against a wall and leans against it as though we're talking casually. He hands me my glass before he turns up the vibrator a notch.

"Do you wish to use a better tone, or do you wish to come in front of three hundred people?"

"Do you know what the only reason is that I'm not pissed at you?"

"You have a habit of answering a question with a question."

"Only when I'm negotiating. The only reason I'm not pissed is because you are a master negotiator, and I know you wouldn't stop until you came out on top with them. Except there is someone better than you. Me. If you make me come in front of everyone, I will say no tonight. And I know you will never, ever force me. I've given in so far, but that's because I've never really wanted to say no. Discover whether or not I do."

"That's not negotiating. That's an ultimatum."

"That's one way to negotiate."

"I don't like ultimatums, *malyshka*. I will punish you for it."

"Not if I say no."

He turns the vibrator up another notch. How fucking high does this thing go? Any higher, and people will hear it. I'm clutching the glass so tightly I'm afraid I'm going to snap the stem, so I put it on a nearby table.

"I think it's time we find our seats for dinner, *malyshka*."

"I'm going to use the restroom first."

"No, you're not. You went before we left, and you haven't drunk enough to need to go again. You just want a reprieve, and I'm not giving you one."

"No. I wish to wash my hands. We've shaken a lot of them, and they feel gross."

"Fine."

Maks leads me through the crowd until we get into the hallway. He stands outside the door with his arms crossed. I know better than to delay. I slip into a stall and pull the panties down for a moment. I just need to catch my breath. As my discomfort subsides, I realize I have a solution. I pull them off and turn them around. The thong is hardly comfortable like this, but at least I don't have the vibrator against my clit. I slip out of the stall and find Maks standing there. Fuck.

"I needed a moment alone to compose myself."

I don't even bother to mention that he can't be in here. Maksim Kutsenko does what he wants. I wash my hands and accept the paper towels he hands me. He takes my arm and leads me back to the ballroom where we find our table. He turns up the vibrator once more, and I pretend to shift. It feels weird having it against my ass, and I can't ignore that it's still arousing. But at least I don't feel like I want to crawl out of my skin. Maks glances at me. He knows something's up. He turns it up to what must be full blast. Thank God, my ass has some meat to it and silences the sound it would surely make.

I play the part. I clench a fist around the edge of the tablecloth and take several deep breaths. I lean a little toward Maks as though I need his support. Instead, his hand slides up the slit and to my inner thighs. I know the moment he realizes the vibrator isn't where it's supposed to be. His fingertips bite into my thigh. He leans to whisper in my ear.

"Daddy is not happy with his baby girl. You disobeyed me

and thought your little ultimatum gave you the upper hand. You may have an iron will, but remember that tungsten you didn't want me to buy? That's what my will is made of. It will not break."

I swallow. I don't have the vibrator to make my clit throb. It's him. I squeeze my thighs together, trapping his hand between them. I never wanted to say no. I still don't. And we both know that I won't. Maks draws his hand away as other people take their seats. He leaves the vibrator on high throughout the entire meal.

"I'll be back. Stay here with the other wives."

I glance at Maks as he stands. I exchanged pleasantries with the women sitting with us, but I don't know any of them. But they seem to know each other well. Maks walks to a group of men who are standing near the patio doors. One of them hands him a cigar. I have never seen nor smelled Maks smoke anything. I look around for Sergei and Stefan. I spy my cousin-in-law near the patio doors that Maks just went through. I look for Stefan, but I can't see him. Maybe he went to the restroom.

"Mrs. Kutsenko, none of us knew Maks was dating."

The youngest woman at the table besides me had her eye on Maks nearly the entire evening. He paid no attention to her, or any of the other women, focusing only on the men who he discussed politics with. I don't know who she is, but I feel the barbed comments coming. The other women seem amused and eager to see what happens.

"We've kept to ourselves since we started dating. We enjoy one another's company."

"But it was only a couple of months ago that he brought a stunning blonde to the mayor's last cocktail party. You must not have dated long."

Maks never mentioned bringing anyone anywhere. Just the

opposite. He said he went to these events alone or with one of his brothers. Who the hell is this blonde she's talking about?

"We didn't. We just knew."

"I didn't take Maksim for the impetuous type."

This comes from a woman to my right. She's old enough to be my mother, but she's still very attractive. Her husband was more attentive to her than the other woman's. I feel less vulnerable to her, but I know that letting my guard down is a mistake. Some of the most viperous snakes in the world appear harmless.

"My husband isn't impetuous or impulsive. But he is decisive. So am I."

"Did you meet him at work?"

"I did."

That's an odd question. And we did meet at work, but how would they know?

"Which of his clubs do you perform at?"

My heart stops. They think I'm a stripper. They think Maks married an employee. One of his exotic dancers. Is that what the blonde was that he brought to the last event?

"My husband doesn't date his employees."

"Date." The woman scoffs. She means screws.

"I was the attorney representing a company Kutsenko Partners merged with. We met during negotiations."

"You're a lawyer?" A third woman, one who is sitting directly across from me laughs. Laughs. They don't believe me. What about me makes them think I'm a stripper? Kudos to women with the confidence to do what they do, but that isn't me. And I hardly think I have the body anyone would want to give money to gyrate in front of them.

"Until recently, I was with Stanley, Hughes, and Barnes. I was a junior partner."

That shuts up the woman across from me. She must recognize the name, but the other two don't.

"How quaint. I—" The woman who began this conversation doesn't get to continue because Larry and Tom approach our table.

"Laura, we considered your husband's offer of your services. We accept."

Fuck me with a pogo stick. Perfect timing. Not only did they think I was a stripper, now they think I'm a whore.

"Have an assistant draft a memo with the details of the merger and acquisition. If you have my husband's email, send it to him. Otherwise, you can send it to the general Kutsenko Partners inbox. I'll get it. I have other cases ahead of you. I will get in touch when I can. Once I have an idea of the scope of this case, I will send you a projected invoice. Whatever you paid your last attorney who failed so miserably against me probably won't cover half my retainer, but I will win. I'm certain my husband will be in touch, so you can share your appreciation for the favor he's doing you. Good night, gentlemen. If you'll excuse me, ladies."

I leave all five of them aghast as I walk away. Screw them all. I'm headed away from the patio doors. I don't want to deal with Maks right now. I look for Stefan, but I still can't find him. I'm going to the restroom, and I'm taking these damn panties off. If Maks isn't ready to leave, I'll get an Uber. I look around the hallway, but there's no one in sight. I hurry to the bathroom and don't even bother going into a stall. I pull the blasted underwear off and shove them in my clutch. I yank the door open and freeze. Salvatore Mancinelli is smiling at me.

Chapter Twenty-Six

Maksim

I know Laura is annoyed with me. Again. She's a shark in a conference room, so I thought she would take my manipulating those two idiots better than she did. Maybe she's not used to having a partner. I tried to remain stern when I discovered she'd turned the damn panties around. I assumed she'd try to take them off, but I knew she hadn't. I could hear the slight buzz when she came out of the stall. I didn't expect her to outwit me, but I should have.

She's still at the table with a few wives. Sergei is nearby, and Stefan is at the other end of the room. I'd signaled him to stay put when I escorted Laura to the restroom. He was in his place when we returned. I don't like being away from her in such a crowded place, but I need to try to finish this deal I started at dinner. I keep reminding myself that now that she's my wife, the other syndicate leaders know she's off limits.

"Kutsenko, my company is going public in two months. The value rises every day. Now is the time to invest."

I watch the middle-aged man who looks like he just stepped off a boat in Martha's Vineyard. He's what Americans call preppy. Everything about him screams wealth and entitlement. Even the way he speaks to me. There's a command in his voice that chafes.

"I'm considering it. But why do I need to invest in your biotech firm when I already have one of my own?"

"Because mine not only deals in pharmaceuticals but chemical weapons. I would think that's right up your alley."

Asshole. I look at him questioningly. Go ahead. Say it. Say that you think I'm interested in chemical weapons because I'm Russian.

"I figure you know of some foreign markets we could expand into."

And there you go. I have no ties to the Russian government, and I don't want any. I have no ties to any government, and I'm not interested in finding private buyers. I don't trade in skin or weapons of mass destruction. Guns and bombs, yes. Biowarfare, no.

"I doubt I can help you there. My international connections are in banking, real estate, construction, and plain old pharmaceuticals. Nothing so exciting."

"But they could be."

This comes from the man who sat next to me at the table. He's short, paunchy, and balding. The stereotype of a businessman who isn't aging well and doesn't take care of himself. He has more money than sense. I need to steer this back to the banking conversation we were having at the meal.

"It seems to me that you wish to get my money into your company without any guaranteed return on investment. That's not a sound business model for me. If we were to find something more mutually beneficial, I would consider it. I have bids on three commercial developments in Brooklyn that need silent investors. If I get those bids, which I don't see why I wouldn't, the construction will start almost immediately. Rent from the units will be coming in before the end of next year's first quarter. That's sooner than your company going public. Show me a sign of good faith, and I'll see about investing."

What none of them know is that my investments are going to drive the valuation down. When the company goes public, the price per share will be below the margin they need to remain open. I intend to acquire this company for a fraction of what this guy thinks it's worth. Then I will bring my backers in and drive up the share prices. But that's a secret only my brothers and I know.

"Send us a proposal next week, Kutsenko."

This comes from the third guy who's been quiet throughout most of the conversation this evening. He's the only one I worry might have a clue what I'm up to. He listens and studies rather than speaks. Still waters run deep with this one. He might be quiet, but it doesn't mean he doesn't have plenty of thoughts on the matter.

"I will. If you'll excuse me, I've left my bride alone long enough."

"They do get testy when they aren't the center of attention."

Mr. Martha's Vineyard grins and claps me on the shoulder. I want to break his hand. I look down at it then at him. He's quick to pull it away. I reenter the ballroom and immediately notice Laura isn't at the table with the other women. I scan the crowd, but she's nowhere to be seen. I know I haven't missed her. My wife is like a homing beacon to me. It doesn't matter who's around, I will find her. I look for Stefan, but he isn't at his post anymore. Maybe he took her to the restroom. I walk over to Sergei.

"Did you see Laura and Stefan leave?"

"No. I saw her get up about twenty minutes ago, but I didn't watch where she went. I assumed Stefan would go with her."

"You assumed?"

"Don't get pissy with me, Maks. You posted me here, and you posted him there. She went his way."

"Fine."

"Just wait a moment. I'll radio him."

I watch as Sergei presses his earpiece and speaks quietly. He looks at me and shakes his head. He tries again. I see him searching the ballroom before he looks back at me. We both head toward the doors that lead into the mansion's main hallway. I look around, but neither Laura nor Stefan is in sight.

"The restroom is this way."

I tug at Sergei's tux jacket. I reach under mine, reassuring myself that my gun is against my lower back. As we round a corner, I spy a group of men surrounding someone. I look toward the floor and recognize Laura's shoes. I stare at the men as we approach, then I recognize the one who has Laura pinned against the restroom door. I'm going to fucking murder him. Sergei recognizes him at the same time. I hear Laura as I approach.

"Mr. Mancinelli, I know you deny what happened at Pussycats, but why shouldn't I think it was you when I was at Envy the night your men attacked? In fact, I recognize two of them."

I watch her point then the men's posture become more threatening.

"Simmer down. I'm not calling the police to identify any of you. That's attention neither my husband nor I need. What I want to know is why you aren't taking credit where credit is due. You didn't hesitate to make sure everyone knew it was you at Envy. What's to be gained by being so sly? You're already on the bratva's radar."

"You talk a lot, Mrs. Kutsenko. It seems your husband hasn't taught you not to be so nosey."

"If he didn't want a nosey wife, he shouldn't have married a lawyer. Tell me this, if it wasn't you, then who was it? Last I heard, you're still on decent terms with the Cartel. Are you covering for them?"

"What would you know?"

"Not what, Mr. Mancinelli, but who. Who don't I know? Neither you nor my husband are the first men I've dealt with who walk both sides of the line. Are you covering for the Diazes?"

I watch Salvatore go rigid. What is my *malyshka* doing? Why can't she be quiet? I watch her pretend to shift her weight, and our eyes meet. She isn't surprised to see me. She knew I was there. I dip my chin and signal to Sergei to wait. She wants me to hear what's going on.

"What do you know about the Diazes?"

"Again with the 'what,' Mr. Mancinelli. Who. Who do I know with the Diazes? Honestly, I'm a little insulted. Or perhaps my ego is too big. I would have thought you'd investigate your enemy's brand-new wife. I figured you'd started poking around the moment you saw us together. By the way, that ruined our first date. I didn't appreciate that."

"Fine. I'll bite. Who do you know?"

"Let's just say that I bet you miss your friend. He's been in a Colombian prison longer than ever before. I hear his son—the older one—is a chip off the old block. Do you get along with him as well as you do his father and uncles?"

"I thought Kutsenko had a pair of big balls. Do you have him by his, or are you carrying your own under that pretty little dress? Maybe I should find out."

"Oh, that wouldn't be a good idea. My husband is a little on the possessive side."

I watch as Laura makes a sign with her thumb and forefinger pressed close together.

"And I've been like a niece to Enrique Diaz since nearly the day I was born. His younger nephew and I grew up almost like brother and sister. I even called him *tio* for the first half of my life. That might not be good for business. He's always looked out for me like a father. I think he always wished he'd had a daughter. I was the closest thing to it. Oh! And don't forget that younger nephew has a whole other kind of connections. He's almost as protective as my husband. Maks really is the worst though.... Actually, I think he's the best."

"You're rambling, Mrs. Kutsenko."

"It's hard to keep it brief when you know so many people. But we digress. Pussycats. If you didn't do it, are you covering for Enrique and Pablo? Or was it someone else? If it was the Cartel, I might be able to get my husband to call off his hounds."

"Hounds?"

"Oh, yes. Russians are like dogs with a bone when they've decided to do something. Worse than the Latin Americans. They're loud. Russians are sneaky. How sneaky are the Italians? Sneaky enough to break into a strip club? Sneaky enough to take Caribbean vacations?"

I watch Salvatore's brow crease in confusion with Laura's last comment. It wasn't him who ordered the photos taken.

"Sneaky, Mrs. Kutsenko? Like you leaving the ballroom without your guard?"

"What did you do with him? Knocked out or dead so you could have a chance to gossip with me?"

"Knocked out. You would do well to keep a better guard assigned to you. I'm surprised your husband was so lax."

"You've neither denied nor admitted that it was the Diazes. Since that's the case, I'm going to assume you're protecting them. I also know that this is not the place where you would kill me. If you were going to take me, you wouldn't have lingered so long. I'll be sure to let Enrique know that you did a valiant job keeping his secret."

"That wouldn't be wise, Mrs. Kutsenko. I suggest you stay out of my business."

"Or what? You dump me like those bodies on my husband's site? Revenge makes for strange bedfellows, Mr. Mancinelli. Harm me, and you will find the Russians and the Cartel are suddenly best friends. Neither will ignore it. But they may race to see who rips you apart first. My *tio* or my husband. I wouldn't want either of them at my door. Imagine what it would be like if they showed up to your restaurants' doors together."

"You heard about the bodies, eh?"

Laura offers a nonchalant shrug.

"It was my husband's land, and I have a connection at the NYPD. Not exactly a secret from me. Now does the plot get juicier? Did you off those girls and carve the C into them then dump them to slow down another project? Or did someone else? Because I know none of the Cartel are quite that sloppy. At least not these days, and I heard those bodies were pretty fresh."

"Your husband talks too much."

"Have you met my husband? He barely talks at all. I have other ways to learn things, Mr. Mancinelli. Like I said, I'm a lawyer. It's in my nature to be nosey."

"Curiosity killed the kitty, Mrs. Kutsenko."

"But this cat has claws, Mr. Mancinelli. Claws dug into more than one branch of New York's syndicates. I don't think you want to stand here much longer and risk someone seeing us. I don't want to have to explain why I'm talking to you. Let's be done, Salvatore."

I watch his eyes narrow at Laura's familiarity.

"You and my husband don't get along. I know that. We all know that. But you do get along with the Cartel, which is practically extended family to me. That makes me Laura and you Salvatore. You deny having anything to do with Pussycats, but you haven't refuted that the Cartel did. Silence is consent, Salvatore. Or in this case, agreement. If you are still such good friends with the Cartel, they must be pissed that you used their kills to derail my husband's projects. So either you aren't on such good terms with the Cartel, or you're hoping your silence about Pussycats will make up for involving them with the build site. I think I'm right. Remember, silence is agreement. If you don't give me another explanation, then I'll have to assume you agree."

I wait for Salvatore to say something, but he doesn't. He glowers at Laura, and she has the audacity to grin. She sticks out her hand and waits. Salvatore looks down at it in shock. She flicks it palm up for a second. She doesn't reach farther forward. He has to come more than halfway. The same move she used on me. He eventually takes it, and they shake.

"What's the price of your silence, Laura?"

"To the cops and the Diazes? Stay away from all things bratva. We've already established that I'm untouchable. But I will sing like a fucking canary set free if you mess with my husband, my family, or our business. As for my husband? He's not as lax as you think."

She turns to look at me, and all the Italians whip their heads around. They reach for their guns, including Salvatore. She puts her hand on his arm before he draws it. She clears her throat.

"You don't want me to sing, Salvatore. I sound like a

magpie, and it'll just draw attention. I suggest you find your way out. I have a Russian bear to soothe. You don't want to stay in his path."

I watch Salvatore and his men let Laura pass. She comes to stand beside me and curls her arm around mine. She shoots Salvatore a cheeky grin and waves as he and his men brush past and storm out the door.

"Find Stefan. Meet us at the car."

I don't look at Sergei, but I know he's following my command. I look at my bride as she bites her bottom lip. She speaks before I get a chance, and I'm not prepared for it.

"You told me you hadn't seen Nadia in years. If she wasn't the blonde you took to the last event, who was?"

"What are you talking about?"

"One of those bitches you abandoned me to told me you brought a blonde as your date to the last cocktail party. If you can't remember, let me give you a hint. She was one of your strippers. They confused me for your employee since you seem to date them."

"What the fuck are you talking about, Laura? I haven't brought a date to any event in five years. Even then, half the time I didn't take Nadia. She's lying. I came with Aleks to the last event."

She narrows her eyes at me as she stares into mine. She nods finally.

"That doesn't change the fact that they assumed I was a stripper. One of them laughed when I said I was a lawyer. It didn't help that those two asshats came over and said they accepted your offer. It sounded like some type of indecent proposal, like you were going to let them fuck me. I had to tell them to send a memo about the deal, and I warned them that they probably couldn't afford me—as their fucking lawyer. You left me to that on my own while you smoked a cigar and scored some big-time deal. Please tell me you made billions off your conversation, because your time out there also left me vulnerable to Mancinelli."

"Why did you come out here alone?"

"Because Sergei was at the back door. Stefan was supposed to be at the front. When I couldn't see him, I was too embarrassed to walk back across the room, past those trolls, to get Sergei or you. I was too annoyed at you. I looked around, and I didn't see anyone. Mancinelli must have seen me, watched me."

"I'm furious and proud of you. Part of me wants to spank you, and part of me wishes to worship your feet. You played a dangerous game tonight, Laura. One that you couldn't possibly guarantee you would win, regardless of who you know. Salvatore isn't a man to play with. You gained invaluable information and put us in a better position than my brothers or I could do. But you risked your life doing it. I hate that."

"I know, Maks. Can we please deal with this at home? I don't know if it's just catching up with me, but I suddenly feel ill. I—"

She doesn't finish before she ducks into the restroom. I charge in after her and gather her hair as she throws up.

"Get out, Maksim. Now. Leave."

"No."

"Get the fuck out."

She swats at me and tries to push as she heaves again. I step out of the stall, but there isn't a chance in hell I'm leaving the restroom. I can hear her heaving, but she doesn't throw up again. Once she flushes, she steps out. She walks past me and washes her hands before rinsing her mouth. She pulls a hair tie from her clutch, where I spy the panties. She pulls her hair back in a messy bun before wetting a paper towel. She drapes it over the back of her neck before wetting another and wiping her brow.

She grips the counter with both hands before rushing back into the stall. We suffer through round two. My heart hurts as I listen to how miserable she sounds. When she comes out a second time, she's so pale I fear she's going to pass out. I help her to the sink where she washes her hands and mouth again. I don't wait after that. I scoop her into my arms. She's too tired to fight me. She burrows into my chest and sighs. She's asleep by the time we're in the car, and I have no idea what to do. What the hell just happened?

Chapter Twenty-Seven

Laura

I don't remember getting home last night. I barely remember Maks helping me get undressed and brushing my teeth for me. I barely had anything to drink since the alcohol just didn't taste right. I wonder if it was something I ate. I don't feel sick anymore, but I also slept for like twelve hours. When I wake, Maks is sitting up in bed next to me with his laptop in his lap. He's in a t-shirt and sweats. He's never this casual during a weekday. It's Thursday, and I thought he was going to a meeting on Staten Island about a housing development he and his brothers are bidding on.

"Maks?"

"How do you feel, *meelaya?*"

"Better. What are you doing here? You had a meeting this morning."

"I had a wife who was unwell. Why would I go to a meeting?"

"Because people get sick sometimes. The world doesn't end for it. You have work to do."

"And I'm doing it. My brothers went without me. I'd already decided to stay here, but they insisted anyway."

"Thank you. I can't believe it's already two in the afternoon. I've been asleep for like fourteen hours."

"I know."

"I'm surprised you didn't wake me to make sure I was okay."

"Your mom and my mom told me not to."

"You called our moms?"

"You've been sleeping for fourteen hours."

I sit up and inch closer. He puts the computer aside and draws me even closer. I relax against his chest with my eyes closed. I feel so much better until suddenly I don't. I scramble over Maks's legs and bolt into the bathroom. I slam the door shut. I lock it and barely make it to the toilet in time. What the hell is left in me to throw up? I dry heave over and over. I roll off my knees to my ass and rest my head on my arm that's on the toilet seat.

"Stop banging, Maks. You're making my head hurt."

"Let me in, Laura. Now."

"I hate having anyone see me when I'm throwing up. Ask Michelle or Lanie or Maddie. I don't want anyone hovering. I don't want anyone holding my hair back. I want to be left alone. Please."

"Fine."

I hear a soft thunk. I don't know if it's his back hitting the door or his arm, but I sense he's still there. I feel badly for the guy. He hates being out of control and not able to help me. I hate being out of control and needing someone to help me. No wonder we're a couple. We're like a pair of matched socks.

Another wave of nausea hits me, but I don't heave. I just

feel tired again. What the hell is wrong with me? I look at the counter and spy my birth control. I don't have a placebo week, so I rarely get a period. I wouldn't know if I've missed one because I don't usually have them. I stand up and brush my teeth. I can't stop staring at them. I'm not wearing any clothes. Shocking. I turn on the shower and wait a moment for it to warm up.

When I step in, I let the water run over my face and breasts. I cup, then massage them. They're tender, but then again, they have been since I met Maks. I've been assuming it's from how we like to play. Maybe our rough sex isn't the only explanation. They don't seem any bigger. I press against my lower belly, and that's a little tender. I wasn't prepared for that.

I hurry to wash my hair and the rest of me. I could order what I need online, but I'll have to wait at least a day. And even then, most packages get opened by security before they come in the house. That's the last thing I need. When I'm done, I wrap my hair in a towel and dry off.

"Maks?"

"Yes, *malyshka*."

"I'm feeling better, but I need some fresh air. I'm going to the store to get some ginger ale and saltines."

"I'll send someone."

"No, Daddy. I want to get outside."

"I'll take you."

"You have work to do. I'll take Bastian for a walk, and one of the guys can come with me."

"I'm coming, Laura."

I sigh. If we take Bastian, I can make him wait outside. He'd never let me wait while he goes in. Bastian hasn't warmed to most of the men, and they aren't so sure of my enormous cuddle bug. He might have someone come with us, but I can say I'm getting some feminine products when he sends the guard in with me. Maks would still have to wait outside with Bastian.

"Fine."

I put on some eyeliner and deodorant before combing my hair. I step out and instantly feel guilty for shutting him out. Maks looks miserable. I stand on my toes and wrap my arms around his waist. When out lips meet, he grasps my ass and lifts me. He spins me against the wall as I yank at his shirt. I think for a moment about a condom, but it may not even matter anymore.

"Maks."

I cry out as he enters me. As he bites my nipple and tugs, I remind myself that this could be the only reason why my tits are tender. We move together as his fingers bite into my ass, lifting and lowering me on his cock. I cling to him as I reach the edge.

"Come for me, baby girl."

"Yes, Daddy."

I squeeze my legs around him as I moan. It's pure pleasure just like it always is. I feel him coming inside me, and I suddenly know exactly what I hope the results will be. He carries me to the bed and sits so I'm straddling his lap.

"If you need space, *meelaya*, then I'll give it to you. But please don't shut me out. I don't know how to handle that."

"I know, *moya lyubov'*. I don't like needing to depend on people when I'm throwing up. I hate it. In future, just let me do what I need to. I'll ask if I need anything, and when I'm done, I'll come to you."

I feel him relax as I call him my love. He nods and eases me off his lap. I hurry to dress before I grab a bigger purse than the fancy clutch I carried last night. We round up Bastian, and Maks asks two guys to come with us. Okay, that's a little more inconvenient. The pharmacy is a ten-minute walk. I want to rush, but I stroll alongside him. There's a breeze with a bit of a bite. I love how he huddles with me, sharing his heat. I hold my dog's leash while he keeps me close. When we get to the store, Maks waits with Bastian as I predicted. I remain with Maks as the two men sweep the store.

Once I have the all-clear, I head to the soda aisle and get three bottles of ginger ale then two boxes of saltines. I suspect I'll need all of them. One of the guys is roaming the store, while the other is my shadow.

"Um. I need some feminine products. I'll just grab them and check out at the pharmacy counter. Can you give me a moment?"

Please, please, please. I imagine crossing my fingers. The guy looks doubtful and glances around for his partner. Finally, he nods.

"Can you wait here, please?"

He frowns but nods. I hurry past the tampons and maxi pads to the family planning section. I puff an exhale as I walk past the condoms. They seem a bit pointless at the moment, and it may be a while before we use up what we have. I grab a two-pack box of pregnancy tests. I head to the counter and check out. The clerk puts everything in a bag and hands me the receipt. I stop to look at the vitamins and think about how my next trip may include picking out prenatal ones. While I appear to browse, I watch both guards. One is coming toward me. I'm quick to drop the tests and my receipt into my purse and zip it closed. I meet the guy halfway.

Maks smiles as I come back outside, and Bastian wiggles. He really has no concept of time. He's happy to see me whether it's been ten minutes or ten hours. He's such an easy-going dog, I don't doubt he'll make an excellent family pet.

Don't get ahead of yourself, I remind myself. If I convince

myself that the test is going to be positive, and it isn't, I'm just going to be disappointed. I need to slow my roll for a minute.

When we get back to the house, I offer to make Maks a sandwich because I'm suddenly starving. Once we're done eating, I encourage him to get some work done in his office. I tell him I'm going upstairs to watch TV in our room. Once I'm up there, I run to the toilet. I drank half the damn bottle of ginger ale in one sitting to make sure I had to pee. I fight with the wrapping and finally get the box open. When I'm done, I pop the cap back onto the test and put it on the counter.

I pull out my phone and force myself to play a game of solitaire before I look at the test. When I do, I nearly burst into tears. There is no doubting the results. I'm not sure what to think. I just sit and stare. A wave of emotion hits me, and I don't know how to describe it. It's kinda like relief, but that doesn't quite seem right. I head downstairs to find Maks. I don't want to be by myself so much after all, and I want to talk to him about last night. I knock on his office door even though I know I can walk right in.

"I thought you were going to watch TV."

"I was, but we need to talk about last night."

"Salvatore—"

"No. That's not what I'm talking about. I'm talking about the part where you used me to negotiate a deal. I'm talking about the part where you left me with strangers. I'm talking about the part where your compliments were backhanded at best. I'm talking about the part where I looked like an abandoned bride because you left me alone for so long. Maks, I saw people staring at me. They were wondering why I was alone since it was obvious I'm not friends with any of the women who were at that table."

"I know you're trying to learn how to be a bratva wife. I'm still learning how to be a husband, let alone one who brings so much danger to my wife's life. I assumed things I shouldn't have. I expected you to read my mind, I suppose. I was wrong about Hanson and Taylor. It was a dick move. But I see how people look at us, how they look at you."

"What's that supposed to mean?"

"I noticed it with my men at the ceremony, but it didn't matter there. When we got to the reception though, I realized other people would see the same thing."

"See what, Maks? Just say it. I'm not a mind reader."

"They see how much you mean to me. They see I love you, and that makes you a target. Exactly what I wanted to avoid is what happened with Salvatore. He tried to get to me through you. I thought if I showed less interest and put some space between us, people would think that we weren't as close as they believed. That they might even believe we were arranged. It's not unheard of among our types of families. I hoped it would provide you the protection the no wives and children provision is supposed to give."

"What types? Russian?"

"No. Among the ruling families in the various mafias. Salvatore and his wife were arranged. Enrique and his wife were too. Even Luis and Margherita were arranged."

"They were? They always seem in love."

"They're one of the few couples who are. I thought if I made it look like we weren't as close as people gossiped, then Salvatore and men like him wouldn't think you were worth approaching, that they would respect the unwritten rule. Obviously, I was monumentally wrong. Last night could have been so incredibly worse."

"Why can't you tell me these things before they happen?"

"Because I'm not used to confiding in anyone about bratva matters who aren't my brothers or cousins. I'm still trying to figure out what's safe for you to know. Remember, I wasn't even sure if you should know the bratva structure."

"I know, but Maks, this isn't going to work if you do this. I'm not arguing with you about what you believe is wrong or right. I'm upset though that you won't tell me. If you'd said, 'Laura, we can't appear too attached because it might not be safe for everyone to see us madly and passionately in love,' then I would have understood."

Maks walks around his desk and wraps his arms around my waist.

"Madly and passionately? Is that what we are?"

"Mhmm. Punch-drunk in love. Head over heels."

"That we are, *malyshka*."

"Look, Maks. There is plenty I know you can't tell me. I'll try not to pry. I really will. But there are some things you need to tell me, even if you're not sure if it's the best choice. I need to be better prepared. I don't want another incident like the one with Salvatore. I know I got lucky. But I'm pretty positive that if I'd cowered in front of him, he would have pounced. He would have taken me."

"I'm still surprised he didn't."

"But what I said to him wasn't anything you told me. I was lucky that I knew stuff. If I hadn't, I wouldn't have had any leverage. If it were someone else, if it were the Irish for example, I wouldn't know what to say. I don't even know who to watch out for. I know what Donovan O'Rourke looks like now, but I don't know what's between you two if anything."

"You're right, *meelaya*."

"So how do we move forward? I don't want you to think that I can't be by myself for even a moment without freaking out. But I also don't want to feel abandoned again. I don't want you to ignore me like you have at previous dinners. It's embarrassing."

"I will tell you more about who I expect us to see, and I'll point people out as I can."

"Are we going to play it cool between us?"

"No. That's been a colossal failure. It didn't fool Salvatore. It probably just emboldened him. If people know I love you, they'll know I won't hesitate to kill to protect you."

I consider what to say next. We've made progress, so I don't want to derail it.

"I'm glad we talked, Maks. I need us to be on the same page because it's not going to be just about us anymore."

I see his confusion. I reach into my pocket and pull out the pregnancy test and hold it up for him to see. He glances at it, then he's staring at me.

"You're pregnant?"

His voice is barely more than a whisper. I can't help the ridiculous smile on my face as I nod. I'm not prepared for the hurt in his next words.

"You took the test without me."

I see the disappointment in his eyes, and it breaks my heart. I thought I needed to prepare myself for telling him. I was scared he might not be excited. I never dreamed he would feel left out.

"I'm sorry, Maks. I wasn't sure how you'd react since we haven't talked about having a family. Not even once. Most couples do before they get married, but we didn't exactly take our time. I thought I needed to gear up to tell you and be ready if you weren't excited."

"Not be excited? We created a life together, *malyshka*. One that we will love and share for the rest of ours. I know we didn't talk about having kids, so I get why you were nervous. I suppose I don't really give off a paternal vibe despite what you might call me. But I want children now that I'm with you. I want as many as you want to have. Whether it's one or ten. As long as you and our children are safe and healthy, then I couldn't ask for more."

He lifts me off my feet with his hands at my waist, and I wrap my arms around his neck as he kisses me. We're both smiling and laughing as our lips meet. I run my fingers through his hair as he sets me down.

"I'll need to see my ob-gyn soon for blood work to make sure everything is progressing and to get a due date. Would you go with me to that? It won't be exciting or anything."

"I'll go to any and all appointments that you want me at, *meelaya*."

"And can we keep this to ourselves for a little while? I think it must have happened that night in Turks and Caicos when I didn't have my pills. We've been careful except for this afternoon. Until we know that everything is good, and I make it to my second trimester, I don't want to tell people. Just in case something does happen."

"That's fine. Is that why you were sick and so tired?"

"I think so. I don't know if I'm going to get sick often or never again. I don't know what to expect."

"Just tell me what you need, and I'll do whatever I can. I can't believe you're going to be a mama, and I'm going to be a *papochka* for real."

"We are. I'm so happy, Maks."

"I am too, Laura. I can't wait to see what our future together brings."

Chapter Twenty-Eight

Maksim

Laura's conversation with Salvatore proved more useful than I expected when Detective Diaz shows up to a meeting with his uncle and brother. I narrow my eyes at Juan as he saunters in. We're at a restaurant in Brooklyn, a place that's neutral and with enough people that none of us want to make a scene. It's been two weeks since the mayor's fundraiser. My brothers and I spent a night at the warehouse after picking up a mid-level Cartel member.

Bogdan brought him in and tied him to a chair two days before I showed up. Bogdan worked him over, but just enough to keep him scared shitless. I arrived midmorning after taking Laura to her first appointment. She had blood drawn a couple days earlier, so the doctor had the results when we arrived. Laura's estimation was right. She must have gotten pregnant that night in Turks and Caicos. I can tell she's happy that our romantic getaway has created an entire new memory. We're going to have a summer baby.

As I took my turn with the Cartel member we scooped up, I reminded myself of how dangerous the threat is to Laura. The words painted on the wall in the Pussycat office along with the photos are etched in my mind's eye. The guy admitted that he was there the night of the break-in. He squealed like a stuck pig each time my blade cut into him. He admitted that it wasn't a sanctioned attack. That a friend of his put him up to it. I believed him when he said he didn't know more than that. But he'd already seen my face and Bogdan's. He was a part of an attack on my business. He breathed his last before becoming ash that floated away in the Flushing River. Now I sit across from the *jefe* and his nephews, and I'm doing everything I can to keep from losing my shit.

"Why did you call us here, Kutsenko?"

"When I called you here, I expected you to bring one nephew, not both. How much are you paying the NYPD to protect you these days?"

Juan looks like he's about to say something but snaps his mouth shut. He sits back, knowing that his uncle will do the talking.

"I don't need to pay anyone to protect me."

"Maybe you should. You have a little rebellion in your cartel, Enrique. Seems someone might be vying for your position."

"And you think you're doing me a favor by telling me?"

"No. I'm not here to do you a favor."

I turn my lips down, as smug as ever, as I watch the three men. I sit back in my chair, appearing casual as I fiddle with my butter knife. I watch them with an air of disinterest and wait. I don't mind silence. But other people do, and inevitably, someone always speaks up.

"I haven't all day. Why'd you call me here? If this is it, you could have emailed me."

"I'll be honest."

"That would be refreshing."

"I'd keep your bad mood to the person who really deserves it. I called you because I was going to demand you hand someone over to me. But you saved me the trouble."

"And why would I hand over anyone to you?"

"Because I know who broke into my strip club and trashed it. I know who threatened my wife."

I watch Juan flinch. I was certain he knew Laura and I were married. It's been two months now. But it's obvious it's still a sore spot. I talked to Laura last night about this meeting. She was the one who figured out the Cartel was responsible for the club, and she remembered what was spray-painted on the wall. After my night at the warehouse, I had her join me for her first bratva meeting, and she asked to see the picture again. She zoomed in then held the phone at a distance. She let out a steam of curses in English and Russian that made my men stop and stare. I thought she might demand the keys and directions to the warehouse. She also figured out that we didn't have a mole. It's someone taking advantage of her.

"I still don't see how this involves me, Kutsenko. Get on with it. Your theatrics are boring."

I turn to Juan and stare at him. I give him the chance to speak up, but he glares back at me.

"You know the problem with revenge is that sometimes emotions overshadow reason. You want so badly to get back at someone that you make careless mistakes like leaving behind evidence the victim can identify. Handwriting is so specific to a person, isn't it, Juan? It's something that can be so easily identifiable if you've been looking at it for twenty-odd years."

I watch Juan shift in his chair. His uncle and brother see him and turn to look. Pablo continues to stare at his brother, but Enrique turns back to me.

"Your nephew thought he could hide behind his badge and you. He thought he could trash my business and threaten the woman who spurned him. He thought he could make the Italians take the blame. But the problem with that is that there's always someone somewhere willing to talk. I will say he went to a lot of work to make it look like someone else. I even thought it was Simms who sent the men. But nope. It was your nephew and a couple of his friends."

"What did you do?" Enrique's voice is quiet but lethal. I love it. I cross my arms and watch the family drama that ensues.

"So I broke some furniture and some bottles of booze."

"And killed one of my guards and practically sterilized another. That kick to his balls practically castrated him." I'm quick to add a couple more details.

"I didn't do that."

"But you organized it?"

"Yes, *tio.*"

Juan doesn't take his eyes off me. I pull out my phone and open it to the photo of the spray painting. I hand it to Enrique. His nostrils flare as he curses in Spanish.

"You wrote this about our Laurita? You threatened her because she didn't want your *pequeña polla.*"

I try not to laugh as I listen to Enrique insult his nephew's small dick.

"It was to piss off this *gilipollas.*"

I don't speak Spanish, but I know the insults. I don't care if calls me an asshole in slang. He can call me whatever he wants. I'm not pissed anymore, but his uncle and brother are.

"Not good enough. Laurita is family. You don't talk about the women in our family like that. You don't talk about our Laurita like that."

"Oh, but that's not all." I grin at Juan as he shoots me a confused look. I shake my head.

"What are you going on about, *ruso*?"

"He didn't tell you about the bodies? Juan, secrets, secrets are no fun. Secrets, secrets hurt someone. In this case, I suspect it will be you. Do you want me to tell?"

"Fuck you."

"No, thank you. We both know I don't need any offers. I'm happy at home with my wife."

Juan lurches forward. His uncle's guard yanks Juan back into his chair as my men step forward. I wave them away.

"Speak, *sobrino*."

I'm pretty sure Enrique is wishing he didn't have to claim Juan as his nephew.

"I planted some bodies, but I didn't expect someone to call the cops. I thought this asshole and his brothers would assume it was the Italians trying to frame us. I thought it would derail their construction, which would have helped the Italians."

"Did Salvatore know?"

"No, *tio*."

"Salvatore didn't mind since it did slow my construction. But I think your little boy here didn't check the bodies before they wound up in the dirt. They were marked."

"What the hell, *trunco*?"

"Shut up, Pablo. It was dark. I didn't see they were marked. I thought it would slow things for them, and they would think it was the Italians fucking with them."

"You risked the bratva going to war with the Italians. You assumed Salvatore would keep your secret. He did because the Kutsenkos haven't declared war. If they had, your ass would be in the Russians' meat grinder or their vat of acid."

"Pretty much. You should listen to your brother, Juan. Salvatore didn't sell you out because he poached my workers. He didn't tell me you did Pussycats because he benefited from the bodies. You walked a fine line. But the photos, those were too much."

"What photos?"

I can tell he doesn't know what I'm talking about. Fuck. Once I found out that he was behind the club and the bodies, I thought he was behind the photos. I still don't know about the car following Laura or the roof. Those have been dead ends. I haven't gotten anything out of Simms. I can't even track the fucker down.

"Someone sent photos to Laura at work. They were intimate photos of my wife with me. They were taken at our places and while we were on vacation."

"That wasn't fucking me. But what are you doing to protect her? How'd you let anyone get close enough to take photos of her?"

"Sit the fuck down, Juan." Pablo's voice is a whisper, but it's got such a bite I think Juan might piss himself.

My men are ready to draw their guns when Juan jumps to his feet. I wave them off again, but Enrique's man doesn't try to restrain him again. The *jefe* doesn't look at Juan, and he ignores Pablo's demand. He focuses on me.

"What do you want, Kutsenko? What's it going to cost to get you to forgive and forget?"

"He gets to live for Laura's sake. She wants nothing to do with him ever again, but I doubt she'd forgive me if I asked for what I really want. He disappears for good. If I find out he's anywhere in this time zone, he's mine to do with what I want."

"What?"

"Shut up, *sobrino*. Consider it done." Enrique stands and reaches out his hand. I accept and shake it then Pablo's. I look at Juan and glare.

"Every time you wake up, say thanks to Laura for keeping

you alive. If you do anything to contact her or come near her, I know she won't stop me."

I walk away from the table, my men falling in behind me. I'm satisfied that Enrique will take care of Juan to my satisfaction. His nephew took matters into his own hands and could have cost the Cartel the tenuous truce they have with us. He'll be gone by nightfall. And I doubt he'll be in any kind of condition to ever come back. It's time to go home to my baby girl and spoil her for a bit. We have plans tonight, and I can't wait to see her in the dress that should be on its way.

Laura looks incredible in the sapphire-blue evening gown. It hits floor length, but the slit shows off just enough of her shapely swimmer's legs to get my cock hard without me wanting to choke any man who looks in her direction. Let's be honest though. Any time I look at her, or even think about her, my cock gets hard. For the first time in my life, it's not just appearances that get me aroused. It's thinking about her laugh, the way she outwits adversaries, her trusting heart. All of it. She's so much more than I ever imagined.

We're walking into The Peninsula for the first time since our reception. We're here for a charity gala. Laura's put together three silent auction baskets, including one with a weekend at a villa near the one we stayed at in Turks and Caicos. Let whoever wins it remember that it's Kutsenko Partners that they owe for their getaway. Hopefully, whoever gets it is someone I can leverage—in the name of charity, of course.

My hand is at the small of Laura's back as we enter. It's brisk as we approach winter, so we stop at the coat check. I'm not having a repeat of the last event, so my brothers and cousins are here. But I'm not counting on Bogdan tonight. He scored his own invitation with some woman he met a couple weeks ago. She's a petite redhead. His type, not mine. My only type is my *malyshka*. As we make our way into the main ballroom, I can already see it's going to be packed. Niko and Aleks walk ahead of us with Sergei and Anton behind. The crowd parts like the Red Sea. I'm not sure if it's our sizes—we're all among the tallest in the room and definitely the broadest—or our reputation.

"Try not scaring everyone tonight, Maks. We want people to bid on the baskets, not be terrified."

"That might make them bid higher."

"Just smile a little and tell the guys not to look like mobsters. It's not exactly discreet."

"We are mobsters, *malyshka*."

I lean over and kiss her temple. But as I do, I spot Salvatore and Enrique. They look thick as thieves, which they are. Salvatore spots me and narrows his eyes. I merely nod and steer Laura away. She follows my gaze. Once she sees them, she lifts her chin to Salvatore but smiles like she sees family when she moves her attention to Enrique.

I didn't keep my meeting with Enrique a secret, nor did I hide what was said. She knows Juan won't be around. She grew quiet and went to our room. I gave her half an hour before I couldn't wait any longer. Her eyes were puffy as she tried to hide her tears. Jealousy spiked, but I forced myself not to react until she explained. I couldn't help but have my heart break a little as she mourned the loss of a friendship she's had since she could crawl.

She assured me she wouldn't miss the Juan she knew now. It was the dear friend she'd thought she had. I wonder if I shouldn't have forced the issue with Enrique. Maybe with time, they could have repaired their friendship. Laura knew what I was thinking and told me she doubted that would ever happen.

She'd gotten married. That was the ultimate rejection, and she didn't think he'd ever forgive her for that.

We make our way to the bar, where Laura orders a Sprite. For all anyone else knows, it could be a gin and tonic. At least unless they look too closely at the tiny bubbles. I order a double shot of vodka. Thank God I can get a real drink rather than the grape juice they pass off as wine at these events. It's rarely award winning at occasions like this when they need so many cases. The cheaper stuff gets people drunker faster, which gets their wallets and checkbooks out faster.

I spy two council members approaching. Laura recognizes both of them and their spouses from our reception. She greets the women and their husbands with charm and humor. She eases the conversation into the women's reelection bids and suggests we might be interested in donating. She doesn't commit, since she mentions we're focused on getting our construction projects back on track. It's amazing how quickly both council members assure us they welcome the developments in their neighborhoods and will ensure things move along. She accomplishes more in five minutes of chatting than I can in weeks of coercing the city planner.

"You amaze me, *malyshka*."

I lean over and kiss behind her ear, feeling that shiver that makes my cock twitch. We agreed we were abandoning the public coldness. Let people think we'd had a disagreement or something before the last event. Let them think we're falling more and more in love as the days pass since the wedding. We are. I'm too damned proud to pretend I don't love my wife. But it means the extra security. I scan the crowd again and spot Niko near the employees' doors to the kitchen. Aleks and Anton are near the front doors. Sergei is near the fire escape. Bogdan and his date stand near the stage. Our eyes meet, both of us keenly aware of who is near our women. From the way he stands with his date, I think there's potential for something serious. That would be a first.

"Maks, isn't that one of the men who was sitting with Donovan the night we had dinner with our families?"

I casually adjust my position to see a man looking at us. He's Donovan's second-in-command. I've known him since we were teens. I went up against him countless times in the ring. We took turns being bare-knuckle champions. He'd love nothing more than to knock me out since the last time we fought I put him in the hospital. He shouldn't have said anything about my mother. A comment about my brothers: fine. My ex-girlfriend: fine. My mother is another story.

"Yeah. That's Colin O'Rourke. He's Donovan's right hand man and his cousin. I used to box against him."

"He doesn't look pleased to see us."

"Me. He holds a grudge from our last match. He has some false teeth now."

"He looks like he wants to go another round."

"I also gave him a concussion that's kept him out of the ring ever since."

"Ah. Pride and his bank account. No wonder he looks pissed."

"Stay away from him, *meelaya*. He has a reputation for hurting the women he's with. He's been banned from our strip clubs for a decade." I watch Laura shift closer to me, so I wrap my arm around her waist. She leans against me as she nods. I can tell she's still looking around the room. "The mayor is coming."

"At least it's before dinner. He turns my stomach over, Maks. He gives me the creeps with the way he looks at you. It's like he wants to make you his next meal."

"He's hinted at it. Since I never brought a date to any events, there's been speculation."

"And his wife doesn't care?"

"She'd have joined in."

Laura's eyes jump to the woman who's accompanying her husband. I see the wariness as she shifts again, this time putting herself slightly in front of me. I slide my hand to her hip and squeeze.

"Play nice, *malyshka*, and I'll reward you tonight."

"I might be getting punished. I don't like the way she's looking at you. It's just as bad as her husband."

We greet the powerful couple. I can tell our newly on-display affection rattles them both. They're trying to tell if it's just for appearances. I don't know if it's our tone or our body language, but it's clear they soon lose interest and extract themselves from the conversation.

"A reward it is, baby girl."

"Thank you, Daddy."

Laura grins up at me and waggles her eyebrows. We make our way to our table. Bogdan and his date join us. Laura seems to have hit it off with the woman since the beginning, so they are soon chatting. Bogdan and I make small talk with the other people at the table as we sip our vodka. The meal progresses painfully slowly, since the wait staff has hundreds of people to serve each course. Laura looks a little green as the main course arrives.

"Are you all right?"

"The smell is a little much. I'm going to the restroom for a moment."

"I'll come with you."

"No, stay. It'll look odd if we both leave the ballroom. Can one of the guys come with me?"

I signal Anton. Bogdan and I both rise as Laura stands. Our father trained all of us, but it throws the other men off. They're not sure if they should stand, too. Laura and her newfound best friend both head to the restroom. Sergei now accompanies them.

"I'm glad we brought the others." Bogdan keeps his voice low, and I nod.

I look around and notice Colin is nowhere to be seen. As I watch the doors Laura just passed through, something doesn't feel right. I search the crowd again, but I don't see anything suspicious. It's just a feeling. I need to find Laura.

"Something's going on. I need to find Laura."

Bogdan and I push away from the table. I've just gotten my feet under me when an explosion knocks me backwards. I grab Bogdan's tux jacket and barely pull him out of the way before a chandelier shatters to the ground. Where's Laura?

Chapter Twenty-Nine

Laura

I'm sideways against the wall of the bathroom when a blast rocks the building. I barely miss hitting my head against the sink. My shoulder slams into the metal trash can. I slide to the floor as my legs collapse beneath me. As a second blast goes off, I look for Bogdan's date, Christina. She's still in a stall.

"Laura!"

"I'm by the sinks. Are you okay?"

"I can't get the door open. The stall wall came loose and is pinning me."

"I'm coming."

I can hear screaming outside the restroom and the sound of people running. Where are Sergei and Anton? They were right outside the door. Why haven't they come in? Are they hurt? What the fuck is going on?

My mind spins with questions as I push myself to my feet and hurry to Christina. I can see what she means. I lean over and see her feet pointing sideways. She must have been standing already. I think there's room for me to slide under the door. I crouch low and look up at her. Her head is bleeding, and the partition is pinning her chest.

"I'm going to slide under the door and come up next to you. We have to push together. Can you get your arms up?"

"Yeah. I already tried, but it's wedged."

I lie on my belly and push myself under the door. I come to my feet slowly. I won't be able to stand upright, but I can get my shoulder under the stall wall. I kick off my heels, grateful I didn't wear pantyhose.

"We're going to push together. Are you ready?"

"Yeah."

"All right. Now."

I push with all my strength. I can feel a tug in my belly, and my hand goes to it. I don't have even a hint of a bump, so it feels weird. But I keep going. It moves a couple inches. I shift and put my foot on the opposite partition and try harder. It moves just enough for Christina to drop to her knees.

"Come on."

I slip back under the door and move out of Christina's way. Her head's bleeding worse, and there's a gash across her chest. Bruises are already showing on her bare arms. I hurry to the sink and grab a handful of the rolled terry cloth towels. I hand her one while I hold two more.

"Press it against your head. I'll press these to your chest. We need to wait here. Bogdan and Maks know we came here. Anton and Sergei have to be nearby."

The words are barely out of my mouth when the restroom door slams open. It's not Maks or any of the bratva men. It's Donovan O'Rourke. He has the most malicious grin I've ever seen. Before I know what's happening, he's yanking my hair, making my neck snap back. I bite my tongue and can barely gasp. His hand goes around my throat, but not before I release a bloodcurdling scream. His hand releases my throat and lands across my cheek. Then he's choking me. He isn't trying to scare me. He's ready to strangle me and leave me for dead.

"Shut the fuck up."

His face is almost touching mine. He keeps squeezing.

"Going—to—puke."

I'm not, but it gets him to let go. I recognize Colin O'Rourke as he burst through the door. He looks at me then at Christina. His fist lands against her temple, and she crumbles like a sandcastle.

"No!"

"I told you to shut the fuck up. Want to wind up like her?"

I'm smart enough to not use Christina's name. I'm not giving them anything to use against either of us. Colin holds the door open as Donovan drags me out. He pulls a rag from his pocket. I fight as best I can to keep it away from me, but he's too strong. He's still dragging me down the hallway, and we're headed to the kitchen. Never let them take you to a secondary location. I keep thrashing and biting at his hand every time it comes near me. I catch the meaty part of the side of his hand and sink my teeth in. My head hits the wall as he flings me against it. I see stars as the rag covers my mouth and nose. My last thoughts are: is this chloroform, and will it hurt my baby?

I keep my eyes closed as I come round. I have never felt so nauseous in my life. And my head. Holy fuck. I feel like I've taken a dozen blows to my temples. I can't open my eyes even if I want to. It hurts too damn much. But I'm becoming more aware of my surroundings. I'm tied to some type of chair with armrests. The bindings are so tight I don't have much feeling in my hands. The rope chafes against my bare ankles. I remember I left my shoes in the restroom stall. Oh God, what happened to Christina? I never saw her come out. They must have left her there. I never saw Sergei or Anton. There's a rope around my chest and my stomach. It's only a smidge looser than the other bindings. It's hard to breathe though.

I listen for anything that might hint where I am. There's no blindfold, so I'll eventually be able to open my eyes. But until then, I strain my ears. I can hear dripping, and the air is cold. It makes me wonder if the Irish have their own warehouse. The sound echoes, so I'm somewhere large and empty. I can hear the low rumble of voices, but I can't make out any words. I think it must be Gaelic, which I realized Donovan and Colin spoke at the restaurant. A door opens, and I do my best to keep my body from reacting. I keep my breathing steady.

"She should be awake by now."

"I didn't put that much on the rag, Don. But then you gave her that shot. Everyone reacts differently. You know that."

"She's been out for five hours."

What the fuck? Five hours. Maks must be going crazy. We'll be fucking lucky if anything is left of the city by the time he finds me. I refuse to think anything else but that Maks rescuing me is going to happen. I refuse to even harbor a second of doubt that Maks is alive. But what about Anton and Sergei? I tried to look around when Donovan dragged me out. There was no one on the floor. Did they kill my cousins-in-law and dump them somewhere before they came for me? Did the blasts knock them out or kill them?

"Get a bucket of water."

I hear footsteps after Donovan's command. I try not to tense, but I know what's coming. My head is already lolling to one side. When the frigid water hits, I can't help but jerk. But I know my unconscious body would do that, too. I let my head droop to the other side, but I don't do anything else. I force myself not to shiver. I was already fighting that battle when I woke. Now my body wants to practically convulse. My fingers flex open and closed behind my back. It's the only reaction I allow myself.

I hear footsteps approaching, but I'm not ready for someone to practically rip the hair from my head as they yank backwards. Several hard slaps land across my cheek, making me bite the inside. My eyes snap open, and I spit blood into Donovan's face. He's shocked enough to ease the tension on my hair. I headbutt his throat. I'm going to take a beating for that, and it was stupid, considering I'm responsible for the life growing inside me. But I won't let him think I'll cower. I glare at him before my lips curl into a smirk. His hand goes around my throat like it did in the restroom. I stick my tongue out at him.

"Unless you want me to start by cutting out your tongue, I'd behave."

I cock one eyebrow as I pull my tongue back in. I look past his shoulder and spot Colin and three other guys I didn't hear approach. They're staring with mixed expressions of shock and laughter. I don't know if they're daring to laugh at Donovan while his back is turned or if it's because they know I've sealed my fate. I lean as best I can and return their smiles. Suddenly they're serious as Donovan spins around. It jerks my head forward since he still grips my hair.

But Donovan's new position allows me to see Sergei and Anton hanging from meat hooks. Their arms are stretched overhead, and their toes barely touch the floor. There are gags in their mouths. Their eyes are wide as they watch me. When they see me looking at them, they shake their heads furiously. I shift my attention back to Donovan when he lets go of my hair and steps back far enough that I can't headbutt him again. I spit more blood, this time at his feet.

"Unless you want me to puke from swallowing my own blood, don't make my mouth bleed. I'll just have to keep spitting. My aim's not bad for a girl, is it?"

I see his men smirk again. I still don't know if it's because Donovan isn't watching or if it's because I'm slowly killing myself.

"You talk an awful lot. Maybe I should gag you like I did them."

Donovan gestures toward Sergei and Anton.

"I'm pretty sure you want answers from me. I can't speak if I have a gag in my mouth."

"I'm a patient man. I can wait to get my answers."

He walks over to my new family members and draws a blade. The men are hanging naked, and their bodies are already riddled with bruises and shallow cuts. I can tell they're deep enough to hurt and bleed, but not deep enough to kill them. Yet. Donovan's fist lands in Anton's gut. Neither of them reacts. Donovan punches Anton again and again, but neither Russian makes a sound. Their faces don't show any emotion. The only sign that the abuse registers is I can see Anton's abs flex before each blow. It must feel like hitting a brick wall. I wonder if it's hurting Donovan more than it is Anton. When Donovan steps back and flexes his hand, I know at least he's in pain too.

He's quick though. I don't anticipate the cut he makes on Sergei. It's as low on his belly as he can get. I try not to notice that he's manscaped, but I watch the blade. I glance at Anton, and something flashes in his eyes as he watches Donovan. I look back at Sergei, who seems to be pleading with Anton, even though his face appears expressionless.

Holy fucking shit! They're a couple. Or at least, they're in love. I never imagined that. They're not related by blood, so the only thing that is keeping them apart is the antiquated notions

347

Russians have. I'm positive Maks and my brothers-in-law must know. They don't seem to care, but I'm certain there are plenty of men in the bratva who would. I'm trying to wrap my head around my realization when a man old enough to be my father steps forward.

My brow furrows as I turn my head a fraction toward him. He's nearly a mirror image of my father. I look at the other men still standing with Colin, and I stare harder. They resemble this man, but they aren't replicas like this man is of my father.

"Who are you?"

"Recognize the similarities, lass?"

The accent is Irish, but it's dulled. My father's family has been here for a few generations. I don't understand what's happening. I glance back at Donovan, who's now watching me and this man.

"Who do you think is older? Me or your da?"

I blink several times before I rake my eyes over him. I notice the fine lines around his eyes. I see the freckles across his nose. I see the same slightly receding hairline as my father. Then I see it. The scar through his left eyebrow.

"Uncle Peter?"

"Smart lass. Thought I was dead, didn't you? Killed in that car crash that supposedly killed our parents and me. That's what your da's always told you."

"Why do you sound Irish, and my father doesn't? The crash supposedly killed you when you were in your twenties."

"Probably because I'm the one who's spent twenty-eight years living in Ireland."

"Why?"

"It started out as a way to get away from your husband's predecessor. Then it became good for business."

"Are you buying or selling the weapons?"

"Maybe you're too smart."

"So both."

"Shut her up, Uncle Peter. She's supposed to be giving us answers, not the other way around."

My head whips toward Donovan.

"He's right, Da." Now it's Colin speaking. I look at the other men, and my gaze hardens. There's no humor left in my expression.

"I'm your cousin, and you have me strapped to a chair after you drugged me. What the fuck kind of family are you?"

"The kind that expects our own to be loyal." Uncle Peter leans toward me.

"Loyal? You knew I was family, but I didn't know. How the hell was I supposed to be loyal? It's not like you showed up to Christmas or invited us over."

"Yes well, your parents should have explained that. My brother thought he could run away from his family. That a respectable job and a respectable wife wouldn't make him what he's always been."

"Why'd you suddenly take an interest in me? It's because of Maks, isn't it?"

"It was fine while you were fucking that wetback, but you crossed the line." Donovan waits to see if I react to the racial slur, but I don't. It's not like I condone it, but I won't give anything else away. "So you really are on the outs with our friend Juan."

Their friend? What the hell?

"He was a good informant for how little we paid him." I look at Colin, trying to work through everything I'm hearing.

My oldest friend turned on me, not out of jealousy but for money. Or maybe he accepted the money and was happy to do the work because he didn't get what he wanted. Either way, I think I want Maks to change his mind about how he handled Juan. He worked with these men to hurt me, to hurt my husband, to hurt my family. I don't know if I'll ever forgive, but I sure as fuck won't forget.

"Explain to me how we're related."

"We don't answer to your demands, lass." Uncle Peter grins and shakes his head.

"Oh yes, you do. If you want me to cooperate for even a moment, you will explain."

"Have you already forgotten that we hold your new cousins' lives in our hands?" Donovan cackles.

I turn a dismissive look at him. I pray he thinks that hurting Sergei and Anton won't faze me enough to use them to manipulate me. I pray it doesn't make him see them as useless and kill them sooner. I keep my attention on my uncle.

"What happened to my grandparents? Are they alive?"

"No. I wasn't in the car when Vlad blew it up, but my parents were."

That isn't the car accident that was described to me. I remember telling Maks about how my dad lost his family. I didn't see even a hint that he already knew. It was well before he came to America, so maybe he never heard. Maybe he never made the connection. I pray he hasn't known all along and kept it from me. I seem to be doing a lot of praying.

"Has our family always been in the Irish mob?"

"Since we stepped foot on American soil. It was necessity back then. It's how my grandparents survived, put food on the table for my parents."

"Was my dad?"

"No. My parents always doted on how smart he was. How he would make something of himself. When we started getting in trouble, they kept us away. When Vlad took our parents, I committed my life to the cause. Your father ran away like a little bitch."

"The cause? Fighting the Russians over guns and drugs? Licking the Italians' asses for lasagna? Some cause."

"You have quite the mouth on you, lass. Maybe your mother should know that all those lessons in manners failed."

My eyes narrow at my uncle, and he sees the venom I wish to spew. It's the same consuming need to protect that I felt when the men on the roof were shooting. My eyes widen and such hate fills me that it scares me.

"It was you. You tried to kill me on the roof."

"No. That was supposed to be when we snatched you. We should have done it ourselves instead of hiring it out."

I look back at Donovan as he speaks. I just need to keep them talking. It's keeping him away from my cousins-in-law, and it's giving Maks time to find me.

"Why? Were you going to ransom me to Maks? To my parents? Scare me away from Maks? Make my parents tell me to stop dating him?"

"You ask a lot of questions for a hostage."

"What else do I have to fill my time, Cousin Donovan? Give me a rosary, and I'll say some prayers for you."

"If we'd known you could shoot so well, we would have recruited you to our side." Uncle Peter chuckles, but I keep glaring at him. I want to know more about my family, what they hope to gain from this.

"If my father avoided joining, did you cut him out of the family?"

"We kept him close while he did some business for us. But he let his company reassign him. He thought it could free him. You can never be free of the blood that runs through your veins."

I listen to Donovan and think about the baby inside me. I don't believe what he's saying for a moment. My baby's

351

ethnicity might be Irish and Russian, but his or her blood is mine and Maks's. It has nothing to do with anyone else.

But even as I tell myself this, I know it's bullshit. If we have a son, he'll be trained to succeed Maks. I'm carrying the next generation of Russian bratva. I need to make sure these men don't discover that. My arms tied behind my back are a blessing because all I want to do is wrap them around my middle and shield my baby.

"What do you want from me?"

"It's been obvious from the beginning that Maks has been chasing your pussy like it's fucking solid gold."

"That's how you talk about your female cousins? And you want me to think we're family and that counts above all else. Fuck you. Is your dick tiny? Is that why you're doing this? Trying to measure up? I know you know exactly what I'm enjoying. You were behind the photos, weren't you?"

"You can be a real cunt."

"Apparently, one made out of gold."

I hate that word most of the time. When Maks says it, I want to come. Hearing Donovan say it makes me want to scratch his eyes out.

"Your golden cunt has him pussy whipped. The great Maksim Kutsenko is being led around by the balls. He'll do anything to get you back, and every criminal in New York knows that. Probably the entire eastern seaboard. If he wants you and his baby back, then he's going to have to answer to me."

He knows? They know?

"Medical records aren't private when they're digital. June twelfth is supposed to be the auspicious occasion. If Maks wants you both back alive, then he'll cooperate."

"How Irish are you, Donovan?"

"What the fuck are you talking about?"

"How Irish are you? Are you as Irish to the blood and bone as you claim?"

"What do you think?"

"I think you won't touch me or my unborn baby if you're as Irish as you say. I see the cross around your neck. I'm surprised it doesn't burn. But a good Catholic knows an unborn life is precious. You won't do a fucking thing to hurt me."

I know no such thing. I don't even believe what I'm saying. But it's making him think. While Donovan's talking to me, he isn't carving up Sergei or Anton.

"I can keep you for the next seven months. Once I have your baby, you won't matter. I'll lock you away somewhere where even God can't find you."

"You were behind the car following me, the rooftop, the photos, and the bombing. You were a part of Pussycats too, weren't you?"

"Who do you think sold Juan the weapons he and his friends used?" I turn toward Uncle Peter as he chimes in.

"Weapons I suppose you imported."

"Aye, lass."

"Does my dad know you're alive?"

"No. It was best that way."

"Were you protecting him or just your own ass?"

"Both."

"You went to that much trouble, and now you're holding your niece hostage."

"He shouldn't have condoned you marrying Maks. He knew he should have broken you up."

"Was he never free of the mob?"

"He could have stayed free if he'd remembered his own loyalty."

"His loyalty is to my mom, my sister, and me. He knew what I wanted was Maks."

"And he knew it put you in danger. He had to know we wouldn't ignore this."

Such a fucked-up sense of family. How could my parents not warn me? I think about my mom's reaction to seeing Donovan. She knows everything. Neither of them tried to protect me. Even if they thought Maks could keep me safe, they didn't tell him. I look at Donovan.

"What exactly do you want from Maks, Donovan?"

"He defaults on the new developments and lets the city take them back. I already know they will undersell them. He withdraws his bids on the Staten Island projects. He ends his arms imports, and he sells his strip clubs. They bring in more money than his regular clubs and bars."

"You want to bankrupt him. He loves me, but not enough to sacrifice all of his men and their lives and families. You think too much of me. He's as loyal to the bratva as you are to the mob. He's young. He'll find a new wife."

"A man like that doesn't love as hard as he does and then just finds a new wife. He'll sell his soul to have you back." Uncle Peter seems so sure as he shares his assessment.

Part of me hopes that's true. I want to feel that loved and precious. I need him to feel that way to protect our baby. But I don't know that a rescue is possible no matter how much he wants to. He can't forsake the bratva and his duties. I always feared the day the bratva would have to come ahead of me. That day is now. He'll come for me and his cousins. But he may not leave with us.

Chapter Thirty

Maksim

"What the hell happened?"

Bogdan and I are running toward the door our women went through. We're pushing past people and leaping over overturned tables and chairs. Smoke fills the air as we get into the hallway. Aleks and Niko are calling to us from behind, but neither Bogdan nor I slow down as we race toward the restroom.

"Maks, look."

Bogdan is pointing to a piece of silk on the ground. I recognize it as Sergei's tuxedo pocket square. I grab it and look around, but there's nothing else. I glance down the hallway as the door to the women's restroom opens, and Bogdan's date tumbles out.

"Tina!"

Bogdan hurtles himself forward and catches the bleeding woman. The entire side of her face is bloody and bruised. She's pale as a ghost, and her chest is oozing blood. Bogdan scoops her into his arms. I approach as he pushes hair from her eyes. He's kissing her forehead as he cradles her.

"What happened, *malyshka?*"

It's odd to my ear to hear my brother use that term. I've never seen the look in his eyes before. It's the same kind of fear I feel right now not knowing where Laura is.

"They took her, Bogdi."

"Who, *malyshka?*"

"Irish. I recognized a tattoo on the man who hit me. He's not the one who got Laura. She fought, but they took her. The guy knocked me out and left me in the restroom. She saved me, Bogdi. I was pinned in the stall. She helped me get out from under the partition. Then I let them take her. I didn't save her when she saved me."

Guilt and shame mar this woman's attractive face. I can't be angry. I'm certain it was Colin and probably Donovan. Neither woman stood a chance.

"Take her home, Bogdan. Get Boris to check her out. If it was Colin who hit her, she's got at least a concussion."

"I will kill that motherfucker."

When Christina whimpers, he kisses her forehead again and moves back toward the hotel's backdoor.

"Aleks, go with him. Niko, stay with me."

"No. Michail will take us home. Aleks and Niko stay with you. I have my own men once I get to my penthouse."

"This is Anton's."

Niko holds up a near-matching pocket square that's outside the restroom door. It's one of the only subtle signs the couple can share. There can never be matching rings or tattoos. But they wear matching socks and pocket squares. The backs of their watches are engraved with their partner's initials.

"They have them both and Laura."

I'm fighting to control my rage. I don't know where they

have her. I'm certain they have a warehouse or some abandoned building like we do. It's probably in Pearl River, which is at least an hour from here. I can't just start busting down doors. That's a good way to get arrested before I find her or my cousins. I pull up my phone and open the tracking app. Anton and Sergei's watches, and the bracelet Laura's wearing, have trackers. She knows because the bracelet has a special key that unfastens it. Nothing can get it off without it. I look at my phone and want to hurl it at the wall.

"Fuck. None of the trackers are working. They must be jamming them. We go back to my place and plan. Aleks, see if you can find Salvatore. He probably knows where the fuck they went. If he doesn't tell you, take him to the warehouse. I'll fucking kill him if he knows where my wife is."

"I don't know."

I spin around and find Salvatore with his arm around his wife, who looks dazed. I march over to him and barely keep myself from grabbing him.

"How do you even know who I'm talking about?"

"Because I'm not stupid enough to take your woman. Enrique considers her family. That only leaves Donovan. That bastard isn't right in the head."

"The Italians and Irish have a history. Tell me what you know about where he goes."

"They've got businesses all over the place. It could be Pearl River, like you said. Or it could be the docks. They could be on their way out of the city for all I know. You need to talk to your in-laws. They're not quite the suburban yuppies you think."

"What the fuck does that mean?"

"They have ties they tried to cut decades ago. I think they're not as severed as they thought. Your father-in-law has history with them."

I'm reeling. I'm not pissed that Laura's parents have ties to the Irish mob. I'm fucking beyond furious that they never told me or her. They had to know the risk they allowed by letting their daughter marry me. I didn't protect her properly. And I should have fucking guessed a long time ago that it was Donovan. I shouldn't have discounted him and focused only on Salvatore and Juan. This is my doing as much as it is Killian's and Susan's.

"Thank you."

"Is this war?"

"Yes. No women and no children. He took both."

I see the understanding in Salvatore's eyes. Even his wife, Sylvia, is alert enough to understand. We weren't going to tell anyone, and I hear my brothers' shock. I'll deal with not telling them first later. I watch my nemesis's arm tighten around his wife.

"What do you need?"

"You're siding with me?"

"If I don't, then I'm condoning what he did. I can't do that. I can't let anyone think I believe women and children are fair game. It endangers my family."

"I don't know what I need yet. But I expect you to answer my call. Enrique may get involved. Can you deal with that?"

"For this, yes. I'm a selfish man, Kutsenko. I'll do what I need to protect what's mine."

I look down at Sylvia before I lock eyes with Salvatore and nod. My brothers and I head to the car. I'm dialing my father-in-law before we pull away from the curb.

"Maksim. How nice—"

"Donovan has Laura. Tell me why the fuck he's after my wife."

"Susan!" I pull the phone away from my ear as Killian bellows for his wife.

"Put me on speaker. You're on mine. Two of my brothers are with me. They have our cousins, too."

"Maks? What's happened?" I hear the panic in Susan's voice.

"We were at The Peninsula. Donovan bombed it and took Laura and my two cousins. Who the hell is the Irish mob to you? Tell me now."

There's a pause before Killian launches into a story that makes my head feel like it's going to explode.

"Vlad Lushak killed my parents in a car bomb twenty-eight years ago, so long before you came to America and met him. My brother wasn't in the car, but we let people think he was. Peter fled to family in Ireland, where he stayed. I only found out this morning that he's back. He texted me and asked if we wanted to get together for a drink. I haven't seen him in fifteen years, the last time I went to Ireland. He's Colin's father."

"I thought Colin's father was killed by a hit from the Boston Italians."

"No. Donovan's father, Liam, concocted that story. Liam's sister is Peter's wife—or was before she died of cancer not long after he fled. Peter didn't know until she was gone. It was fast. Indirectly, Donovan and Laura are basically cousins. I was never a part of it. My parents did what they could to keep Peter and me out even though our father was a top-ranking member. My family has been in for generations. I was already married, and Laura was on the way when my parents were killed. I refused to join. Peter more than made up for my refusal. He threw himself into it once he got to Ireland. He's been dealing arms and drugs between Ireland, and New York and Boston."

"Is your family in this, Susan?"

"Not for two generations. It stopped when my grandmother married a Frenchman. She was kicked out of the family, disowned completely."

"You should have told me that night we saw Donovan. You should have told me before the wedding. I should have pressed you to explain your reaction to Donovan."

"We didn't want to ruin your engagement or wedding."

"You left her vulnerable because I didn't know. I thought the threats we've dealt with were from the Italians. They must have been Donovan all along."

"What threats?" Killian's voice hardens in a way I never pictured. If I'd known his ties, I probably would have told him. He could have handled it, even helped me figure out it was Donovan.

"We didn't tell you because we didn't know you understood this world. Laura was followed on the way to church right after we started dating. There was an attack on my rooftop. My cousin was shot, but Laura wasn't injured. There was a threat spray painted on the wall of a club that was broken into. I know it was Juan who did it, but I'm positive Donovan supplied whatever guns Juan had. He wouldn't have used his service pistol. Someone sent photos to Laura the day she left her job. They were shot while we were intimate. Now I'm certain he has her."

Killian releases a flow of curses in English and Gaelic. I'm certain I hear a few from Susan, too. I let them vent for a moment, but I need information.

"Where would he have taken her? Mancinelli said it could be Pearl River or the docks. My gut's telling me that's too obvious."

"It is. He's got some buildings in Rochester on the Lake Ontario docks. They aren't on any map or city plans. I only know because I saw them in some shipping manifests when I was handling his investments. It's part of what got me to maneuver my transfer. I made my bosses think it was their idea, but I wanted no part of it. I'm fairly sure Peter sends the weapons and drugs down the St. Lawrence River, through Canada, to Lake Ontario. That's why the police can't bust Donovan."

"Rochester is five hours away. Would he drive?"

"Yeah. He hates flying. His dad died in a plane crash taking off in a snowstorm. He refuses to go near them if he can help it."

"What else do I need to know?"

"Colin isn't Peter's only child. He had two before he married his wife. They have different mothers. I don't know anything about them as adults. I don't know if they know him or not. He wasn't much of a father to them before he fled. But they're likely with Donovan since they grew up together."

"Maks, you'll know it's him because he looks exactly like Killian, except he has a scar through his eyebrow. There's no way Laura won't know who he is." Susan's voice holds the same steel as her husband's.

"Would he let Donovan hurt her?"

"I don't know."

Susan and Killian answer at the same time. I debate whether to tell them that Laura is going to have our baby. Secrets got us into this mess.

"You need to know Laura is pregnant. She didn't want to tell anyone for a few more weeks, until she's in her second trimester."

I look at Niko and Aleks and hope they can understand. Their smiles tell me they do. Despite this shitstorm, knowing they're going to be uncles makes them happy. My smile is tight, but I return it.

"We're coming to your place." Susan makes the announcement, and I'm unprepared.

"I don't—"

"I don't care how long it takes you to find our daughter. I

am going to be there when you bring her home. You will not stop me, Maksim. I guarantee you that."

"Fine."

"And I'm coming with you."

"No. I'm not taking you into this, Killian."

"I'm certain you know Laura can shoot. Who do you think taught her? She doesn't know, but I've killed more than one man in my life. I'll put a bullet between my brother's eyes if she's got even a hair out of place."

I can hear a gun being assembled as Killian speaks. These are more family secrets than I imagined when I woke up this morning.

"How many men do you think he'll have there, Killian?"

"A dozen. Probably not more than that. He'll want to keep this discreet."

"What's he going to want in exchange for Laura?"

"I really don't know, Maksim. He could try to bribe you into giving up some of your businesses. Or he could kill her right before your eyes just so you don't have an Irish bride. He's yours unless I have to act."

The stockbroker who had me to dinner at his home, the one who was there when I made my former proposal, the man who walked my wife down the aisle, is gone. This is a man who sounds like he could be one of my *brodyaga*, a foot soldier.

"We'll be at your place in forty-five minutes."

"No. Meet us at the airport in Fairfield. We're flying. Susan, two of my men will take you to my house in Queens. I'm taking Laura there."

"If you're flying, I'm coming. I stay with the plane, but I'm coming."

I'm not going to argue. I don't know what condition I'm going to find Laura in. She may need her mother, especially since she's a doctor.

"Be there in forty-five minutes, or I set off without you."

I hang up with them and start making calls. Aleks and Niko are on it, too. Aleks calls Bogdan to tell him what's happening. I know he can't join us, even though I wish he could. He needs to look after Christina. Niko is arranging for men to meet us at the airport. We can accommodate up to nineteen if we have to, and there's five of us already. I have to remember we're bringing three back. That leaves room for eleven of my best men. I get them organized with orders to go to the warehouse for a full arsenal. They'll have to run red lights and drive like bats out of hell on the highways, but I trust they'll get there without keeping us waiting.

When we get to the airfield, the jet is rolling out of the hangar. I get out of the limo, and I can't keep from pacing. It's an hour and a half flight. They have nearly a two-hour head start. I don't know for sure where she is. My phone still isn't tracking her. I pray we're right about Rochester.

We're wheels up an hour after I call Laura's parents. We're flying into a headwind the entire way, so what should be a ninety-minute flight is closer to two hours. I strategize with Aleks, Niko, and Killian. Susan silently listens. No one on my team knows their way around Rochester. We're looking at maps on our phones, trying to figure out the most likely place. There's not enough of us to split up. We have to make our choices carefully.

We land outside the city limits. We can't exactly hire a car service or roll up to a regular car rental. I called someone who knows someone who knows someone. Three large black SUVs are waiting on the tarmac, keys in the ignition, with no one in sight. I didn't say anything to Killian when he arrived with his gun case. I walk around the trunk of one of the SUVs as he's about to load it into the vehicle. He puts it down and opens the case. It's not what I expected. It's a high-powered rifle with a scope. It's almost sniper quality.

"Why do you have this if you aren't in? If you thought you needed it, why didn't you tell Laura and me who you are?"

"It's an older model. It works like it's brand new, but I've had it since I was a newlywed. Despite keeping us out, my father made sure Peter and I had certain skills. I wasn't far enough removed when I got married to think I didn't need it to protect my wife. I did. You may have killed Vlad, but I left him with scars and shrapnel to remember me by."

I check my phone, and I still don't have a location on Laura, Sergei, or Anton. If they're in Rochester, they haven't been here long. We pile into the vehicles and head toward the docks. We're thirty minutes away, and the minutes are crawling. I have my hand fisted around my phone when it pings.

"I have them. Whatever they were in blocked the signal, but they aren't moving. They're in a building by the water."

All of us are wearing earpieces and vests. Susan is still with the plane with the pilot and two of my men. I couldn't in good conscience leave her unprotected, but I hate being down even one man, let alone two. I radio Aleks and Niko who are each in a separate SUV. It's nearly dawn, but it's still dark out. When we pull up, everyone slides their night-vision goggles into place. I know what we look like. Anyone who didn't know we were bratva would think we were some type of paramilitary.

"Stay with me. Everything will be in Russian if we have to talk at all."

Killian nods as he falls in behind me. It's my father-in-law who spots the first threat. I watch him pivot and aim. A body falls backwards on the roof. All our guns have silencers, so no one is the wiser. I'm impressed, but I'm more impatient than anything else. I need to see Laura, feel her in my arms. Until then, there's nothing else that matters but getting to her. I don't care how, and I don't care who we kill.

Aleks takes out the guards at the gate. Niko cuts the wires, and we push it open. We stay to the shadows as we run across the distance separating the gravel lot outside the fence to the building. Three of my men break off and take out the tires of the two SUVs. Unlike the ones we're borrowing, these are bulletproof. I can tell from the metal plating. We can't afford them being able to follow us.

Aleks leads four men around the back while Niko and I enter the building first. Killian is behind us and aiming between our shoulders. I can hear voices, but I still can't see anyone. There's a gravelly one that I recognize as Donovan's. I sense Killian tense when a second man speaks. It must be his brother. Then I hear the sweetest sound there has ever been. It's my *malyshka*.

We draw closer on silent feet until we can see into the cavernous space. I spot Sergei and Anton immediately. They look like shit, but they're alive. I follow where they're looking and see bare feet bound to a chair leg. I can see them between an older man's legs. Donovan saunters over to where I'm certain Laura is tied. The slap rings through the air, and it takes everything in me not to open fire. I can tell Killian feels the same way.

There's a female trill of laughter before I hear another slap. I think my teeth may crack from how I'm clenching my jaw. We're in a darkened hallway right now as we creep forward, but in three more yards, we'll be exposed.

"I'm telling you, Maksim knows his duty as *pakhan*. I may be his wife, but I'm hardly the first woman he's fucked. He'll replace me if for no other reason that he needs an heir. That's the real reason he married me. Killing me won't stop him, Donovan. It'll just make your life so much worse."

I can tell Killian isn't comfortable with what his daughter says, but what does he think we do? We're married, and he knows she's pregnant.

"You keep trying to convince me of that, Cousin. But we all know that's not true. He'll burn the fucking world down to get you back. All he needs to do is back out of those jobs and find somewhere else to sell his guns and drugs."

"Even if he did that, *Cousin*, that doesn't stop the Cartel from swooping in and taking his place. You might be sucking Salvatore's dick, but he's not going against Enrique. He can bring way more men across the border faster than you can get your little clan over from Ireland. Maks and Enrique might not be on good terms, but that doesn't change how Enrique sees me. Hurting Maks is the same as hurting me. Enrique won't ignore that."

"You have a pretty high opinion of yourself."

"It's not an opinion. It's fact. Next time you see Enrique's left arm, look closely at the cross. The tip has a P, the bottom has a J. Pablo and Juan. The left has an L for Laura, and the right has an M for Madeline. If I didn't mean shit to him, then why is my initial on his arm? He treats me like a niece, since they see me like a sister to Juan and Pablo."

"Ah, but you and Juan aren't so close anymore, are you?"

"That's his fault, not mine. Juan fucked up helping you. Enrique may value family, but he's not quick to forgive. Juan's probably in a vat of acid if he's lucky. If he's not, he's probably on his way to stay with his dad in a Colombian prison. Enrique is going to be pissed when he finds out. So go ahead. Take from the bratva, but the Cartel will take from you."

"I should kill you."

"But you won't. Not unless you're going to stop being Catholic."

"Bitch."

I listen to Laura laugh again.

"Do you think Salvatore is going to back you up? He's already got enough problems with Maks between getting in the way with the city planner and trashing Envy. He kept quiet about knowing Juan was behind trashing Pussycats. You're going to have to shove your tongue a long way up his ass for him to want to save you from this shitshow. You still haven't convinced me that he'll side with you. From where I'm sitting in this luxurious accommodation you've given me, you already have the bratva after you. By morning, Enrique will know, so he'll take his own pound of flesh. And Salvatore won't let you hide behind him. Uncle Peter, I hope you booked a roundtrip flight."

"Shut up, lass."

"How do you think your brother is going to react when he finds out his own brother is involved?"

I turn toward Killian and cant my head at Peter. Blood squirts from the back of both knees before Peter collapses. Blood soaks his shirt from each shoulder. Killian fires off four rounds before anyone can react.

"I'll tell you how your brother's going to react, you fucking piece of shit. Turn around so I can put a bullet between your eyes, Peter. I won't kill you by shooting you in the back. I'll do it looking right at you."

My men and I pour into the room. The Irish are scrambling, but we're already shooting one after another until Laura screams. With Peter on the ground, I can see my baby girl. Donovan was at her side in a flash, and now he's poking his knife into her belly. Laura is remarkably calm and still. She screamed to get my attention.

"What do you want, O'Rourke?"

"The Manhattan strip malls and Staten Island projects."

"Done."

Let the fucker think I'm giving in. He's not walking out alive.

"Sell your guns and drugs somewhere else."

"I could do that, but my wife is right. You aren't going to get ahead. The Cartel will just fill my place. You don't have the strength to stop them."

"I've dealt with Enrique before. He owes me a few favors."

"He won't pay if you hurt my wife. You heard her, just like I did. She's as good as family to the Diazes."

"Who knew your pretty little cunt was so well connected to three syndicates?"

I watch Laura grin as she looks up at Donovan. What the hell is she going to say now?

"I forgot to tell you who's had me on retainer. I'm sure you've met them."

"Shut the fuck up, bitch."

"I don't think Mr. Huang, Mr. Sun, or Mr. Cheng will appreciate knowing this is how you treat family."

"What?"

I watch Donovan pull back slightly on the knife.

"My bosses might not have known they let the Triad hire us, but I did. My firm knew it was useful having an attorney on-staff who speaks both Russian and Chinese, but what they didn't bother thinking about was what we said when other people couldn't understand."

She looks at me and offers what's supposed to appear like an apologetic expression. I can see in her eyes that it's nothing close. What the hell is she going to surprise me with?

"You know that crystal decanter and glasses that arrived as a wedding gift? I didn't say anything, but it was from Bingwen

Huang. It was part wedding gift, part thank you for getting a shipment in without tariffs. I don't think it was just pottery that arrived on that container ship."

I knew it was from a former client. I had no idea that it was from the leader of one of the dragons. Who the fuck doesn't my wife know? We need to have a talk about any more connections I'm not aware of.

"You're lying."

Donovan lunges toward Laura. My bullet hits him between the eyes. Killian's lands in his heart. And Niko's leaves a gaping hole in his belly. I look around and see Colin aiming for Aleks, who's running toward Sergei and Anton. Niko takes him out. The rest of the Irish are frantically trying to get out of the building. Aleks and Niko rush to help our cousins while I bolt to Laura. I pull my knife from my belt and cut away the ropes. I pull her into my arms as much as she lurches into them.

"Daddy." It's barely a whisper, but it's a balm.

"I'm here, *malyshka*. I'll always be here."

"I know. I kept him talking as long as I could. It distracted him."

"And Anton and Sergei are probably alive for it."

I look at her battered face. There are scrapes all over her arms and fingerprints wrap around her neck. If Donovan weren't already dead, I would have tortured him for that alone. Never once, no matter how rough we are, have I marred her neck with even a hint of a bruise. I kiss along it, wishing my lips could lift away each mark.

"I'm all right now that you're here, *solnste*. I promise."

"I'm getting you out of here."

I lift Laura out of the chair and turn to find Killian has a pistol to his brother's temple.

"You should have stayed away, Peter. But you didn't. You picked a life that Mom and Da never wanted, and you pulled my daughter into it. You were my best friend until the day you left. I've grieved you like you were just as dead as Mom and Da. But you hurt my little girl. You let other men hurt her. I can never forgive that. Put your hand on the stock and wrap your finger around the trigger. I'm not going to kill my own brother. You're going to own the consequences of what you did."

"You talk about protecting your family. Where were you to protect my boys? Where was your loyalty after what the bratva took from us?"

"You think I don't know what they took? I watched that car explode. My wife carried our daughter in her womb while she stood beside me and watched. But you were too busy to come to dinner that night. You were off cheating on your wife and doing whatever with some stripper. You weren't there to hear Mom and Da make me promise to keep my little one far away from this. I swore I would. So don't tell me I wasn't loyal. I've kept that vow for as long as I could."

I push Laura's head against my chest and turn my back as Killian wraps his fingers around Peter's hand and forces him to pull the trigger. There's no sound but Peter hitting the ground. I hurry to get her outside. I know my brothers are taking care of our cousins, and they'll make sure all our men come home.

"*Meelaya*, your mom is waiting for you. Your parents know you're pregnant. I'm sorry, but I felt I had to tell them."

"I don't care. All I care is that you are here. I'm glad my parents are too, but what I need most is you."

"Did they do anything to you I can't see?" I hate asking the question, but I need to know how to help her. When she remains silent, I don't know if I've offended her or if I should be scared. "Laura, I just want to know if you need medical attention. That's all. Nothing changes between us unless that's what you need."

"No. They didn't do anything. I'm related—or I was related—to all of them one way or another."

I lift her into my arms and move to the trunk where the tailgate is open. I sit and hold her against me. As she often does, her fingers slip between the buttons in my shirt. When her fingertips touch my skin, she relaxes. I breathe easier, too. She's asleep in my arms before my brothers, cousins, and men return. Laura sleeps through all of it, only waking when the explosion rattles the car. She sits up to see the building go up in flames as we drive away. We didn't lose any, but my cousins and a handful of men benefit from having a doctor when we arrive at the plane. Susan stitches up several wounds on Sergei and Anton and removes three bullets from three men. She asks no questions, so we tell her no lies.

Laura stirs as I walk toward the plane. Susan can no longer wait to greet her daughter. She hadn't wanted to disturb her, but now that's she's awake, she won't be deterred.

"Laura!" She watches her daughter, and I can see a flash-forward to Laura as a mother. Susan gives us space, but I can tell she desperately wants to hold Laura, too.

"Can you stand, *malyshka?*"

"Yes."

I ease her to her feet, and she falls into her mom's arms. I stand back, giving them time even though I don't want to let go. But I don't have to wait long. Laura reaches back for my hand while she continues to hug her mom. I take it, and she tugs hard until we're making a sandwich with her in the middle. I feel her sigh.

"Mom, they drugged me with something over my mouth and then some shot. Could it have hurt the baby?"

"I don't know what they used, boo bear."

"I think chloroform to knock me out at first."

"Do you think they held it over your face for long?"

"I don't think so. They said something about the shot not wearing off as fast as they expected."

Susan looks at her daughter as she presses her lips together, deciding what to say.

"Prolonged exposure to chloroform can cause permanent damage or death. If it was midazolam – a powerful sedative used for anesthesia – or propofol, I don't have an answer. It's only used as anesthesia if the benefits outweigh the risks. It's unadvisable to use it. We need to get you to a hospital and get labs run to know what's happening."

Laura looks at me, panicked.

"Susan, can it wait until we get home? We have a doctor on staff who can draw labs and run them discreetly."

Susan glances at me then gazes into her daughter's eyes. Her expression softens as she nods.

"Tell me if you get any cramping or spotting."

"Yes, Mom. Maks, I need to sit down."

I carry her into the cabin and settle her in one of the chairs with a blanket and pillow. She falls back to sleep and remains asleep throughout the flight and drive to our home in Queens.

Her parents spend the night, and so do my cousins and brothers. We check with Bogdan and learn Christina is doing fine. He's keeping her at his place until morning when he agrees to come here. I suspect he'll show up with her. As I curl into bed next to my wife, I pray for the first time since I stopped attending church as a teenager. I pray for thanksgiving that Laura and our baby are home with me. I pray that they're healthy and nothing happens to either of them. I pray that this is the end of the threats to my family.

By midmorning, I've spoken to Salvatore, who repeats his offer to help. I take it on face value, but I don't turn it down. I don't know how soon the Irish will regroup with Donovan and Colin gone. Enrique calls Killian and demands to speak to

Laura, who accepts. I listen to their call, and from what I can tell, she has to convince him not to burn every Irish pub in the tri-state area.

I refuse to step out when Susan and our on-staff doctor, Boris, thoroughly examine her. Susan draws blood, and Boris takes it to a lab that doesn't ask questions. Laura sleeps most of the afternoon and into the evening. I stay beside her, accepting food when my mom brings it. She arrived first thing in the morning. Apparently, Bogdan decided to take his woman to our mom's instead of his place in Manhattan, and they're still there while she recovers.

Boris calls with the results as everyone else is sitting down to dinner. Laura is still sleeping, and I'm sitting next to her in bed. I'm just watching her sleep. If there weren't bruises on her face and neck, she would look so peaceful. No one would imagine what she's been through. I gently wake her, pulling her against my chest as I slide down the bed.

"Boris got your results back, *malyshka*. Everything is normal. There's no trace of anything left in your system. Your hormones are exactly how they should be—"

When I pause, Laura jerks away and looks up at me. I'm still getting used to the news. No one but Boris knows. Not even Susan. It must have been too early for this to be detected when she got her initial bloodwork done.

"Maks, what's wrong? You're scaring me."

"Twins, *meelaya*. We're having twins."

"What? Do they run in your family? I don't think they do in mine." Her voice is soft with awe.

"I don't know. Are you all right?"

"Two babies?"

"Yes."

"Two."

She seems dazed. Then she yawns. I wonder if Boris got the

results wrong. Why is she still so tired? She's slept for twelve hours.

"Baby girl?"

"It's tiring growing one person. It's exhausting growing two. And I'm starving."

"Do you feel up to seeing everyone?"

"Yes. But I desperately want a shower with you, Daddy."

"Come let me take care of you, baby girl."

She's soon biting her lip as she tries to keep from screaming as I suck her clit. My tongue swipes across her seam before I press it into her pussy. Finest honey I've ever tasted. She's whimpering and begging, but I don't relent until her fingers practically pull the hair from my head. With a growl, I lift her beneath her ass and thrust into her. We cling to each other, our heads resting on each other's shoulders. It's rough, just like we enjoy. We're left breathless and grinning like fools. We're safe and together, and that's all that matters right now.

"Daddy, I was so naughty while they had me. I used bad language and talked way too much."

"I know, *malyshka*. Once everyone is gone, you're going over my knee."

"Do you promise, *solnste*?"

"Absolutely, *zaychik*. Are you ready to face the world?"

"With you? Yes."

Our kiss threatens to keep us from ever leaving, but neither of us is in a rush to rejoin everyone else. When we finally do, it's hand in hand. Just like it's always meant to be.

Epilogue

Laura

I've finally stopped throwing up most mornings, and I can stay awake for more than three hours at a time. Maks makes sure there's always three bottles of ginger ale and two boxes of saltines in the house at all times. We've decided to find a new home in Queens. We like this one, but Maks wants one with a wing that allows him to work from home and meet with his men there. He doesn't like going into Manhattan if he doesn't have to. He also wants there to be room for my parents, my sister, and his mom to visit whenever any of them want, and especially all together for the holidays. Christmas was a tight fit despite how large this house is.

I spend most of my day in the home office with him. He and his brothers decided to pension off Dmitry and bring me on as their corporate attorney. I've met Valentin, their criminal lawyer, but they haven't needed to call him since before I met Maks. I warned him that it might not be a good idea to get rid of Dmitry when I'm five months pregnant, but his brothers pushed, and he gave in. Once the four of them learned about my connections to the underworld, they decided I was the only one who should negotiate anything in the future. The syndicates existed on the periphery of my life before Maks swept in and swept me off my feet. Now it's my everyday life.

The Irish are still causing rumbles, but they're mostly quiet as they regroup. That makes Maks more nervous than dealing with them outright. My kidnapping has created a tenuous truce between Maks and Salvatore. Enrique is caught up with business in Miami, so Pablo is handling most of New York. He's as ruthless as they come, but he also feels guilt in a way none of the other men seem to. He's checked on me weekly since the kidnapping. I don't know the details, but I know Juan can never contact me again. I didn't know how to react to that. I was just numb. Aleks and Niko have been keeping an eye out for even the whisper of trouble, and it lets me sleep easy at night.

Michelle got worried when she couldn't reach me for a few days, so she came by the house. The guards almost turned her away, but I happened to see her through my bedroom window and recognized her car. Security was extra tight, and I ended up explaining why. I left out as many details as I could. I asked her about Lanie, and she was noncommittal. But she offered to take me to brunch that weekend. Maks came with me, and we went to Catherine's Bistro. Blessedly, there weren't any servers from Maks's past, but we did run into someone I knew from one of my clubs. I thought Maks was going to break the man's hand when they shook. Laughing earned me a spanking on the way home.

It shocked me when Lanie walked into the restaurant. She looked at me then Maks before sitting down next to Michelle. She didn't exactly apologize and neither did I. We just picked up where we left off, but it was uncomfortable. Michelle worked hard to get us to repair our friendship, and we have. It took a solid three months, but the best thing to move along our reunion was Lanie seeing me with Maks. He dotes on me, makes me laugh, and loves me in all the ways I need.

I meet Christina for yoga at least twice a week and have lunch with her afterward. She's become one of my closest friends. I can talk to her about things I can't even tell Michelle or my sister. I really enjoy her company, and she makes me laugh so hard I nearly pee myself every time we're together. I've never loved clothes shopping, but she has an eye for fashion. I feel like the most stylish pregnant woman in the world. She keeps me from feeling and looking frumpy since Maks and I are still attending social events.

Maks gave Sergei and Anton time off after what happened in Rochester, but they continue to accompany us to all the events we go to. Now that they know that I know, they're both much more relaxed around me. Especially since I gave them matching luxury travel shaving kits. I considered monogramming them on the inside with their letters overlapping, but I got scared that it would be dangerous for them. So I just stuck with their personal monogram on the outside of each.

"*Malyshka*, what the hell are you doing?"

"Packing for when we move."

Maks enters the living room with a face like a thundercloud. He wraps his arm around my rounded belly and lifts me off the chair I'm standing on and sits on it. I shriek as I tip over his lap. Before I know it, my yoga pants and panties are around my ankles. His hand rains down five slaps on each cheek. As my pregnancy progresses, he's gotten gentler. But they still send fire through my ass.

"I was being careful, *solnste*."

"If you were, you would have asked for help. You wouldn't be climbing like you're on a jungle gym."

"It was a chair. I was fine."

Two more smacks land where my ass meets my thighs. Fuck, that burns. He turns me the right way up, and I straddle his lap. He puts his hands on my belly.

"Let me help you, *malyshka*."

"I thought you were busy."

"I'm never too busy for you."

"In that case, I think I have some other things to confess."

I wiggle off his lap and race toward the stairs. I know I can't beat him to the top when I'm not pregnant, so there is no chance now. He scoops me into his arms then tosses me on the mattress, and I try to scurry away. He grabs my ankle and tugs me back to him.

"Come here, my darling girl. Daddy hasn't even started."

God, I hope that's true.

Don't miss the next installment

Preorder and have it ready when you wake on Aug. 9.

She thought it was only for one night...

I've never let anyone into my life.

At least not like her. Not until her.

She sees a side of me that isn't the bratva monster everyone else believes.

Now that she knows, she's mine.

Mine to keep and protect. Mine to please. In return, it's her love I crave. She's my soulmate.

Every kiss, every touch will take her to her limits, and I'll be the one to catch her.

Bratva Sweetheart is an interconnecting, standalone Dark Mafia Romance with a HEA and no cliffhanger. It contains extra-steamy scenes that will make your toes curl and your granny blush. This is book two in *The Ivankov Brotherhood*, a six-book series that'll keep you warm at night.

Preorder now for Aug 9.

Thank you for reading The Bratva Darling

Sabine Barclay, a nom de plume also writing Historical Romance as Celeste Barclay, lives near the Southern California coast with her husband and sons. Growing up in the Midwest, Celeste enjoyed spending as much time in and on the water as she could. Now she lives near the beach. She's an avid swimmer, a hopeful future surfer, and a former rower. When she's not writing, she's working or being a mom.

Subscribe to Sabine's bimonthly newsletter to receive exclusive insider perks.

www.sabinebarclay.com

Join the fun and get exclusive insider giveaways, sneak peeks, and new release announcements in
Sabine Barclay's Facebook Dubious Dames Group

Do you also enjoy steamy Historical Romance? Discover Sabine's books written as Celeste Barclay.